AWAKENING
THE BALANCE BRINGER

THE BALANCE BRINGER CHRONICLES
BOOK TWO

USA TODAY BESTSELLING AUTHOR
DEBRA KRISTI

Awakening: The Balance Bringer (The Balance Bringer Chronicles, Book Two)

Copyright © 2018 by Debra Kristi

All rights reserved. Published by Ghost Girl Publishing, LLC. www. GhostGirlPublishing.com

Library of Congress Control Number: 2018907856

Paperback ISBN: 978-1-942191-11-7 / eBook ISBN: 978-1-942191-10-0

Hardcover ISBN: 13: 978-1-942191-19-3

Cover design by Rebecca Frank

Book layout by Under Wraps Publishing Services

Professional editing by Eden Plantz and Tiffany Johnson

Awakening: The Balance Bringer– 1st ed.

Visit the author: http://www.debrakristi.com/

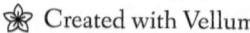 Created with Vellum

FOREWORD

Welcome adventurer,

Quick. Before you begin. Did you read book one, *Becoming: The Balance Bringer*? If not, please turn around and read that book first! In this series, order matters. Grab book one here: http://www.debrakristi.com/books/becoming-balance-bringer/

You did read book one? Awesome! Please take a quick look at the copyright page in your copy of *Becoming: The Balance Bringer*. If it says "2nd edition," you may skip the rest of this message and jump, headfirst, into this story. Enjoy!

Does your version of *Becoming: The Balance Bringer* say "1st edition"? If so, you may have missed the proper ending to book one. The original ending, as the story was written, was cut from the first printing but added back into the story with the second print. You don't want to miss the *true* final chapter of *Becoming: The Balance Bringer*. The start of *Awakening: The Balance Bringer* may not make sense to you if you skip that read.

If you own a verified purchased eBook copy, you may

simply update your version and head to chapter 31. If you read the 1st edition of book one by any other means, you can read chapter 31 of *Becoming: The Balance Bringer* here: http://www.debrakristi.com/awakening-the-balance-bringer-begins/ Password: Bringer

Happy reading!

OTHER WORKS BY DEBRA KRISTI

THE BALANCE BRINGER CHRONICLES:

Becoming: The Balance Bringer

Awakening: The Balance Bringer

Empowering: The Balance Bringer

The Frist Balance Bringer (Coming Soon)

MOORIGAD DRAGON COLLECTION:

The Moorigad Dragon, Part One Moorigad Collection

Reap Not the Dragon, Part Two Moorigad Collection

Plight of the Dragon, Part Three Moorigad Collection

Moorigad, Parts One – Three

CURSED ANGEL COLLECTION:

Blood Promise: Watchtower 7

For Christy,
This book and every book in this series is dedicated to my
sweet, departed sister: my soul twin and writing partner. I
love you always.

"Magic is believing in yourself. If you can do that, you can make anything happen."

Johann Wolfgang von Goethe

Loreitta Village

Painted Stones

Gaea's
Temple Ruins

Palinot Woodlands

City of Palinot

Ivey City

Hushman's Meadow

Listless River

Norde Sorlonte
Homestead

Old Cottage

N

HIDDENKEL

ONE

There are only three things of which I am certain...
One, I found Crystia! Two, I need to find Kaia. And
three, the level of pain in my body is beyond the use of my
go-to curse word. The hurting is seriously outrageous!
Which means I am less likely to immediately set out in
search of Kaia and the magic blocking her.

A harsh ache beats at my temples. Every muscle and
tendon complains of discomfort. It's as if I have tumbled
down a mountain in a landslide of boulders and I barely
survived.

I release a long, steady breath and struggle against the
desire to fall into a coma.

The idea of a long winter nap sounds all too inviting. I
don't want to wake up, not with the pain coursing through
my body. I'd prefer to sleep through the sting of change and
healing. I want to roll onto my side, find some small bit of
comfort, and slumber endlessly. If only my body didn't

protest at the slightest twitch, which it does. So, I lie unmoving, suspecting the escape of sleep will, for now, elude me.

That's alright, I guess. As I recall, my slumber wasn't all that blissful. The oddest nagging sensation persists that, while I slept, the crazy mystic from my computer, Madame what's-her-name, kept beckoning me over and over and over again.

Madame Marrouske. That's right. That was her name.

And stranger yet, that Bree girl from school was bouncing around in my head, too. What's up with that?

I internally groan at the physical and mental discomfort. My head hurts with skull throbs and unwanted confusion. My body aches with... with... well, everywhere. It doesn't help that the surface beneath me is lumpy and stiff. I want to study my surroundings, figure out where I am and what's going on, but my eyes sting and resist opening. Instead, my hand gropes for the bottle of aspirin I keep on my nightstand. I can't say I'm surprised when my fingers cut through citrus-filled air and find nothing. No nightstand and no aspirin.

Agony and disappointment escape in a moan.

The truth I've been living the last few weeks is no fairytale, and I no longer want to believe. When I open my eyes, I want to discover that today is an ordinary school day. I want to be home with my mom and my sister, Crystia. And I want to laugh at the wild dream that explains away everything from the past few days because nothing really did happen.

Seriously. The idea that I'm some sort of foretold savior, the Balance Bringer, is the stuff of a teen-focused movie script. Such things don't happen in real life, and I'm just me—freak Ana, high school outcast.

But... this definitely isn't my bed.

Gaea give me strength.

The throbbing shifts to the sides and back of my skull, exaggerating every movement, every whisper, into crackling fireworks and making sleep an impossibility. As much as I don't want it to be true, it's clear that the previous events were not a dream. My father's evil sister, Dreya, who tried to kill me, is probably still out there and still after me; Kaia is lost; I left my mom behind in my old world, and Crystia died, only to now magically exist in this other realm.

The only positive I can glean in this ugly turn of events is finding Jaden. Even now, my skin flushes and tingles at the thought of him. Traitorous skin.

A few feet away, something rustles, "Would you mind fetching some fresh water? She is awakening and will be parched." Although he whispers, Jaden's voice is unmistakable, and it sets my skin afire with dozens upon dozens of buzzing fireflies. Though, the fire is quickly tamed by the cannon fire of receding footfalls.

He's right; I am thirsty. I swallow and practically choke on the action. It's as if my tongue has swollen, closing off my throat. The inside of my mouth clings to movement like Velcro, and everything tastes like paste. My eyes pop open.

Jaden is watching me from across the room. My heart leaps into my throat. Stupid heart. It's probably now trapped against the Velcro presiding in my esophagus. In a laggard and stiff move, I prop myself up on my elbows and try to grin to cover my anxiety. Failing, I deliver some sort of weak and pathetic simper.

Will I ever get comfortable with Jaden's special feel-what-Ana-feels superpower?

"What happened?" My voice cracks as if I haven't used it in a long while. The words are torn from my interior, forced from my lips. But... in my save-face mental state, if I succeed in drawing his attention away from my overactive feelings, it's worth the pain.

"Don't you remember? You collapsed." Jaden studies my reaction, and he doesn't appear surprised when I neither flinch nor shrug. I'm too tired to try. "That was quite a show you put on at the lake," he continues, "... but you were already running on fumes, and that was a rather grand feat."

The lake. The mere mention of the place has memories rushing back to me. We made it through the doorway to Hiddenkel only to find ourselves deep in a body of water. My gaze wanders from my dark, woven blanket to the thatched roof, then to the support beams and walls. Something similar to bamboo has been used in the structure, and everything appears to be anchored and built around a large tree trunk that sits in the center of the space.

The space is cozy, hosting my bed against one wall, a side table and shelf on the wall at my side, and a dressing table or desk on the wall at my feet. Over the side table is a small, covered window, and the door is on the wall opposite me. It, too, is covered. Most of the light filters in through small holes in the ceiling.

I blink and recall rising out of the lake. I was panicked, rushed, and I somehow removed all the water from the lake, pulling it back and up like a blanket. I needed to get to Ry and Jaden, and when I eventually managed to join the guys on the shore, we were surrounded by hostile villagers. I anticipated a fight that never happened. Instead, they bowed to me.

To me! It was crazy nuts.

Lost in the memory, I fixate on my mattress. I'm lying on a bed of hay or straw, or something similar. I chew on the inside of my lip and allow my gaze to wander back to Jaden.

Where are we?

And then the most important part of our journey springs to the forefront of my mind—my sister.

"Crystia?" I ask and sit up. Agony hits me like a hundred of Aunt Dreya's rocks pelting my skull. Clamping my jaw, I squeeze my eyes shut, press my hands to my head, and breathe, in and out and in and out, until the pain level... becomes tolerable.

Jaden's feather touch runs down my arm, setting off a chain reaction of goosebumps along my flesh.

"Focus on your core." His breath warms my cheek.

I focus and breathe deep three more times. Testing the pain, I slowly open my eyes to find him beside me. Back at school, I deeply desired a close and attentive Jaden. I now wonder if the attraction is a product of what we are to each other and the role destiny expects us to play. Does he have a choice where his feelings for me are concerned?

Avoiding the awkwardness between us, I focus my attention on the unusual tension pulling at my right eye. For reasons unknown to me, my right eye is taking longer than my left eye to adjusts to the light.

"Weird," I mumble a croak and massage along the edge of the troubled eye.

"Let me see." With a gentle hand, Jaden tilts my head.

At his nearness, my eyes flutter and my mouth twitches, threatening a grin. I bite my lip.

He gravitates closer, and I am captivated by his lips, parted ever so slightly. I can't... turn away. I want...

"Would you look at that?" He peers into my eyes with a gaze so intense I believe he can look straight into my soul.

"What?" My voice is small, hardly recognizable. My throat still scratchy and dry.

Where is the water he requested? I could swallow gallons without getting ill. I glance to the side table just out of arm's reach. No water awaits. My chest tightens, and my fingers clench at the dark knit blanket.

Jaden scans the room, and I watch him, almost hoping that, *this time,* he *has* read my thoughts and will somehow magically produce an endless supply of water. He doesn't. From the long dressing table shoved against the adjacent wall, he grabs what appears to be a primitive mirror and holds it to my face.

Only, I'm not studying my reflection in the mirror as I suspect was his plan. The style of the mirror, its imperfect glass, streaked and cracked reflective surface, has me once again pondering our location.

"Ana, look in the mirror."

Right. I swallow the lump in my throat and peer into the mirror. The girl blinking back at me has limp, oily hair, and her face is drained of color. Our adventurous journey has left me haggard and worn. My cheeks redden. This is not how I want Jaden to see me. I want to turn, look away, only I can't. I'm mesmerized by the brilliant blue peering back at me.

Blue! My right eye is blue!

The crazy collage of colors is no longer scattered across my iris, but rather, one hue dominates.

A change... for one eye only? *So unfair!*

What does this mean? And since when does sectoral heterochromia correct itself? I knew that doctor was wrong. My face drops into ugly disappointment.

"This explains the intense adjustment you're experiencing... now that you have finally opened your eyes after all this time." Jaden lowers himself onto the side of the tiny bed.

Shivers rattle through my body, and a crease presses into

my brow. I abandon my reflection to regard Jaden. "What do you mean by *all this time*?"

"Ana." His hand finds mine. "You have been sleeping for three days." His lips curve with concern.

"Three days!" I jolt, and my little cot of a bed shakes. Everything inside of me is buzzing and spinning and churning. I lost three whole days! I glance around, take in the minimal furnishings and cloth door. I recognize the place from when we first emerged from the lake.

Or as the people here call it, the reflecting pool.

How do I know that?

I rub my temples and try to remember all the tiny bits about our arrival. I manipulated the water. The very water that called me *peturi*, meaning princess. In fact, the water called me princess in many languages. I recall that now. Totally *Gaea insane*. And the power that surged throughout my entire body... *Damn crazy*.

I gaze down at my hands, flipping them back and forth. When I glance up, Jaden is watching me.

"What?" I ask.

The corner of his eye glistens. "Nothing."

I know it's not nothing, and in this moment, I wish our roles were reversed. I wish *I* could read *his* emotions.

"Excuse me a moment. Ryland will never forgive me if he's not immediately informed of your awakening."

Jaden dips his head out the door and quietly speaks to someone outside the hut. Every other word drifts to my ear unheard. The events of our first evening this side of the portal, here in Hiddenkel, are too busy playing out in my mind.

Why can't I remember how I ended up lying on a cot?

"When you collapsed, we brought you here to recover."

Jaden turns back toward me.

My lips torque to the side. He did it again, like he did when we were in the caves. "You're reading me, aren't you?" In a moment of truth, he told me he's my Tracer, or seer. He can supposedly feel my emotions and foresee my future, but he can't outright read my mind. So he says.

"When you project as strongly as you are right now, it's hard not to listen." His chest heaves, and he walks back toward me. "You can choose to project or not."

My body stiffens. "So... you've been hearing my random thoughts ever since we met?"

"Longer." He glances to the side.

Heat rises up my neck and flushes my cheeks. Aware that he's likely picking up on some or all of my emotions, I try to control my reaction, both internal and external, only the task borders on hopeless.

When I first found out about his ability, I was in awe of the magic and of him... the sincere improbability of him. Yet, the more time I spend with him the more I come to understand how much he has been privy to. How many times have I had incredibly embarrassing thoughts about him? This ability of his suddenly has me fuming inside. What I share, when I share, and with whom I share should be my choice.

Frozen in uncomfortable silence, Jaden pretends to study something on the other side of the room, and I'm unwilling to speak the first word. My rebellious mind is focused on our first kiss, our only kiss, and comparing it to the many I have shared with Dohlan.

A girl shoves the cloth door aside, interrupting the moment. She bustles in, holding some sort of horrendous, dried gourd in her hands. Whatever it is, she sets it on the side table, removes the top, and proceeds to pour water into the cup-shaped lid. My fingers start twitching, my hands reaching. *So thirsty!* Salivating. I could swallow an entire swimming pool right now.

I snatch the water from the girl's hands and gulp the liquid as if trying to put out a fire in my belly. I gulp and gulp, and my gaze wanders the room. My picture of Crystia, Ry, and myself is propped up on the far edge of the dressing table. I'm guessing Ry set the picture there. The sight of it warms my heart.

When my thirst is satisfied, I return my attention to Jaden.

"So..." I hesitate, thinking about our arrival. "I passed out before I could reach Crystia?"

Ry ducks into the not-so-private hut. My gaze instinctively flashes to him and then back to Jaden. I catch a flicker in Jaden's eye that sparks worry.

"I'll give you two some privacy," he says and steps toward the door without answering my question.

"Jaden," I call after him.

"I'll be outside if you need me. I won't be far." And then he's gone.

My gut twists into a knot. I don't know what to make of Jaden or his ability, but his simple departure has left me hollow. I hate the feeling.

Ry moves to my side, and I turn to meet his quizzical nature, fully aware of the pain that must show through my features.

"Wow! Look at you!" He steps beside me, bumping the bed, and I grab at the sides of the cot, fearing the little frame's collapse. He brushes my limp hair behind my ear. "It's finally begun. Astounding."

"What's begun?" I reach for the gourd, wanting more

water.

The native girl grabs the gourd before I am able, and she fills my cup. She is one of the natives I saw when we first emerged from the lake. Finished, she sets the water on a small table and pushes the table within my reach. Her task complete, she goes to stand by the door. She ogles me, and after the reaction I received at the lakefront, I suspect she's curious, slightly awed, and intimidated by my presence, yet I can't help thinking myself to be some kind of freak. I roll my eyes and glance away.

Same thing—sort of—different world.

The cloth door swishes, announcing her departure.

"You're *becoming* what you were meant to be, Ana. This is proof." He studies my eye, and my skin begins to itch.

I shift on the clumpy cot-bed. "About that. The strangest thing happened to me in the water." I refill the water mug, again.

"Jaden told me," he interrupts. "Your ability to control the water..." He shakes his head, eyes sparkling.

My back straightens. "Jaden told you?" He used our connection thing. "Did you know he could perceive my emotions, thoughts, and all that?" I shoot Ry a tight glare.

"Don't be too hard on him, Ana. These last two days, he's been sick with concern. I may have questioned his motives before, but not anymore. There's no denying how devoted he is to you and your safety." Ry folds my hands within his own. "As for feeling your emotions or picking up on your thoughts, that's all part of who and what he is. And what you are. What the two of you are, together. He's been bound to you by the fates. It wasn't a choice he had any say in."

"But..." Ry puts his finger to my lips.

"However, with time and discipline, I have no doubt

you'll be able to master the skills required to control what you share, if that's what you desire. He tells me it's within your ability spectrum. If you'd like, we can find someone to help you learn." His lips draw into a tight line. "But let me point out, there are benefits in having this type of connection with someone."

I glance toward the door, wonder if Jaden is listening. Ry follows my gaze, his lips twisting into a smirk. His words are muddling my thoughts; like water mixed with dirt, everything about me and my purpose is coming up sticky mud.

Ry squeezes my hand, pulling my attention back to him. "With Jaden in the group, he'll know when you're in need before anyone else does. He'll be able to find you or get you anything necessary without the wasted time of words. It's handy."

"You make his ability sound as convenient as the language option on a rental movie, only it's not that black and white."

"Listen, he's already proven himself, and..." Ry leans closer. "He can sometimes glimpse the future. Knowing when and where the big bad is coming... come on, Ana! Tell me that's not invaluable." He gives me an incredulous stare.

"Was he really sick with concern?" Out of everything Ry said, those words dug in the deepest.

Ry takes a deep breath and readjusts his position on the little cot. "What you need to understand, Ana, is Jaden has spent most of his life connected to your thoughts and emotions. From what I've seen, he's incorporated them into who he is. These last two days, while you were sleeping, there was a void. He got nothing from you. And I think..." Ry appears deep in thought for a moment. "I was worried for both of you." He squeezes my hand again.

My eyes widen and Ry nods.

"He said it was unusual, even in a slumber state. Of course, you've never been through such a transformation. I suspect the silence was driving him a tad mad... and making him rather difficult to be around." Ry huffs. "Can't say I blame him. I'd probably be the same way if I were in his shoes."

"Nothing, huh?" I glance toward the door, imagine him standing on the other side.

"That's what he said. You were deep in the clutches of change. But you're here now, and a transformation has definitely occurred." He motions to my blue eye.

"It was really driving him mad?" Logic tells me I should be concentrating on what Jaden can do for me, but it's how he's been feeling that most interests me.

Ry stands and paces the room. "Can we focus? You're like a schoolgirl with a crush. You need to be above such behavior."

"Why? Because everyone decided there was this bigger purpose for me?" I throw my hands in the air. "Because Ana is this big Balance Bringer thing she's not allowed to crush on anyone? That's bull, and you know it." I thrust my finger at him. He doesn't flinch. "Haven't you ever felt more for anyone?"

His eyes spark, and he glances away. My stomach flops. Unknowingly, I've stumbled onto something interesting. Except, the stern set of his jaw tells me now is not the time to press.

Throwing back the blanket, I swing my legs over the edge of the little cot, and the room spins. My hands grip the cot's edge, my knuckles whitening. It takes a second for the room to steady.

"What are you doing?" Ry asks.

"What does it look like I'm doing? If I've been asleep for three days, then we've lost a lot of time and need to get moving. I need to find that old mystic and fix whatever is happening with Kaia before it's too late." I hesitate and muse over what I'm wearing. I'm dressed in an extra-large pillowcase. Or could be, anyway. My garment is as fashionable as one. I frown and meet Ry's gaze. "Where are my crystals?" I've grown so accustomed to my wristband, I am incomplete without it.

"They're safe," he answers, referring not only to my crystal band, but Crystia's band as well. I started wearing hers after... well, you know. I'd rather not dwell on the why since being here in Hiddenkel is going to change all that.

"Is Crystia waiting outside?"

His face crinkles in what appears to be confusion. "The sun will be setting soon. Let's head out in the morning. I believe Jaden could use the rest before our next adventure. Now that you're out of the fog, there's a chance he may actually sleep."

Like Jaden before him, Ry avoids the topic of Crystia. Something dark and rigid slinks up my spine. Pushing the sensation away, I slip from the cot, stand, and test my weight. My legs are stiff, and the grassy, weaved rug scratches my bare feet, but the cuts I received while running in the rocky dirt at the mine don't cause me any discomfort.

I sway—only slightly. Once I am steady, I lift each leg in turn and check the bottom of my feet. The base of each is covered in the sign of healed cuts—tiny, disorganized lines running in every direction. I set my foot firmly on the ground.

I'm not human. But I already knew that. It's just, wrapping my head around that truth is somewhat difficult.

"Let me help you." Ry extends a hand.

Pushing him away, I skirt around the side table and head for... *where*? If we aren't leaving right now, where am I going? "Where's Crystia?"

"Crystia?" Confusion rattles Ry's voice.

"Yes, Crystia." I turn back and pin him with a glower. His face is awash in an emotion I don't quite understand. "You and Jaden have both avoided the topic. Why? She was here, remember? Waiting for us when we climbed out of the lake?"

He steps toward me, his hand lifting to sooth. I back away. Already, I want to cover my ears, shut out all sound. I don't want to listen to what he has to say.

His hand drops short of my arm. "The only thing here, waiting for us, was the tribe of the lake gate."

I want to scream, but I don't. Not yet.

"I'm sorry, Ana. I promise we'll fix your sisterly bond."

My body stiffens, and my hands ball up into fists. "No. I know what I saw. Crystia was here." My arms flail, as if trying to determine which direction to point. "She was here, Ry. I swear it. Why didn't you see her?"

"Calm down." Ry presses his hand in the air like the gesture will soften my mood. "I believe you."

"You do?" My shoulders relax.

His lips pull into a straight line, and his brow furrows. "I believe you believe," he says softly.

My jaw drops, my gut flops, and I want to... *oh for the love of Gaea*, I don't know what I want. My body is frozen and my head clouded, unable to wrap my mind around the idea that I could have imagined Crystia. I'm not crazy... am I?

TWO

"She's not wrong," Jaden says, from behind me.

I suck back a breath. Thank Gaea, someone else saw Crystia. I turn to face him. He has pulled back the cloth cover and is standing in the doorway.

"Crystia exists on another plane, only visible to you." His gaze is gentle, piercing, direct, and his words are like a punch to the gut.

My mouth pops open, and I stumble backward, Ry's hands clutch my elbows. "Like a ghost?" I don't want to believe it. Except, I thought of her as a ghost shortly after her death. Only, that was back in our dusty California town of a home. Somehow, I thought it would be different here. I believed the magic of Hiddenkel would change things.

Jaden shrugs, lifting his hands at his side. "If that's what you would like to call her. Her energy is simply in a different form. Energy is forever, Ana. It can never be destroyed."

"But I thought..." I start to shake. *Crap*. I don't want to breakdown. Not here, in front of the guys. *Crap. Crap. Crap.*

I hug myself and rub my upper arms. "I thought I'd get to touch her again, sister to sister—real flesh and blood." My resolve cracks, and a small tear forms at the corner of my eye.

In one fluid movement, Jaden's hand relinquishes Ry's hold, then glides up my arm and wipes away my tear. A beat later, I'm in his embrace. Soothing comfort sails through my system. A handy and irritating ability of his Tracer traits, to manipulate or guide my emotions. I can't even tell which emotions are truly mine and which have been fabricated by his ability.

Using my knuckles, I wipe the corner of my eyes and step away from Jaden. My chest once again starting to squeeze the air from my lungs.

With a somber gleam in his eye, Jaden reaches out and brushes my hair to the side. The edge of my lip twitches. I'm instantly self-conscious of my cleanliness... or lack thereof.

"I believe a bath would do you a realm of good. Relax your body, mind, and soul all at once," he says. "Possibly help you put things into perspective."

A horrendous grimace permeates my soul, and I let out a heavy sigh. "I don't feel like doing anything."

Jaden plants his gaze upon Ry. "I think it's the best thing for her right now. That and some food in her belly."

My stomach growls, and I press the palm of my hand to my gut in an attempt to silence the beast.

"Right," Ry replies and then grabs my hand. "Come with me."

"What if my lack of will results in me slipping under the water and drowning?"

"You won't drown, Ana." Jaden's eyes spark, and I'm reminded of when we first came through the gate, being under the water for an impossibly long time. And yet, I'm still alive and conscious and completely aware.

"Fine." My shoulders droop. "Which way to the shower?"

Beside me, Ry shifts and chuckles. "I'll show her the way. You get some sleep," he says to Jaden. Without another word, Jaden nods and excuses himself.

Ry tugs on my arm, prompting me to follow, and he trails Jaden out the door. I'm so absorbed in my loss, I almost miss Ry grabbing a satchel from a chair beside the door. Outside, the full force of the sun slaps me in the face. It's blinding and envelopes Jaden, leaving me clueless as to which direction he went. I blink rapidly and shield my eyes.

In a few quick breaths, my sight adjusts, and everything comes into view. The hut we've exited is made of massive bark shingles. Every hut is bark, tied together and supported by a center tree trunk and bamboo-thick beams. Row after row of huts, each with a plume of tree branches and leaves on top, like a fluffy, green hat.

The air is mild and dry, a nice change for the pungent, citrusy air from within the bark shingle homes. The glassy ocean of clear sky above stretches only as far as the towering mountainside on my right and what appears to be an enormous log wall surrounding the village on my left.

Who needs a wall that high? What are they trying to keep out? King Kong?

"Thank you," Ry says. I tear my gaze away from the monstrosity of a wall in time to witness a girl handing him something. He passes it to me. "Eat up."

I spin the item in my hands. It's warm with a hint of green and has a rather firm surface. Although the color is slightly off, I'm fairly confident it's bread. Excitement rumbles in my belly.

Ry leads me along an unpaved path as I devour my stale-tasting mini meal, each bite turning to paste in my mouth. Thatch buildings sit on either side of us, camouflaged beneath the tree cover, likely making the village invisible from the sky.

We're headed toward the edge of the settlement and to the lake beyond. "Is this a community bath situation? Because I don't know if I'm comfortable with that."

"Look around you. Do you expect them to have modern conveniences?" Ry shakes his head.

I don't need to look; I've already seen. If I want to get clean, I need to take a dip in a cold lake. *Awesome.* My insides tighten and drop.

Gravel crunches beneath my feet, and the sound reverberates through my head like exploding boulders. I rub my temples, attempt to soften the pain, and slowly scan our surroundings. It's as if our swim sucked us through a time vortex and dumped us sometime in the past... or in a remote area of Papua, New Guinea... rather than in a different world or dimension.

Behold, Ana the interdimensional time traveler.

Sarcasm sweeps through my soul, and I scoff at my ridiculous notion. Time travel aside, a more grueling truth burrows into the pit of my stomach. I am the Balance Bringer, and this world, whatever and wherever this is, is where I came from. I'm like Alice in Wonderland, if Wonderland was stripped of its bright colors and magic.

Worse yet, my sister isn't here.

Our feet carry us forward until we're standing beside a sparkling pool, sufficiently sheltered from the village. The clear, blue water appears unnatural in brilliance, and I have the strangest suspicion I've been to this place before. A just-out-of-reach memory plucks at my gut. Molting trees, vivid vegetation in various hues of green and purple, and boulders of all shapes and sizes surround the pool. Together, they create the illusion of privacy. There is also the sweetest scent of lavender. It's unarming, and with each inhale, my muscles relax a smidgen.

And then it hits me, as if I've face-slammed the surface of the lake. *This is it.* This is the wooded lake that invaded my thoughts and dreams so many times in the past. It's here that I foresaw Crystia. My searching gaze takes in the surroundings, exploring every shadow and dark place.

My thoughts swim... I saw Crystia when I first got to Hiddenkel. I swear I did. *Where is she now?*

Ry drops the satchel onto one of the larger stones. "Your clothing." He presses his hand to the clump of fabric. "You'll also find a towel and some soap." He glances toward the tree line, then back. "Would you like me to stand guard, make sure no one bothers you?"

"Do you think that's necessary?" I blink.

"You never know." He shrugs. "You are sort of a big deal here."

My tongue is frozen. I have no response to that. I've never been a big deal. Not ever. Except maybe on the swim team. Sort of.

He smirks at my silence and turns to go. I watch him leave, unease draping over me like a body bag. Everything I've done to get here, where here is—I tug at my pillowcase of a gown—how I'm dressed, and the change in my eye, is the kind of stuff you read about in storybooks, not real life.

A mild tremor runs through me, I hug myself and face

the lake. My feet don't want to move, don't want to carry me to the cold water. My hands resist compliance, unwilling to pull the tunic from my body. Can I wish myself back home like Dorothy in the Wizard of Oz?

If only.

My options are to either slip into the cold water or stay slime-under-a-rock gross, frozen on the shore.

Taking a deep breath, I muster my inner strength and prepare to face my insecurities. Feeling comfortable in my skin was never one of my strong points. I shuffle toward the lake with the tunic still on and the soap clutched to my chest. Goosebumps parade across my skin.

Before I am mentally ready, I'm there, one step into the lake water. Only, when the water laps over my skin, a calming warmth sweeps through my body, not the chilly bite I was expecting. It's like slipping into my bed back home—a belonging—an overdue homecoming.

And once again, I am connected with the Ondine, the water spirits.

With newfound bravery, I lose the tunic and move forward, immersing myself in the pool's liquid depth. The touch, the sensation, it makes me sense... more. More of me and more of the world around me.

Brimming on the edge of my internal receptors, I perceive a connection with water systems spreading far beyond this sparkling pool. Water gliding and rushing everywhere. Hiddenkel. Faredale. Places I've never been.

Vibrant, liquid energy tingles around and within me, and with the energy, blooms a confidence regarding my sisters and myself.

I bathe and swim and laze until the aches in my body diminish and my skin prunes. Without a phone or ticking clock, the concept of time eludes me. I duck beneath the water. My hair swims around me, suspended in slow motion. Bubbles float past me, and suddenly... I'm not me anymore.

I'm living a memory; to whom it belongs, I do not know.

That's the problem with this peculiarity, pulling experiences from blood relations I've never known and who have long since passed... I'm too new, too green, to understand what all the memories mean. I've been told it's a gift from my mother's side, being able to witness what past relatives have experienced in order to make the living relation more efficient, more skilled, and more successful in battle. But I am half Fae. It's quite possible my father's side has contributed a nice twist to the trait.

The hair of the memory's originator is still blonde, although fairer than mine. White fabric billows around me, and something heavy at my feet drags me down. I am falling too quickly or too slow to the bottom of a lake. My frantic motions and wild-eyed fixation are aimed at the surface, now covered in a thick layer of ice. I am dying, I know it to be so, and some part of me blames him, now nothing more than a shadow sourced above the ice. Only, more than I blame him, I scream out for him, expecting him to save me, because he loves me and he always comes to my rescue.

Who is he? I haven't a clue.

I thrash and scream and finally let go. Or, she does, anyway.

And the memory is gone. I am floating peacefully beneath the water. What good has it done me to experience so intimately the death of someone I never knew? Will it be relevant in my future? Is it something about him or her or the water? I want answers now, but there are none to be found.

I push forward through the water, and a space in front of

me shimmers. I stop, my limbs oscillating at my side. The shimmer darkens, takes form, and becomes a recognizable face—the old mystic who emailed me a million times and destroyed my computer with electricity. Or was the destruction my bad?

Me, I think. I was the source of the electricity. Electric discharge being a product of my abilities manifesting outside of my home world.

Out of reflex, I cover myself. Memories and magical visits, where is the sense of decency? I want to enjoy my bath alone and in peace.

"Glad you are well, my dear," she says, her voice fluctuating in the water around me. "Now don't dawdle. Please make your pilgrimage to me right away." She disappears.

I push up, break through the surface of the water, and swallow a massive gulp of air. What is with this lady? Instead of using a crystal ball, she uses computers and water to reach me? Can she use any reflective surface as a conduit for communication?

First Jaden, now this. My privacy is nonexistent.

I storm from the water, grab my towel, and dry off. I'm guessing I might need to get used to the strange and unusual in my life. After all, *I'm* clearly strange and unusual.

Leaving my hair wet, I slip into my comfortable, battered attire and make my way through the darkening treescape toward the warm glow of the village. There's a buzz I failed to perceive the last time I walked this path. Villagers dart along my route, an air of excitement infused in their hushed tones and rushed movements. I capture many a glance... or gawk. Even the occasional head bow. The attention makes my skin warm and my gaze avert.

It's along the central passage that I find my brother Ry sitting on a carved-out log bench set before a large campfire.

Brother.

The title is strange to me, after living with the lie for so long. If I ponder the truth and all the deceptions too much, my thoughts start to muddle into a fuzzy puddle of indecipherable emotions.

Ry appears deep in thought and is leaning so far forward on the makeshift bench, I half expect to see him tumble over. I plop down on the ground right next to his leg and warm myself by the flame. The smell brings back memories of family trips and summer nights by the campfire with Crystia and my mom. Mom always insisted we learn how to do it all, pitch a tent, start a fire, find and clean our own drinking water. Guess I now understand why.

Ry's fingers pull at the tangled mess at the back of my head. "This is a disaster you have going on back here."

"Yeah, well." I shift on the hard ground in search of better comfort. "I was forced to make do."

"This isn't the Ritz Carlton."

"I noticed," I lament and lean back into the log. Reaching behind me, I grab his hand and hold tight. "I'm happy you're safe and at my side."

"Where else would I be?" His voice cracks with laughter.

"I'm serious." I twist to look at him. "I was really scared when Dreya stabbed you. I thought..." I swallow a breath. "I thought you were dead. Thought you were stabbed by the Fire of Gaurdoone." A small tear forms at the corner of my eye.

Ry grimaces and dips his chin into his chest. "I'm sorry," he says. "Both Jaden and I regret what we put you through, but it was with good reason; we needed to keep you moving.

The moments following Dreya's attack weren't the time for mortal concerns or frets."

I release his hand and turn onto my knees to better face him. "What is that supposed to mean?"

He breathes in and out, slowly, leaving me to hang on the edge of anticipation. "The weapon that stabbed me *was* kissed by the Fire of Gaurdoone."

I study him. "Okay. But you said your blood..." I shake my head.

"I know what I said." He reaches for me, and I pull back. He sighs and lifts his shirt. Among the many warrior tattoos, I regard the wound, a red, puffy-lined scar, with a mapwork of red lines crackling outward. I suck back a deep breath. Shortly after Dreya's attack, the area had been clean, free of any sign of attack. "It was killing me slowly, from the inside out. I didn't want to take the chance of telling you and slowing our progress to get here." He drops his shirt back into place. "It was the small trace of Bringer blood that kept me alive long enough to get here."

He didn't lie to me. He just didn't tell me the whole truth. I file away my anger to be revisited another day, and with the tip of my fingers, gently touch his shirt at the spot of the wound. "Is it still killing you?"

He takes my hand in his and gives me a classic Ryland, everything-is-grand grin. "I don't believe so. The people here treated me, and I've been feeling much better."

"There's a cure?" I gaze into his eyes, searching for any sign of dishonesty. I see none.

"Apparently so," he says with a shrug. "Who knew?" He takes a sip from his mug. "It's the sap of a plant that only grows near the edge of the reflecting pool. They gave me some cuttings to take with us."

"Huh." I flop back around and lean against the log once more. "That's good. And oddly convenient." The words taste foreign on my tongue. I scrutinize the fire, unable to focus with my emotions in a tangled mess. "Thanks for lying to me, by the way." I don't try to hide the sarcasm in my voice, nor does Ry respond to it. Moments of silence pass between us, and it's like I'm holding my breath, waiting. Waiting for something, but I know not what.

My thoughts run to Jaden, as they often do. "In that fight where Dreya stabbed you," I say. "Jaden also got hurt. Dreya's sword sliced his upper arm, and he fell, smacking his head heavily against the rocky ground. He seemed alright when I saw him. Of course, I have been out for three days. Has he really healed?"

"He's recovered alright," he says, matter-of-factly.

I gaze at the flickering light of the fire, blinking and blinking to focus my sight. My view clears, and someone walks by, ogling me. "The people here look at me funny."

"You're like a rock star to them." Ry leans into his knees. "It's the Balance Bringer legend. They're hopeful you will fix this ailing world."

"That's a tall order," I say. "Sucks to be me." Several sparks pop from the fire. I watch the swirl and curve of red, orange, yellow, and blue flame. "Kaia told me as much."

"You already knew?" He tilts his head, curiosity gleaming in his eyes.

"I had some idea. It's a large concept to wrap one's head around. I mean, this *is* me we're talking about. And Kaia mentioned worlds, plural." I let out a heavy sigh.

"Don't underestimate yourself." He rubs my shoulder.

I frown at the midnight blue sky and its twinkle of gold. I don't recognize the stars. Orion's Belt, the Big and Little

Dippers, I can't find them anywhere. I twist my hair between my hands, work my fingers through the tangles, and ponder the difference in the night sky. I decide to try to memorize the new-to-me star pattern, for guidance purposes.

I barely have the chance to set the design to mind when a girl appears at my side. She's holding a mug in one hand and what looks like strips of beef jerky wrapped in cloth in the other. "Eat. Drink," she says, handing me my meal. I scrutinize the yellow chunks floating in my drink.

"What is it?" I say and sniff the rim of the mug.

"Let me see." Ry grabs the mug, takes a sip, and returns it to me. "It's Aloe water. It's good for you. Don't be afraid. They aren't going to poison you after going to such efforts to make you comfortable."

I narrow my gaze on him and take a sip of the water. *It's good.* I follow up with a bite of the jerky. My stomach growls in appreciation.

"I almost forgot. This is for you." Ry drops Jaden's magic backpack at my side. It's filled with everything I need and more. "Jaden said there were things in here you might want." Ry nudges the bag.

My arms shake. I greedily pull the bag into my lap and immediately dig in. "I never would have believed I could be so excited over finding a hairbrush." I pull a bristle brush from the bag. In no time, I've put it to work on my tangles, and I start to feel almost half human. But, of course, I'm not. Human, that is. I'm half Immortal Warrior Clan and half Fae. "Remind me again why I am so important. Not the why but the what."

His foot taps twice as if pressing a gas pedal. "The people here grew up with the legend of the Balance Bringer. They probably know it by heart. When the scales are tipped to the point of breaking, a Balance Bringer is born—three sisters, one balancer at the core. This time, Ana, it's your burden to bear. You are that one destined to keep the balance among the worlds." He watches me, a mixture of pity and tenderness drawing the lines on his face.

My chest heaves, heavy with mental and emotional weight.

"The story is older than time, having been passed down through the ages," he continues. "It's always a trinity with one at the core. You are the synthesis of yourself and your sisters. You are the core, and with the power of the three, you will become everything you were ever meant to be. You have your parental blending of blood to thank for your foretold destiny."

I lean deeper into the bench, wishing to blend with the wood, become the log. Then no one would expect anything from me other than to just be. Too many have expectations, and there are too many chances for me to fail. My face crinkles into an uncommitted and, likely unattractive, what-the-heck expression.

Ry flashes his teeth. "The mingling of our mother's warrior race blood with that of the magical Fae race of your father. What they took for love or convenience or whatever, resulted in the unique individual you are *becoming*. Legend says that the first Balance Bringer entrusted the warrior race to watch over her seed until the time of the next calling. So has been the case each time thereafter. It would stand to reason that you are a direct descendant of the original Balance Bringer." His eyes twinkle like a cat who swallowed the canary.

"Are you trying to tell me that my sisters are within me?"

I stop mid-stroke, the brush lodged in a strand of hair near my ear.

"Sort of, I guess. I don't really know how it works, but once we fix this issue with Kaia, you should feel something... I think." He squeezes my shoulder and releases.

My fingers instinctively brush the edges of Kaia's crystal. After all I've been through, it still hangs at my neck. It's cold to the touch, and its lines are smooth beneath my fingers. I lift the stone to my sight, and my chest folds in on itself. Something is stomping on my chest. The stone is no longer clear. It's now smoky in appearance. I twist and shake the crystal at him.

"It's smoky. What does that mean?" A tear threatens to slip from the corner of my eye, and I fight to keep it at bay.

"I don't know, but we'll figure it out. I promise you." He grabs me by the shoulders.

"Did you know my father's sister killed Kaia?"

Ry takes a deep breath and exhales slowly, "We expected as much, but there has never been any proof. Those bruises on your body the other week, you lived one of her experiences, didn't you?"

"Yes." My voice croaks. "It was horrible. In all these years, Kaia has never mentioned it to me, and I don't think she ever planned to share that information with me either."

"That's actually an important thing to know. She should be more forthcoming." Ry sighs.

"Did you know Kaia well?" I blink.

"I worked with her as I work with you. Only, we didn't need to live a cover story. We lived as a family, here in Hiddenkel." The lines on his face are easy to read, and it's clear he misses her more than he's letting on.

I reach for his hand. "I'm sorry," I say, wanting to ease his pain, although I have no idea how. I can't imagine anything anyone could say to me that would ease my pain over the loss of Crystia. Kaia is my sister, too, and I should feel a pain equivalent to Ry's. Only, I never knew her when she was alive—and so I mourn her differently. She is the voice in my dreams. The voice I don't want to lose, and yet I am.

"She was only twenty-three years old," he says, his voice a mere whisper.

"Twenty-three?" My voice squeaks. "She doesn't look twenty-three!"

"Immortal-Fae hybrid, remember?" He adopts a cocky grin, and his sadness appears to melt away. "We can live for countless years without signs of aging. But as you well know, we're not impervious to injury or a fatal blow."

What does that mean for me and my lifespan? Will I get bored after a hundred years? I toss my unspoken questions into the flames, watch as they flicker and lick at the night sky.

Ry leans forward to gaze around the fall of my hair. "How are you feeling? Tired at all?"

I just slept for three days! I start to say no but freeze when a chill caresses my ear and the familiar scent of peaches wafts around me. "Crystia?" I whisper.

"Rest. You're going to need it."

I drop my head against Ry's knee.

THREE

It was so clear—Crystia's voice at my ear.

Had she somehow caused me to fall asleep? I don't remember walking back to the hut, nor crawling into my cot of a bed.

I rub my eyes and glance down at the disheveled blankets. I've been awake for a few minutes—ten, maybe—only without the convenience of a modern bathroom, there isn't much to do to prep for the day. I should be jumping up, eager to start searching for Crystia and Kaia. Especially after getting so much sleep.

Three whole days!

Only, at the moment, I have no desire to move... or think. Sitting up is about as much energy as I am able to muster. A peaceful calm resides outside the walls of my little hut, and I am reluctant to disrupt the silence.

Something delicious tickles my nose. It's the mouthwatering aroma of breakfast. Ham? Possibly bacon? Assuming they have pigs in this world. I close my eyes and envision

Sunday morning's spread with my family. A yearning pang presses into my chest, and I sigh. I miss my mom. I miss my family.

"Get dressed. We need to go."

My eyes pop open. Ry is leaning in through the door, his entire person buzzing with anxiety.

"What's wrong?" I throw back the blanket.

"Just get dressed and meet us outside." He disappears, leaving the cloth doorway cover to fall back into place.

I glance down at what I'm wearing.

I am dressed.

A jumble of voices sounds outside, followed by the clamor of feet jogging and running upon the dusty earth. I quickly pull on my socks and shoes, toss any of my belonging—which pretty much consists of my now bent and wrinkled picture of Crystia with Caesar and the picture of Crystia, Ry, and me—into my magical Jaden bag and spy something within the dark depths of the bag. I reach in and pull out the sliver of rock I retrieved from the school parking lot when Jaden slammed the main object to the ground.

Why had he done that? Had he seen what I later observed, when I studied the piece in the safety of my own home? Had he also witnessed the girl glaring back at him? Right now, the cut of rock appears to be nothing more than a glossy, broken stone. No faces watching. Nothing out of the ordinary. I drop the stone back into the depths of the bag and make a note to remember it is there.

In fact, the stone is all I can now think about. Is it magic like the backpack? Is it a way to communicate? Instead of calling someone up on a phone, they use a smooth, glossy rock?

I weave my hair into a braid, snap on my crystal wristbands, toss the pack over my shoulder, and step outside.

Ry and Jaden are not immediately detectable among the busy bodies crowding the path. And when I say busy, I mean moving quickly with a clear purpose and destination, except they aren't all moving toward the same destination. I decide to follow the majority, which leads me toward the King-Kong-sized wall.

"Are you ready?"

Jaden appears out of the crowd. I startle. I'd been so busy following everyone else that his approach from the side catches me off guard. My gaze falls upon the crystal pendant hanging at his neck. My skin warms and tingles. Casually, Jaden lifts the weight of the small pack at my back and slings it over his shoulder.

"Yeah. I think so." I glance between him, the wall, and the people rushing toward it. They are working a massive pulley system and opening a gate the size of a two-car garage door. The gate must be unbelievably heavy to require so much manpower. "What's going on?"

Jaden hands me a delicious-smelling morsel. I'm guessing it's more bread, but again, it's a mossy green. The heat permeates the cloth in which it's wrapped, and I find myself gently tossing it back and forth between my fingers. It's as if my meal was pulled immediately from the oven. Or, off the fire. However they cook things here.

"Earlier this morning, one of the village scouts returned with distressing news. One of Dreya's regiments is headed this direction." He motions to the food in my hand. "Eat up. You're going to need your strength. We leave shortly."

Dreya's coming here? Of course, she knew where to find me. She'd been there practically at the point where we crossed over. And if her goon squad is on the move, then it's likely she survived the crystal cave. *That's just great.*

I break the doughy meal into pieces, deem the rising steam bearable, and take a bite. It's okay. Not something I would ever search out when hungry.

There's a glint in Jaden's eye, and I'd swear he's suppressing a laugh. "It's not the tastiest stuff, but it's loaded with everything your body needs."

I scrutinize the remains held in my hand and decide delicious meals are overrated. "And Ry?" I ask. "Where's he?"

"He's been planning our departure from this village since the day we set foot on the shore. He's now organizing everything, since we are leaving a couple hours before originally planned."

I nod, keep walking, making my way toward the wall. I spin my greenish bread in my hand, no longer confident on how to act in Jaden's presence. No longer confident on how to act in regards to anything, really. I steal a glance in his direction. "So..." I bite the edge of my lip, look away. "Are you feeling better?" I glance his direction again.

He blinks hard, and his head flinches back. "I feel fine. Why?"

"Oh." My feet are suddenly extremely interesting. "It's just something Ry said."

The morning sun casts our shadows out before us, and I can make out enough movement variation to discern the moment his understanding is clearly evident. Ry told me Jaden wasn't sleeping and was distressed during my hibernation period. I hold that tiny knowledge close to my heart. Even if my feelings are confused. I want Jaden to like me because he sincerely does, not because of some magic binding between us.

"Over here." Ry beckons us with the swoop of his arm. He and a couple of the villagers are huddled to the side of the gate, studying what appears to be a map. Between them are a few loaded packs. We step up beside the huddle just in time for them to wave and walk away. Ry is still holding the map.

"Was it me?" I ask regarding their departure.

"Don't be silly." Ry shakes his head. "They need to fortify and prepare for the arrival of the enemy at their gates."

I study the activity around the gate more closely. A platform, fitted with some type of bungee support and harnesses runs along the top of the log wall. Midway down the wall, sits a large reinforcement and platform, which is loaded with contraptions reminiscent of medieval artillery. Catapults, ballistas, and whatnot.

I didn't study medieval artillery in high school.

"One for you." My attention snaps back to our little group. Ry has pushed one of the packs into Jaden's arms. "And one for you." He tosses one at me. I drop my breakfast crumbs and catch the pack.

"Can we make these smaller? Like somehow toss them into Jaden's magical backpack?" I ask and bounce the weight of the pack in my arms while making a silly holy-cow-this-is-heavy expression.

Jaden smiles at my clever idea, and Ry's gaze shifts from me to my Tracer. He shrugs. "I don't see why not."

"Awesome." My victory beam warms my entire face. I really didn't want to lug that uncomfortable pack around. "Do we know where we are going?"

Jaden snatched the pack from my hands and sets it on the ground at his feet, next to his own load. Once his magical backpack is open, he starts finagling the squeeze past the opening.

"Pretty sure." Ry's gaze sweeps from the map in his hand to Jaden. "But I am hoping this guy's Tracer gift would keep us on point," he says, motioning to Jaden.

"I'm not a compass." Jaden's response is quick. He's in the midst of dropping the pack Ry handed me into the endless-space-available backpack he's been carrying since our adventure began. Within seconds, the larger pack is gone. He drops his own inside next. Now, instead of three bags, we have one that is smaller and easier to handle.

I wonder if the backpack has an infinite amount of space or if the space is limited.

Jaden extends his hand to Ry in a silent request for my brother's large bundled burden. "Ready?" The question, spoken by neither Ry nor Jaden, comes from my left—a villager.

"Yeah, yeah," Ry says in response. He hoists his gear over his shoulders, turns toward the gate, and follows the villager. He glances over his shoulders. "Coming?"

Jaden shrugs and, accepting Ry has chosen to carry his bag, waves his hand, motioning for me to follow our leader. I hasten after Ry and the villager. Jaden is right behind me.

"Who's this person?" I point to the leader of our little procession. It's a girl with long, to-her-butt, black hair.

"This is Yuromo," Ry says over his shoulder. "She was the scout that spotted Dreya's people. She knows the terrain and is going to be our guide."

My mouth drops open. The siren-red streak in Yuromo's hair is unmistakable. I saw her at the front of the group gathered at the lake side when we arrived. Her body was tense, ready to fight. "But..." I stammer. "Can we trust her?" I whisper.

"Of course we can." Ry scoffs.

Yuromo turns around, walks backward, awarding me with a full view of her half -naked body. She's dressed in something akin to rawhide short shorts, and her top is small and tight and shows all the curves. I never considered it wise to go out in the wilderness with your arms and legs and abdomen exposed, not to mention the low-cut neckline. Her lips twist in an upward curl, and her hues seem pleasant enough, but I have little to no understanding of the colors and their means.

My mouth is agape. I snap it shut and press my lips into a firm line.

"I am Yuromo of the lake gate tribe, and I am most completely at your service," she says with eyes wide and a mild nod of the head. "*Princeza.*"

That's not the same word Jaden and the water Ondine used in reference to me. Yuromo has chosen a different language by which to call me princess, something I can't relate to at all.

"Don't call me that."

"As you wish." She bows her head, then turns forward and walks through the front gate. The rest of us follow. All the while, I keep glancing Jaden's direction.

Once we are outside the village fortress, the gate begins to lower, cutting us off from all the villagers wishing us luck and shouting their goodbyes. We wave and head toward the tree line. We are in the midst of a large mountain range and have a ton of downhill hiking ahead of us.

Since Ry's original plan had us entering Hiddenkel somewhere completely different than where we ended up, we need to make up for lost time. Translation: more walking, less resting. We will attempt to avoid Dreya's regiment and cover as much ground as possible before nightfall. Hopefully, all my training has properly prepared me for our quest.

"Well, at least we got here," I mumble. And it's true. We'd probably still be driving across the United States if Ry hadn't remembered the abandoned gateway. Or if Jaden hadn't been there to collect me when I escaped from Ry's stolen car. Or Dreya could have succeeded and we could all be dead. But we're here and we're alive, so I need to remember to count my blessings and not give in to my fears or anxieties.

Before stepping into the cover of the trees, I glance back at the village one last time. It was the last place where I saw Crystia, and, even if no one else saw her, now it's like I'm walking away from a piece of myself. Leaving one sister behind to find the other. The desire to stay, opposed to the desire to go, it's like rabid dogs and feral cats in my chest. Yet logic dictates the greater hope can be found ahead, verses back in the shadows of where I've been.

I say my final farewell and put the village at my back, deciding to move toward my future. Trying not to dwell over Crystia or the puzzle that is my connection with Jaden, I occupy my mind with the surrounding sights and scents. I once heard that it's the journey that makes us who we are meant to be. I want that future me to be someone who takes the time to truly absorb the world around her.

I've never visited any wooded areas before. I grew up in the middle of the California dessert. Sure, we had trees, but there wasn't any place nearly as densely populated as the mountainside we now traverse. Everywhere around us, everything is so green. So leafy. So breathtakingly stunning.

The trees vary in height, some standing ten to twenty feet tall, while other's tower over us like skyscrapers. There are as many shades of green as there are stars in the sky—endless. The ground is lush, covered in moss and tiny ferns. And we are all wrapped in the robust aroma of sap and cedar and pine.

This is Gaea's cathedral.

There is a peace to be found among the bark and leaves. A hushed calm unlike the one I'd experienced in the vast desert landscape of my hometown. There's plenty of life in the desert, among the dirt and yucca trees, but here, I detect the rustle of the leaves, the chatter of birds, the singing of bugs, and something else... a sadness, and a glimmer of hope.

The first leg of our journey is downhill, and we keep a steady pace following a barely there path. Yuromo leads the way, weaving through trees and climbing over, under, and down rocky ledges. When the sun is directly overhead and the light shimmering upon the branches and leaves drops deformed sun puddles upon the ground, Ry allows us a break for lunch.

By the time I settle in against a thick-rooted giant of a tree, my stomach is growling with the anticipation of food. Ry is already biting into his bread before I can even pull my lunch from my pack. Yuromo gathers the canteens and excuses herself. I watch her retreat and contemplate what I'd be like if I'd grown up here as she did. Would I have become a tree climber? Possibly a tree hugger? Would I know my way around the forests and mountain sides as well as I know how to throw a knife?

I slap my arm and kill a bug. A tiny, shrilling stab pierces the side of my head, and I wince.

Or would I be constantly covered in bug bites?

"Is this what you expected?" Ry asks between bites.

I tilt my head in thought. "I've seen this place in so many different states—sparkling with life, completely dead, in the process of dying—I don't know what I expected." I survey the trees surrounding us. "It's hard to imagine things are much different here than they are back home." I stammer. "I mean, where I grew up."

Ry snorts. "Well, if you're waiting for talking trees or fire breathing dragons, you'll be disappointed."

"No dragons?" I fake a frown, even though the idea of trying to talk to one intrigues me. A vision pops into my head of me as dragon kibble. Or maybe not.

Ry shakes his head, his eyes twinkling with laughter. "Things are definitely different here, Ana. This world appears primitive because civilization is built in balance with the land. No toxins to destroy the environment. That is, besides the toxins of illness you are meant to heal. The unbalance. But..." He swirls his finger toward me. "...if you keep your mind open and your observations sharp, there are endless hints of magic to be witnessed."

Yuromo returns from her quick trip to the waterhole and passes out the canteens. Jaden takes two and hands one to me, his fingers lingering on mine in the exchange. I find myself gazing into his eyes, and it's as if he is the center of a magnetic pull and all I want to do is let go and crash into him. Butterflies take flight in my belly, swirling in tiny circles. In that moment, my conflicted emotions about his *ability* seem insignificant, even stupid. I have faith that some-day, maybe, I'll be able to look beyond what he can do and will be able to focus on who he is.

A shudder rolls over me, and with it, the strangest of

thoughts. It's as if Jaden and I have always been. Lifetime after lifetime.

I flinch, breaking the moment, and try to cover the awkwardness by taking a sip from the canteen. "I'm assuming this water is safe?" I ask after swallowing a mouthful.

Jaden grimaces. "Totally unsafe. I saw this as the perfect opportunity to poison your mind."

I gasp.

"Of course it's safe. I wouldn't give it to you if it wasn't," Yuromo says. She's sitting directly across from me.

My gaze jumps between Jaden and Yuromo. Jaden starts laughing.

"Were you actually joking?" I ask. Jaden's head nods between chuckles. "That's the first time I've ever heard you joke around."

"Most of the situations we have found ourselves in have been rather serious, don't you think? Many a no-joking matter."

I nod once in agreement. His body heaves with a heavy, slow breath, as if releasing the burdens of past events. "May I," Jaden asks, gesturing to my free hand. My eyebrows pinch together, and I place my hand in his. He pulls something from his coat pocket and slips it into my hand.

"Oh." The tiny word involuntarily escapes my lips. Sitting in the palm of my hand is a small chocolate square. There was a bag of them hidden in his pack at the beginning of our journey. So much has happened since then I completely forgot.

I flip the chocolate in my palm, turning it over and then over again. "Thank you." I meet his gaze. "Your knowledge of me is like a box of constant surprises. If you're not careful, you're going to spoil me."

He grins. "I don't see that as a bad thing."

I bite my lip, and his soft, harmonious laughter serenades me. The sound is beautiful, a delight to my soul, and then I remember why he knows so much about me. My fingers jump to my lips, hold my mouth closed even as my breath lodges in my throat. His ability has allowed him to spy on me for years. I blink and peer into his eyes, searching for signs of deceit. But it's not deceit that I find. In fact, I'm not sure what it is I've found. I perceive him differently than I ever have before. It's like I'm gazing upon his soul, and something about him is intimately familiar.

"Lifetime after lifetime," I whisper and quickly busy myself unwrapping the chocolate, watching the slivers of silver unfold.

"What is that?" he asks, tilting into me.

I'm fairly certain he was asking about my whispered words. Instead, I show him the daily wisdom I have revealed, and together we read it in silence.

Never look back. That's where the shadows wait.

That's ominous, I muse, and then remember I thought something eerily similar a few hours earlier. It's probably nothing. I shake it off. "Looks like it's only forward from this point on," I joke.

Jaden moves to face me straight on and grabs both my hands. "Ana, I..."

"You've got to move."

I recognize her voice immediately. Crystia is hovering at my side. I squeal her name.

"Where have you been?" I ask her.

Ry abruptly hushes me. He's moving past me, staring

through the trees. Jaden's eyes have gone murky, and Yuromo is gathering all evidence of our stop and shoving it into Ry's bag.

I could fly; I'm so excited my sister is here. Even if it appears to be the worst timing *ever*.

"Go!" she shouts at me and points in the opposite direction of whatever has Ry's attention.

Jaden returns in a snap. "Get out of sight," he whispers.

Without a word, I let him lead me at a quick jog, hand in hand. Ry and Yuromo follow close behind. And I'm hoping, hoping, hoping, Crystia is following, too. We drop into a gully and hunker up against a gnarly mess of massive tree roots. I motion to Jaden, plead to be clued in on what his vision revealed, but get silenced by Ry's finger.

Ry surveys the landscape, then, with a point of his finger, directs us to move deeper into the woodlands. Keeping our heads low, we sprint away from the barely-there-path until we find an outrageously mammoth tree to use as cover.

"I want to get an idea what we're dealing with," Ry says. He tilts his head toward Jaden. "Take Ana and Yuromo and keep moving. I'll catch up."

"Ry, no." I grab his arm. I have no idea what is out there, but based on Jaden and Crystia's reactions, it has to be troubling, and I don't want Ry to get hurt. Or worse, I don't want to lose him. We're here in a land completely foreign to me, and I can't, simply can't, go forward without him.

"Don't, Ana. Not now." He peels my hand free. I'm prepared to argue when Yuromo jumps in.

"I'll keep him safe," she says to me. "And I'll find you. I know this land like I know my tribal oath, up and down, backward and forward."

I want to argue, only Ry makes one quick motion to

Jaden, and before I understand what's happening, Jaden has tossed me over his shoulder and is running the opposite direction. Tree after tree races by, and the ground turns into a blur of motion. My body bounces and jerks, my stomach lurches and rolls, and my skin burns like the surface of the sun. I can't believe Ry, my best friend and brother, did that to me.

Well, actually, I can. But it doesn't stop me from wanting to shake him until his brain unhinges. It's not fair that Yuromo gets to stay, and fight if needed, and I don't. I have every right to be at Ry's side.

"If you're still with me, Crystia, I could use a little help."

Jaden's momentum shifts and slows. Seconds later, he sets me beside a massive redwood-type tree. It blends with all the other large trees surrounding us. I no longer recognize the beauty of the place or the subtle differences. I only envision my fist slamming into Ry's face.

Out of frustration, of course.

Without thought, my arm swings around, my hand curled into a fist, destined for Jaden's nose. He is, after all, guilty of aiding and abetting. My fist smacks into his palm.

"Nice right hook," he says, a grin wrapping his face. "Might I suggest we keep quiet?"

Right. How silly of me. I fume.

My anger thaws, leaving me to feel minuscule and childish.

"Sorry," I whisper and push myself against the base of the tree. Forward and back, left and right, no Crystia. Why would she show up only to leave again so quickly?

The world around us goes silent, deathly still, and it's clear to me that the trees, birds, and bugs sense something we don't. A chill shivers up my spine, and I recall the darkness that chased me at school, in my home, at the ghost mine, and in the tunnels. I pray to God and Gaea that's not what now comes our way.

Like Ry, I need to know. Need to know what it is we're running from. I close my eyes, breathe deep, and reach out with my senses. When I'm searching for it, the sound swiftly travels to my ear. Trampling footsteps. A step-and-drag motion. A horde of them, following a confident stride. The path through the trees is too small to contain them all, so they spill over into the surrounding flora.

I *wonder*.

A few days ago. when Jaden, Ry, and I made our way through the dark, searching for the forgotten doorway to Hiddenkel, I experienced vision issues. Like other abilities of mine, has my sight received an upgrade? If so, how do I tap into that ability?

Twisting onto my belly, I inch forward and press tight against the tree's oversized roots. I'm focused and determined and peering as far as I can—between the trees and across the landscape. The scene gradually comes into sharp view like I'm squinting through a long tube. A dark mass of bodies is shifting and marching in our direction. There's zero fashion to the order in which they move. They drag; some even waddle; they push and shove, all the while continuing to press forward.

Late night zombie movies. That's what they remind me of. Walking corpses. The many members appear devoid of life. The light in their eyes is gone, and their flesh is pale and flaking. Few sport odd patches of pink warmth. *Goon squad. Ghoul squad. What are they?*

Jaden's hand drops onto my arm, and I jump. With a quick wave, he motions for us to shimmy down the slope behind us. I agree with a nod. He starts down, and I take one last memorizing scan of the half-dead army before retreating.

I'm about to follow Jaden down the bank when something registers in the back of my mind, a familiar calling. Like the pull of a magnet, my gaze is torn back to the mass of walking un-dead corpses.

The air squeezes from my lungs, my heart quickens, and a lump lodges in my throat. Striding down the middle of the un-dead army is Dohlan. My Dohlan.

FOUR

D ohlan's glory illuminates the woods around him. The spectral is likely a figment of my imagination. One I can't unsee. Something inside of me claws and kicks, wanting to run to him.

I'm too easily influenced, but I don't want to be. I don't want the weak side of me to win.

Run, the voice in my head whispers. *Run far, far away.*

Dohlan stops mid-stride. He's surrounded by demonized un-dead men and monsters. And he doesn't spot us.

Or does he?

His gaze is off to the side. Not searching in our direction, at all. Yet... the tiniest hint of a grin graces his lips, and the softest whisper of my name touches my ear.

Run!

Dohlan is here. Physically here. So close I could run to him, touch him. But why is he leading a group of... of what-ever they are... un-dead monster soldiers?

After Jeremy died, I fantasized about Dohlan. That was

before the flesh and blood version of Jaden came along. Even now, I sense something. A need? A want? I don't know why. I only know I can't *not* feel for him. And yet, he scares me.

Jaden returns to my side. Touches my arm. I jolt. "What are you doing?" he asks.

"What are they?" I motion to the army, gluing my gaze upon them once more.

"No idea. I have not seen their kind before." He keeps his gaze glued on the approaching procession. The horde loops in and out of the surrounding tree line, browsing at anything and everything, searching.

Chills race across my skin, and I rub my arms.

I want to turn away, and yet I can't. They're a puzzle in need of solving. Are they monsters? I peer harder, my gaze averting to Dohlan and then back. Based on their clothing, hair, and shoes, they're farmers, merchants, pirates, and bullies. The army is comprised of everything and nothing at all. It's as if they once lead productive lives and then something sucked the will to live right out of them and made them puppets.

"Those poor souls." I sigh and return my attention to Dohlan.

"She has him pretty well twisted up in knots," Crystia says, now perched at my side.

"Dreya?" I respond, refusing to shift my gaze away from Dohlan.

"Yeah. She's done a real wackadoo of a number on him. And the army of monsters, you were right to consider them as undead. They are men, women, and children touched by her mad darkness. Their lives and souls are held in suspension, their physical form twisting into the ugliness you see." She glances back toward Jaden, and I follow her gaze.

Jaden taps my arm, motioning for a take-two on the shimmy down the slope. Without glancing his way, I nod, spare Crystia a quick peek, and then continue to gaze at Dohlan. His jacket flares out around him, exposing his beautiful build and perfect taste in attire. His hair falls with just the right kind of flip that makes my belly summersault. I inch closer.

"You sure do have it bad. Don't you?" Crystia whispers.

I sigh, hate the idea of admitting to such a truth.

Dohlan moves his head in such a manner I freeze, fearing I've been detected. *Did he motion for me to stop?* My head spins with options for my next move, and I make none. I study him, and it's like he's aware of my watchful eye.

His hand presses into the air before him, motions for me to run away.

He knows I'm here.

Jaden grabs my hand, severing my connection, my pull, to Dohlan. All traitorous thoughts are instantly obliterated. I blink and let out a deep breath, hopeful the simple effort will clear my mind and emotions.

Never forget, you belong to me, Ana. Dohlan's voice wraps around the curve of my ear and slides across my skin.

With a shiver, I follow Jaden down the slope. I slip and slide in loose dirt, pine needles, and fallen leaves. We weave through the trees toward the sound of running water, leaving the un-dead army far behind.

A considerable distance begins to stretch between us and them, and yet, I'm not comfortable allowing confidence to bloom in my chest. Instead, I push forward, one quick step at a time, my hand held tight in Jaden's. I can't tell if Crystia is keeping up with us or not, but every once in a while, I catch sight of a transparent blur of color. Maybe it's her.

"We've run so far. How will Ry and Yuromo find us?" I ask, keeping pace with Jaden.

"He's Ryland. He'll always find you." He chances a glance in my direction, and the confidence in his eyes doesn't match his words. He turns away. "And Yuromo, well..."

Yuromo. She is as familiar with the territory as she is with her tribal oath. I hope that wasn't a lie. Either way, find us or not, I have zero control over what will be, so I try not to let worry overrun me. Instead, I concentrate on where we are and where we are going. Which, in my current mood, isn't ideal. The trees, the landscape, the rocks, ferns, and weeds, they are all the same. One big blur.

That is, until I catch sight of something so unusual, so different, my forward progress falters. My hand slips free from Jaden's hold, my attention stuck upon a dark crack in the earth.

The crack runs diagonally across our path like a mini fault line splintering the forest into sections. Only, that isn't what I find so curious. After all, I grew up in California, land of earthquakes and fault lines. The curious part is that a tarry substance fills the crack, and along the torn lines of land, clusters of trees and vegetation are withering in death and decay. And not just dying. Stuff is turning a rot black.

"Something isn't right with that," Jaden whispers, grabbing my hand and pulling me away from the site. Reluctantly, I follow.

I remember the vision Kaia shared with me of the land dying, turning brown and then black. Now, it's as if I have witnessed that truth in action. Dark, dried, crumbled are the tiny fern blades along the path. The bark on the trees flake and crack like age-old black paint from a wall. And ahead, a wall of a tree. The giant has succumbed to the illness and fallen, blocking our path.

"I should have expected this. I should have taken us in a different direction." Jaden rakes his hand through his hair and weighs our options. The tree is forever long with no visible end in either direction. Our run has come to a temporary stop.

"Don't beat yourself up, handsome. You'll figure this one out." Crystia flicks her fingers through his hair. Jaden flinches and scratches the side of his head at the spot where Crystia touched him. I bite my lips, muffling a giggle.

"Maybe if we find some branches, we can climb over?" I offer and remember climbing the pinyon pine that took Jeremy's life.

If it hadn't been for the unexpected vision, I would have easily made it to the top. Unfortunately for us, this tree refuses to be so helpful. It is oddly bare of any branches, no matter how small. Almost as if they were purposely removed to create an unscalable barrier.

"You don't think this was put here on purpose?" I ask, scanning left to right, attempting to determine which direction is the top of the tree, then glancing at Crystia in hopes she'll hold an answer.

"No idea." Jaden takes a deep breath.

Crystia shrugs.

I rest my hands on my hips. "You don't happen to have any rope in that handy bag of yours?" When last I checked, Jaden's magical pack dropped everything I could possibly want into my lap. "That would come in really handy right about now..."

My gaze scans the top of the tree for any remaining broken

branches. I've never beheld a tree so massive. I once saw a picture of the biggest tree in the United States. It was wider than my mom's SUV. I suspect this tree would rival that one.

"...if we can find something to loop it around," I add.

Crystia's head sways from side to side, like we're boring her, and she shuffles out of sight.

"You know I do." He slips the pack from his back and starts yanking the bag open.

My mind is still obsessed with the picture of that enormous tree, of how I wanted to take a family trip to see it in person, and how I'm standing in front of one just as large or larger, only without my family. "Maybe we can tie something to the rope, use it as an anchor, and toss it over the tree."

"Huh," he says.

I glance his direction. Jaden isn't holding any rope. He isn't even perusing through the bag. It sits at his feet next to the two larger bags he's pulled free. He's pointing to a spot several feet along the tree to my left. There's a dip in the dirt, a small tunnel beneath the wooden beast. The kind a large animal or child would have carved out in order to crawl to the other side. I'm fairly certain the space wasn't there several minutes ago. Do we have Crystia to thank for the opening?

I study the hole and try to gauge the depth and width. It'll be tight, but I can shimmy through.

"Will you fit?" I mentally compare the space to Jaden's wide shoulders.

"I think so." His lips twist into uncertainty.

I move to the dip, drop to the ground, and glance back. He is slowly dropping his pack inside the magic backpack. I don't understand why he pulled the things out in the first place, and I decide not to ask.

I slide through to the other side. The tree scrapes at my sides as I wiggle and scoot my way. When I pull free of the tunnel, Jaden pushes the pack through. I grab it, take a step back to allow him space, and...

"Ana!" His voice is filled with panic.

"Duck," Crystia orders sharply. A millisecond later, I register the sound of a snapping twig.

I don't think, don't question, simply act, dropping to a quick crouch. Something from behind lunges over me. Arms swing through the space that seconds ago I filled. Whatever is behind me, it's large, surprisingly fast, and rank. The lurch of his arm may not have knocked me out, but his body odor might.

My gut drops. I suck back a breath, steel my nerves, and abruptly stand, swinging the backpack around me in hopes of a damaging connection. I'm not disappointed. The packs hit a wall of twisted flesh sending the monster stumbling. The impact was more than I anticipated, and I also stumble, a foot, possibly two, yet manage to remain standing. I spin around and find my attacker on the ground. He's down, not out.

He is one of three undead soldiers situated in front of me. My attacker on the ground, fumbling to get back up, and two more standing a far-too-close ten feet away. They're snarling and smiling and drooling and carry with them the smell of rotten eggs.

So gross.

I know better than to enter a space blindly. I should have checked before diving under the tree. I was trusting Crystia, and that turned out to be a mistake. She might not have been the one who made the opening. I made the mistake of assuming.

"Reckless," I mutter.

Behind me are the scrapes and struggle of Jaden pulling himself through. Of course, awaiting his aid isn't my style. My skin crawls with the thought that these monstrous men have been watching me, biding their time until the pounce. I highly doubt they will give us the courtesy of waiting. I tighten my hold on the pack and secure my footing.

With a battle cry, I charge, stepping hard and vaulting off the mongrel still struggling on the ground. I swing the pack over my head, bring it around and slam it into the nearest foe. He stumbles. I follow through with a butterfly kick, and it's like kicking a rubber wall. What happened to the all-powerful warrior Ry led me to believe I was becoming? My punch and kick are weak, ineffective, nothing like what I know I'm capable of, and in an instant, I land butt to the ground.

"Girly," a gurgling voice rasps in my ear, his arms locking down around mine and drag me to a stand. My captor has me facing the wrong way, away from Jaden. How can the monster at my back use me as leverage when he has me facing the wrong way?

He's stupid. Untrained. Use that against him.

His breath is hot and putrid, sending creepy-crawly chills running across my neck and shoulders. The stench makes me want to vomit, possibly pass out.

"Ew," Crystia says. "He smells like cat piss, spoiled eggs, and vomit, if they were mixed with moldy onions in a stew."

I ignore her. Try not to picture the visual she's thrust into my head.

Stay alert. Don't breathe through your nose.

I blink hard and fight to keep my eyes open. The other two revolting monsters narrow their gaze at something behind me. Something jolts at my back, and the beast behind me is pushed sideways. I'm knocked clear, hitting the ground in a hard skid. I turn over, ready to defend. Jaden is on top of my captor, attacking him with some sort of sharp weapon.

I should have weapons!

Of the two men still standing, one advances on Jaden, and the other heads toward me. I scamper backward and scan the area for something I can fashion into a weapon, a long, strong branch, a heavy rock, anything, only there's nothing. The spiked metal ball dangling from his hold tips the scales in his favor, and that's something I need to change. I stand, back up.

The ghoul moves closer, and I close the distance, taking a couple steps and then launching into a jump kick. My foot slams dead center into his chest. It's like kicking a block wall. Splinters spark across the bottom of my foot. Of course, I refuse to let that interfere with what needs to be done. I shift into a spinning hook kick to his cheek and land in a crouch ready to spring. He twists and falls like a tree.

My execution was less than perfect. I'm capable of stronger, sharper blows.

What's going on with me?

Maybe this new realm has knocked me off balance? An off-balance Balance Bringer. How would that work? Maybe my less-than-stellar performance has to do with the change I'm going through. Whatever is causing the issue, I hope it doesn't last long.

"Believe in your own strength and ability, Ana. You need to stop trying to channel Kaia."

I wince at Crystia's words. Is that what I am doing? Relying on Kaia's knowhow to get me through a fight?

Despite my imperfect form, the thug is down, and I've managed to knock the angry weapon from his grasp. A fleeting fear for Jaden's predicament flashes through my mind. I shake my head. *Focus.* My foe rouses and reaches for the baton, but I jump into a roll-spin, and my hand clasps around the handle first. I yank the baton far from his reach.

Weapon in hand, I twist away and stand, my gaze locked on the enemy. He may be devoid of emotion; still he's quick, misses nothing, and is now moving all-too-fast toward me. I swing my leg around in a wide sweep, collide with his feet, and rock his stability. The baton is in my hold, the metal ball of spikes already in full swing when his firm grasp tightens on my foot, yanks my support out from under me. My head collides with the unyielding earth.

I moan, imagine my name being called, only the sound is lost to the ringing in my ears. I blink hard.

The beastly man towers over me. I turn to my right, arms struggling to twist and pull away, and it's as if the world has flipped the switch to slow motion. My head throbs, my muscles ache, and my eyes sting. I have dirt in my eyes, digging into my skin, beneath my nails, and sticking to my lips and tongue. I gasp, gag on the earth, and wish it would envelope the monsters in the same manner it is attempting to inundate me.

I crawl and pull myself from the monster's reach, knowing all too well that I am moving too slow to be effective. I wildly search out Jaden and spot Ry instead. He's standing on top of the mammoth fallen tree.

Am I seeing things? Has Ry really found me?

In a flash, Ry is soaring through the air, sword in hand,

his entire body exuding confidence. He hits the ground with the grace of a gazelle and rushes past me, taking my attacker with him. I don't need to witness what happens next to know he has bested his target.

I pull myself to a stand and run-stumble toward Jaden. He is fighting near the base of the tree, one foe engaged and another fallen at his feet. Clearly, Jaden has the upper hand, but I swing the baton and run at the beastly man's back anyway.

I'm about to slam the metal ball into his skull when he grunts and slumps to the ground. Jaden stands before me, a bloody knife in his hand. I screech to a halt and toss the weapon away from me before it has a chance to hurt my Tracer.

"You alright?" His gaze bouncing between me and the weapon I tossed.

"Mostly." I don't want to discuss my throbbing head, so I pop a weak grin into place and allow my shoulders to relax. "You?"

Jaden shrugs, tilting his head into his left shoulder.

"That was concerning." Ry slaps a hand on my shoulder. "Your fight performance lacked luster."

I wipe the dirt from my lips and swallow the coppery taste of blood. "Thanks for the rescue," I say. "And the critique," I add.

"Anytime." He wraps an arm around me and squeezes me to his side. "But I didn't really rescue you. You rescued yourself. I took out the guy emerging from the brush." He turns and points. Sure enough, there is a monster lying face down beside a group of bushes.

"If you didn't take out my attacker, what happened?" I survey the area, and Ry directs my gaze. In the midst of a wide ring of disturbed earth are the fingers of the buried undead poking up from the ground.

"It was the coolest thing ever," Crystia says, overflowing with excitement. "It wasn't as astonishing as when you kissed Jaden at the party. I mean, all that electrical charge. Wow, wow, wowie. This was a whole different level of cool. This here, though, you made the earth swallow the dead dude whole."

I what? My stomach drops into a knot. I stare at the guys fingers and contemplate what that means for me. A burn in my chest ignites. I killed a man. With magic. And I didn't just kill him, I buried him alive. But... but that can't be possible. My gut slams to the ground. A violent rush of bile surges up my throat.

Visions of me manipulating water push against my disbelief. Me, mastering the elements? If water, why not earth?

I gag, throw my hand over my mouth. Try not to gag again and breathe deep. So immensely deep. I inhale as far as I can reach, all the way to the tips of my toes.

I intended to kill the other one, too, but I never expected the onslaught of emotions that come in the aftermath. They were trying to hurt us, so what else could I have done? Crystia said they were people, just regular people, caught in Dreya's web of darkness. Could I have saved them rather than destroy them?

I guess that is the question that will continue to haunt me.

But, magic? Me... here... in this place?

Plus, I don't even know how I managed to do such an incredibly horrid thing, so how do I prevent it from happening again? I regard the fingers, saying not a word. Neither does anyone else.

We still have a ton of ground to cover before nightfall, so sitting around and waiting out Ana's internal crisis is not an option. We move out, and I walk silently beside Ry and Jaden. Once again, we're all following Yuromo.

"It's pretty quiet most of the way," Crystia says. "I think you guys will be safe." She ducks her head down to look at me, then nods at my unspoken response. I make no effort to hide the conflict ripe within me. "You'll get through this." She wraps her hand around mine, and her energy warms and tingles my skin. "I gotta go take care of something, but I don't want you to worry. I'll be back."

My head snaps up. My eyes are wide, and I don't understand. Where does she need to go? What does she need to do? She's a ghost.

She shrugs and disappears.

A tiny, strangled yelp escapes my lips.

Jaden's hand enfolds mine, mingling her lingering energy with his own. Our fingers slip together effortlessly, and my eye finds his concerned gaze. Something hums within my soul, and I want to push closer, find comfort in his arms. "Okay?" he asks, and I decide I wouldn't be if it weren't for him.

"You're stronger than you think," he says. "Stronger than you may ever give yourself credit for. I need you to embrace who you are. Don't fear yourself and never shy from yourself, either." He turns his gaze back to the path.

His choice of words has confused me, and I don't know if my confusion stems from my jumbled state of mind or from the fact that he purposely chose a bewildering delivery.

"Stay alert," Ry whispers.

My gaze wanders in a wide arc, taking in the trees to my left. The gruesome undead Dohlan-led soldiers are still out there somewhere, covering the mountainside like ants on an anthill. I definitely don't want to encounter anymore of them.

"What did you and Yuromo learn when you investigated the fugly army?" I ask Ry.

"That the lake gate village has a serious challenge coming their way," Ry says. "There are far too many of them for the four of us to take on."

I bite my lip and study the back of Yuromo's head. She shows no physical signs of acknowledging her village's impending danger. Now the King-Kong-sized gate makes some sense.

We move silently among the cover of the trees, adding mile after mile to our journey. The thick canvas eventually gives way to smaller tree patches interspersed with clusters of house-sized rocks. We dart from one cover to the next, vigilant not to remain in the open longer than necessary.

Admittedly, I have failed my training. I let the outcome of the fight mess with my head, and now I've completely lost my bearings. I have no idea if we're moving north or south, east or west. I only know to follow Yuromo, and so that's what I do... I keep moving.

I run from a cluster of five trees and flatten myself against a ginormous rock. Yuromo is beside me, and a sound startles us still. Something is moving around the side of the rock, just out of sight. Only, the random shift, pause, shuffle, sniff doesn't make sense. Ry lifts his finger to his lips and scales the rock to better assess the situation.

"We need to get over there," Yuromo whispers, barely audible, and points to a spot that will require us to be in the open for a longer period of time than I am presently comfortable with.

Another sniff, and then a bark, followed by a pack full of barks.

Dogs, Yuromo mouths. Jaden pushes in front of me, protectively, pressing me between him and the rock. I shove at his back and slip out of the tight squeeze. I hope dogs are something I actually don't *need* to worry about. Except, talking to animals was Crystia's affinity, not mine. Not that I've tried to talk to any animals since I got to Hiddenkel.

The guys and Yuromo are silently communicating through hand signals, making plans for our next move. It's like Yuromo is just another one of the guys. Why have they seen fit not to include me? The backs of my eyes burn. I turn, skim my fingers along the black and grey and white speckled stone, moving away from them and their so very guy-ness.

Will every day here be more of the same? More running. More hiding. More guys being guys. I consider the stone speckles and the way the colors slip past my fingers becoming nothing more than recorded blotches in my memory.

I slam into warmth, the scent of spice, and... I blink away from the rock, gaze up, and forget how to breathe. Dohlan wraps his arm around my waist, pulls me tight against his chest, leans forward... I close my eyes to the waft of intoxication swimming around my head... and he brushes his lips against the edge of my ear. A kiss that's barely there.

It happened in a nanosecond, I'd let my defenses down and stopped paying attention for a three count. That's all it took to collide into the arms of the enemy.

I should fight him. I need to fight him. But...

I can't fight him.

"You weren't supposed to be anywhere near here," he says.

"Finally, I get to meet the infamous Dohlan," Crystia whispers from behind me.

I want to tear my gaze away from him and turn toward Crystia, yet I don't. I'm so stupidly enthralled, I'm probably drooling.

Dohlan shifts and lifts his gaze to ponder Crystia. *Can he see her?*

"Not bad," she says. "But you really shouldn't be wasting time."

Dohlan grins and pins me with a stargazed ogle. "Listen to your sister." He raises a finger. "And give Dreya a wide berth. Do not try to go home."

Home. *Mom.*

I jerk, throw my arms out at my sides. This. Everything. It needs to be a dream, and I need it to stop. Like Dorothy in the Wizard of Oz, I want to go home. *Wish* to go home. My hand slams into the rock beside me, and Dohlan's hand slams on top of mine, his gaze unwavering. Dogs bark and the earth shakes. He doesn't let the chaos sway him. He weaves his fingers through mine. "Did you hear me, Ana? Don't go home."

FIVE

"A na." Ry and Jaden are calling my name. They should have been right behind me, and yet their voices sound distant.

"I will buy you time," Dohlan whispers. "But you must hurry. She is coming."

Dreya? A shiver races up my spine. "How did she..."

"She saw you through the eyes of her children." Dohlan steps back, grins, and vanishes in a blur of motion.

"Half-dead flunkies for kids. That's not creepy at all," Crystia says.

Children? As in the undead soldiers? I gaze at the spot where Dohlan stood a heartbeat ago.

"Brace yourself." Crystia smirks.

In a blink, I'm on the ground with Ry protectively splayed over the top of me. No doubt, that act of heroics was for my safety. I shove him off.

"That was weird," Crystia says, regarding herself. She's standing at my feet. When Ry tackled me, I fell straight through her. "Let's not do that again." She glances at Ry who is brushing the dirt and grass off his pants.

I agree, for multiple reason.

"Was that him?" Ry asks. "That low-life, soul-sucking... why'd you let Dohlan touch you?"

"Why would you walk away like that?" Jaden asks, now standing at my side. Yuromo hangs at the edge of the group, shifting her weight and studying the dirt at her feet.

I get it. She's the outsider. She hasn't figured out her role within the group dynamics.

I put my finger to my lips. With the dogs nearby, they shouldn't be talking so loudly. "I didn't wander that far," I whisper to Jaden, ignoring Ry's outburst. "It was only three steps." I turn around, and my mouth pops open; a waft of air escapes.

There must be thirty yards between where I stand and where I started. I have no clue how I crossed so much space. And I find the not knowing scarier than Dohlan.

The dog barks have been replaced with howls. They are more distant, softer, and that sort of explains why Jaden wasn't talking in such hushed tones. I don't think the dogs have move so much as we have.

"What's happening?" I ask.

"What's happening is you are getting everyone out of here," Crystia says, with a bounce and swing. She's glowing, literally pulsating with excitement.

"You tell me," Ry responds, oblivious to Crystia's presence and contribution. "Why didn't you call for help? Why did you appear so content in his arms?"

"Right." I nod at Crystia, and avoiding Ry's question, sweep my gaze over everyone—Ry, Jaden, Yuromo, and Crystia. She's nodding enthusiastically and pointing to the side of the rock.

"Sorry." A tiny, nervous giggle escapes my lips, and I sound like a little girl. "I don't understand." I'm talking to Crystia but shift my gaze to Ry and sigh.

"I don't know what you want me to say. I have no idea how I ended up like that." I wave my hands in the air as if that explains how I was wrapped in Dohlan's embrace. "It just happened, and I couldn't stop it. I don't know why." Ry's face is blistering, steaming, preparing to blow, so I snap my attention to Crystia.

Crystia sighs; her glow and pulsating dims. "You need to follow." She turns and disappears into the rock.

I scan the massive rock wall into which Crystia vanished. Lines in shades of grey and black wave from top to bottom across the rock's surface. I trust my sister, but, what if I'm going mad and my visions of her are a delusion?

I take a step forward.

Ry grabs my arm. "What's going on with you?"

"It's alright," Jaden says, gently removing Ry's hold on me. "Just watch."

I flash him a nervous simper and then flatten my hand against the hard, gritty surface of the rock at my side. *I need to know.* I drag my fingertips toward the other end of the stone. Within five steps, my perception changes. Shadows across the surface darken, and my hand slips around a corner.

There's a break in the middle of the massive stone that I hadn't noticed among the lines and speckles. The pattern created an optical illusion, camouflaging the passageway. The space is tight, yet a pathway none-the-same. Hopefully, not a dead-end.

Crystia's head pops up in front of me. "Told you. Come now." She vanishes, becoming one with the shadows of the passage.

"What have you found?" Ry asks, seeming to have dropped the Dohlan inquest. At least, for now.

I turn to the group and wave my arm in the open space between the rocks.

Ry scratches the back of his neck. "Narrow," he whispers. "Not sure I trust it."

"We need to make a plan," Jaden says, peering back toward the howling. Eventually, those dogs are bound to catch our scent. "What do you think we should do, Ana?"

Me? I'm supposed to lead the group now?

Ry targets Jaden with a nasty glare before sweeping his gaze past me to the crevice in the rock. A serious pinch of concentration is trying hard to cut a crater in his face. His glower snaps to me... or my shoulder, rather. His expression softens.

A butterfly flutters at my side. It lands on my upper arm, remaining all of three seconds before taking to the air once again and drifting down the tight tunnel. I watch the butterfly become absorbed by the shadows as Crystia did.

"Okay, then," I say. "Let's do this." Before I can change my mind, I dash into the shadows of the crevice-tunnel.

Carefully running my hands along the side walls, I make my way deeper into the passageway. The shuffle of three individuals follows me. I don't glance back. I trust that it is my new family clan.

There is something about the darkness, something unknown to me, that makes me feel alone, turns my thoughts inward, reflective, as if I were sitting in a Catholic Church confessional booth. I admit truths to myself, truths I'm not prepared to speak out loud. I didn't want to push Dohlan away. Not really. I relished the warmth of his arms around me, the press of his body against mine. The sweet spice of his breath makes me want for nothing more than the touch of his skin.

I shouldn't feel that way. I'm so confused. And what of Jaden? Is he currently experiencing my turmoil?

I chew on the inside of my lip and press against the pangs that thrum in my chest. Each thrum yelling guilty, guilty, guilty.

The narrow path drops us below the enormous bolder and into a fissure beneath the surface. It's a tight fit, but not so tight that we can't walk normal with our backs and shoulders straight. The light emanating from the opening at our back gradually fades, and, as it does, the walls around us come to life in glowing streaks and blotches of brilliant blues, apple greens, orangey reds, and regal yellows. It's as if a bunch of glow-in-the-dark paint cans exploded all along the path.

I reach out and touch the rock wall. The streaks and blotches in the stone aren't the only things glowing. The swirls, lines, and strange symbols upon my skin have illuminated, as well.

I forgot about the markings upon my skin. I had seen the them only briefly when we entered the cave back in California. I wonder if they are present all the time and only visible under certain lighting conditions or if they come to life when ignited by an event or something?

"My geology teacher would have killed to explore this space." Crystia slips up beside me. I throw her a sideways glance. "Okay, maybe not kill, but you know what I mean." I nod. Back in school, we used the word "kill" freely and without thought. Now that I have actually taken a life, I feel different about the usage. "What you've created here is amazing."

"This wasn't me," I snap.

"Yes, it was." She moves in front of me, turns around, and glides backward, so that she can meet my gaze. "When your hand pressed against the rock and the grumpy earth rumbled, this was happening. Subconsciously, you were wishing for an escape, and the earth responded. This was being made... because of you." Her lips curve up in triumphant.

My eyes blink wide, and for a moment, I am stunned. It takes only a second for me to recognize the truth. My shoulders relax. "Dohlan did this. He told me to get out of here, said he'd buy me time. He must have made this tunnel to move us out quickly. Or maybe he made it to trap us. I don't know. But he's strong, powerful, and completely capable."

"I'm fully aware of what he's capable of," she blurts. "And this is not his doing." She rushes ahead. "I have something waiting for you on the other side." Her voice drifts back to me making the distance between us displeasing.

"How are you doing up there?" Ry asks. "Giving in to talking to yourself?"

"It beats talking to you," I retort.

The colorful glow of the surrounding walls fades, and a modest beam of light appears in the distance. I assume that's where Crystia went and where she waits. A breeze kisses my skin. Fresh air wraps around me. The scents of pine and sap tickle my nose, pull me forward. The light grows wider and wider until a white glow engulfs the space, broken only by the silhouette of the fluttering butterfly.

Shielding my eyes, I step away from the tunnel and into

the open air. My sight quickly adjusts, and a small sound of awe escapes me. I don't recognize our surroundings as being part of the same mountainside we were actively descending. The area doesn't resemble anything near the ginormous tree kingdom that leads to Yuromo's village. The surrounding trees aren't nearly as tall. In fact, I could jump and tap their lowest branches.

The branches plume out above us like smashed gumdrops, and the color... soft pinks and purples. The leaves appear to float in the air as they softly fall from their places on the branches. The grass at our feet is a lush carpet of vibrant kiwi green, and nearby, I detect the trickle of a small stream. It's so unreal, I expect a magical melody to be playing softly in the background.

The only music present, though, is the sweet song of birds and the whinny of horses.

Horses.

I move away from the tunnel exit, slowly turn in a circle, and when I've spun a third of the way around, I spot them—four magnificent creatures. Crystia stands next to one. Although I can't discern what she's saying, it appears like a lively conversation... even if it's one way. Her hands are moving through the air, mimicking waves and jumps and strides. The horse simply shakes its head up and down.

Is this what Crystia meant when she said she had something waiting for me? Did she mean the horses?

Jaden is the last one to step out of the tunnel, and everyone wastes no time in relocating any movable rock to block the tunnel opening.

My gaze washes over them and focuses on Crystia. She's beckoning me.

"Oh, for the love of Gaea and God." My shoulders and

jaw drop. She expects me to talk to the horses, like I talked to the tiger, Caesar. "Nope." My lips pull into a tight line, pushing the edge of a frown. Horses are scary strong, and the four together could trample me like wine grapes.

"What's wrong, sis?" Ry leans into my side. "You did good. It turned out to be the right move, using the fissure as an escape."

"Yeah, you should learn to trust me more." I shake my head. "But it's not that." I throw my arm up in Crystia's direction and wave wildly to indicate Crystia's presence. "It's the horses."

"Horses?" Ry's head snaps toward the small herd. "What great luck."

"You'd think, but Crystia actually brought them here or something."

"Crystia?" His gaze sweeps from left to right. "She's here?"

"Yeah." My head drops in an over exaggerated nod. "And she wants me to talk to them."

"And?" Ry prompts.

"I can't do it." My voice rises an octave. "It's Crystia's thing, and, sure, I talked to Caesar, but this..." My hand cuts through the air. "Can't."

"Sure, you can." He shakes my shoulder. "You've got this."

"You don't understand." I'm like a child begging not to go to school. "I've felt oddly off, lately. I mean, my water thing is way cool. I've got that going on, but my fight... well, you saw. Totally off my game. It's as if that part of me is somehow missing. Crystia said I was relying too much on Kaia for my fighting strength. Well, I totally rely on my bond with Crystia to communicate with animals."

"You just told me Crystia was here," Ry says. "So, I fail to recognize the problem."

I recall all the mistakes I've made just today. Like, I killed a bug, a bug I should have been able to communicate with. The shrill of his death rattled through my head when I smacked him flat during our lunch break. I'm an emotional mess when it comes to myself, my Tracer, or Dohlan. My fighting was horrid. And I buried a person or thing alive. I tell Ry as much in as few words as possible.

"Sounds like something you should be talking about with Jaden."

"No way." I fan my hands across the top of my head and pull my hair tight, like I'm trying to pull the strands from my skull.

Ry heaves a heavy breath and glances in Jaden's direction. I chance a glance at Jaden, too. He's leaning against the collected stone barrier in front of the tunnel, pretending to be busy, pretending he isn't aware we're discussing him. Which we now totally are. And I have no doubt he totally knows. Embarrassment burns across my skin.

Ry rubs my upper arms. "Listen Ana, you need to get past this whole high school crush thing and build a working relationship with the guy." Using his finger, Ry tilts my face to his. "He's your Tracer, and he probably already has a good idea what's going on with you. He's just waiting for you to broach the subject."

I close my eyes, let my shoulders sag.

"I'm quite sure he's not judging you." Ry leans closer. "You'd have to be a fool not to notice the way he looks at you."

My eyes snap open, and I pin Ry with an incredulous

glare. My relationship with Jaden is not something I want to discuss with my brother.

"I thought you already knew." Ry frowns. "Surely, you don't need confirmation from me."

Maybe confirmation is exactly what I need. Confirmation that his interest in me isn't anything magical but simply a boy liking a girl.

I gaze at the empty air in front of me. My heart is pounding so hard I half expect to hyperventilate and pass out.

"Don't worry, sis." Crystia's voice is like a tiny bird at my ear. "Jaden's interest in you is *so* obvious."

"Yes, but is it real?" I ask.

Ry's head jerks back. "I don't understand. You think he might be faking his feelings?"

I blink and focus on Ry. "Even if I do talk to Jaden, which I'm not promising I will, that's kind of a lengthy conversation, and right now we do need to keep moving." I reluctantly glance toward the horses.

"That's true," Ry agrees.

"Don't worry," Crystia says. "I got your back." The slightest tingle of energy dances across my hand. It tugs and pulls and leads me forward. Reluctance slows my feet, but I let Crystia guide me anyway.

The closest horse, the one I spied Crystia talking to, rears her head. Her nostrils flare, her hoof digs at the dirt, and then she breaks into a run straight for me. The other three horses follow suit.

I stumble backward and fall flat on my butt. I let out a gasp. All I can register are hooves. Hooves racing straight at me. Hooves kicking up earth and stomping grass. Hooves that are, at any second, going to make tenderized meat out of me.

Several feet before trampling me, the horses skid to a stop. There's a fair chance every hair on my head has now turned grey. My heart races, and my blood pumps with the rapid pulse of a hummingbird's wings.

Cautiously, the front horse closes the space between us. She lowers her head and presses against my upper arm. Her breath is warm, strong, as is she. Energy rolls off her body with the strength of a massive waterfall. When she stood in the shade, I thought her to be an unadulterated snowy white, but when touched by the sunlight, she glistens of gold. Like someone sprinkled golden glitter all over her body. She's stunning and I can hardly tear my gaze away to take in her traveling companions.

"Don't you just love animals?" Crystia whispers dreamily, ending with a sigh. Her image is fading, becoming more translucent, less defined. I want to grab her, hang on to her, which of course, I can't. My breath hitches.

I consider her question. I like Oscar well enough, but he was mostly Crystia's cat. And he's back in California with Mom, and my room, and everything I understand.

Animals have always been Crystia's thing, not mine. Mom was never keen on allowing furry things into our lives. She never even took us to the zoo. So, I guess, for the most part, I'm neutral. I pick myself up off the ground and brush the dirt from my backside.

"I don't know what to do," I say to Crystia. She's now nothing more than a shimmer at my right. I don't understand why she isn't showing herself more clearly.

"When are you going to start believing in yourself?" she says.

"When I realize this isn't a dream and I won't suddenly wake up in my own comfy bed?" Just saying the word makes me miss my bed even more. I had four pillows and a super fluffy comforter.

"Funny, girl," she says, firm sarcasm in her voice. "Go ahead, talk to her. Her name is Velsa."

"Velsa," I repeat, and the horse lifts her head as if I've called her to attention. I get the odd feeling she's expecting me to say something brilliant. Only, I haven't a single brilliant thought in my head. Right now, I don't think a brilliant thought has ever resided within my brain. Not ever. In fact, my mind is suspiciously blank and my gut, oddly tickled with the brush of a thousand horses' manes.

"What should I say?" I take a tentative step forward.

"You already know what you need to say." The electric tickle of Crystia's presence warms my side. "Listen to your heart."

I bite my lip and recall talking to Caesar, the Siberian tiger at the Feline Preservation Center. In theory, this shouldn't be any different.

I peer at Velsa and at the trees and at the ground, and then I close my eyes and search my soul. Tucked deeply away, I recognize the truth in Crystia's words. I'll talk to the horse as I would any other respectful person or being. My muscles relax, the fluttering weight on my chest dissipates, and I take another step forward.

You are magnificent. I pause a moment, let the factuality sink in that I am speaking to a gold-speckled horse. *Thank you for coming to our aid.* I allow my thoughts to travel out into the ether around me and watch Velsa's ears perk. She tilts her head in my direction.

I *can* talk to her as I talked Caesar. My lips jump into a

crooked smile, spread wide across my face. As it was with the water in the reflecting pool, a sense of purpose with regards to the horses flourishes within me.

It's another small victory and a slightly stronger hold on my confidence. Only this time, I believe the change within me is more likely a gift from my sister and not so much because of who or what I am.

Velsa stomps her feet, flares her nostrils, and shakes her head. I lay a shaky hand upon her soft, golden-white face, run my hand along the side of her nose.

"You have the power," she says. "You are the Bringer."

I bite the side of my lip. Maybe I'm the Balance Bringer, and from what I understand, so are my sisters. Animal communication can be Crystia's gift, not mine. Of course, I don't project such a thought. It would be rude to disagree so early in our relationship. Instead, I opt for a topic lighter in tone. "I've never ridden a horse, never even been close to one, and riding a horse has to be easier than riding a tiger."

Velsa's head bobs as if in agreement, and a tiny laugh escapes my lips.

"She is a hoot, isn't she," Crystia says. "And she has the most agreeable friends. Their names are Belmiso, Clemens, and Timbers, and they've all agreed to help you. They know the land well, possibly better than your guide girl over there."

I glance over my shoulder at Yuromo, who, to my horror, is gawking at me. I snap back to Crystia's shimmer and Velsa, the golden-white horse. As for the other horses, I decide to call each name in turn to identify who is who.

The results, Belmiso is a stunning black stallion with a small white crescent on his forehead. Clemens is a majestic, soft grey mare with a smoked face, smoked lower legs, and black mane. And Timbers is a warm chocolate beauty with a black tail and mane. Like Velsa, he appears to morph in color depending on how you gaze at him. He's brown and then he's black and then he's brown again.

"I think I've got it," I say after repeating their names for a third time. Each horse courteously reacts with a nod or a hoof stamp when I run through the roll call.

"I need to tell you," Crystia says. "Velsa has informed me that, although they are happy to help you for as long as you may need them, your destination is best reached by water. So, anyway, they will take you to a boat or all the way. Just let them know."

"Got it." I turn toward her shimmer. "What's going on with you?" I motion to her lack of form. "Why are you all..." My hand waves up, then down, then drops against my leg. "Less."

"I'm sorry," she says.

Her words send a chill racing across my skin. My mood instantly deflates.

"Held on as long as I could, but my time's up, and you're going to be alright." Warm, tingling energy wraps around me, and I picture her hugging me. "Thankfully, I achieved my goal and got you to Velsa and her herd."

"What? Why?" I say.

"Don't stress so much. There are forces at work that are stronger than me. You're going to fix this, right?" She slides back, and she is no longer the shimmer, or the whisper of white, nor the glowing spirit I saw when I first arrived. She is the Crystia I couldn't save—the pale-skinned, dying in the park Crystia. A trickle of blood emerges from behind her ear and slowly makes its way down the length of her neck. I gasp.

She shrugs. "We can't all be pretty all of the time."

"Is this a joke to you?" I say.

"Of course not." She shakes her head. "Listen, Ana. I don't want things to end on this note."

"I don't want things to end," I argue. "First Kaia, now you."

Crystia bows her head. "The forces have a strong hold on our sister. You'll have to be strong if you're going to save us both."

"Forces? Don't you mean Dreya?" I frown. Crystia shrugs. "But what if I..."

"Believe in yourself." A meek smile flitters to her lips, and then she is gone. It's as if someone opened a trapdoor and she dropped through. Her warm, vibrant energy simply slips away.

"Wait!" I drop to the ground, slam my hands against the grass. "You said I was stuck with you. That means you never leave. Do you hear me? Never." My pleas are pointless. Crystia, and any sign of her existence, is gone.

SIX

"Crystia is gone." Maybe saying the words out loud will help me accept it as truth. "Crystia is gone." Velsa neighs and I turn my head to her. "Did you sense my sister leave?"

I wait, but Velsa doesn't answer.

"Are you giving me the silent treatment?" I ask.

Again, she says nothing. I wrinkle my nose and frown.

"Are you talking to me?" I ask.

She nods and suddenly I find it difficult to breathe.

Crystia left, and with her went her animal communication ability. My hands clench at the grass, tear lumps of blades free. A wave washes over me, pain, sorrow. Only, the pain and sorrow are not mine. Hot and dizzy, I open my palm and study the grass in my hands. I jerk, then shake the blades free and clutch my chest.

Did I just... kill the grass? Something inside of me wants to scream. The circumstance I find myself in is crazy. This world is crazy. My power, ability, gift, whatever you want to call it is crazy.

Breathe. Breathe deep. Neither Dorothy nor Alice freaked out when they found themselves stuck in nonsensical worlds.

I can do this.

I can and will believe in me.

I simply need to make sense of the situation first. It appears, Velsa is talking, and I can't hear her like I could at the start, or as I heard Caesar or the ants. At least, not anymore. That's okay, we can make this work—somehow.

I take another deep breath and receive the slightest sense of encouragement. I peer into Velsa's large, luminous eyes. She nods, and again I sense her encouragement.

Different. But we can work with it.

Warmth races through my body, and I sit up straight.

"We can communicate?" I whisper. She nods. "We can communicate!" I yell and jump to my feet.

Velsa takes off at a run, moving in a wide arc with her head bobbing up and down.

Thanks be to Gaea and God. I cross my hands, press them into my chest, and beam at Velsa as she circles back toward me.

Ever since I came through the doorway to Hiddenkel, it's like I've been trapped taking a forever long test for which I failed to prepare. My sisters, the water, the half-dead grossed-out monster-soldiers, Dohlan, our escape, the threat of Dreya, even Jaden and Ry, and now Velsa. Everything and everyone wants something from me, and I can't believe I'll ever fulfill everyone's' needs.

One thing at a time.

And right now, that one thing is communicating with the horses. It would seem that I am sensing, rather than out-right hearing, Velsa's thoughts, and I can deal with that. I wonder if this is how Jaden feels in relation to me.

Spinning on my heels, I head toward the group. "Come on." I wave the horses to follow.

"The horses have agreed to help us get to our destination."

"Great," Ry replies. "Everyone pick your partner. I'll take black beauty, here." He winks at me. "Get it?"

Oh yeah, that joke has me doubling over with uncontained laughter. He walks over to Belmiso and introduces himself. I bite my bottom lip and turn away. Velsa presses to my side. I guess she has picked me as her partner. Never was I picked first when it came to teams in school. Except, maybe swim. And that's probably because I swim incredibly fast... because I'm not human. But they didn't know that. Now that I do, it feels like cheating.

Everyone jumps on their horse, and within minutes, we're making our way out of the pink and purple forest.

It's nice to give my feet a rest, even though walking side-by-side was more social than riding horses together turns out to be. The distance between us isn't huge, yet it's enough that I have to raise my voice to be heard, and the things I want to talk about are not things to be spoken loudly.

I still have *so* many questions for Ry, and since his car got stolen back in California, the only quiet moment we've had alone together was at the campfire in Yuromo's village. There wasn't enough time to cover everything then.

Now that Yuromo has joined our group, a stranger whom I know nothing about, I'm incredibly self-conscious bringing up any personal questions. A lot of time is fleeting past us, and I'm not feeding my need to know, nor am I making small talk. And if I'm not talking, I'm thinking. At present, if I'm thinking, it's about something I don't want to be thinking about.

Crystia's gone.

Like that. Push the thought away. *Don't go there.*

Yuromo rides Clemens, leading the way from one fantastical setting to another. Ry rides beside her, and Jaden and I follow. The horses jaunt through a forest of twisted trees, beyond the woods, over a hill, and descend into a breeze-blown ocean of burnt-gold and olive-green grass.

The splintered blades reach past Velsa's belly, and I can almost touch them. I pretend that they want to connect and are stretching for my fingertips.

I briefly catch Jaden's gaze. He's watching me attempt to reach the tall grass. My cheeks warm and I sit straight, look away. I've been so wishy-washy where he's concerned, and I don't want to be. I want to be accepting. One hundred percent accepting. If I am destined to be the Balance Bringer, then I should be able to find a balance between our individual wants and needs. I want to be able to stand near him without an air of awkwardness wafting between us.

I need to talk to him. I promised Ry I would.

Not yet. Now is not the time.

The sun's glow is brilliantly blinding. Like a last hurrah before slipping out of sight for the night. It's so silly, I know, but I'd swear, if only for the briefest of moments, the sliver-thin rays of light are singing.

At a hopeless distance, beyond a stretched-out curving blanket of yellow-green, lies a tiny cluster of buildings. It's a beacon of hope at the end of an all-too-exhausting day, but even I'm aware, with my uneducated eye, that the space between us and the signs of civilization cannot be successfully traversed before nightfall. It's, without a doubt, more than an hour's ride.

"I know a place," Yuromo calls over her shoulder. Beside him, Ry is motioning us into a curved right turn, toward the setting sun. It's winking goodnight, painting the sky in brilliant pinks and blues and lavenders.

We drop to a quick trot, weave through a barrier of trees, climb a small hill, and emerge on the other side of the sloop in time to catch the last bit of sunlight disappear over the range. A full and un-ordinarily bright moon is left to light our way.

Laid out before us is a wide lake surrounded by trees and meadows in various shades of brown and green and yellow. The moon's luminescence gleams off the water's surface casting a soft glow and sense of serenity. Nestled near the lake, and at the heart of the tranquil scene, sits the ruins of what was once an enormous structure.

Broken and alone, amongst a circle of rubble and ruin, stands a high, curved wall with long, inset windows and a wide, arched doorway. The darkened ground around the perimeter tells a story of unnatural destruction.

The horses come to a stop beside the doorway. No sooner do I jump off Velsa than she is headed to the lake for a drink. I'm rather parched, too. I grab my canteen and swallow a mouthful of day-warmed water. I watch the horses for a few minutes, and various flutters skip through my chest. I contemplate if the flutters are connected to Velsa or one or the other horses or if the sensation means nothing substantial at all.

Why must communication be so much harder for me now, when it came so easily before? So *unfair*.

"This should be good," Ry says.

"I agree," Jaden replies.

They've wandered within the walls of the ruins. I step through the archway and follow their voices. They've found a spot against a back wall, near a corner, limiting our exposure and the direction by which anyone—or thing—can detect us. Ry catches sight of my approach and points to the tents Jaden is setting up.

"We're going to make camp here for the night," Ry says.

"Obviously." I slap him with sarcasm.

Yuromo watches Jaden and the tent erecting with great intensity. She reaches out, touches the tent siding. "What is this?" she asks. "I know no grain or animal hide that can be used to make anything so slippery. Is this a fabric weaved of magic, like the kind one finds in the city?"

I hold back a giggle and listen to Jaden try to explain. From my understanding, Jaden was only recently introduced to such things. She watches him with intense curiosity, pulls her hair from her face and leans closer... A spark ignites in my mind. I glare at Yuromo, study her keenly. Is she flirting with Jaden?

Ry takes a swig of water from his canteen and studies the ruins. "I know this place," he says. "Tracer, isn't this one of your people's temples?"

If Yuromo was flirting, Ry's interjection has pulled her actions into line.

My body straightens, head tilts, and I examine the structure, taking in all the remaining bits, piecing them together in my mind. Along the foundation, on the side facing the lake, the remnants of a grand entrance still stand. The entrance I used. The doors are no longer present, but the detail of the frame is magnificent with ornate elements.

"This was once Gaea's Temple." It is Yuromo, not Jaden who responds. "I have stood on that ridge." She points to the place where we emerged from the tree line. "That is as close as I have ever been. Until now." Her gaze meets mine. "It is an honor to be here with you, princeza."

I want to remind her that I told her not to call me that. I don't feel anything like a princess, and I surely don't want people treating me like one. But I don't. Given the circumstances, and her possible flirtation with Jaden, I decide it might be best that she remembers who I am. I remain quiet.

"I thought this might be one of her temples," Jaden says, a soft reverence in his voice. "Before leaving Hiddenkel to find Ana, I had not made a pilgrimage this far from home."

Ry nods his head and glances from me to Jaden. "Hey Yuromo." The girl immediately straightens. "Can you help Jaden with the tents?" Confusion covers her face for a nanosecond.

"I thought that was what I was doing," she says.

Ry doesn't acknowledge her response. He turns away from Yuromo and Jaden and walks toward me. Walks past me. "Let's you and I take a walk," he says over his shoulder.

I frown and set my canteen on the ground. Why do I sense a big-brother lecture coming on? Of course, he's not the only one with things to say. This might be the quiet alone time I've been hoping for. There are so many questions bouncing around in my head in need of answers. A second later, I'm jogging to catch up.

"That was subtle," I say about his exit.

Ry shrugs. "A guy's gotta do what he must to get some alone time with you."

I laugh and follow him several yards beyond the ruin. He stops at a safe distance. Safe to talk without being heard while not being so far that we couldn't easily and quickly get back if needed.

"Why does Yuromo call me princess but doesn't call you prince?" I ask before he can start into whatever it is he has planned.

"It's because of your father," he says, matter-of-fact. "I'm only royal by marriage, whereas you are royal by birth. Your father was the king, not mine."

My father, the Fae king. I nod. "But we have the same mom, so where's your father?"

He gazes out at the lake. It's so still it mimics glass. "I lost my father in battle many years ago." Ry's posture exudes pain. "After his death, Nerine, our mother, gave up the fight and became the liaison between our people and the Fae. She was determined not to leave me orphaned. Of course, I was old enough to take care of myself. I never truly believed her story. If you ask me, she lost the taste for battle after my father's death. In all honesty, it's hard to say, though." He dips his head. Kicks a rock. "Maybe it was all meant to be. If it hadn't been for her position as liaison, she never would have met your father. Of course, it was many more years before she agreed to marry him."

He crosses his arms. "She knew how it would be perceived by his people, and she was right. Ours were slightly more understanding, waiting for the time of the prophecy to once again come to fruition." He nods as if checking his facts before speaking them. "They did eventually marry and live happily for a time. Kaia was born and, as she grew, trained to be a great warrior. She was a real natural."

He turns toward me with his arms wide. "You should have seen her! Well, I guess you have." His arms drop to his side, and he returns his view to the lake. "After her life was cut short, everything changed. Your father's sister rallied the people against him, and eventually, the realms went to war. It wasn't long after that, mom discovered she was with child. For your safety and the safety of your sister, we fled to the mortal realm. Your father stayed behind to lead the fight, and I stayed with mom to keep you both safe. You probably know the rest."

He's given me far more information than I asked for, and I'm grateful. I would have eventually asked. But I'm sad for his part in the story. Duty and loss. What kind of life had that given him? I reach out, touch his upper arm. "I'm sorry about your father. If he was anything like you, then he was a great man."

He nods in silent acknowledgement. My gaze wanders to the horses. They are sleeping in a cozy herd under the shelter of a tree cluster.

I weave my hands together and study the way they inter-twine. "What happened to my father?" I ask.

"I'm sorry, Ana. I don't know. One day, the letters to Mom abruptly stopped. We assumed he was either captured or worse."

I never knew my father, and I want to say the loss means nothing, makes me feel nothing, but that would be a lie. He is a part of who I am, a part I want to understand better, and he could help me do that. It seems God and Gaea have other plans and wish to keep my father a mystery.

I glance back at the broken building. The sight of it is beautifully distracting. I envision the temple as it once was; towering, lustrous, and white. Extraordinarily white. Delicate cut glass filled the windows, each with their own unique design. Designs like none I've ever seen.

And then, with a blur and a swirl, it's no longer night and I am standing in the middle of Gaea's Temple. Sunlight pours through the windows, casting colorful designs across the pearly floor. People bustle past and around me. It's like the exiting congregation after a church service. The desire to follow the people pulls at me, so I do, follow them, right through the main entrance, the massive wood and iron doors standing at the open.

At the front of the temple, the air is filled with the delightful sounds of children's laughter. People are greeting one another and engaging in conversations, and beyond them, at the edge of the lake, a multitude of children play. They play a game involving colorful ribbons.

A little girl breaks from the group and runs toward the temple.

I watch her approach with curiosity. Her white dress billows out around her, and her long red hair flows and bounces. Oddly, this feels like a memory. Maybe this is part of my warrior blood thing Ry mentioned and this *is* a memory, just not mine. Like the one I experienced of the girl drowning when I bathed at the lake.

The red-headed child runs up to me, her deep-set hazel eyes sparkle, and her small voice sings, "You're going to join us, aren't you?"

I want to both laugh and cry. I don't know how I'm supposed to feel. I'm confused, and everything is disorienting. Maybe these emotions belong to the owner of this memory because we have yet to answer the child.

Someone at my side fake coughs, and I glance over, meet

Jaden's amused smile. It's not exactly his face, yet I know it's him. I'd recognize his stunning green eyes anywhere.

Slowly, I lean toward him and whisper. "Tracer?"

His brow pinches and the edge of his lip quivers, curving upward. Now it's his turn to lean closer. "Balancer?"

Balancer? I jerk back and inspect him. Him. The child. The entire scene.

SEVEN

"**E**arth to Ana." Ry nudges me.

I jerk and blink; the scene is gone. There are no children at the lake's edge. No astounding Temple beside me. Even the guy who reminded me so much of Jaden has vanished. Yet, I'm sure they were once all here, in the place, and so was I in a past life. My shoulders slump, and I chew on my lower lip.

"Are you so tired that you plan on sleeping out here, standing up?" Ry quips.

I let out a nervous laugh and turn to walk back into the temple ruins, but Ry grabs my arm and stops me.

That's right. He brought me out here for a purpose. He wants to talk *alone.*

"Only a fool wouldn't notice that there is something going on with you, Ana," he whispers firmly. "I'm here for you, you can talk to me. And if it requires special help, then please, I'm begging you, open up to your tagalong Tracer.

After all, we brought him along. Might as well make use of him."

"Rude." My upper body jerks. "This is a person you are talking about. Not an object."

Ry bows his head. "My apologies. You're right." He fixes his gaze upon the sky. "When the guy first showed up on the scene, his mere existence irritated me. I'm going to chalk that up to my overly keen sense of protection where you are concerned. I have since come to see the error of my ways."

"And when did this happen?" My head hums with skepticism.

"While you were sleeping," he says. "We had three days together to worry about you. Three days without your input. Three days to pound out any issues between us. I can now say, we are good." He gazes out at the lake and scratches the back of his neck. "If something should ever happen to me, it's important that you have someone who is willing to risk his own life to protect you. I can say, in all honesty, Jaden is that man." His gaze snaps back upon me. "So, don't allow a lack of communication to come between the two of you. Or between us. Stop being stubborn or shy or whatever and talk to me, or that guy over there." He motions toward Jaden's location.

My lips pull to the side, no words finding their way from my lips. I can't tell Ry how I feel regarding Dohlan. His hatred for the guy borders on explosive. Yet Dohlan helped us at our last encounter. Not that Ry has any knowledge of that. That's twice now Dohlan has helped me. In the crystal cluster cave when we fought Dreya and now with the escape from his half-dead army. It's not like I'm completely suscep-tible to Dohlan's manipulation, and the connection could have its benefits.

Would he, too, be willing to risk his life for my safety? Has he already risked his life the couple of times he helped me?

As for everything not Dohlan, I'm lost in the shadows as much as Ry. What's the point of worrying him over stuff I either need to deal with or learn to control. Last thing I want is for everyone in our small group to be stressing over me and my change. I guess that is the reason Jaden is here, to help with the process.

I take a deep breath and lower my head.

"Okay," Ry says, sounding defeated. "Have it your way." He squeezes my hand. "Just don't forget what you promised me."

I raise my head and make eye contact.

"Jaden," he reminds.

My mouth slowly opens. I'd promised Ry I would talk to Jaden. I haven't forgotten. It's almost all I've been able to think about. Almost.

"This evening... or now... might be an appropriate time." He turns and walks away.

I make my way back into the temple ruins, weave through the mini maze and find Jaden. His head snaps up at my approach, I'm stunned stupid. It's not only the color of his eyes, his magical, mesmerizing eyes, it's also the unnatural pull he possesses. There's no question in my mind that the guy I saw in the dream, the guy with a different face, was him—my Tracer.

Why am I so afraid to talk to Jaden?

We already kissed once. And he was beyond extraordinary to me at my sister's funeral service. Maybe my ancestors are trying to tell me something. Like the little voice that yells at me to run when I'm around Dohlan. Or maybe it's simply teenage girl hormones causing me to act stupid and nonsensical. Maybe that's why I'm scared. I am having trouble believing it isn't magic that makes him like me.

Plus, it's strange that he literally knows everything about me. The things I feel, think, and dream.

I gasp, spin around, and go search for Ry.

I find him standing in the corner of the temple ruins, his pack of supplies placed at his feet. He's chosen a spot near a window, so that he can easily peek out onto the landscape beyond... and in case a quick and easy exit is needed. One of the things he taught me during my after-school training. In addition, the window makes for a handy look-out. It's not the best scenario, but it will have to do.

"This will do nicely, don't you think?" Ry asks. "If need be, we can use some of those old planks to create a shelter." He gestures to a small pile of weathered wood. Possibly old panels or platforms or alters. "I'd like to avoid a campfire. We could still have someone on our trail, and we don't want to draw any unwanted attention."

"Makes sense, I guess." Standard rules of survival... sort of. *Serious bummer.* "A little warmth would've been nice." My attention wanders to my cold feet. Better to be safe than end up Dreya's dinner. Dohlan did say she could spy on us through the eyes of her undead soldiers.

I shiver.

"So, I'm thinking..." He glances over at Jaden and Yuromo. "If I decide it's safe to do so, Yuromo and I will hunt for small game. We'll handle all skinning and cooking an ample distance from camp." His lips quirk to the side, and his head nods as if he's mentally calculating. "We should be gone two to three hours."

"You and Yuromo? Gone for three hours?" I ask, hooking my hands on my hips.

I'm starving, and the thought of food should excite me, only Ry's put me on the spot, and the thought of being left alone with Jaden for an extensive amount of time causes my stomach to contract and squeeze tight. Of course, that also means Yuromo will be far away from Jaden. Ry is expecting me to come clean to Jaden, and the prospect weighs heavily upon my chest.

"The way I see it, you and Jaden have some air to clear," he says with a flip of the hand. I inhale deep.

"Hey, Yuromo," Ry hollers to the girl. "Gather your supplies. We're on dinner duty." Without another word to me or even a glance back, Ry heads out. He's already wearing his weapons, so he's got nothing to grab. Always prepared. That's what he's been trying to teach me. Yuromo grabs her bow and follows.

I rush after Ry and grab his hand. Yuromo tosses me a sideways glance. Ry turns toward me, but before I get a word out, he raises his finger. "Don't be afraid, Ana. Talk to him." His hand slips from mine.

"But..." I greedily grab for his hand again, only I miss and my fingers brushes along the side of his abdomen.

He flinches and pulls away. My mouth pops open, and then my eyes narrow, my gaze shifting between his give-nothing-away face and the spot where Dreya stabbed him.

"It's all good." His voice is sharp. "Take care of yourself." His glare jumps to Jaden. "Secure the campsite and make it semi-comfortable. Then pry it out of her." He turns and leaves.

My hands curl into fists. He made me sound like an object in need of fixing. I want to smack him in the back of the head, yet I don't. I remain planted in the doorway, where I stay and watch as Ry and Yuromo ride off on Belmiso and Clemens.

When they are no longer in view, I turn to Jaden. "Is he going to be alright?" I ask, regarding Ry and his injury.

Jaden has set up two tents and four sleeping mats. Two in tents and two outside, one of which is by the window. The spot Ry select for himself. Jaden, being the gentleman that he is, probably plans for Yuromo and me to take the tents, leaving the guys to sleep beneath the stars.

"I don't know," he says. "I am not connected to Ryland. And I'm not so sure he'd tell you the truth either way."

Jaden's right, of course. Ry can be a stubborn fathead. I frown and nod, then turn back and gaze at the lake and the moonlight shimmering across its surface.

"Jaden," I say. "May I talk to you about something?"

"Anything." He sets something down with a thump. "No topic is off limits."

His approaching footsteps are soft, almost silent upon the cracked stone foundation. I consider all the things we should discuss and the things I ought to tell him. My chest tightens, and my palms start to sweat. I swiftly wipe my hands along my hips and then hug myself... a tad too tight.

I don't want to end up sad and resentful because I never stepped outside of my comfort zone. Never spoke the truth to the guy I... to the guy I what? Love... like... kind of like-love? I'm not sure I even understand my own emotions. Mountains upon mountains of emotions exist for Jaden, and then Dohlan comes along. I sigh and resolve to simply speak whatever truth my heart chooses to send to my lips.

I fancy the moon, the massively large moon, and blink. "She's gone." The words whisper from my lips.

"I'm so sorry, Ana." The feathery touch of his fingers runs across my shoulders and down to my elbows.

I turn and throw my arms around him, hugging myself to his form. This wasn't how I intended this conversation to begin, but there's no turning back now, and I might as well embrace the moment, quite literally. I lay my head upon his shoulder, close my eyes, and reacquaint myself with his woodsy scent.

"I've lost both my sisters," I sniffle. "And with them, I've lost some of my fighting skills and the ability to talk to animals."

His fingers comb through my hair and massage the back of my skull. "This will only be temporary. You have my promise on that. I will do whatever it takes to get you wherever you need to be and to whomever you need to see."

I blink. Again and again, I blink and dip my chin, then shift and pull away. Pain pulls at my face—my internal pain and the pain I am about to cause him. He's the last person I'd want to cause pain, but I owe him honesty.

"You wouldn't say that if you knew the truth." I turn away, not wanting to see his reaction when the words spill out.

He clasps a gentle hold upon my arm and turns me around, lifts my face to his. "There's nothing you could say to me that would change the way I feel."

I brush his arm away. "Don't be so sure." I start to pace and start to rant. "There's all this stuff between us, you know?" I spare him a glance. "It's not fair that you know what I'm thinking or feeling, sometimes even before I do. And it's not fair that you know practically everything about me, been privy to my life since forever. You've seen my private moments and my not-so-private moments. And it's certainly not fair that I can't tell if my feelings for you are some sort of predestined thing or because I actually like you."

Jaden steps in my path and takes my hands in his own. He's got the goofiest grin on his face, and for a second, I believe he's going to kiss me. "Ana." His face softens. "One step at a time. We don't need to have all the answers right now. We've got God and Gaea on our side. They'll help us figure everything out."

"No." I shake my head. "You still don't get it. I don't deserve you. I don't deserve anyone's kindness."

"Is that what you think I'm doing?" His goofy grin falls into a frown. He releases my hands. "Being kind?"

"I'm responsible for my sister's death." I continue my rant, ignoring his question. "I'll soon be responsible for my brother's death. My mother's probably dead, and my sister's cat, too. Responsible for those."

Jaden cups my face in his hands, and my throat thickens; my words freeze, and all I can do is absorb all that is him.

"Stop this right now. You're not responsible for any bad that has happened. If anything, it is the rest of us who are to blame for keeping you in the dark." His gaze is almost as tight as his lips are straight.

My shoulders relax, and my head drops, and Jaden lets his hands fall back at his side. "Maybe I could get past all my issues..." I raise my gaze to meet Jaden's. "...if I didn't continuously find myself captivated by a dream incubus." I immediately bite my lip to stop myself from disclosing anything more.

Jaden's lips pull to the side with clear irritation, only not at me, at the situation... I hope. "That's not you. That's him.

The power of an incubus. It will get easier for you to withstand him the more time away from him you have."

"Time away. That doesn't seem to be working out," I say. "Since we arrived, I've seen him twice and heard him a third time."

"Three times?" Jaden forehead creases.

"I didn't tell you about the first time, the time I only heard him, because I took a seriously long nap before I had the chance." I rake my fingers through my hair and remember Dohlan's greeting upon my arrival to Hiddenkel. Always calling me his. Always trying to claim me. "But that time we saw him in the woods, my body ached with the desire to run to him. It was my head that kept me from making such a monumental mistake. The second time was when Ry tackled me beside the rocks." I study my feet and heave a heavy sigh. "I didn't want to push him away, and I didn't want you guys to hurt him." I tilt my head to the side. "Or him, you. I really didn't want you to see him, and as a result, I don't believe you did. It was strange and so surreal, and I suspect I blocked you from sensing me."

Jaden's head flinches. "But how?"

I let out a deep breath. "By sheer desire." I allow a frown to decorate my face and permeate my soul. "My want for him and my want to protect him is so overpowering that I kept you out of my head without any effort and without a clue as to how I managed it." I rub my temple. "I'm not a fool. I know what he is. And I can tell you that I don't want him with this." I touch my temple. "Or this." I cover my heart. "But that the feeling comes from everywhere, as if it has infected my blood." A tear forms at the corner of my eye. "I want Dohlan, and I don't know how to figh..."

My vision blurs. I blink and shake my head vigorously

and still only perceive blotches and fuzz. I stumble a step forward.

"Ana?" Jaden's voice sounds distant, like he's running down a long hallway, away from me.

Whistling. Somewhere. Everywhere.

Dohlan is whistling.

"What's happening..." My world tips. Jaden catches me. His touch tingles through me, and his green eyes fill with concern.

Sweet Jaden, what have I done?

Did I somehow summon Dohlan?

The drag, it's impossibly strong. I don't want to fight. I close my eyes.

EIGHT

M y eyes snap open, and I sit up with a start. "What happened? Where am I?"

I am surrounded by walls of stone, camouflaged by a lacework of narrow trees and vines. Strange exotic blooms dot color within the tangle and weave, creating an all-natural alternative to wallpaper. At varied heights and locations, the trees and vines branch out above me creating mini canopies. Everywhere around the perimeter, water drips and drizzles. It falls from the branches and vines and glides down the tree trunks, trickles like clear pears from the blooms.

And yet, none of the water seems to be falling upon me.

The ceiling is impossibly high. And the floor is covered in a lush green, much like moss. I allow my feet to dangle over the side of the bed. Then I touch my big toe to the surface.

"Yep. It's moss. Wet, mushy moss."

Strange as it may seem, the furniture fits, as if it's meant to be here. Their presence makes this strange place oddly functional. And the bed *is* comfortable. I press my hand into the mattress.

"Ana."

Dohlan leans against the wall. His arms are folded behind him. He flashes his usual cocky grin and takes a step forward. My skin begins to buzz, yearning for his touch, and my body flushes with heat. My fingers clench at the bedspread, and I don't move. I won't move.

Before our last meeting, I thought I was overcoming his effect on me. I glance around the room. Ry said Dohlan was a dream incubus. If I'm dreaming, then I'm in his domain where he's the most powerful.

I whimper and fixate on him. I forgot how insanely beautiful he is. How could I have possibly forgotten?

Jaden, my mind answers. *Jaden has the power to eclipse Dohlan.* Jaden, not Dohlan, is the key to unlocking who I am meant to be.

Dohlan whistles, switches to hums, and moves ever closer to my position.

"Am I dreaming?" I ask.

"And if you are?" he counters.

"But how?" I shake my head. "The last thing I recall, I was in the middle of a conversation..." I stop, not wanting to say Jaden's name in front of Dohlan.

"You called to me, Ana." He leans forward and presses his hands into the mattress on either side of me. "And I answered. Brought you here."

"You just brought me? Dragged me into a dream without my permission?" I remember he did that once before. I'd been in the middle of a swim meet. I knocked my head on the side of the pool, contaminated the water with my blood, and required saving. "What did I tell you about that?"

"Aw..." His hands slink forward, like the predator advancing on the prey. "You said the other world was dangerous, but you're not there now, are you?"

He's right. I didn't clarify that it was *never* okay to pull me into a dream. I'll have to be more careful with my word choice in the future.

His breath brushes along my collarbone, and I fall back to the bed.

If there is a next time.

This temptation is going to be the death of me. I close my eyes.

"Do you fear me?" His voice is at my ear. His body warmth mingles with my own. He's so close. So very unsafely close. I could touch him. My fingers tighten their hold on the bedding, and I pinch my eyes closed harder. I refuse to look. Refuse to be confused and overwhelmed by his power.

"No," I say, my voice escaping in a high-pitched squeal. I grimace.

"Haven't I helped you, Ana?"

I nod.

"Haven't I been keeping you safe?"

I shrug. He may have helped me with the most recent escape and with Dreya before, but safe... that might be stretching it.

"Do you trust me?"

I open my eyes.

Mistake. Mistake. Mistake.

I catch my breath.

"Ana." He slips his arms around my waist and gently plants the tiniest of kisses upon my forehead. Shivers run down my spine, and my entire body trembles.

He pulls away and stretches out beside me. I release my hold on the bedding and turn to face him. This time, he doesn't smile. He's busy studying me. Sizing me up somehow.

"Your mind is full of many wondrous things," he says.

I can no longer fight the buzz, so I stop trying. "What do you mean?" I say and let my hand run a curved line across his chest. It's a relief to allow my body to follow through on its desire. "I have been through a lot, yes. And I've seen some things, yes. But wondrous? I'm not sure about that."

Dohlan places his hand over mine, stopping its exploratory travels. His gaze narrows, and I sense he wants to ask something. I've never seen him like this, and I rather like it. I tilt my head and kiss the edge of his chin.

In a flash, his lips are upon mine. He pushes me back to the bed, holds my hands above my head, and kisses me with equal parts tenderness and danger. I want to pull him closer, push him away, hold this kiss forever.

A hurricane of emotions rips through me and pushes to the surface. I'm suddenly raw and vulnerable, quivering and crying.

"There you are." Dohlan pulls away, catches my tears with his finger. "What has you troubled, luv?"

That's the second time he's used the 'L' word with me. I don't know what it means. I shiver, then open my mouth to speak. I have no idea what I'm going to say, yet I'm compelled to say something. Only, instead of words, I give him sobs. Deep, powerful sobs. And within seconds, I am a weepy, snotty, saltwater mess.

"There, there," he says, petting my hair.

"I don't know what to do," I say between sobs. "Everything is falling apart."

He lays on his side, I curl into his chest, and he wipes the tears from my cheek. "Why don't you tell me your troubles. Maybe I can fix them."

"I think Ry is dying, and I don't know how to cure him." I curl tighter, press harder against Dohlan.

"Your warrior?" His tone borders on boredom. "And this would make you sad?" His arms wrap around me.

"Oh my Gaea and God, yes!" I stretch out and meet his understanding and tender return gaze. I bow my head and kiss his chest.

Using his finger, he lifts my head. "What ails him?"

"That horrible sword wound from Dreya."

He nods.

"And then there's my sisters."

"Hmm. I'd heard the merging is difficult," he says.

"That's not it at all," I say. "I want to merge. I'm eager to merge. If it will bring my sisters back to me. Only, I fear we won't make it in time." I sniffle. "We have so far to go, and there are so many obstacles, and my sisters... they are already gone."

Dohlan sits up and peers at me, his face a mask of serious intensity. "What do you mean? Tell me what has happened."

"I. I. Don't know." I sit up and wipe at my eyes. "Ry says some sort of dark magic has been used to block them from me. But the thing is..." I pull my knee into my chest. "When I last saw each of them, they appeared dreadfully dead. It was horrible, Dohlan!" I drop my face into my hands.

He gently moves my hands away and cradles my face in his palms. "If it is magic of any kind, then there is a way to undo it."

I brave a smile. "That's what Ry said. But I can't drag him across the country in his dying state so that I can search for the mystic Kaia said could fix us." I sniffle. "How do I choose between my brother and my sisters? I shouldn't have to make such a choice. And anyway, this mystic appears to be further away than I anticipated. There are just so many obstacles we hadn't planned for." I sigh and lean my cheek into his palm.

He leans forward. "How far do you have to travel?"

"Far!" I shake my head. "Honestly, I don't know. From the ruins of a Gaea Temple to the cabin of some old mystic by the name of Marrouske, I think."

My fingers fly to my lips. *I told Dohlan where to find me. Did I just put us all in danger?* I regard him and decide *no*, he already knew where I was. We are in no more danger now than before I spoke.

"And these obstacles?" he prompts.

"That freaky army you were leading through the woods." My voice pitches. He was there; he should know what we're up against.

He laughs. "Sweet, Ana. That can be easily dealt with."

"The way you did last time?"

He raises a brow. "Why do you think I was there?" He cracks a crooked smile. "Do you trust me?"

I'm lost for an answer. I can't deny that part of me that wants to rub my hands all over him, and yet I'm unfamiliar with that girl; she is a stranger to the rest of me. And there's always that little voice in the back of my head screaming for me to run. Run, Ana, run. And lately, the oddest feeling has plagued me that there's another reason I shouldn't *want* to be here, only I can't recall what that reason is.

I don't answer. Instead, I gaze at him and recall how I felt when I thought I saw him walking among that army of the twisted and dying. Dohlan has helped me, and I wanted to go to him.

"Ana?" His hands slip from my face. "Remember, this is *your* dream." He steps away from the bed.

His words confuse me, but I don't say anything. Instead, I reach for him, not wanting there to be any space between us.

"Do you trust me, Ana?" His voice is a mere whisper.

Tilting my head, I watch him back away from me. He backs up until he is leaning against the dresser. He adopts a stance that is a mixture of casual, arrogant, and cocky.

The hairs on my arms rise, and a fervent desire to claw my way out of the dream courses through my veins. Unfortunately, I am once again rooted in place. Only this time, I don't believe fear is the cause of my frozen state. I glare at Dohlan, suspecting the pompous prince is responsible. A sneer decorates his once beautiful face. And then the sound of shifting earth and breaking ice drags my attention away from him to the moving walls. Suddenly, this uniquely pleasant bedroom has turned into a prison.

The trees and vines bend and move with the shift of the earth, and a dark, wide gap opens. From it, a woman steps forward and glides to the middle of the room.

My jaw drops. "This is *my* dream. How did *you* get in?" I say, remembering what Dohlan told me.

"Dohlan left the door unlocked." Dreya's gaze shifts between me and Dohlan. "Oh, silly girl," she says with a laugh. "Did you think he loved you?" Her hand fans out across her chest in feigned horror. Every time she shows up, she appears to favor a different style. Does she suffer from dissociative identity disorder? This time, she is all in white, wearing a shimmering, billowing white gown. Her skin is powdered white. Her hair is white. Everything except the glimmering, golden rings adorning her fingers is white. "He says that to all his fools, but he couldn't possibly feel that way for any of them. He belongs to me." Her voice is harsh, and her steps take her to Dohlan's side. "Isn't that right, my pet?" Dreya slowly drags a lone finger down his cheek.

Dohlan snarls and turns his head away. Excitement flashes in her eyes. She's one seriously messed up aunt. Clearly, she enjoys her role as predator a tad too much. Dohlan's gaze flickers to me, and it's so brief I'm not sure if I imagined it or not. He wants me to trust him, but I'm not sure I can. Especially now, when he's brought Dreya here.

Dreya turns to me, throws her arms wide and advances. Immediately, memories of Kaia's death dream flood my thoughts. My chest sucks back, tries to press against my spine, and my arms tighten against my sides. Her eyes sparkle, and her lips curl into the cruelest of sneers. When she gets a foot away, her arms drop, and she glances over me.

"No, you are not her," she says with the slightest shake of her head. "I can see a glimmer of her within you..." She wags her finger at me "...but clearly you are you and not her." She sighs, turns away, circles the room and comes to stop a couple feet in front of me. "But you *are* the one I have been waiting for." She rests her palms on the backside of her hips. "Aren't you?"

I'm not a hundred percent sure, but I suspect she just compared me to Kaia. That being my only frame of reference, it's the most obvious assumption. As for me being the *one*, if I am to believe all the hyperbole about me, then yes... I am the one. Of course, I don't trust my witch of an aunt, and I don't feel all-mighty powerful, so I keep my mouth shut.

"Nothing to say?" She leans forward. "That's too bad."

She straightens, stands tall. "I believe you are the one, whether you are brave enough to admit it in my presence or not. Of course, you are right to fear me." She smirks. "I am stronger than you and will crush you in the end. Be sure of that, girl." Her cheeks rise with her smile, and her bluish-violet eyes sparkle. I imagine her hatred running like a stream of filthy cast-off water. The ugliness glides through her veins and bleeds into her irises. Suddenly, everything about her looks muddy and gross.

I chance a glance at Dohlan. He stares across the room, his expression vacant.

"Eyes here, girlie." Dreya flags me with the wave of her hand. "He will not help you. Did you fail to hear me when I said he's mine?" Her lips twist to the side. "I meant that in more ways than one." She laughs, and I'm reminded of a hyena. "You are in my territory now, and we're going to have so much fun together."

I've experienced her kind of fun, and I'm not interested in participating. It's like being the mouse in that game Mouse Trap, only with falling boulders and flying swords. I chance another glance at Dohlan. He still avoids looking our direction. He's like so many of the cats at the Feline Preservation where Crystia worked—caged and bored. If this were my dream, I'd release him.

My eyes widen. *This is my dream.*

Dohlan made a point of telling me that seconds before Dreya arrived. Was he sending me a message?

My back straightens, and a fire sparks in my belly. If this is my dream, I should be able to manipulate things. I should be stronger, wiser, and more confident. And Dreya should have zero power over me. The campfire in my gut spreads like wildfire through my body, increasing in intensity with every pump of my heart.

Dreya giggles. "I've stirred your pot. Good." Her musical voice only angers me further.

I refuse to break eye contact but notice from the corner of my eye Dohlan turning to face me, his mouth agape.

"Now listen here, Auntie." I narrow my gaze and imagine burning a hole between her eyes. "I know the things you've done. You're going to pay for your crimes against the kingdom and its people, and you'll also pay for what you did to my sister, Kaia."

Dohlan flinches. His lips curve toward the floor, and his brows pinch together. A split-second later, he's once again composed, a bored expression settling comfortably over his features.

Holy jealous monster. Did another girl's name pull a reaction from the god of stone? And not just any girl's name, my sister's?

I gasp. What if Dohlan knows something about Kaia's disappearance?

Here and now is not the place to delve into that particular subject. I quickly compose myself and glare at Dreya. "I'll make sure your payment for your crimes is substantial."

"Silly girl, you're young and inexperienced. I am far more talented than you will ever be, and you never stand a chance, so why even try?"

"Because you need to be stopped," I say.

"And you are the one to stop me?" She raises a brow.

"Oh, yeah." I nod and slip off the bed to stand before her.

Dreya tilts her head and studies me as if judging a potential purchase. Her arms are crossed, and I half expect the constant oscillation of her index finger against her lower lip to draw blood. I wish it would. I want to shove her nose up through her skull.

She huffs. "I believe that you believe you can defeat me. Unfortunately for you, that shall never come to pass, and in the end, you will meet a pitiful demise." She shoves her fingers into my chest, pushing me back to sit on the bed.

"Enough!" I shove her hand away. The fire in my veins has morphed and now travels throughout my body in never-ending electrical pulses. My fingers tingle and need to move. The electricity sparks across my skin, and my tiny arm hairs stand on end. "No more. Not another word!" The intensity of my words presses into the crease of my forehead. "You have taken advantage of too many for too long. It's time you release your hold on all the poor souls you force to do your dirty work."

I spare Dohlan a glance and consider all the things I've heard or witnessed. Dohlan may not have the appearance of a prisoner, only that's exactly what he is. An unwilling incubus chained and bound to do the evil queen's bidding.

"And you're going to start with that one." I throw my arm out, sharp and straight, and point at Dohlan.

Dreya throws her head back, and her shoulders lift in a strong, bold laugh. A second later, she brings her palms to her chest and throws me a devil-stern leer. "I don't think you have the slightest clue who you are dealing with."

"I said. No. More. Words!" I stand, swing my arms around, and thrust the full force of my electric pulse through my palms and into her chest with a slam.

Dreya is thrown across the room. She laughs, her return strike flying at me before she's even on her feet. I don't move out of the way fast enough and catch the hit in the arm. I'm swung around and tossed into a beside tree.

"Damn," I mumble. I was kind of hoping Dreya wouldn't have that ability. I collapse to the ground and roll. Her second attack sails over my head, and satisfaction blooms in my chest. *Call me inexperienced!*

"Stop this!" Dohlan steps between us. "You are both acting... *so... cattish* right now."

"Ana." He turns the fierce force of his heavenly blue eyes on me. "What are you doing?"

"It's a dream, Dohlan. I can beat her." I pull myself into a crouch.

He shakes his head. "You're ill-informed." His face softens, and I spy sadness in his eyes.

"Don't be so cavalier, boy. Her youth has made you weak." Dreya shoves him aside, swings her arm in my direction, producing a scepter mid-swing.

I throw my arms up to block the blow, and then everything is red and yellow and white, and I'm falling backward. Blazing white needles everywhere. I've become her pincushion. Then I slam into the back wall. The air is knocked out of my lungs, still, I shake my head and dig my heels in for purchase. I don't know what I'm going to do, but it will be something grand, I'm sure.

I scurry to a stand, and before I can determine who is where on the game board, a curtain of black wraps around me, strong arms secure me, and the world beyond us starts spinning. It spins, and it spins, fading into nothingness and taking Dreya's screeches of betrayal along with it.

"I could have held my own. I want the opportunity to end this, Dohlan." I cling to him, fearful of where I might find myself if I let go in a spinning world of darkness.

"One must not be rash but fight with reason. You are not

ready. And this was neither the time nor the place." His answer is smooth, as if it has been rehearsed.

"Then why did you let her in?" I speak into his chest, savor the slow rise and give of his breathing.

"I did not. But nor can I ever keep her out."

"You said it was my dream. I thought you were telling me I could turn things to my favor," I say.

"I meant you had the power to escape." He sighs. "All you had to do was wake up."

Like a child's spinning top, we keep revolving. My stomach lurches and I swallow hard. My head starts to pound, and my body drags, as if I've suddenly doubled in weight. I close my eyes, press into Dohlan's chest, and breathe in his rich exotic spices. Never again will I be able to walk into a spice shop and *not* be reminded of him.

"That's right, Ana. Rest your head." His hand brushes the length of my hair, and then his finger traces the line from the top of my neck to the end of my collar bone. I prickle with want, and yet, that tiny voice within me screams for me to run. Run where?

I sigh into his chest. I wish I knew what I wanted and what I will do in regards to him. Why does the closeness of Dohlan muffle my clarity of thought?

His sweet fevered breath washes over me, and I release the fight. It is then, my thoughts clarify. I want reason when it comes to Dohlan. I don't want to stay, and I don't want to run. I want to be able to think straight. But that will be a task for another day because right now, I'm tired.

The last of my strength wanes, and my body falls slack. Dohlan compensates, holding me tighter and snuggling my head into his chest. Still, I fall farther, everything around me melting and fading away. Dohlan lifts me into his arms, and the world ceases to exist.

"This meeting was not without its rewards," he whispers at my ear.

My body slips, jerks into a drop, and I lurch forward for his shoulders, his arms, anything I can grip.

NINE

I open my eyes to the morning light awakening life around me. Last night, I slipped from Dohlan's arm and fell straight into our camp and straight into a nightly slumber. I missed dinner, and now morning is here. The shimmer creeps through the colossal windows in the wall beside me, and somewhere in the near distance, a chorus of birds sings a joyful wake-up song.

My stomach gurgles off key, adding to the melody. I suck in my belly, hoping to silence the squawking with the constriction of my muscles. Soon, I promise myself, soon I will venture out and find food, but I'm not ready to move.

I'm laid out comfortably on my bedroll, in a tent, and have Jaden's jacket as a pillow. I turn my head into his jacket and inhale his woodsy scent.

Jaden. The thought of him warms me.

We were talking last night when I simply crashed, mid-sentence, standing up. He must have carried me to bed.

Dohlan stole my Jaden time.

My jaw clenches, and my hands curl into fists. I blink hard and release the frustration. Somehow, I'll fix this. Curb my attraction to Dohlan.

I rub my eyes, sit up, and fluff my hair. I check the pendant hanging around my neck. It's still cloudy. Thankfully, the crystals on my wrist bands have remained clear.

The guys... or Yuromo... are nowhere in sight, but a few feet away, their stuff is neatly gathered together, packed and ready to go.

I'm not sure if I'm disappointed or pleased that the group isn't present. Ry would probably have a hundred and five questions for me if he knew of last night's adventure.

Jaden, me, Dohlan... *help me, Gaea.*

Beyond the crumbling wall of the temple ruin are the calm waters of the lake, and I detect the faintest refrain, a morning melody. It's not only the bird song; it's the chatter of bugs, the yawn of flowers, and the whisper of the water. For the first time since arriving in this strange world, I feel blessed.

My lips slowly lift to the side in a crooked smile. I sigh and then roll my head and stretch my arms and shoulders. A stiffness has set in, and muscles I am unfamiliar with cry for attention. A hot shower and a pain-relief rub would be a welcomed comfort yet might do little to ease the pain.

When was the last time I exercised? I count the days on my fingers: the longest day ever on the run, three days sleeping, the day after Crystia's death, her funeral, and the crazy trip here. A week, maybe more? I'll have to figure out some sort of routine while we're on the move.

Standing, I release one final yawn and then make my way to the lakeside. My stomach is grumbling. I missed dinner the night before. I'm certain the group saved some grub for me, I just need to find them.

Even beyond the temple ruins, the group are nowhere to be seen, leaving me curious regarding their whereabouts. I'm surprised they left me alone after all their Ana-fretting. That can get so tiring, the fretting. The horses are relaxing in the grass, appearing content, so I suppose, I won't worry yet.

The water is inviting, so I kick off my boots, wade a few feet in, scoop a handful and splash my face. My body hums, fills with information and understanding the water Ondine have chosen to share with me. They show me the spot where I stand through generations of seasons, events, and emotions. The emotions have me internally floating to the clouds. The sensation is better than a mug of tea or cup of coffee. Good thing, too, because I doubt we'll come across any java huts along our travels.

After another face splash and a few quick sips to quench my dry throat, I settle into a comfortable spot beside the lake and meditate, attempt to tap into any residual emotions lingering here. The temple at my back is thousands of years old, and during the time when people gathered here in worship, both the temple and the surrounding land were a place of happiness and serenity. I could use some of that serenity now.

Somewhere behind me, far behind me, a girl giggles, making me curious as to what Yuromo finds so funny on this first true morning of our wayward adventure. I try not to care. I try to stay focused on being in the moment, on sensing the energy of the universe moving around me and through me.

An image of Yuromo shamelessly flirting with Jaden, in the same way Skylar used to throw herself at him, flashes in my mind.

I huff, breathe deep, let the image go, and try to meditate once again.

Yuromo flipping her hair, batting her eyes, peering at me sideways.

It's no use. Meditation isn't going to happen today.

I open my eyes. Ry is standing in front of me. His arrival was as quiet as a breeze, making his approach practically undetectable. Either that or I wasn't paying attention, in which case, he'll probably have a few things to say about my awareness.

His arms are crossed, and his eyes are scrutinizing me. "How'd you sleep?"

"Fine," I lie. I don't want to get into a nasty Dohlan conversation with him, only somehow, I suspect he already knows.

His chest heaves, and he lets out a slow breath. "Jaden says you need a few refresher courses to help you compensate for the change in your sisterly connection." His gaze flickers toward the temple, and I glance over my shoulder. Yuromo is pulling all the packs out into the open, mine included. "I'd like Yuromo to participate, if you don't mind."

"Ahh... okay." What I really want to do is roll my eyes and complain, but I don't. I bite my lip. "So, um, have you seen Jaden?" I'm kicking myself internally. I sound like a lovesick girl. I might be, when I'm not around Dohlan. I need some Dohlan-free time to sort out my messy emotions.

Ry laughs and turns his gaze to the sky.

"Sure. He's over there." Yuromo walks up and points to the line of trees closest to our position. "He's doing some of that stuff you were just doing. Said he had to work something out."

Work something out? Why does Yuromo know Jaden's business? Should I be worried?

I gaze at the nearby trees and contemplate Jaden's abilities. It must be horrible to know things you'd rather not know and feel things you'd wish you could forget. I thought I'd feel inadequate and less of a person after admitting my faults to him last night. Oddly, it's quite the contrary. But what if I transferred all my mixed emotions over to him and that's why he needs to work through some things?

I sigh and try to imagine Jaden meditating among nature.

Until this morning, I failed to recognize how strongly that emotion runs through me. Never have I felt a sense of belonging like I do with Jaden. I shouldn't have been afraid to come clean. I don't want to lose him because I'm too closed lipped.

Ry waves his hand in front of my face. "You with us, Ana?"

I jolt. "Yeah, sorry. But um..." My stomach growls. "Do you mind if I eat first?"

"You can eat while we ride."

Making my disappointment clear, I shuffle forward and stand next to Yuromo. Ry leads us through a morning of fight skills 101.

I express concern that we are spending too much time in one place, but Ry assures me we'll be on our way within the hour, hour and a half tops, and it won't behoove us to head out into unknown terrain with flawed defense finesse. I can't argue his point.

It's the dreaded catch twenty-two. We need to hurry in order to save my sisterly connection and find a cure for Ry, but in order to succeed at either task, I must be dedicated to bettering myself, which means practice, practice, practice.

Since I've already mastered the mechanics of the various fight moves, my job is to search within, reach out to my higher senses, tap into the universal power, and find my way back to killer execution and follow through. Be excellent alone, without Kaia's help influencing me.

The message from Jaden was that I need to believe in myself in order bring my ability to fruition.

I kind of hope that the moment I decide to be fabulous, I will be. Apparently, the universe has other plans. It wants my sweat and concentration. Too many times, I find myself grinding my teeth and stomping the ground. In the grand scheme of things, a mere fraction of time has passed, even though the ticking clock in my head urges me to learn faster and become quicker. And so, I keep trying, concentrating with all my will.

I breathe deep and close my eyes. Focus. The world beyond whispers, a simple, soft quiet. Except for the flapping. Flap, flap, flap. The gentle flapping fills the air.

Annoying. My eyes pop open, and I scan the area.

Strange. I get the sense that I am the only one bothered by the noise.

I straighten. My eyes widen. *Have I successfully tapped into my extra senses?*

The sound slows, and a delicate butterfly lands on my forearm. I hold my breath and observe the beautiful creature, fixate on the slow open and close of its wings.

Whap... whap... whap.

The world and all its delicious sounds have fallen away. There's only silence and the little blue butterfly. And what's that...

"Something not right."

My brows pinch. Did the butterfly talk to me?

Whap... whap... whap...

"Should leave."

I tilt my head and turn my attention to the horses. Velsa stands at attention, and understanding washes through me.

Velsa was the one speaking. I did it! I can once again hear the animals speak!

My eyes avert to the sky above. *Thank you, Crystia. Thank you, God and Gaea.*

"Yes." Velsa's head nods. *"No longer feel safe. Something is wrong."* Her movements are agitated.

Ry and Yuromo continue to drill as if nothing has changed. Farther down the lake, a hundred yards or more, Jaden emerges from the tree line, running. He's safe. Everyone is safe and accounted for. Only, something smells off, like rotting fish. My gaze drops to the water. I spy no floating bodies. But still...

The butterfly flies away, skimming over the surface of the lake. I watch her go, and as I do, time slows, sounds mute, and I am pulled toward the water.

I walk past Ry and Yuromo, ignoring Ry's inquiries. I move forward until my reflection peers back at me in the lake's smooth surface. Something dark swirls deep below.

An image of the old mystic, Madame Marrouske, materializes on the water, and I jerk.

"Be ever vigilant, my dear," she says. "Deep within you lies your strength. Don't be afraid to seize who you are, nor release who you are not." Her eyes dart from side to side, and I pull a fraction of an inch away. "Where is the girl?"

My nose wrinkles. "What girl?"

"The girl I sent to meet you at the tree?"

The only girl with whom I share any kind of tree experience is...

Oh my God and Gaea. Does she mean Bree?

Madame Marrouske's image disappears.

I lean closer, tilt my head, and bite my lip in concentration. Why would she leave before answering my question? If she did mean Bree, why would the old woman expect me to bring a girl to this world that I barely know and only know because of school? Besides, I wasn't really in control of our California exit. That one is on Ry. He didn't give me permission to invite a friend... or my mother.

Sarcasm sweeps through me and quickly evaporates.

My nose wrinkles. When I took my three-day nap, I had dreamt about Bree, which made no sense to me at all. But then, normal dreams, the kind I rarely have, are supposed to be nonsensical, aren't they?

Bree's a strange one. Kind of like Madame Marrouske.

My lower lip puckers.

The old mystic's image is gone, and yet something dark in the water remains, pulsing and billowing below the surface.

I'm new to this world and thereby unfamiliar with all its inhabitants and unusual quirks, but there is something very not right about the inky black churn in the lake. It reminds me of the darkness that chased us at the old mining camp.

There's a tension dwelling amongst the water's depth, something foreign and unwanted, and I need to know what it is. Even if it is the darkness. The Tenebrousian.

On pure instinct, I reach out to touch the water.

"Ana."

I pull back and glance over my shoulder at Ry.

"What are you doing?" He walks toward me.

"I don't really know, but you might want to stay back," I say, returning my focus to the lake.

I will not shy away.

Embracing both Jaden's and the mystic's words, I lean closer to the disturbance in the water and cling to confidence. My braid slips forward, the tip slapping the water.

Rings and ripples burst into motion. I scrutinize the fold and billow. Among the dazzling swirls and shimmers of blue are two red glowing dots, like eyes in the dark.

Something glares back at me. Rises to meet me.

My instinct is to tumble back, scurry away. Except seconds ago, I made a promise to myself to be strong and believe in myself. I will not break that promise this quick.

I don't glance over my shoulder. Don't care if Ry is advancing or not. I've already decided I'm not going to let him stop me. Be it a wise decision or a foolish one, it is mine, and I will suffer the consequences either way. My fingertips break the surface of the lake.

The crystals on my wristbands illuminate ever slightly.

A rush of knowledge floods through me faster than a lightning strike.

Tenebrousian, the Ondine say.

I pull back, still the inky black fog moves quick, culling up through the water, reaching for me. Like a whip, it wraps around my wrist and braid, yanking me forward, toward the glowing eyes of red. The whites of the eyes, or in this case, cloudy-day grey, are now visible—a mere sliver of a crescent moon.

The octopus-like tentacle morphs, and, suddenly, claws are digging into my skin. My blood pumps beneath the pressure, and tiny pinpricks of pain cut along the edge of the Tenebrousian's hold. It yanks me down, and if I were the human I grew up believing myself to be, it would drag me to the lake's floor. Only, I have become more, and I have a way with water.

At least, I believe I do.

The Ondines acknowledge my presence, and I sense they

are planning something. The light of my crystal bands increases and illuminates the lake water in a brilliant blue. Tiny jet streams rush around me, push against me, spark against my flesh. Their thoughts whisper against my skin and travel along my veins. When the Ondines and I are together in the water, we are as one. I know as they know, and so I know what I need to do.

Why would the Tenebrousian attack me where I'm at my strongest? I wonder.

A commotion erupts behind me. Things moving. Ry, Yuromo, even Jaden yelling. I don't pay it any attention. I hold my focus where it needs to be.

The Tenebrousian yanks again. This time I'm prepared, with my feet anchored and my weight braced firmly against the table. Only, there is no table. The table is the water, supporting me and holding me steady, keeping me from tumbling forward into the murky depths. The pull on my braid is firm. My head jerks, and my arms instinctively slap the water as if preparing for a fall, yet my body remains out of the Tenebrousian's reach.

Ondines press against my hands, and it's like a watery hand flat against my own, moving us as one. My fingers fan out, and the lake stirs beneath my touch, churning and spinning like a cyclone into the water's depth. In a mere instant, I understand what I can do, what I will do, and what I want to do.

But doubt creeps around the edges of my resolve.

I toss a bucket of water upon the ugliness of doubt and wash that barrier away.

The fury that possessed me in Dreya's presence the night before is nothing more than a memory now. I have no desire to destroy or mar. If I could heal the Tenebrousian, remove the black sickness, I would, only I don't know how, so for now, I want to send him... or her... home.

Thin whirlpools like antennas extend from my fingertips. They stretch clear to the lake's floor and move in a search pattern. The once calm lake gyrates and splashes, the water curving and whirling around the pond until it finds the Tenebrousian and the hole through which it crawled.

Working the lake is becoming like second nature to me. As if I've always been able to manipulate water. The motions are becoming as simple as one, two, three. It's a mere flick of the wrist, a flex of the hand. They may be minor motions, yet each move communicates my wishes, and the water responds.

All my crystals, besides the clouding one from Kaia, hum. Hum and glow. I move my hands along the lake's surface in a question mark motion. Ten small whirlpools merge into one massive, sucking and pulling, vortex. The Tenebrousian clings to me, fights my maelstrom pull, even as the pressure of the lake's vortex continues to build. My head begins to pound, and the Tenebrousian is slipping, cutting my skin.

There's no emotion in the face of a Tenebrousian. There's nothing more than two red glowing eyes and a multitude of deep black swirls. But if I were to deduce anything from the way it clings and claws, drawing blood from my skin, I would say the thing is scared... or extremely determined.

Either way, it needs to go.

My strength is ebbing, and I'm unsure how much longer I'll be able to keep up the fight. I shove the heels of my palms against the lake's surface, sending a heavy pulse through the volume of the lake. It's similar to an underwater sonic boom. Everything is swept toward the vortex, and the Tenebrousian gets caught in the spin. It's stretching and stretching, spinning down into the forever gone, and it has yet to release me. I teeter, lose my balance, and start to pitch forward.

I scream.

Hands clasp around me. Around my waist and legs. Four, five, six hands hold my body upon the shore. The Tenebrousian screeches, rips free from my skin, and disappears into the void. The spiraling water washes my wounds clean.

The lake drops to a calm, and my crystals sleep.

"Ana," Ry says, holding firm to my arm. "It's done. Please step back."

I sigh, and my shoulders droop. That was exhausting, and I don't want the group privy to the toil it has taken upon me. If all I do is sleep all the time, I wouldn't put it past Ry to start calling me sleeping beauty. I pat his hand to let him know I'm alright.

My concentration remains glued on the water. I thoughts tied to the Tenebrousian. It had clearly come from a pathway beneath the water. The same pathway used to send it away. A pathway that could be used by the darkness or anything else to return again and again and again.

"Ana, please," Ry echoes.

"One more thing." I plunge my hands back into the water. The crystals on my wrist explode with light and pulse with the energy coursing through my body. I'm not sure why I'm doing it, I just know that I need to. I need to do something. My hands move together in the direction of the underwater door. Water is an extraordinary, powerful force, and I am going to put it work. Nadir waves—floor skimming waves

—form and push heavy rocks and sediment into the gap, permanently closing the passage.

Now it is done.

No one can see what I have done, but if Dreya learned our location through the eyes of that Tenebrousian, then she won't be getting to us through that pathway. I've bought us time, and we're all safe... for the time being.

I flick the water from my fingers and stand upright, a wave of exhaustion slams into me. *Wooha. That took more energy than I realized.* I wipe the back of my hand across my forehead and collapse... straight into Jaden's awaiting arms.

"Thanks." I whimper and close my eyes.

He gently guides my body to the ground, and I rest for a minute or ten. I don't know how long I stay that way, and when I do finally open my eyes, I spy Ry pacing at the lake's edge, ready to whip his electric wands into action.

Doesn't he realize there's nothing left to fight? I huff. Blow a stray hair from my vision. Rebellious, the hair returns to almost the same spot.

A few feet away, Yuromo sits on the ground watching me. It's not a creepy kind of watch but one, rather, of concern. Her gaze jumps from me to the crystals I wear then back to me. Jaden's pack lays on the ground at her side and sitting upon the pack, the sliver of glossy stone. I can't help but ogle. Had Jaden taken the rock far from my view to attempt communication with whomever is on the other side? Does he not trust me enough to share his plan? I avert my gaze and fixate on Jaden, the guy cradling my tired body.

"Hey." My words are barely audible. "Sorry about last night." After everything I just went through, I am slightly hung up on how I left him the night before.

"Nothing to be sorry about." He brushes the unruly hair from my view. "Are you alright?"

My breath heaves. "Will it always be like this?" I ask, deciding not to bring up the subject of the stone. Not now, anyway. "Will everything I attempt be so draining?"

"I can't believe that it will be." He smiles wearily. "But in truth, little is known about you and your abilities."

I sigh. "Will you always be here to catch me?" I don't really mean for him to answer the question. I don't know why I even asked. It wasn't fair of me.

His thumb brushes along my cheek. "I will always be here for you. Until the day I am no more." His lips brush across my forehead, and he lifts me into his arms, carries me toward the sanctuary of the temple ruins. I want to tell him that he needs to set me on a horse. That we need to move, put space between us and the area around the lake, yet my mouth doesn't move.

Instead, I find myself mesmerized by the crystal pendant hanging around his neck. It's one of mine. I made it as a gift for someone who failed to appreciate its value. Jaden claimed the gem from her pile of discards. But that's not why I stare. It's the slight swirl of purple and red threads twisting and churning within the stone that has me captivated. I blink, turn my gaze to my crystal wristband, the one worn on the arm I have wrapped around Jaden's neck. The same dance of colors is visible within my own. It's quite the curiosity. What does it mean?

"I know what you think," he says, and my attention snaps to Jaden. His face tightens, his brow pinches, and his forehead gleams. "That my interest in you is a manifestation of the magic binding us. I don't believe that is so." He glances from the path to me. "And I meant to say as much last night, before our conversation put you to sleep." His smile twists into a smirk.

My eyelids are heavy, and yet I force them to remain open. I want to see his expressions during his confession. Plus, I like watching him, even when he is aware of my watchful eye.

"I think you should let go of the notion that our feelings are being influenced and simply allow yourself to feel whatever it is you feel. That's what I plan on doing."

For a moment of whispered wind, the world seems to stop and there is only us. Him, with his piercing jade eyes. Both of our gazes locked upon the other. He does have a solid point. It shouldn't matter where the root of our emotions lies. If they feel real, then why can't they honestly be real? I see no reason why they can't be.

My hands itch to reach up, cradle his face, and my lips burn with the desire to kiss him. Kiss him silly. But I haven't enough strength to move my pinkie, so for now, that thought will remain exactly that... a thought or wish or a hope for a future action.

He looks away, his expression turning serious, and he focuses his attention on the uneven path. I'm guessing he doesn't want to trip or drop me.

"We can't stay here," I croak, with my small and strained voice. Jaden doesn't react and doesn't slow in his movements away from the horses. I should push the subject, only, I have zero energy to say more than I have already.

Jaden takes us to a back corner of the temple ruins, leans against the wall, and cradles me in his lap. I don't object. Exhaustion is excellent at taming one's desire to make a fuss. Not to mention, I enjoy the gentle rhythm of his heart and the snuggly warmth of his body. I gaze at his face, memorizing every line and muscle twitch. He has a tiny scar on the side of his right eye that I failed to spy before, and another more predominate one slightly off-center on his chin.

"Close your eyes," he says. "Rest."

I raise my chin in protest.

He shushes me. "Don't fight your body's efforts to restore."

I groan. My eyelids are heavy, as are my limbs. And my body does ache. Not in the way it ached after sleeping for days, but in a I-fell-down-the-stairs after running an around-the-world marathon kind of way. I concede to his wishes with a slight nod and close my eyes.

"Is she alright?" Ry asks.

"She needs time to replenish, but she will be fine." Jaden brushes a soft finger down the side of my face and rests his palm against my cheek. "She'll likely be good as new by late this evening."

"I hate to be the militant big brother, but we can't afford to stay here. Not after what happened."

My eyes unwillingly open, and I peer up at Ry.

"I'm sorry," he says. "You'll eventually thank me for this when we get you to our destination." He leans forward with his hand held out to me. "Can you get up?"

Without argument, I grab his hand and allow him to pull me to a stand. I sway and stumble backward, into Jaden. His grip tights on my arms, holding me steady.

"She's weak. If we must move, I recommend she ride with one of us until she recovers."

Ry shifts his weight awkwardly, considers me, and considers Jaden's recommendation. "Very well," he says. "We wouldn't want anything happening to our precious princess." He smirks at me. He knows I hate being called a princess. "Like falling off her horse." He winks, turns to leave, and then glances back at Jaden. "She's riding with you, by the way."

My heart jitters to a pause and then jumps into my throat and gets comfy. All the close-to-Jaden time, riding double on a horse. Will I need to come up with conversation? Or will I pass out and drool on his arm? My cheeks flush.

TEN

J aden and I ride Timbers together. I sit in front, and
Jaden's arms provide a sturdy barrier between me and
the ground. Velsa trots at our side. With Yuromo in the
lead, we follow a worn dirt road. The surrounding grass
encroaches on the path, softening the edges.

I visualize the track once serving as the main route to the
temple at our back. Once upon a time, the dirt road was
likely busy with people coming and going. It's shocking how
detailed my imagination can be, but even the images of a past
long gone can't keep my eyes trained on this new-to-me
world. My eyes close, then open, then close again, allowing
me short glimpses of our travels. Jaden's words weave in and
out of my consciousness. He's saying something about his
ability to sense my emotions not being one-sided. That I, too,
have the talent, only I don't appear to recall the time when I
used that talent naturally and with ease.

Checking my confusion and frustration to the side of the
road, at least for now, I lean against him and rest. His

warmth, the rhythm of his heart, the slow saunter of the horse is like a mother rocking a baby, and I want to sleep. And, I don't want to sleep.

I close my eyes.

My eyes flutter open, catching sight of a piled rock wall. The next time my eyes flutter open, we're marching through a sea of purple flowers exploding with beech trees. I'm fuzzy about how much time passes before I open my eyes again, but when I do, the density of the trees lining the road gives the illusion of a hallway. A nature-made, mile-long hallway. In my half-awake state, I envision us as warriors wandering the course in search of the ruling lion king. The branches on either side, reach across the pathway, connecting and weaving together with the trees on the opposite side. It's a latticework of green, and it does a darn good job at blocking out the sky. If it weren't so lovely, it would be scary.

"From Gaea's temple to God's cathedral," I whisper.

Jaden rests his face against the side of my head. "It's breathtaking, isn't it?"

Bliss warms my body and lifts my lips, and, again, I close my eyes. The rhythm of his breath is soothing.

Once more, I lose time.

It's strange. Before I came to Hiddenkel, I thought I knew myself, as much as I guess anyone can know themselves. I had a handle on my talents, and I felt good about the choices I was making in regard to my life plan. But life can change so incredibly fast, like you are a dot on the Wheel of Fortune spinner. With one quick whirl, everything changes. You may remain on the board, or you might be the lucky dot that gets toss off the table and into another zone.

I am that dot, the one in another zone. I no longer know who I am or what I want. All I know is...

Something isn't right.

My eyes pop open. Yuromo and Ry are both riding at the front. Velsa is still at our side. Her head bobs, sending funny vibes to my belly. Everyone in our group appears to be tense. Yuromo's searching gaze is darting all over the place. Ry is alert, as always. It's what he has taught me. *Always be aware of your surroundings, or your surroundings may get the better of you.* A warrior never rests and never lets his guard down.

I've been doing a lot of that lately. Resting and letting my guard down. Not this time. I pull myself upright and sit straight. I keep my gaze glued to the surrounded flora. Everything is as beautiful as the last time I opened my eyes. Wouldn't it be just like this world to house a human-sized Venus fly trap? Or worse yet, an entire forest of them. All it takes is one to pull us in with the beauty, then devour us.

We ride for another hour and nothing happens. And I mean nothing. Not even a horse poops. Okay. Maybe it's only fifteen minutes, even though it feels like an hour, and my muscles ache from the tension. I close my eyes.

Snap.

Crack. Snap.

I rub my eyes. "How long have I been out?" I mumble.

Jaden's lips graze the end of my ear, and he gently shushes me.

My eyes pop wide. I'm suddenly terribly awake. And the tightening in my belly is buzzing. The world around us is no longer pretty, purple flowers and cathedral-worthy, lanky white trees. The path might be wider, easier to travel, but the walls are dark and confining, thick with moss and shadowy shrubs. The plant life is consuming, covering, and devouring everything in sight—trees, rocks, dirt—until there is nothing but green, green, green everywhere you look.

We are mere tiny specks moving in a towering verdigris forest. Nature has swallowed us whole, communicating our incredible insignificance to the ecosystem.

We're all extra quiet as we make our way, attempting to match the silence of the world around us.

Snap.

My gaze flies to the branches above, then back to our party. I am not the only one studying the trees. Ry and Yuromo are ever diligent in their watchfulness.

Green and grey flashes across the edge of my view. Before I can react, something smacks into me, into us, knocking Jaden and me off the horse. Timbers squeals—it sounds like a roar. He rears, kicking the air, and leaps into a bolt. Velsa takes off after him.

One minute, I'm searching the trees for signs of swinging activity. The next, I'm on my butt among the moss and lichen. I sit up and rub my back, twist around to assess the situation and get a handle on what is happening.

Down the path, Yuromo has also been knocked from her horse. Ry has his weapon pulled and has somehow managed to remain on Belmiso. The horse dances or gallops in a circle. Something dark bears down on them from all sides. Even from above.

They're in the trees!

I need a weapon. I drag myself off the ground and quickly scan the area in search of one of the packs. There aren't any to be found, nor are any of the horses present, other than Belmiso.

Jaden is deeply engaged, fighting the darkness. Except, it isn't really darkness at all. It's men clad in dark green and grey, with clumps of mossy ground cover clinging to their bodies in camouflage. *Stupid smart.* The moss made them harder to spot... until *now*.

"Ana." The sound of my name rolls over my skin, low and shallow. Another quick scan of the area. *Who's calling me?*

The flashes of black. The voice calling my name. The reaction of my skin. The person present and left unseen has to be *him*. Dohlan. I groan and roll my eyes... get slammed backward.

I hit the ground, back flat, with a thud. This time I moan. *That's going to hurt.*

I'm pinned beneath one of the ugliest men I've ever seen. He's uglier than the mutant soldiers we fought in the forest of cathedral trees. He laughs, and foul, make-me-want-to-faint breath washes over me. I try not to gag and then try not to breathe.

The guy is the same as the mutant soldiers, only uglier and possibly, slightly less dead. Instead of uniforms, this group drew the lucky camo straw.

His breath is like hot, rotting fish. So gross. I press my eyes shut and turn away. Reach for the rock a few feet away.

Maybe he saw what I was going to do. Maybe he deemed me unworthy. Because one second, he's pushing me to the ground, and the next, he's gone, nowhere in sight. Who knew they could move that fast.

Yet it doesn't make sense. He clearly had the advantage.

Sitting up, for the second time, I note everyone heavily enthralled in the fight. There are more mutant soldiers than there are resistance fighters in our weary gang.

Ry moves like lightning, defending and destroying. Yuromo creates her own wave of damage—I guess we're lucky to have her with us—and Jaden takes on several at once. I'm blessed to have such an amazing team.

For a three count, I watch Ry. Fully aware that he's in a weakened state and could be in danger, my heart squeezes to a shudder-stop. I shouldn't worry. He's skilled and hasn't shown any decline in his abilities. I'm confident he still has the strength and knowhow to best his opponents. Although ugly and strong, the mutant soldiers have not shown themselves to be particularly bright.

With a sweeping gaze, I take in the scene and find no sign of my own attacker. I turn in a circle, my search pausing on a pile of dark rags.

I gasp, my hand flying to my lips. *It couldn't be?* My attacker is dead and lying in a heap some thirty feet away. Did I unknowingly somehow do that to him, like I pulled the other soldier into the earth?

A cyclone of emotions whirls in my gut and is swept clean by wildfire.

I release the guilt, if only temporarily. *I want to fight.*

My blood boils and turns into a liquid inferno. Heat rises off my skin, and the corners of my vision warp; my eyes sting. Ignoring the irritation, I focus on my target, grab the dead attacker's weapon and stride toward Jaden.

He defends himself with the agility of an expert, even in the eye of atrocious odds, four against one. A fifth attacker lies dead near their feet. With my help, he won't need to take on so many at once. We'll end this squabble all the quicker.

A flash of black zips between me and my target. Suddenly, Jaden is fighting two instead of four. Two of his attackers have disappeared, just as mine did.

I pause, my feet shifting right, then left. I'm fairly sure I didn't cause the sudden disappearing act. Something else is going on here. I want to help, moreover I want to understand what is happening. I assess Jaden and his two attackers.

He no longer needs me. I glance to my right. *Maybe I should help Yuromo.* I turn toward the village scout and warrior and fall witness to the event happen again. A flash of black and suddenly, the number of Yuromo's attackers is reduced. My gaze darts to Ry. Swoosh, one less mutant to fight.

What the...?

I spin in a circle and find no hint of black, at least, not when it isn't busy stealing and killing our foes. The ground is littered with the remains of torn and broken soldiers, none of which have been put down by us. And despite the numbers that have been taken out of the fight, more and more keep showing up.

Where are they coming from?

My heart pounds against the crushing pressure of my chest. The number of attackers coming down on Jaden has once again increased, and the will to unstick my feet ignites. I take a step and stop dead to the growling howl of an attack cry at my back.

I spin, barely raising my weapon in time. Our swords clash, and his slides to the side. I clutch his arm and fall into a backward roll, pulling him with me. It's a move I've practiced a hundred times with Ry. The monster slams onto his back, and I flip around into a ready to pounce crouch. My weapon begs to be swung, until it remembers my previous fight outcome. The attacker sneers and rises in a clumsy lift. I holler, swing, and catch... nothing but air.

I can't let myself be derailed by a past already set. I need to be strong and smart and willing to be my absolute best. But before I can undo him, something unseen pushes him with the force of a nuclear explosion. The mutant flies sideways and slams into a nearby tree with a splat. No longer recognizable, he's a mess of flesh and blood and bone. I gag, look away.

My gaze falls upon the black blur, my sun-kissed prince—Dohlan.

He's a picture of ferocity— in a crouch, ready to fight. His hair, tipped with blood, drips down the sides of his face, and his eyes burn with intensity. I suck back a breath and press my hands into my chest, trying to calm my overwrought heart. Am I scared or excited or a little of both? I wish I knew, and I wish it were neither. He looks a bit like a blood-crazed killer.

"Ana." His lips barely move, yet there's a potency in his voice, and as if I'm in a trance, I'm drawn to him.

I drift closer and closer without actively choosing to move. He straightens, towers over me, and appears completely unmoved. When there is little more than a breath between us, my clear thought ability vanishes.

I'm doomed.

His mouth curves into a wicked grin, the next second, we are joined. His passion is fierce and completely divine. He tastes of eagerness and a strength I cannot match. My kiss wipes the blood from a cut on his lip, and something inside of me hums, like the after vibrations of a rung bell. His body brings me fever and ignites me like a match.

The fight still continues. It's all around us, I have no doubt. But it's nothing more than a blur in my peripheral vision, and I no longer care what's happening. My rage is subsiding. I'm melting into him. His lips are a welcome distraction along the journey I am trapped within.

And yet... something is building. It weighs heavily on my

heart. It's a need, a want, a something I forgot. Something green.

Our kiss ends too quickly. Dohlan pulls away, his eyes alight with a different emotion than previously. Could it be he no longer seeks the fight and has become enveloped in an all new plight?

I can't give in to speculation before his eyes hold my attention. His exquisite, impossibly-blue, god-like eyes. They fuddle my ability to concentrate.

I jolt, my heart taking flight.

I remember...

The man with the eyes. The man of my heart. Not Dohlan... Jaden. He's the one I want.

Dohlan grins, kisses me, and erases my thought. Again, I am forgetting, and I am completely his for the committing. How could I ever desire another when he embodies everything? He is my one, my only, my golden ring. And with our bond, I promise to shudder with every kiss and to never love another.

One more kiss. And still, I want another. Dohlan pulls my lower lip in an all-too-loose tooth grip. When he releases, I do as promised: I shudder.

Dohlan arches his back, looks up at the sky, and lets out a long whistle to the wind. "I find you hard to resist." His gaze drops upon me. "My dear Ana, I'm sorry I am not a stronger man. When you fight, your beauty is magnified, making you irresistible. Nevertheless, I should not have let you see me."

"Dohl..." He presses a finger to my lips, stopping me mid-word.

He traces my lips with his thumb, allowing his hand to travel off to the side and skim along my cheekbone. His eyes follow his slow-traveling hand as it glides along my neck to my collar bone. He lifts the pendant hanging there, studies its cloudy condition, and then releases it, returning to his previous exploration. His gaze continues sweeping down my body; then his hand slips around to my back and yanks me firmly against him.

"Sorry, Ana." His voice is soft and gentle.

Blham.

ELEVEN

"A na, come on, love."

Something softly taps on the side of my face. With a flip of my hand, I knock it away. Somebody muffles a laugh. A rapid blinking motion helps me gather my senses, and I open my eyes, find Jaden kneeling beside me, looking mildly concerned.

"What happened?" I sit up. Slightly woozy, my body sways. I sturdy myself with one hand, and, with the other, I rub my head, find a lump. *That really smarts.*

"You must have hit your head when we were knocked off Timbers." Jaden hands me a cloth to press upon the wound. "Looks like a good one, too."

An awkward tickle scratches in my belly, and I sense that it is somehow coming from Jaden. Like he's holding something back. I quirk my head.

"You missed one heck of a fight, but we somehow managed. I'm just glad you're alright." He offers an assisting hand. I take it and slowly stand.

That's not how I remember things. Didn't they see me trying to fight? Or see me with Dohlan? I scan the site, take stock of all the dead. Could the guys have done all this carnage on their own? Did I dream the incident with Dohlan? I question myself and my memory. I find it hard to believe that none of them would have seen me with Dohlan had he really been here.

But... putting my fingers to my lips, it's like I can still *feel* him.

Something glints on my finger. I drop my left hand to the side and glance sideways at it. There is a delicate golden band on my ring finger where, previously, there was none. A slight gasp escapes my lips. Did Dohlan slip this on my finger when I was under his trance? I remember something about gold and bond. *Holy Gaea and God!* What does this mean?

"How do you feel?"

I shift to face Ry. He steps over a body to get to me. He looks exhilarated from the battle, despite the fine sheen of sweat across his forehead and the discoloration on his shirt where Dreya dealt him a death sentence.

I casually slip my left hand behind me. I don't want to be bombarded with a thousand and ten questions from him. I'll figure this out. I'll deal with Dohlan... and the ring... soon enough.

"Okay, I guess. I don't remember getting knocked unconscious from the fall." I begin brushing the dirt and grime from my outfit. I shake out my physical knots, too.

"I understand, I guess. Hasn't happened to me, so I can't really relate," Ry boasts.

Showoff. It's been a while, twenty-four hours maybe, since he's made me feel like punching him in the face. I guess the timing was overdue. "Think you can ride? I'd like to get out of here."

Me too.

He hands me a canteen, and I take a conservative sip. I have zero idea how long it might be until we find our next water source, so no matter how thirsty I am, I want to be smart. I hand the canteen back. "I can ride."

"Then shall we?" Jaden offers me his hand. I accept, with my right. Together, we walk toward Timbers. I stop before we reach the horse.

"You know." I turn and look at him. "I think I'm really okay to ride on my own."

"Oh, alright." The flash in his eyes, the inflection in his voice, it's clear I've disappointed him. I didn't mean to. With my thumb, I twist the new ring on my fingers. Dohlan made things a whole lot more complicated. "I am glad you are feeling better. Will you need help mounting?"

I shove my hands into my pockets. "No thanks. Velsa will be accommodating." I turn and walk toward my horse, stop, look back. "Thank you, Jaden." I start to walk again and then glance back a second time. "It's not because I don't like riding with you. You know that, right?"

I'm rewarded with a grin. "Never worry, Ana." He slips his pack over his shoulder and walks away, toward Timbers.

I don't move. I stand there, watching him. I sigh and let my eyes wander from the soft, dark waves of his hair, down the hinted-to-muscle curves across his back and arms, all the way down the length of his pant leg. I chew my lip and soak in the vision.

What have you done, Ana? What... have... you... done?

It's not Ry, but me, who deserves a punch in the face.

Jaden turns, catches me watching. Chagrined, I stifle a

laugh and turn away, hide the new color blossoming across my face. Maybe Ry was right, I'm acting like a schoolgirl with a crush. Is that so bad? There were things that bothered me about Jaden earlier, and I seem to be working my way through them.

Probably mucked everything up accepting this damn ring on my finger. My wedding ring finger! How could I have been so dumb?

I drop my head and shake, shake at my monumentally stupid mistake.

I chance another glance at Jaden. This time, he's not looking. Things have been different with him today, since we sorta talked last night. I sense a deeper connection, even with his uncomfortable ability. And when Dohlan's not around, I can't help but feel some greater pull toward my Tracer. A pull I can't explain nor fully understand. Plus, it doesn't hurt that he's so deliciously attractive.

Ugh. Jaden probably picked up on everything I was thinking and feeling.

I moan.

I'll have to work on controlling my thoughts and building a mental wall of some sort. I glance his direction for the third time, and I can't tell if he's aware of my emotions or not. He gives nothing away.

Damn, he's good.

In a matter of minutes, we're making tracks, hightailing it out of that moss-encrusted forest in record time. The road wanders up and around a low-lying mountain and eventually splits, continuing in two different directions. We take the east fork, which heads deeper into the mountain range and higher ground. Why go around the mountain when you can go over and save time, right? Time is currently our enemy.

It's only after we've covered considerable distance that Ry agrees to a short rest. We pick a small bluff for our stop and send the horses to graze in a nearby glen. Ry settles in to a spot a fair distance away from the rest of us. I've never seen him look so haggard and suspect that's why he's choosing to be anti-social.

Maybe he thinks he's protecting me by not letting me see him in his current state. The problem with that is, I already know what's going on with him. I'm not going to suddenly forget. And if he needs anything, I want to be there for him.

As we all settle down for a late lunch, no one seems to be in much of a talkative mood, and I don't mind that at all. I'd probably get myself in trouble if I struck up a conversation.

I rub my tailbone and shake my legs before grabbing my snack sack from one of the oversized carry-all packs Jaden has yanked free from his magic bag. I sit alone and quietly unpack my meal. Set out the various components of my meal like I'm preparing for a lovely picnic at the top of the world.

I have the shade of a charming tree at my back and the taste of a juicy red apple and day-*ish*-old bread to look forward to. I also have something neatly wrapped in flattened leaves and tied with twine. I call it my sustenance surprise. But the real surprise, and the best part of my entire meal, is the tiny foil-wrapped chocolate square.

I glance at Jaden. He sits perfectly still with eyes closed. His meal sits untouched at his side. I think he's meditating, but I'm not entirely sure.

I know he's the one that slipped the chocolate into my lunch. I wonder when he found the time or how he knew which sack I would grab? Maybe every lunch sack has a chocolate? I crane my neck to view Yuromo's meal. There isn't anything square or shiny. I decide I don't care. I also decide the chocolate will be the first thing I devour.

Like always, I carefully unwrap and neatly flatten the foil so that I can read whatever wisdom it has chosen for me today. I find myself oddly excited. It's a ritual from a life I no longer have. A life of normalcy. A life of chores and school and swim meets. All things I grumbled about and all things I want back.

I gaze at today's words of wisdom. Four short words. I frown.

This too shall pass.

That's all it says. Something more helpful or more specific would have been appreciated. I'm clueless on how to interpret these words. What will pass, exactly? My fear of Ry's emanate death? The disconnect from my disembodied sisters? My confusion over Jaden? Or the problem wrapped in gold around my finger and the dangerous guy who put it there?

I cough up irritation. I wasn't nearly as focused on all my issues until the silly little foil pulled them all in front of me with four little words. "Thanks," I say to the air around me.

I glance toward Yuromo. She is working on her technique with a Chinese Sai, and she has stopped to regard me. I avert my gaze. She probably thinks I'm crazy. Playing in the lake water and now talking to the sky. I crumple the foil and toss into the bottom of the sack, hoping for an out-of-sight-out-of-mind affect.

Someone takes a seat beside me, and I look up expecting to see Jaden. Yuromo half-smiles at me. *Great.*

"You are the prophesied one?" she says with a slit of a grin.

"So they tell me," I answer sarcastically. "Where did you get the sword?"

She raises the sword between us so that I can get a better look. "Your Jaden gave it to me. Isn't it beautiful? I've never had a weapon as nice as this one."

"It's pretty amazing." What's amazing is how much stuff Jaden seems to have packed in his magical backpack. I take a bite of my bread and gaze at the bluff beyond. *Nice of Jaden to make sure she has a weapon to protect herself but to overlook my weaponry needs.*

Yuromo makes a tiny whistle, and I look back at her. She's fixated upon my finger and the little gold ring. I drop my hand. "I did not know," she says. "Is it Sir Jaden?"

All ability to think abandons my brain, and I fall mute and dumbfounded, with a blurry-eyed stare.

"The courtship ring," she clarifies. "Is it Sir Jaden."

I glance at Jaden. He's still meditating. When I return my attention to Yuromo, I find my voice again. "This silly thing belongs to a friend." I lean forward, and she does the same. "Do me a favor. Let's not speak of this again. Keep it quiet, if you don't mind?"

She straightens, and her brow deeply creases. I fear I've made a mistake. She looks over her shoulder and gazes at Jaden. I picture the wheels in her mind processing this new knowledge and determining how to best use it to elevate her standing. I'm anxious she'll go straight to Ry or Jaden with the discovery.

To my relief, her features mellow, and she gives me one solid nod, then looks away and studies the world at our side.

Discreetly, I twist at the ring on my finger. It resists my efforts, not wanting to release my skin. I twist and I spin, and the ring finally agrees to let go. I slip it off my finger and slide it safely into my pocket.

Yuromo releases a deep breath and turns back to me. I suspect I've made her uncomfortable by asking her to keep a secret from the others. Yet, I'm thankful she has agreed to go along with me. "I noticed," she begins. "You were talking to something unseen a few minute ago. Were you talking to your sister?" She swings her hand through the air at her side.

Her chosen topic is a distraction from our previous discomfort, but I'm not sure I care to discuss the subject matter at all.

"What?" I look around at the empty air. "No. Who told you that?"

"Lord Ryland said..."

"Hold on." I stop her with a raised palm. "Lord Ryland. Seriously? You've got to stop that stuff right now, or you will only inflate his already too-large-for-this-world ego." I glance over at Ry. He's looking back, so I wave.

"Lord Ryland is good people," Yuromo continues, unaware that Ry is rising from his seat and now moving our direction. "When he told me about your sister and how you can still see and talk to her, I was most intrigued."

My lips involuntarily pull into a tight line. I try to imagine how the conversation got started. *Oh, yeah. My sister here, she's the mighty Balance Bringer, ya know. The other two sisters are dead, but don't you worry. She can still communicate with them like they are standing right next to her.*

Of course, I imagine Ry with a totally ridiculous accent. I huff a laugh and immediately feel guilty. Yuromo is still sharing her story when my mind wanders off, taking my attention along for the ride.

"My people have spoken of the trinity. Of you." She motions to me with a respectable hand gesture. "I never imagined the power would transverse the veil of life itself." Her smile is the size of a kid's grin on Christmas morning. "Can you see your sister now?"

"No. Not right now," I say to the scattered remains of my lunch. "I saw Crystia. She helped us find the horses. I used to see Kaia in my dreams all the time. Not so much, lately. She passed away a long time ago." I guess this mealtime was meant to be depressing. First the chocolate pulls all my issues into the light, and now the downer questions remind me of what I've lost.

"Both your sisters are confirmed dead, then?" she asks.

Why is she being so rude? Has she never lost anyone? Why would there ever be any question over the confirmation of my sisters' deaths? I watched Crystia die with my own eyes, and Kaia I experienced. She *is* dead, right?

Yuromo's one question was like the spoon's edge to the egg, causing multiple splintering cracks, each with their own individual reaction and level of pain. It's all making my blood temperature rise. How can she not see this? Is she completely unaware of the pain her question inflicts?

My nose wrinkles, and I take a calming breath. Something tells me I'll be taking a lot of calming breaths during this journey.

"May I join you?" Ry doesn't wait for me to respond. He takes a seat somewhat between Yuromo and me. "What's up?"

I tilt my head and unpack my sarcastic voice. "I don't know, Ry. Why don't you tell me why Yuromo is asking if my sisters, and by sisters, I primarily mean Kaia, have been confirmed dead?"

Ry's eyes widen, and he inhales deep. His shoulders straighten, muscles tense, and I'm betting he wished he'd never walked over. He glances at Yuromo, and then lands his gaze upon me. A tiny muscle in his temple twitches. "You told me you experienced her death, did you not?" He turns to Yuromo. "It has been confirmed." His voice is steady and calm, and yet it gives me pause.

"Yes, but... you found her, right? Gave her a proper cremation? Those are her ashes we're carrying with us, aren't they?" I gesture to the pouch of ashes tied to his belt.

"Yes Ana, feel safe in knowing we have the correct ashes." His fingers skim across the small leather pouch.

"Oh. Kay." I squint my eyes. "Then why do I feel like you're not telling me the whole truth?"

He shrugs, but the small muscle at his temple twitches again.

"You have to tell me," I say and lean forward. "I command it."

He flinches and turns to face me. I gloat in return. "Pulling rank, are you? I'm not fond of this, Ana." His face resembles a stone mask. I discovered, quite by accident, that I can pull rank on Ry and force him to do my bidding. Out of respect for him and our relationship, I haven't taken advantage of that fact until now, but I need to know Kaia's situation. And I sense he's holding something back.

"Tell me," I say.

His nostrils flare, and his expression suggests he wants to hit me. "There was never an official cremation. There was no body to burn."

"Wuh?" My hands fly out to my side. "But then how can there be ashes?" My shoulders droop, and my face muscles slacken.

"Kaia was smart, and she planned well," Ry says. "She used to keep a small treasure chest on her dresser. When Kaia was brought home in need of healing, Nerine went to place Kaia's crystal inside the chest and discovered Kaia had been keeping all her nail and hair clippings. She even had small vials of blood and small bags filled with flakes of skin."

Gross.

"It was as if she started collecting everything her body shed from the moment she learned to walk." Ry scratches his collar bone. "You see, Kaia always knew who and what she was, the first member of the Bringer Triune, and she apparently prepared a failsafe plan. I don't know what gave her the idea or the incentive, but it turned out to be a destiny saver."

"Hair and nails?" My nose crinkles. "Blood and skin?"

"Combined with all the baby teeth Nerine saved. It should be enough DNA to work, in theory, anyway." His lips curve into a questioning sideways grin.

I glance at Yuromo. She's getting a firsthand taste of what it's like to be trapped inside an American soap opera, and she's been exceptionally quiet. Her lips pull into a tad-too-wide, upward curve.

Why would Kaia leave a box of that manner? It only makes sense to me if she was planning to run away, or if she was afraid for her life. Possibly both. I bite the inside of my lip. If she was keeping me in the dark to protect me, then I think her plan backfired big time.

I study my hands and remember them covered in thick-as-blood punch the night Jeremy passed over, then covered in dream blood the night I thought I'd lost Ry. And, of course, I was covered in real blood the night Crystia died. I've experienced enough loss. I don't want to lose anyone else. My gaze bounces off Ry's wound-soiled shirt. He's cleaned himself and his shirt up fairly well, but it doesn't change the fact the mortal issue exists.

"We need to retrieve Kaia's body from the meadow," I say. "She deserves a proper burial or cremation or whatever it is you do here." That was at least seventeen years ago. Would anything even be left?

"The meadow?" A funny pinch in Ry's forehead forms. "She *was* retrieved from the meadow and brought home. She was a broken mess, and the poison in her system slowed her healing, but we saw that she received the best of care."

I look away, cover my mouth, and then snap back toward him. "But if you brought her home, how come you don't have her ashes?"

"Kaia wasn't dead, Ana." He reaches over and takes my hand. "I thought you knew that. I thought she told you everything." I shake my head. His gaze narrows, and he glances at the ground before looking back at me. "She was brought home alive. I believed she would have recovered, even if it took a year for her to do so. But she disappeared a month into her recovery."

I was certain she died in that memory of hers I experienced. I never even considered any other possible outcome.

"How? If she was so ill..." My hands fly to my lips. My sister is still out there somewhere. *I need to find her.*

"Your father, King Marduk, never stopped looking," Ry says, as if he could read my thoughts. "Your mother and I would have never left, never stopped the search either, if it weren't for your safety."

I mouth pops open. "Kaia could have been saved if it weren't for me?"

He squeezes my hand. "I didn't say that. You can never

think that way. Nerine and I have never regretted the choice we made." He rubs the back of my head. "I love you, Ana."

I pull my hand free from his grip. "I know, but... Kaia."

"Like I said, Marduk never stopped looking. Up until the day he went missing. The same fate might have befallen all of us had we stayed." He shifts closer, grabs both of my hands, and gazes into my eyes, sharing the depth of his sincerity.

I glance at Yuromo. Her eyes are wide, and her mouth is pressed tight. She looks away.

My heart is as heavy as the tree at my back. The weight is crushing everything within me. I know I shouldn't blame myself, and yet... somehow, I carry the burden, the fault for everything bad that has happened to this world and the worlds beyond. It's all because of me, because of what I am.

I stand up. I want to get away. Run away from everything. Ry is immediately standing beside me, pulling me into a hug. He flinches, ever so slightly, when my body presses against his. Another reminder of a horrible situation that has happened because of me.

My arms lay limp at my side. I close my eyes and focus on the rhythmic thump of his heart, and discover that somehow, being wrapped in his brotherly hold takes the sting out of my self-blame. Having him with me is a blessing, one I never want to overlook. My shoulders relax, and, with a thankful sigh, I enclose him in my embrace.

"Are we good?" he asks.

"I guess so. We're good," I respond. And I mean it, mostly. I still need to find out what happened to Kaia.

He steps back, an appraising grin on his face. "Keep something in mind," he adds. "Wherever Kaia is, if she were still among the living, I doubt you would have had the dream connection you seemed to have had all these years."

I bite the inside of my lip. I can't argue with his logic. It's true then, she must be dead. But what happened to her? That question will remain a huge nagging beat in my head.

When we step away from our intense conversation, Yuromo is no longer at our side. At some point, undetected by me, she wandered over to Jaden, and the two of them are now setting up camp. Looks like they are having a fun time at it, too, chatting and laughing. My lower lip puckers.

Looks like the bluff is where we'll be sleeping tonight. The daylight is fading, and everyone is tired, aside from me, the one who slept for half the day's journey. The remaining hour is quiet, everyone finding their center after an all-too-crazy day. And when the group start crawling into the tents, I am content to curl up on my bedroll and hope my dreams wash away my stress.

The night is calm, aside from a few moans from my brother who sleeps beside me. I worry for his health, but my worry doesn't keep me awake. I sleep deep and unmoved by the outside world, until my heart slams and my eyes are jarred open by the sound of a scream.

TWELVE

I twist around, searching for the source of the scream, but
the tent's fabric walls block my view. Ryland no longer
sleeps beside me, but it wasn't his scream I heard. At least, I
don't think it was his holler. I jump up. My blanket tangles
around my feet. I kick and stomp and awkwardly push the
cover away. Dash from the tent.

Everything appears calm. As far as I can tell, nothing is
amiss. The other tent, along with the bedrolls, has already
been packed. A small campfire is burning, with a pot
anchored, hanging, and heating above the flames.

The horses meander to the side of our camp, and
everyone else is standing at the edge of the bluff.

Yuromo lets out an excited yelp, hands a set of binoculars
to Ry, and smiles a little too widely at Jaden. It was her
scream I heard. I realize that now. My momentary fear
relaxes into confusion... and irritation over her smile.

"What's going on?" I yawn and stretch my arms wide.

All three of them, Ry, Jaden, and Yuromo, turn and look my way.

"Come." Yuromo beckons me. "See for yourself." She points to the view beyond the bluff.

I step up beside them, try to pretend their awkward beams don't bother me, and gaze out at the view. From where we stand, above it all, the landscape is something rather magical to behold. There are patches of lavender and pink and soft blue. There are endless shades of green and yellow and splotches of orange out there, too.

I take note of the temple ruins and the quiet lake at its side. Then locate the rock wall that divides the transition of plant life on the countryside. I recall there was a village, one we had spotted and never passed through, and I somewhat suspect it was by design that we missed that particular venue.

It's the beauty I should absorb and marvel after, yet my gaze is drawn to the darkness, the brown and black spots, the places where the world is dying. It's as if the scene below is a picture someone took a match to and the pieces are burning in an organized fashion.

And why, I question myself, am I drawn to the death? Because, I answer my own query, it is my job to fix.

"What do you see?" Ry asks, knocking me free from my reflection and sending my thoughts of death scattering in the wind.

I study the landscape closer, suspecting there's something in particular the group expects me to ponder.

"I see a lot of beautiful country, and I see where we have been." I turn my gaze on him and get the sense I'm missing the mark. "What is it I'm looking for exactly?'

"Look closer," Jaden says, with a hint of tease.

"Maybe try looking near the temple." Ry hands me the binoculars for a closer inspection.

My lip puckers with frustration, and I snatch the binoculars from his hand. Something out of the ordinary or anything that jumps out at me is the goal for which I begin scanning the land. Taking Ry suggestion, I focus on the area around Gaea's Temple. At first, there is nothing worthy of noting, and then something registers as strange. Quickly, I scan over everything before returning to the place in question.

There's an anomaly by the lake. It's a shadow or the angle, an oddity that simply can't be. I drop the binoculars and turn to Jaden for an answer. "It doesn't make sense."

"Can't you piece together what happened?" His eyes are soft and filled with sympathy. They break my heart into a million and one pieces. It's true, I suspect what has happened, and that he understands, only I don't want to accept that reality. The part that is the Bringer burden I never asked to have.

My gaze drops to the ground, and I allow my eyes to fall shut. "Please, tell me what you're thinking."

A tingly warmth weaves around my skin. Jaden has taken my palm in his hand. He pulls me in the direction of the overlooking view, and with the tiniest of grins, he raises his other hand and directs my gaze. "You see the land around the temple, how most of it is dying, withering, or rotting away?"

Yes. That's mostly what I see. The dire cry for healing. Of course, I don't speak that thought out loud. "The land does appear rather unhealthy around that area."

His arm wraps around my waist, and together we gaze at the valley below. His directing point slips sideways from the land beyond the temple to the lake at the ruin's side. "See the area immediately off the lake's shore?"

The spot to which he points is shaped like the outline of a body, overlaid lush with green grass and blooming bright with yellow and white flowers.

I sigh and step away. "You're trying to tell me I had something to do with that? I cannot magically make things grow." I frown and remember my mom. She has a magical touch when it comes to plant life. She can make anything bloom, strong, healthy, and vibrant.

"Come on, Ana," Ry interjects.

"The evidence is clear," Jaden says, keeping me focused on him. He grabs my upper arms and turns me to face him. Disapproval courses through me, and I think it's coming from him. *That's weird.* "Stop fighting who you are," he says with a stern voice.

"But what you're proposing..." I fold into myself, crossing my arms across my body and clamping a hand over my chin and lower lip. "First water and now this? It's not normal."

Tears burn at the back of my eyes. *Stupid emotions.* I don't want to cry. And I don't want to be someone so important that everyone is depending upon me. I don't want to be the one with the magic. The one thing I have always wanted was to be normal and fit in. This is so far the opposite direction from normal.

I consider the change in the land below us, knowing deep down inside that Jaden and Ry are correct. I did that, I healed the landscape, and that's a truth that comes with a massive responsibility. A truth that scares me.

"Don't get so upset. We don't need to talk about this right now." Jaden squeezes my arm and walks away.

My chest squeezes. I don't understand why he up and

left the way he did. Did I do something wrong? I don't want him watching me while I fight with my mental state. And yet his departure makes me anxious, and I am confused by this feeling. I stare at his backside and watch him walk away from me. Emotions and words pop into my mind and dissolve just as quickly, like an exploding fireworks show in my head. I don't know what to make of the internal chaos, or of me, of anything.

"What's all the whining about?" Ry slaps me on the back thrusting me forward. Tears let loose, streaking down my cheeks, and dropping freely. I catch myself with my footing and wipe the evidence clean.

"What the heck, Ry? You made me stumble." I don't glance his direction, afraid my eyes are red and my cheeks wet.

"Ryland, please leave her alone," Jaden calls over his shoulder.

"Well, stop acting so childish about what you can do," Ry says, ignoring Jaden. "You *are* the Balance Bringer, and it's time you start accepting that fact. Only then will you truly become who you were meant to be. Only then can you truly bond with *that* guy." He points at Jaden, who is folding up my tent. "The guy that's meant to help you reach your potential and who happens to kinda like you."

He grabs me by the arm, drags me closer to the bluff's edge, and jabs his finger toward the lake. To the spot where I laid upon the ground after fighting the Tenebrousian. "*That* down there is a part of you and your ability to heal. It's a glaring sign that you are *becoming* that person."

Ry sighs and his shoulders slouch. "Stop fearing the change and embrace it with all that you are. When you do that, you will become greatness. If you teeter on the edge, you are just going to be ho-hum. No one wants that. And I know you don't want that from yourself. So, snap out of this state and *become* already!"

I have no words of rebuttal. He slapped me with a hard truth, and I am stunned silent. I want to argue, but I can't because he's right. One hundred percent right. Not that his being right makes it any easier for me to accept.

"You can't deny that, Ana." He motions to the patch of lush ground. "That is all you down there. You brought life back where it was dead or dying. That's what the Balance Bringer does."

Speechless, I study the odd phenomenon below. Ry is correct. This whole greater destiny thing that has been thrust upon me is overwhelming and will, no doubt, be brutal to accomplish, and on some level, I've been fighting the truth of my nature because it all seemed unlikely and so unreal. But he has no reason to lie to me.

I nod and admire my boots, then gasp. My eyes grow wide.

Two spots at my feet sprout with grass where minutes ago there was nothing more than dirt and rock. All I can think of are my tears. Did my teardrops create life where there had been none?

"I suspect, if we wait long enough, we'll witness flowers bloom from these tiny tufts." Jaden's voice is soft at my side. I spare him a sideways glance. He is gazing at our feet and the new growth of grass.

"Maybe," I say.

"I need you to see something." Ry grabs my hand and drags me over and up the climb behind us, to the top of the hill. From there, we can look over the whole southern territory. "See all that? Really look at it." He jabs his finger to a point far off in the distance. The land to which he points is dark and oddly speckled with white. And it can't possibly be true, but I swear there are islands floating in the sky. "That was my home, your mother's home. It should be your home. Look what it has become."

The word home resonates through me, and I remember Dohlan's words. *Don't go home.* He was so adamant I listen to his warning, but why? And which home does he mean? The one I left back in California or the one Ry points to now?

"That should make you feel something," Ry continues. "Break your heart, make you cry, anything. Soon enough, you will have the power to fix all of this if you want. I need you to *want* to fix that." He forcefully swings me to face him and tugs me tight. He has my full attention. "Do you hear me? I need you to care."

I hadn't realized how emotionally vested he was in the state of Hiddenkel. Although, I should have known, and I am slightly horrified at myself for the oversight. I'm also horrified at how his emotions are manifesting.

"I care. Honest, I do." I sweep my hand across the landscape. "I would have to be completely insensitive to look at that and not care." It's everything Kaia showed me and more. "Destroyed countryside, townships. It's all so horrible. And I could promise you right here and right now that I won't fight my truth any longer, but we both know that words are easily said."

"What do you need from me, Ana? What will it take for you to start believing in yourself?" His flattened palms frame his face and pierce the sky in clear frustration.

"It's not you, Ry, that needs to do anything. It's me." I reach out and wrap my hand around his. "It's all me. I need to make room for the acceptance in here and here," I say, pointing to my heart and head.

He inhales deep and glances up into the morning sky.

"Have faith as I have faith." Ry and I both spin around and eye Yuromo. She climbs the path to our position. "She is the foretold one. Maybe she needs time now, but when the time is right, she will rise to the task. That is what the Balance Bringer does."

I wish I had her faith in me. I frown.

"What are you doing here?" Ry snaps.

"Sir Jaden asked me to tell you that breakfast is ready." Her gaze shifts between us.

"Tell him we will be there shortly." Ry turns back to me, and Yuromo doesn't move to leave. She stands her ground and studies me.

"Why are you still here? Go now," Ry barks and waves her away.

Yuromo doesn't respond. Instead, she looks at me. "I did not always live at the lake's gate village. My mother sent me there when I was very young." Ry sighs. Yuromo ignores him and keeps talking. "I got in many troubles. My quick hands helped me obtain many desired items, and when my mother found out, she thought sending me away to the people at the lake gate was the best thing she could do for me... and she was right."

"Your mother sent you away?" Always having had my mother in my life, having her meddle to the point of frustration sometimes to keep me safe, I can't imagine a mother sending her kid away as Yuromo's did.

"She did, and she was right to." Yuromo spares Ry a quick glance. His shoulders are slumped, and his hands are anchored on his hips. He's focused on the ground. "I love my mother dearly. I love my old village and the people who live there. And I will likely never see them again. As you will likely never see your old home again. The people at the lake gate have come to mean as much to me if not more. They are my family, and I am forever loyal. Such feelings do not make me disloyal to those I left behind, though."

Ry's demeanor has changed. He is now watching Yuromo with what appears to be mild curiosity.

"I know that what I now do keeps the people of my old and new home safe. My actions secure hope for their futures as well as the present. Some of them may never know how different things could have been, but I know, and that is enough for me." She pauses and seems to consider something before continuing. "Your story is not so different.

My brow furrows. Ry's body straightens, making him seem taller, and his head tilts to better listen.

"Your mother took you from your home before you had a chance to know of its wonders. She gave you a new world that became your home. You love your new home, and it is now the home you left behind to come here, your place of origin. In a way, your other home is like my mother's village. You love that place, and you care what happens to it. Now you are here, and you must figure out how you fit into this world, just as I had to figure out how I fit into the tribe at the lake gate."

She closes the distance between us and places her hand upon my upper arm.

"I know you will find your place, and when you do, you will find every motivation and emotion you require to take the next step." She exudes warmth and knowing, and she turns to leave.

"Thank you," Ry says.

"Yes," I chime in. "Thank you."

She half bows and then descends the slope, heading back to our packed-up camp.

Ry and I watch her leave and then allow the silence between us to grow. I haven't the words to follow Yuromo's share. I turn back to the sight beyond our bluff. I study the white-speckled darkness that surrounds the castle. My family lived there, Ry and my parents, as well as Kaia. Had my mother never left, Crystia and I would have grown up there.

"We'll eventually have to go to the castle and figure out what is happening there," I say.

Ry steps up beside me and peers into the distance. He doesn't speak, but he shakes his head in agreement. "What she said..."

"It was helpful," I interject. "Have faith and trust in the divine purpose." I almost cringe saying those last two words, but that's what this whole Balance Bringer thing is, a creation of the divine.

Ry turns and pulls me into a warm embrace. "I'll be with you every step of the way. You know that, right?"

"I know. Best," I say, meaning that together we are the best of the best. It's something he used to say to me a long time ago. I pull back and glance to the small, faded spot of dried blood and puss still evident on his shirt.

Either Ry doesn't notice, or he chooses to ignore my glance at his wound. He grabs my hand and leads me toward the path back to camp. "Let's get this show on the road, shall we?"

After we make the descent back to the bluff, we put a little food in our bellies and once again journey onward. I wonder how far we need to travel and how many days will continue this way; ride and ride and sleep and ride. I love Velsa and her herd, but I don't think I was born for the cowboy lifestyle. My butt and thighs seriously hurt.

We ride most of the day, stopping briefly for lunch, and then get back on the road, making as many tracks as possible before dusk. The landscape keeps changing from trees and rocks and dirt, and I contemplate this gift of mine and how it's supposed to work.

What I've witnessed I can do is minuscule compared to what this world obviously needs. I don't want to let everyone down, but I don't understand how Ry expects me to take my small untrained talent and use it to restore the remaining dying landscape. Am I just supposed to lie down, start rolling my way around? That's a ridiculous notion, and we don't even know if that would work.

Or maybe, since my tears appeared to perform, I should cry everywhere I can. From there, things could grow and fill in the land. I shake my head. *Don't think that would work, either.* There has to be a better way I don't yet see.

We move at a quick pace along the mountain terrain, proceeding down the far side in hopes of reaching a village before night fall. There've been no signs of life since our encounter with the mutated soldiers, and, although everywhere I look the terrain appears rather forsaken, I remind myself how far from everything Yuromo's lake gate village is situated.

I shouldn't be surprised if we happen upon civilization. After all, there are lots of places in California where a town exists far from the next sign of development. The difference being, those locations have paved roads, motorized cars, and electricity.

I really miss those things right now.

As it turns out, there is no village. Only mountain, a wall of rock at our side, and a valley beyond. The valley is a quilt of lush green and sickly yellow, littered with tuffs of jagged rocks hosting leafy lollipop-looking trees.

I'm descending into the land of Whoville.

The closer to the valley floor we descend, the more often we come upon folds and bends in the earth's surface. It's as if a giant blanket has been laid out and wrinkled up at the mountain's base and we are mere miniatures traveling across. We pass unusual highs and lows with stubby peaks and stretched arches, spotted with an endless supply of funny shrubs. They explode from the earth in a random chaotic pattern. I wouldn't be surprised to discover tiny gnomes tracking our progress.

It's a full day traveling the mountain and valley, and come night, we sleep in tents once more. The next morning is a repeat of the previous, without the drama over my possible earthen ability. We eat breakfast and continue the journey. I keep a watchful eye on Ry, fearing he will keel over at any moment. He consults with Yuromo off and on throughout our travel. He appears to be doing alright, and still, I don't trust what I see, so I stay alert.

The horses take us at a trot through meadows, over hills, traversing and splashing in low-lying streams hopping with fish, and across out-of-place bridges in the middle of nowhere. We pass remnants of life, broken statues and grand cities carved into the flat walls of a high-reaching gorge. Never once do I spot a face or a flicker of movement from something human.

That's how the days go, one after the next, blending together. All of us tired and all of us now familiar, like reluctant family. We are comfortable in our silence and equally as comfortable in our banter. Yuromo talks to Jaden and Ry with equal ease, be it serious or joking, and too often, she flirts. Something within me burns when I watch how comfortable she is being herself.

She makes me miss the girl I was before I made the journey to Hiddenkel. The girl who didn't know or understand the important destiny weighing upon her every choice. This bigger plan meant for me keeps me confused and concerned every trot of the way. And I am worried. Worry to the end of Hiddenkel and back, about my brother, Ry. He holds tight to the tough soldier act, but he's tired and anguished and wounded. He refuses to let any of that slow him. And so, we keep going, and I wonder for how long.

We stop at the edge of a wide stream spotted with lily pads the size of large steppingstones. Velsa and her herd have chosen this spot for a rest and a long drink. Yuromo wanders upstream, taking the opportunity to catch us a fish meal or two. I stand beside Velsa, rubbing her legs and back, hoping to reinvigorate her tired muscles. I glance from Velsa to the water, my gaze drawn to the pop of color provided by the lily pads.

"Do you think, with my newly developed water ability, I could walk across those lily pads?" I ask Jaden.

"Would you care to try?" he says, glancing my direction and grinning.

Heck no.

I laugh and flush. Look to the water and imagine the old mystic's face staring back at me, telling me to seize my strength. The last thing I want to do is attempt something and fail, or worse, succeed and come across like I'm showing off.

"If only you would believe in yourself as much as I

believe in you." He returns his attention to the rubbing of Clemens's legs, ending our banter.

The day grows long, and the silence of our little gang speaks volumes. We're all tired and hungry and anxious to get somewhere with civil life. And I'm bored. Bored of doing nothing beyond riding, eating, sleeping. I've now had more time than I would ever care for to contemplate my situation.

I want to know if I'll ever see my mom again. Or if she is forever trapped in the realm in which I was raised. With me and Ry gone, all she has is Oscar, Crystia's cat. Silly, stubborn cat. I even miss him. Wish I could cuddle that orange fluff ball right now. But I can't. Everything about my life as I knew it is now behind me.

My stomach gurgles and roars, as if contributing a thought regarding my mom or Oscar. I press the heel of my hand to my gut and tell it to shush. At that, Ry agrees it's time for lunch.

The food is satisfying, but we are nearing the end of our rations. I guess food can't last forever, not even in Jaden's magical bag. I peer down into his sack, searching for a second apple-pear, the one I had with my meal has left me wanting more. As I ogle the bag, I imagine a refrigerator hidden somewhere amongst the shadows within. I spy no apple-pears, nor anything else delicious.

What I do find is the glossy stone sliver. I'm going to ask Jaden about what I saw reflected in its surface when I studied it in my room, way back when. I close the bag, set it aside, and lay down against the quiet grass.

I'll ask him soon, but first I want to enjoy a quiet moment before we start moving once more.

Only, it's not so quiet when I rest my head against the grass. Something near me is downright noisy. I turn my head from side to side and try to determine where the sound is coming from. It's everywhere, all around us. Only, there is nothing to which I can attribute the noise.

I sit up and search out Ry. He's studying the maps Yuromo's people gave us before we left the village. The paper crinkles beneath his touch, yet I'm certain that isn't the sound in question. Turning from Ry and his maps, I put my hands to the cool, soft ground, savor the grass between my fingers and the pulsing beat of something else. Something more.

"Am I boring you?" Ry asks. His tone is a familiar one. One I've heard plenty of times over our many workout sessions together. On occasion, I've been known to drift off. During a workout, I might suddenly find myself thinking about Jeremy and the car accident, and later, daydreaming about Jaden. Ry always pulled me back to the here and now with some form of the "am I boring you" line. The thing is, Ry never bores me. I must have a strong flee-the-moment desire ingrained in me.

I snap around and focus on him. "I'm sorry, what?"

He rolls his eyes. "I was telling you we are past the halfway point."

My heart leaps with joy. "Great," I say. I can handle four or less more days. I think.

Chatter, chatter. Whoever they are, they continue to babble. My ear tunes in to the sound, and my head slowly begins to turn. Ry's still talking, but I only catch half his words. He's saying something about not expecting me to need maps when I something or other.

"Hiddenkel to Ana"

I spin around again. "I'm sorry. It's just." I tilt my head and jab my finger over my shoulder, pointing. "Don't you hear that?" I lay my ear to the ground. *Yes, there it is.* The sound is coming from beneath the dirt.

"Hear what?" Ry's voice is cut short. I glance back. Jaden is standing behind Ry, a firm hand to Ry's shoulder communicating the universal message for silence.

In another time and place, I might have felt foolish, saying I can communicate with water and talk to animals, but not now. A reasoning, one both recognizable and alien to me, has taken hold of my senses.

Turning my attention back to the ground beneath me, I imagine my receptors reaching from me to the land in long, spindly threads of glowing green and gold. Slowly, I flatten myself to the soil. As I do, the conversations of an entire community become clear in my mind. So many conversations all happening at once, and I am hearing them all!

Wait! I focus harder.

I'm hearing more than one community—I'm hearing several. Ants like before, when we worked our way toward the dimensional door. I recognize their almost militant chant-type speak. There's also something smooth and slow, long and continuous. I'm thinking worms. And then there's something much more informal and rather mischievous. Gophers, maybe? They're warm and fuzzy, but somehow the term gopher doesn't fit. Moles. Yes, that might be it. I believe I may be hearing moles.

All the species are talking among themselves. None of them speak to me. I am merely an enthusiastic listener. An observer of my own, inexplicable talent. I understand everything I hear, salutations, directions, commands. I hear so much it becomes noisy in my head. Too many are talking at the same time. I squeeze my eyes tight, try to focus on shuffling the sounds around. I pull a few, or a couple, to the forefront and shove the rest into the background.

I flip onto my back and swim in the melody buzzing in the earth below me. Song drifts down to me from above. I open my eyes to the pale blue sky and catch sight of a flock of birds flying overhead. I sit up and follow their flight until they fade from view.

A barely-there smile slides onto my face. Never in my life have I ever felt so alive in the moment. So present with life and the world around me. I want to steep in the moment and remember the sensations, the emotions, forever. This, right here—my hands caress the ground at my sides—is what God and Gaea have wished for us and our lives. Peace and happiness.

I want to share this feeling with everyone I touch.

My eyes dart toward the thunderous march of ants upon the bark of the nearest tree. From there, my gaze skips through the branches, following a whisper, and lands upon a camouflaged lizard. He is watching me keenly. When our eyes meet, he begins doing pushups.

He reminds me of the many lizards back home... or, I mean... where I grew up.

I lean forward, prop my elbows against the grass, and rest my chin upon my hands. I watch him watch me. "If I ever asked, requested your aid, would you answer my call?" I ask the lizard.

He lifts and tilts his head and continues to do his pushups.

"You know; you hear. You are different. I feel you," The lizard responds.

Feel me? What does that mean?

The lizard's nervous pushups stop. He freezes. And I

think, his eyes widen. If a lizard's eyes can do such a thing. A second later, he scurries away.

I humph, skim the area. It's silly, but I liken the rush of emotions swirling within me to my once kid-like excitement over trips to the amusement park.

Behind me, I discover a new prattle coming from a yellow splotch of grass a few feet away. I move toward the sad land, ready to investigate. I probe for whatever life is busy at work. My ear detects crickets and spittle bugs going about their nature, not trying to be malicious or purposely destructive. It's the natural order of things, but is it in balance? Guess that's part of the reason I am here—to determine where the balance lies and put things back in order. But I'm not yet up to the task. I don't know enough.

To quote the lizard, I don't yet *feel* it

But I *do* feel the familiar prose coming from the winding nearby stream.

I dance toward the brook, glide my fingers across the surface, exploring the familiar caress of the water. Its touch is welcoming and promptly fills me with knowledge of the surrounding terrain. There are curves and straights, hills and meadows, all loaded before my mind's eye.

The visual is brilliant and intricate, and I can't figure out how to read it like a map to guide our way.

I lay my head on my arm and, using my finger, make circles on the glass surface. The water Ondines ripple the stream and take the form of a face upon the water, pressing their model of communication outward like an ice sculpture.

"*Gaea knows you are here. She wishes for you to remember yourself.*" The face sculpture closes its eyes and disappears, the water is once again smooth and drifting past like normal.

"Remember myself," I mumble. I'm not exactly sure what that means, but I'm guessing it has to do with my destiny—the whole Balance Bringer thing.

Madame Marrouske's face pops across the water with a splash. "Where is the girl?"

I startle. Screech. Fumble backward.

THIRTEEN

That freaky mystic lady is going to give me a nervous tick. I clutch my chest and catch my breath. "What girl?" I scream toward the water, with hands spread wide and slicing at the air. I pull myself onto my knees and lean closer, press my hands to either side of my head. "Do you mean Bree?"

"What is it?" Ry yells.

From upstream, Yuromo sprints toward me through the water.

But it's Jaden who provides what I need most, a wave of calm. In the breath of the moment, his fingers lightly brush across the top of my hands. It's tranquility in a touch. He drops down on one knee and studies the swirls in the water, likely seeking out whatever it was I saw. "We'll figure it out. Don't fret," he whispers.

His breath smells of apples and pears, and I'm hit with the strangest urge to kiss him. I turn, blink, and gaze into his eyes. Our hands are clasped together, resting calmly between us. As if we're trapped in a gravitational pull, our bodies drift ever closer. His lips call to mine, and every molecule in my body wants to answer.

"I don't see anything," Ry says, dropping to the grass behind me. "What scared you?"

I suck back a breath and wiggle my way out of Jaden's grasp. Rapidly blink away any impulsive notions and find the grass worthy of immediate speculation.

Thanks for that, Ry.

Jaden's gentle gaze remains upon me, causing all the hairs on my arms to stand on end. I sense that he, too, is disappointed in the interruption of a potential kiss. I smile the tiniest of smiles and allow the warmth of my suspected knowledge to spread through my chest.

I drop, butt to the ground, and watch Ry and Yuromo as they move along the edge of the stream, examining the water, searching out something they will likely never find. After taking a deep breath, I turn my gaze to meet Jaden's. "Why did you feel the need to calm me when I reacted just then?" I ask.

"I only touched your hand. I didn't try to calm you. You've made it clear that you prefer I not influence your mood."

My hands pull into my lap. If he didn't use his Tracer magic, then what does that mean for the way I felt when he touched me? I ponder him in silence, and he quietly returns my gaze.

Whap. Whap, whap.

I blink, rapidly, three times. I've heard that sound before.

Whap. Whap. Whap.

I can almost recall. Should recall. I heard the sound recently. My mind races through all the things I've heard since finishing my meal. My back straightens, and my eyes search the sky.

Whap... whap... whap.

The sound draws closer, louder, and I am reminded of a helicopter. I suspect such things don't exist here. Yet, in my mind's ear, the sound is defining, drowning out all others. The experience pulls all my attention away from Jaden toward a blur of color moving haphazardly through the air.

Whap... whap.

A dazzling, delicate butterfly comes to rest upon my knee. Slowly, her flapping wings still, and I can't seem to unglue my eyes from the sight. Blues, violets, yellows are the primary kaleidoscope of her wings, and as they start to flap once more in a quick and steady rhythm, the colors blend together in harmonious perfection.

Is this what balance is supposed to bring? Pooling all things together in such a fashion that the lines between them blur, and with a consistent motion, a smooth and even sweep is achieved?

The beat of the butterfly's wings melds with the beat of my heart, and the rest of the world slowly slides away. Soon, only the butterfly and I exist.

Images flash with lightning speed across my inner eye.

Image, image, blur, image.

An onrush of thoughts, visuals, and emotions brought on by my connection with the butterfly. I'm fixated on it, the beat of my heart and the pulsating of its wings moving in time, the music filling my ears, drowning out everything else.

Image, image, blur.

I am being inundated with information that crowds my brain. The blur becomes black... and I lose time.

Did I black out?

I am sitting with my arms wrapped around my legs, and I am ogling Jaden, who now sits across from me. I can't recall pulling myself into this position or him settling in comfortably across from me.

Deciding not to mention my missing time, I run my fingers through my hair and take stock of everything around me. I glance at my knee, then the sky. The butterfly is gone.

"It was the butterfly," Jaden whispers.

"I think I got that part, Mr. Obvious." I'm not trying to be rude. I simply fail to handle my surprise well. And it's undeniably clear, at least to me, that whatever happened was because of the butterfly.

"You misunderstand me." He stands and pulls me up with him. "The butterfly is the symbol for the soul, the symbol of transition and resurrection. All the things you are now going through. I believe she came to you with a purpose. You understood her message, didn't you?" He brushes the grass from his slacks and glances at me, awaiting my response.

"I don't know. That was a lot to take in all at once."

I try to recall all the images in the order they passed through my mind. Like a jigsaw puzzle, I attempt to piece them together until a message is clear. There are so many snapshots and short clips. Flowers blooming, people hugging, the seasons changing. What does it all mean?

I heave and close my eyes. I suspect I'll be working on the butterfly's message for some time. Possibly, too long of a time.

But if my gut knows anything, it's telling me that I need

to accept the changes I am going through. More than that, I need to embrace the changes with every ounce of my soul; like the butterfly embraces her metamorphosis and becomes, so must I. *I am the butterfly.*

Jaden pushes a lock of hair behind my ear. "And what a beautiful butterfly you are becoming," he tacks at the end of my thought.

I laugh. I never thought I would hear someone compare me to a butterfly. A moth, maybe. But never anything so beautiful and graceful. I avert my eyes.

"Are you two going to fill the rest of us in on what the heck is going on? Yuromo and I have been waiting, rather patiently, I might add," Ry asks from behind me.

I'd almost forgotten about them. They'd been so quiet, and I'd been so pulled into the sensation and message from the butterfly.

"Nothing, really," Jaden answers for the both of us. "Ana has simply been listening to the wildlife around us. All the things we cannot hear. It's been interesting, and I think..." He glances at me. "...she's a tad over excited and over-whelmed."

Ry's stature relaxes, and a half-crooked grin cracks the side of his face. "Okay then. Good, good." He says, nodding his head. "I'm happy to see you coming along." His eyes sparkle at me. "But unless we have more business here, we should get a move on. We still have a lot of ground to cover." Ry turns and makes way for the horses.

Sweet Velsa and the rest of the herd never complain, and yet I fear we are walking them to exhaustion. I'm a mere rider, and I feel the lag, the lack of protein, ripe in my bones. But we are warriors on a time-sensitive mission. A mission I question every time I look at Ry and the stain upon his shirt.

At least, everyone but me gets to have fish for dinner tonight. After experiencing the fish's distress, I couldn't bring myself to even be near the group while they ate. Both Ry and Jaden offered to throw the fish back into the water, only I couldn't allow them to make such a sacrifice. They need the protein, more than I do. Ry, especially. Since the gods made me this way, I can only hope they have a solution to my bodily requirements. Time will tell.

We wearily push forward until the sun drops behind the mountains and the sky slips into stunning shades of lavender and pink. The horses pause. We stand, perched at the top of a small crescent hill. Our vantage point overlooks a small lake, reflecting the watercolor sunset. The picture is framed by the dabble of dark shadows amongst the scattering of lake-lining trees.

"Looks as good a place as any to make camp for the night." Ry leans back and pats Belmiso for a job well done.

I'm more than happy to agree and quickly jump from Velsa's back in favor of scouting for a good location to eat and pitch a tent. "I'm so hungry I could eat a horse," I grumble.

Velsa neighs and her group shifts left, right, forward, and back in clear discomfort.

I balk, my stomach clenched, and I wish... oh how I wish... I could erase what I said. I glance up, eyes wide, to find all four horses are glowering at me. *Crap.* My hand flies to my lips.

"It was just an expression. I meant nothing by it. I don't think I could actually eat anything if I tried." My body flushes with heat. I duck my head and turn away.

Ry laughs at my goof, and I want to smack him, but I won't, not in his current condition. I fear a smack from me is all it would take to do him in. Jaden's laughing at me, too, although, he's not as obvious as Ry. When did Jaden earn the right to laugh openly at me? I wrinkle my nose and stomp off to find my own quiet ground for dinner time.

Yuromo cooks the fish, and they all eat greedily. I manage to find a box of crackers shoved deep in Jaden's backpack, and I make do munching on those.

By the time my head hits the mat for the night, I am done, in all senses of the word. Even in Ry's weakened condition, he appears to be handling the journey better than me. I guess, as far as the Immortal Warrior race goes, I didn't get as much of that stamina goodness from the gene pool.

Although, I do recall Jaden once saying something about me requiring more rest than usual while I'm going through *the change*, so maybe I can blame my exhaustion on becoming the Balance Bringer and can look forward to needing less sleep in the future... hopefully.

I'd like that.

The stars are bright tonight, and we have forgone the tents in favor of sleeping directly beneath the big sky. I have Jaden on my left and Ry on my right. I am securely flanked by my warrior men. I hope neither of them snores this night. I close my eyes and fall asleep.

Until... he curls up behind me, matching his form to mine. I'm not even sure who *he* is. I'm barely awake, and my words won't work. His strong sturdy arms wrap over me, ensnare me, as his lips caress the spot behind my ear.

Goosebumps and shivers, spices and intoxication.

In my sleep-addled state, I am dizzy, possibly delirious. My feeble brain can't hold a single thought beyond his name. A name I don't want to acknowledge. Not now, not ever again. Especially after what happened the last time I gave in to him.

"Dohlan," I mumble, and attempt to push away, even as my body begins to tremble. I am determined to remain strong. To hold on to who I am and what I value dear. My choices, my boundaries. I will be in control. I will be stronger than a dreamy dream incubus.

It is Jaden I want. If I choose any guy for my future, it will be Jaden by my side.

But if I believe with my heart that it is Jaden for whom I most care, why do I feel like I am trying to convince myself? I am me, strong on my own. Strong without a man to call my own.

I shove at Dohlan again. "I'm with Jaden," I lie.

In one quick spin, he flips me around, and suddenly I am facing him, peering into his deep sapphire eyes. I want to groan in frustration and temptation. Instead, I bite my lip. Watch as he teases me with the tip of his tongue licking at his inviting mouth. I'm both fascinated and fixated.

The old familiar voice inside my head starts screaming for me to run, run far away. Only, I can't run. I can hardly move. I'm groggy with exhaustion and dizzy with intoxication. I toss my head back and close my eyes. Maybe, if I can't see him, I won't be so profoundly affected.

"You say it is he you are with, but tell me, Ana what purpose does he truly serve for you? Can he please you the way I can? Or protect you in a same or better fashion?" His rough skin brushes along my jaw, and I am turning into putty, losing my rigid resistance. "And do you yearn for him the way you clearly yearn for me?" His breath travels the curve of my neck, and for a moment we are trapped in time, motionless, two souls fighting an inevitable disaster. A gasp escapes my lips, and the moment is gone.

With his hand at the small of my back, he thrusts me

forward, erasing any inch of space between us. His warmth rolls over me like a dark and dangerous tsunami. It's as if I am being consumed, swallowed, absorbed by feelings and emotions I can't allow myself to trust.

My teeth grind, and my spirit wanes, pressing me back from the edge I'm inclined to leap from. My fingers curl in tight, fighting the desire to clutch his clothing and rip the fabric to shreds. There is something within my soul that I can hardly contain. Something of me that I scarcely recognize, and yet I know, I know with certainty that something is me.

When I am around Jaden, I feel an entirely different way. Although I don't completely understand what Jaden and I have, a pull exists, a connection between us that can't be denied no matter how hard I try to fight or ignore it. How can I feel that way for him and feel this way for Dohlan at the same time?

Oh my God and Gaea, is that who I am? A floozy?

I don't... think so. I'm merely confused. Deeply, sincerely confused.

My breath is sharp and unsettled. I need to get away before I fold. I gulp and Dohlan's spices ensnare me, throwing me into a trance with his strikingly chiseled face at the center. And there I might have stayed indefinitely, except for the sparkle of victory set in his eyes and the low arrogance in his laugh. His pretentiousness breaks the spell, and I am free, if only temporarily.

My freedom doesn't last nearly long enough. White hot sears pinch my arm, and I'm spinning, spinning, spinning. His lips are upon mine. His breath melts me, folds me into his palm, and I am content to stay. His kisses cover every inch of uncovered skin. My breath quickens, and I am dying, ecstatic for the end looming near.

In a single beat, one flutter of the heart, Dohlan is gone, taking with him all sense of warmth. He now paces at my side, snarling at what I cannot see. And me, I shiver, curl into myself.

What has happened? What has changed?

Dohlan's head whips around, his glare penetrating our perimeter. His snarl continues, burns low. And still, there is nothing, only a shimmer in the air at my side. I sit up and swoon. I am drunk. Drunk on Dohlan. Lightheaded and dizzy. A few days ago, I thought I was getting better, mastering his control over me. It appears such mastery isn't so.

Tentatively, I reach out, press my finger through the nearest shimmer. Colors shift and distort only to reform over my skin. It's oddly beautiful and completely unfamiliar, and yet, something about it seems all too recognizable. I tilt my head and wrinkle my nose.

"Dohlan?" I ask, hoping he will explain.

He stills, and his eyes fix upon mine. "This one is smart." He turns his gaze to the shimmer. It's growing, widening. "Not such a bad thing if he is to travel at your side." He drops to his knees, straddling my legs. "But you can tell your Tracer that this is not over. He may have won this round, but I am blood-bound to you. Anywhere you go, I can and will find you." He takes me by the hips and pulls me closer. "We are. Understand?"

I gulp, swallow my forthcoming words, and stupidly gawk. I haven't much a clue as to what he's talking about, and I'm set on edge by the words blood-bound.

His gaze swivels to my finger, and he snatches my hand

in his own. "Tsk. Tsk," he says, with a cluck of the tongue. He holds my hand in the air between us. "Where has your ring gone?"

I gasp, fall back on my elbows. He follows, lurching forward, his finger digging deep with in my pocket. Before I can blink reason back into my head, he has extracted the ring and slipped it into place. "This is where the gold belongs," he says, daring me with a steady outstare to protest.

Another shimmer appears a few feet away, diagonally across from the other.

Dohlan's brow arches, and he admires the reflecting light working its way in an arch around us. "What he is doing only makes things much more interesting." He returns his attention to me, rests his hand at my collar bone, feeling the rapid beat of my heart. A wicked smirk dances across his lips, and his fingers slip, linger down to the loop of my bra, hooking a firm hold. "Mine," he says firmly, without a hint of happiness.

Two more shimmer-shows take up residence around us. Dohlan bellows a hostel howl and vanishes.

I drop back on my bed roll and breathe deep. Clutch my hands to my chest, hiding the ring.

That was unhinged.

I'm glad he's gone. I need my sleep, and I need to be free of the complication he creates. I simply can't trust myself in his presence. And what of this ring? Must I always keep it on?

Deep, jagged breaths rock my body as I roll on my side and curl into a fetal position. The night will be a long and unsettling one.

And yet, somehow, I find sleep—wrapped in the comforting thought that we are more than halfway there.

With the first morning bird song, I sense Ry near, pulling me from my sleep with his nearness before he speaks.

"Hey, Ana. Time to wake up." Ry lightly nudges my shoulder.

With a moan of protest, I hug myself tighter and turn away. Ry nudges me again, and I object with a defiant groan before barely cracking my lids. The world is still dark. "The sun isn't even up yet," I croak.

"It's best we get an early start this day."

There's a tone in his voice I'm not completely familiar with, but I sense it's heavy with driven purpose and burden. I decide not to complain any further. Instead, I roll over and rub my head. Rake my fingers through my messy hair.

Jaden is sitting on his bed roll five or six feet away. He's ragged around the edges, with dark circles forming around his eyes and his watch fixed, set upon me. My lips heat with the memory of a kiss, only it wasn't Jaden I was kissing. I bite my lip and consider the possibility that Jaden was privy to my dream of Dohlan. It might explain the way he currently looks.

My thumb rubs, twirls the ring on my finger. *Was it a dream?*

My mouth pops open, and I contemplate the distance between Jaden and myself. Wasn't my bed roll set only inches from his last night? *Why is he so far away now?* With a start, I sit up, back straight, and glance around.

Jaden didn't move. I'm the one who has been moved.

I've been relocated beneath a thinly leafed tree. Things similar to dreamcatchers hang from the branches all around me. I reach out, touch one, and it sways gently to and fro. Something in the action reminds me of the shimmering light from last night's dream.

"Did you do all this?" I turn my gaze on Jaden.

"I did," he says and rests his chin upon his folded hands. "They are enigma loops."

"They're beautiful. But why?" I catch the edge of the one hanging the closest and turn it to better study the design.

"He shouldn't bother you in your dreams anymore. Not as long as we hang those around you each night."

My insides erupt in a rushing liquid inferno, embarrassment too tame of a word to describe my current state. The thought of Jaden being privy to my thoughts and feelings in last night's dream. I can't even... But Jaden said *he*, meaning Dohlan, so he clearly knows.

I seriously want to fall through the ground right now.

My lips pull into a tight line, and my mind makes the connection. Somehow the things hanging around me caused Dohlan to retreat.

"So that's what *he* meant," I mumble to myself and catch Jaden's interest. I decide to explain. After all, back at the temple ruins, I promised him I would be more open. I guess now is as good a time as any, considering he seems to have had a front row seat to the show. I glance Ry's direction. Guess that explains his desire to move out early. I sigh and slouch.

"I dreamt of Dohlan last night, and he knew what you were doing." I motion to the things hanging from the branches. "He said you won this round, but that he would always find me. How did you know, by the way, that he was visiting my dream?"

Jaden gaze wanders from mine, and he suddenly finds interest in the dirt between us. "You mumbled his name." His head snaps up, and he bores into my soul. "You sounded more familiar with him than I would have expected. How often do you dream of him?"

And now might be a good time to start lying, again.

I'm not crazy with this line of questioning. I want to have open communication but not like this. Not when it's so utterly personal.

Crap.

Crap. Crap. Crap.

I peer into Jaden's eyes, and as much as I want to lie, attempt to save the humiliation, I can't. Not to him. Not now.

"Dohlan would creep into my dreams, time and again. I have become... familiar with him. He's been visiting me for almost two years. Until last week, I thought he was just a dream. A product of an overly vivid imagination." I sigh. "Even now, I find the truth hard to believe." I glance around me, my head swiveling. "I find all this incredibly hard to believe."

For a moment, Jaden appears shocked by my disclosure. Then with a breath, he recovers and appears pleasant and calm. "A lot is being thrown at you all at once. I think you're handling it well, though. I can't imagine being in your position. Just know, I am here should you ever need someone to lean on." He stands, approaches, and extends his hand to me. Accepting his hand, I stand. He glances toward the horses. "We'd best get ready to set out." He returns to his bedroll and starts getting things ready to go.

I get the feeling he needs some time to process everything. His surprise at my confession baffles me. I thought he knew the things that rattled through my head. My dreams of Dohlan, I assumed, would be a part of all that. So, why didn't he know?

I chew on that thought as we abandon the camp and make our way into the early morning mist, set upon our journey once again. Yuromo rides at my side, and I find her stealing glances again and again.

"What?" I finally say, allowing my tense muscles to get the better of me.

"I am wondering about this dream warrior of yours," she says.

"What about him?" I try to sound bored, but that's hard to do when the topic of discussion is Dohlan.

"What does he want from you?"

"I wish I knew." I frown and recount the many ways he has played with my heart and mind.

"The way I see things, there are only three reasons why he would bother with you."

"Shoot," I say, and she looks at me oddly. "Go ahead, tell me," I clarify.

She nods. "One, he either wants to help you restore the worlds. Two, he wants to stop you. Or three, he really does have an emotional tie to you."

"I see a fourth option." I flash a humorless smile. Her shoulders straighten, and she regards me with a slight tilt of her head. "He thinks I will become strong enough to destroy Dreya and free him from the chains that keep him bound to her. Maybe he thinks I could someday cure him."

Her eyebrows pinch together. "Cure him of what?"

"Maybe," I say, lifting my finger in the delivery of my brilliant thought. "Just maybe, he hopes I will be able to cure him of his incubus nature and return him to whatever he was beforehand."

Yuromo shakes her head. "There is no such thing. I have never heard of a cure for any incubus or succubus. They are born, not made." She nudges Clemens and increases her pace, moving away from me. I watch her catch up to Jaden, and I am mildly relieved that she isn't wearing her small rawhide outfit today. Today, she is fully covered, complete with a wide brimmed hat to shield from the mid-day sun. If I didn't already know Yuromo was a girl, I wouldn't be able to tell on a glance or even a long gaze.

I sigh and contemplate the scenario I presented her. Until she brought up the subject, I had never considered the fourth option, but what if there is a measure of truth there? If I am meant to cure the world, could I cure Dohlan too?

It turns out to be another long day, only this time the day is flagged with a shadow of hope for civilized comforts. At lunch time, Yuromo mentions a village located somewhere along our plotted path. She's never actually been to the village, but a couple of her friends managed a trade with the inhabitants. "I think it's somewhere near there." She points to a dense basin, probably an hour's ride ahead. "In the thick cover of the trees."

It has been a long trip so far, and Yuromo's information isn't exactly solid, but I am not above inflated hopes. Not yet, anyway.

Another night rolls down upon us as we make our way into the tree cover of the basin. All too quickly, the sun is slipping over the ridge. The sky darkens to a muted shade of navy, and I'm beginning to believe that this is not the night for village comforts but rather another night for tents and tiny campgrounds. Several minutes into the forest and I've already spied several possible locations.

I am ready to settle until a soft cadence beats through the dusk air and our four-legged friends quicken their pace. They, too, are hungry and tired. Poor Velsa, she's ready to retire for the day. Of course, Ry is always cautious, and he motions for everyone to ease back. Our approach is slow and steady with a preparedness to bolt at the slightest sign of trouble.

The trees break away, and we come to a complete stop. Before us is a cliff with a breathtaking view of the valley below and a final glimpse of the setting sun. The lack of trees, in the clearing where we stand, is by design. Low-lying stumps of wooden giants remain, clearly cut down by man.

Fifty or more people, dressed in ceremonial attire, are gathered in the open space. They wear matching robes of soft, mossy green and light bark brown, like the surrounding trees. They stand in a circle around a raised, circular platform. The platform has been painted with incredible detail and is lit by a multitude of candles. As there are candles set upon the ground and the platform, candles also drop in hanging lanterns from the surrounding trees.

One person stands at the platform's center. Most likely the leader, based on his stature and attire. His robe is darker, deeper green and darker brown, and he wears a mask of a wooden tree man. I don't like to make assumptions, yet I'm fairly certain their ceremony is nature oriented.

The tempo stops.

All heads turn toward us.

The ceremonial leader steps forward and throws his arm wide with gusto. "You see, my friends. She has come, just as promised." He steps from the platforms and motions to me. "The prophesied Balance Bringer!"

FOURTEEN

Belmiso rears. Velsa, Timbers, and Clemens, all start angling to bolt. I cling to Velsa's mane and glance to my side, to Jaden. His eyes are murky. Only, they somehow appear different then their usual prolific murkiness.

Timbers lurches forward, and Jaden suddenly slouches.

My heart leaps. What if he falls from his horse? I reach for him, attempt to keep Velsa and myself close at his side. Her body slams against Timbers', pinning both Jaden's leg and mine.

It hurts. Hurts. Hurts. Hurts.

Despite the pain, the extreme closeness enables me to reach Jaden and get an arm around him, keep him from greater injury.

"Please don't go." The ceremonial leader rushes forward. He has removed his mask, revealing his face. Even without the mask, he wears a jeweled headband like a crown upon his head. His eyes are the most brilliant of topaz, and, although there are signs of age in his features, the years have not been unkind. He has more facial hair than I am used to, not that that's a crime.

The sight of him sparks something deep within me. It's as if I should know him from somewhere. The feeling gives me pause for the briefest of moments.

"What's wrong with him?" Ry asks about Jaden. "I don't like this. We should go."

Holding Jaden tight to my side, I throw Ry a look of concern over my shoulder. Jaden takes a sudden, deep gasp, and I snap my attention back to him. His eyes are dull but normal... mostly.

"You scare me when you do that. Could you stop, please?" I say. He's still slouched over Timbers, and his breathing is heavy.

"Sorry." His back straightens. "I sense these people can be trusted and that their leader is an old friend of yours." He whispers the words in my ear.

An old friend of mine? Completely impossible considering I have never been here before. Does Jaden mean a Balance Bringer from a past life? If so, that would be curious, considering the pang of familiarity I experienced when I first saw the guy. My gaze lingers on the man wearing the ceremonial outfit. It's a tad longer than it should be. There is something about him, I'm just not sure what it is yet.

My gaze sweeps from the man with the mask to Jaden. I need to be sure Jaden isn't being controlled in any way by the new, somewhat familiar stranger. This is a curious, unknown-to-me world, after all. And if I have magic, who's to say others don't have the power to manipulate?

So far, I'm finding far more things I dislike about my home world, Hiddenkel, than things I find okay.

One glance at Ry tells me everything I need to know.

Jaden may have spoken softly in my ear, but Ry somehow heard every word. His discomfort is visible in the snarl on his face and the cold glint in his eyes. I close my eyes and nod.

"My people have never had any trouble here," Yuromo says softly.

Ry's wishes are clear, the horses are tired and hungry, and something is off with Jaden. He is slouching and clasping his head between his hands. I lift his face and peer deep into his sometimes-murky eyes. His eyes are clear, and his face is cold.

"Your choice," he whispers.

I don't know what to do. I want Ry to make everything alright, but that isn't really his thing. Despite everyone's physical needs, he still wants to leave. If I only knew if his reaction is based on his tendency to be overly protective or on a gut sense.

Yuromo suggests these people are okay. Jaden says we can stay, only he is clearly in no condition to take the lead. There's no clear course of action. My chest squeezes and the surrounding air presses me toward the ground. The job of decision maker falls to me.

Both guys, if not everyone, are in serious need of rest. And Ry won't admit it, but he's in need of medical attention. And me, I have to admit I am somewhat curious about this past connection it appears some part of me wants to recall.

Sitting on Velsa, as regal as I know how, I turn to face the leader. "Sir, we are merely passing through. We seek one night's meager accommodations and any food and drink for our bellies or supplies for our journey that you may spare."

"Of course, my lady. Anything we can do to help you and your court. You are welcome to stay for as long as you see fit. Our food and beds are quite satisfying, and, if you don't mind me saying, from the looks of your weary crew, you might enjoy a visit to our bath house. The water is warm and the vapors, relaxing." He bows his head.

"Thank you. Very kind of you, sir." I give a petite bow in return.

"Call me, Garr. Sir is so formal, and you are far above that."

"Oh. Okay. Garr." None of the group behind me says a word, but I swear Ry's eyes are rolling. Velsa groans and moves marginally beneath me.

"Your horses need rest, water, food, and a good rubbing." Garr motions to his attending group. Will you allow us to care for them?"

"Oh." I sweep a searching gaze over Ry, Jaden, and Yuromo, looking for some sort of go ahead, but it is Velsa I feel in my gut. She is eager to enjoy the horse quarters and wants to accept the offer. "Thank you, Garr. That would be lovely."

I dismount, and as I do, so does the rest of my weary group. Stealing a few moments with the horses, I walk to each in turn, rub their nose, thank them for all that they have done, and remind them to enjoy this downtime. When I step away from the last horse, a few members of Garr's group lead the horses away. I watch closely, wringing my hands, making sure no harm comes to Velsa and her herd.

"This way," Garr says with a swing of his arm and a turn of his body. "Our home is not far."

Garr is what I would call average height, yet everyone in his group is taller, slenderer, and different in appearance. His skin tone is more similar to mine or Ry's, and he clearly has hair, whereas his people have very little hair and their skin is somewhat similar to the bark on the trees. As if they were actually born from the trees.

The group moves with no rush, which is probably best for us, given our current state. It's with a slow, steady trudge that we make our way deeper into the forest. I look toward the forest ceiling and imagine that I am the equivalent of an ant standing in a giant's world. We are moving amongst some of the largest eucalyptus trees I've ever seen. If they are eucalyptus trees. They're wider, for sure, and possess the colorful bark quality of the rainbow variety.

"Dinner will soon be served. Would you like to wash up and join us?" Garr glances over his shoulder. Members of his group walk on all sides of us, following a tight path toward a soft glow through the trees—their village, I presume.

"A bath sounds delightful," I say, more to myself than anyone in particular.

Garr laughs. "Glorious," he bellows. "Then a bath you shall have."

Ry tugs me to his side. "Be careful with this man," he whispers. "I don't trust him."

I'll be careful, but I'm still getting a warm bath.

I glance at Jaden for reassurance. After all, he was the one who looked ahead and said everything would be alright. Only, when I look at him, there is no reassurance to be found. Instead, he gives me a weak, hardly-there smile, like he's trying to appease, and possibly hide, a state of confusion.

I glance away, scratch my neck, and battle the onslaught of self-doubt.

The forest opens, with giant rainbow eucalyptuses guarding a central clearing. In the center stand five trees, clumped and grown together, expanding in such a way that they create a circle pattern of their own.

"We are here." Garr swings his arm in presentation. "Welcome to Ivey City, our home amongst the trees. May our home be your home for as long as you may need, any time you may need."

The trees are beautiful, a colorful landscape, somehow marvelously set aglow. But a village, no.

"Look to the trees!" Jaden says, pointing above my head.

Oh. My head tilts back, and my eyes grow wide. *Ivey City. As in climbing ivy. As in, these people are climbers. Intriguing. And dreamy.*

The five center trees, enormous as they are, work with a multitude of trees set in the wide outer ring. All of them connected by a web of drippy tentacles. An entire society appears to be supported amongst the many trunks and branches.

Large shimmery pods in a variety of shapes, sizes, and soft green tones are attached to the sides of almost every main branch. Everywhere I look, platforms and bridges and lots of twinkling light. There are rope ladders, traditional stairs, small and big windows, and puffs of white air signaling the existence of chimneys and open flame fires. There's so much illumination, the entire forest around us glows.

Dreamy, I think again.

Jaden wraps his arm and leans close. "You are not dreaming," he says, clearly reacting to my unspoken thought.

"That's not what I..."

He kisses my forehead.

...and I forget what I was going to say. My cheeks warm.

Jaden pauses and gazes at me, intensely.

"Now is not the time to get all lovestruck," Ry grumbles.

I turn on him. His teeth are clenched tight. He's positively irked, causing my mood to fall flat. I knew Ry didn't want to be here, but I hadn't anticipated the situation making him angry. He needs the rest, whether he will admit to the fact or not.

"Lord Ryland is tired. He did not mean to upset you, princess." Yuromo steps between us, nudges Ry with her shoulder. "Did you?" She glances up at him and her face softens. Ry huffs and does not answer.

"Shall we?" We all turn toward Garr, who watches us keenly. He motions for us to continue walking. He leads us around the base of the five center-clumped trees to an opening fashioned like a formal door set in the side of the tree. Beyond the door, stairs are carved into the interior of the tree.

At the entrance, Garr stops and turns to us. In the illumination provided by the abundance of lanterns, the leader of the Ivey City people is far more discernible. He's roughly Ry's height and definitely stockier than the rest of the Ivey City people. He's clearly different from them in many ways. I'm betting he's a different species.

Garr motions for us to move through the door and up the stairs. I hesitate. Bite my lip. Glance at Ry and Jaden. And finally, Yuromo. She shrugs.

Garr steps into the space and Jaden follows. They both disappear.

"Well?" Ry asks at my back.

I stare at the empty space. Jaden is gone. The decision is made. I, too, will follow. I ascend the steps.

The massive beast of a tree is hollowed, creating a tight and steep climb. The rise winds around and around as far as I can see. When we finally step out onto a platform, several stories above the ground, my legs are aching. A rope ladder is used to climb the remaining distance from the platform to the Ivey City above.

We eventually end up on a large balcony of sorts. There are pod structures on both sides, and I find myself reaching out to touch one. It has the texture of a leaf, except thicker, heartier, and somewhat fuzzy. Tiny iridescent hairs cover the surface.

Walkways connect all the trees in the outer ring of the complex. You could walk in one large circle if you kept walking the path, never varying and never stopping. Every tree appears to be a center support for a network of pod-type structures. From the ring of outer trees to the center five trees stretch scary long bridges. The kind of bridges you have to be crazy to cross. The structures built upon the five center trees differ from those in the outer ring.

It's like the structures in the center are first class and we're standing in coach, the outer ring.

Garr points out the gathering hall where we're welcome to meet for dinner. He allows us a peek inside, and I find the space warm, inviting, and full of yummy smells. The room is lit by candle filled chandeliers. I'd be afraid of burning down my house if I lived in a tree. But it's not my call to make for this place.

From the hall, we follow Garr across a suspension bridge or two to a bunch of platforms built around three closely grown tree trunks, each supporting a cluster of pods. Garr stops beside one of the pod clusters. We all stop, and it's like we're a tour group. In some way, I guess that's exactly what we are.

"You have heard of the Purusians, have you not?" he asks.

"Yes," Ry, Jaden, and Yuromo answer simultaneously.

I feel left out. *What's a Purusian?*

Jaden sweeps his eyes in my direction, his hand seeking mine. I help him, folding my palm to his own. The now familiar touch is reassuring under the awkward circumstances. If I had to explain our connection to another, I would tell them our touch was abnormal with an extra tingle and an occasional zap-ya. Something I'm not sure I could now live without.

Garr clears his throat and I startle. I feel like I've been caught doing something wrong. I drop Jaden's hand and peer to Garr at the front.

The tips of my lips curve toward the ground. *Why did I do that?* It's not like Garr is my teacher and I'm a scared schoolgirl.

"The people of Ivey City are Treeites, a branch of the Purusians," he says.

I giggle. Tree people. Branch. He made a funny. Garr shoots me a liquid grey glare, and my intestines turn to lead. I shut up. It's no longer funny.

"We will house Ms. Raine with the other young girls like herself."

A low growl vibrates in Ry's throat. I glance his way and fail to understand why he's worked up.

"Hold on," I interrupt Garr. "What did you just call me?"

"I called you by your name, of course," Garr responds, rather perplexed.

"That's not my name," I retort.

"Actually," Ry cuts in. It is your given name. It might not be the name you're used to hearing, but it's the family name and your name by birth."

"What? Oh..." I remember the book I found hidden at

the floral shop. It had my name on the cover as Anala Raine. Janssen was a lie created by my mother when she went into hiding. I knew this. How quickly I revert to what is comfortable.

"I guess," I say, trying to soften my voice. "I'm having trouble getting used to my proper name since I was raised with another. My apologies."

"None needed, my lady. But it does sound like an interesting story. Maybe you will share some of it with me over dinner?" His face alights with charm, knocking me back a step. Ry, Jaden, even Yuromo each reach toward me in support.

"What did you mean when you said the other girls like me?" I ask.

"The other virgins, of course." He turns and starts walking up the nearest set of stairs.

I balk. "What are you talking about." I turn left and then right, looking at my weary gang of travelers.

"It's common practice," Jaden says, only I'm not listening. All I hear is cartoony parental mush. Something inside of me is burning, steaming. What Garr is saying is downright creepy.

"How do you know if I'm a virgin, and what does it matter? I want to stay with my group." I look to Ry for support. He's glaring daggers at Garr.

Jaden grabs my hand, and I swivel toward him. "It will be okay," he says. "I'll stay with you."

Yuromo has pushed herself up against the rope railing, as if trying to disappear or escape the scene. I want to escape with her. *What have I gotten us into?*

Garr spins around. He looks amused. "My lady, are you trying to tell me, you are not?"

"Not what?" My jaw drops. "No..." I stammer. "I just want to be with my group."

Laugh lines etch deep into the creases around his eyes. "Trust me. This is for the best."

Ry shoots forward, grabs a handful of Garr's garment at the neckline, and shoves him back against the railing. "You do not get to decide what's best for Ana."

Garr's gaze meets Ry's glare. "It protects the purity of all ladies who have not yet committed themselves to a life mate. And believe me..." His focus narrows on me. "I would know if you weren't pure." A light flickers across his eyes. Ry jerks him, demanding his attention. "Of course, you are welcome to look over the facilities yourself, make sure you approve," Garr says, yanking Ry's hold free. Ry's leg shifts in an attempt to hold himself steady.

I blink and focus on Ry. It seems odd that such a small action would knock Ry off balance.

Garr raises a brow and then, without another word, continues to lead the way. "I understand your fire, Lord Ryland, but I assure you, we all have a vested interest in the princess's health and wellbeing."

Ry frowns and falls in step.

Every muscle in my body is tense, and I glance back and forth between Ry and Garr. *What did Garr mean when he said he'd know if I wasn't pure?* I glance at Jaden, figuring he picked up on my thoughts. He simply shrugs. Looks like we're both clueless on Garr's special ability regarding female purity. Ick. *Uncomfortable now.*

I shiver and study Ry with growing unease. Small beads of sweat dot his forehead. I'm concerned he doesn't have much fight left in him before he drops. He needs a good night's rest and medical attention.

"The princess is still young, and this one." Garr thrusts a half-committed gesture in Jaden's direction, "has interests in deflowering her."

My jaw drops. Cheeks flush. My mind is flooding with thoughts faster than I can comprehend. Jaden wants to what? Jaden wants to be with me? My heart hammers faster than I can count. I think... I think... I'm about to burst into flames. Never have I felt such a mad desire to steal away with him to somewhere private.

I venture a sideways glance at Jaden.

His palms are pressed to his forehead.

I glare at the back of Garr's head. How come he hasn't said anything about Yuromo? Is he trying to mess with my group, somehow come between us?

We walk through one quarter of the complex, Garr waving to people, people waving at us, before the man finally stops in a quiet, secluded walkway. He folds his hands together and waits for us to absorb the scene.

Everyone in this tree city appears to like Garr well enough, but I'm not so sure.

We stand near two trees that house multiple glowing pod units. Directly across from the pods, extending from the edge of the platform, a terrifying long bridge. The bridge sways in the breeze, and my stomach drops at the mere sight of the torturous walk. At the foot of the bridge stand two guards, one man and one woman. On the other side of the bridge, in the center five trees, the first-class pod city section.

"I thought this location would best suit your needs. You will all be housed close together. These units here." Garr motions to the pods attached to the trees at our side. "Are for the gentlemen." We all spin toward the finite fuzzy pods. Even from the outside they appear somewhat cozy. But one glance at Ry and any thoughts of coziness evaporate. His Adam's apple is jumping and jumping.

"Ms. Raine will be staying in one of the center units." My gaze snaps back to Garr and he directs our attention across the horrifying bridge. "Those units are the most protected in the entire complex."

I inhale deeply and dip my chin, consider the location. *I don't want to go over there!* But I also don't want Ry to start a fight and get hurt.

I am drowning in indecision. Should I put my foot down and tell Garr I won't go? Ry would definitely support that decision, only he is in no shape to fight on my behalf. Maybe I should go quietly and hope that everyone takes the opportunity to rest? There is no reason to start unnecessary battles, even if my stomach is already dropping, planting roots in the wood at my feet.

Ry takes a step in Garr's direction. "I don't think you've been listening, old m..."

I step in front of Ry and press my hands to his chest, halting both his forward motion and words. "It's fine," I say softly. The confusion on Ry's face is lemon juice on a cut wound. I turn to Garr. "Can I be honest with you?"

"Of course, my lady." Garr tilts his head in a bow.

"I don't want any part of this. I think it's wrong for you to press your ideas and practices upon anyone else, especially people not of your tribal family." He opens his mouth to speak, and I raise a finger stopping him. "That having been said, I have to admit to being rather curious about the fancy looking structures you have clustered in the center trees." I swing my arm out, motioning to the pods in the virgin housing. "And I am willing to take a look before making a final decision."

From behind me, Jaden's hand finds mine, weaving our fingers into a firm hold. Such a simple touch, and it gives me the strength I need to stand firm. I keep my gaze trained on Garr, and for a moment, there is nothing but silence between us.

"As you wish," Garr says. He glances over each member of my party. "As you can see, you all have a clear shot at each other's accommodations. Plus, the area is guarded against unwelcome entry." He swings his attention to Ry. "You, of course, will be granted access." He turns his gaze on Jaden. "As long as it's during the waking hours. No visiting the other young ladies," he says, brandishing his finger.

Ry quietly heaves, snapping Garr's attention back upon him like the release of a stretched rubber band. Ry's lips pull into a straight line, and he sighs in what appears to be resignation. "Understood," he says, stepping forward and bowing slightly. "Thank you for your hospitality." His tone is flat and sounds horribly insincere. And yet...

My eyes widen. I've never witnessed Ry act formal or regal before, but, as it turns out, I hardly know much about him. True to his story, he is royalty by relation. I imagine he's had plenty of training.

Ry turns away from Garr, moves so that his expression is visible to only me, and sneers. His anger and hatred for Garr and our situation seethes behind his eyes, though he hides it well. Only his lips communicate his frustration at our situation. I nod in acknowledgement.

Ry may not care for Garr, but playing nice might earn us some points. I only hope Ry can behave long enough to get the care he needs. Both Ry and Jaden need a solid night's rest and possibly some medical attention.

"Think nothing of it, Lord Ryland." Garr dismisses Ry's

thanks with the wave of his hand and proceeds to give the guys the lowdown on the housing units, the bath house, and expectations from the villagers... Treeites.

I consider the pods in which I'm meant to stay. Soft puffs of white smoke slowly rise from the place in the center, and I picture a cozy fireplace as the origin. Everything about the center complex looks simply amazing. If only it weren't for the knots in my belly and the creepy presence of Garr and his moronic rules, I'd probably be rushing over there right now, in search of the promised washroom and bath.

But for the separation from my family... and the bridge. It can't be safe using something so long or free swinging over a forever long fall.

When finished with the information overload, Garr turns, steps toward the long bridge, and pauses. He looks between Ry and Jaden. "Lord Ryland," he says. "Would you like to accompany us to Ms. Raines accommodations and see where she will be staying?"

"I would." Both Ry and Jaden stand a tad taller.

"Only Lord Ryland?" Yuromo clarifies. Garr nods.

Ry and Jaden exchange something unspoken in a look, and Jaden steps back. Yuromo steps up next to him. I eye her, shadowed in her oversized hat, standing beside him, and my heart drops into my belly.

"You should go. She can call me if she needs me," Jaden says to Ry.

Garr's brow rises at Jaden's choice of words.

"Good decision," Ry whispers and slaps Jaden on the arm. In return, Jaden seizes Ry's arm and hands over a small, thin bag. Again, unspoken words passing between them. Nervously, I glance at Garr and note the man watching everything we do with a keen eye.

Ry accepts the bag from Jaden, gives a curt nod, and moves to my side. As much as I desire some alone time with Jaden, I am thankful for the extra time I can keep a close eye on my brother. I grab his hand and squeeze, then glance back at Jaden and Yuromo.

"What about Yuromo?" I ask. I want to know why I am the only girl being forced to stay in accommodations away from the group.

"What about me?" She looks up and pulls her hat back, lifting the shadows from her features. It isn't her face I see. Well, it is, and it isn't. Her features are far more masculine than I know them to be. My mouth pops open, and I quickly clamp it shut. I have no idea how she manipulated her features, but that's a pretty handy ability. Right now, I wish I could do that.

Garr is watching us, all too closely, and I have now managed to make things awkward. I stammer to cover my error. "You didn't want a chance to accompany me across the bridge?" I ask.

"No." She shakes her head. "Lord Ryland is the appropriate choice."

I bite my lip and nod, note the way Yuromo gazes at Jaden. He looks back at her without any sign of surprise, making me curious if he was privy to her morphing ability. She wraps her arm around his as if meaning to hold him back when I walk away.

My chest squeezes tighter than a clam shell, and my heart bounces off the interior of my ribcage like a Mexican jumping bean. Together, Ry and I set out across the bridge, a few steps behind Garr, the Treeite leader. We take three steps, and I glance back at Jaden and Yuromo. They both wave, half-heartedly.

Believe in yourself, this is nothing Jaden mouths. I slip on a weak smile for show and turn back to Ry. I decide to act confident until it becomes my truth. I take one step after the other until... the bridge moves.

Suspension bridges are designed by sick and twisted individuals.

FIFTEEN

"**Y**ou're not scared, are you?" Ry teases.

"Never." I straighten my back and continue marching across the bridge, always keeping the end goal in sight. I don't stop until I'm standing on something that doesn't sway. I could cross that bridge again and again, only I don't want to. Of course, being trapped out here makes it inevitable. I suspect I'll be forced to cross the bridge several times.

The bridge leads us onto the middle tier of the center tree complex. A circular walkway runs around the outer limits of the five trees. We follow Garr, walking under a decorative archway and over a small bridge to reach the center, larger unit somehow suspended between the five trees.

I'm not so sure I want to stay here, even if it does keep Ry from fighting. After all, what's keeping this giant thing from falling to the ground? I could have a seriously rude awakening come morning, and *that* would surely ruin my day.

Garr throws open the grandly-carved front doors. "This is where you will be staying this night." He steps down into the main room, throws his arms out and spins around. It's clear he wants me to be impressed.

And I am, greatly impressed, I won't lie. But I'm also a little bewildered as to why they have such a grand place out here in what is virtually a virgin security lot. I can visualize it as guest lodging for high tootin' royalty from other territories, or even as Garr's place of residence, but the way things are, it just doesn't make much sense.

Unless they have a princess in their society, I self-edit. I guess this place might work for that situation. I feel somewhat guilty getting to sleep in such luxury while the rest of my group must stay in the commons.

The front room is spacious, lots of plush, comfy furniture neatly centered around a gorgeous rock fireplace. In place of artwork, colorful floral and plant life is decoratively attached to the walls, creating a lovely ambiance. Ry sweeps the room, checking behind and inside absolutely everything. When he doesn't find anything concerning, Garr directs us up the stairs.

At the top of the stairs is a large bedroom. My breath gets lodged in my throat. I miss my bed immensely. Sleeping on a bedroll doesn't even begin to compare. But here, sitting center in the sleeping chamber is a bed fit for a queen. It's amazing beyond comparison, and it makes my eyes want to water. In fact, it looks *so* inviting I want to curl up on it right now.

I glance over at Garr. Maybe not yet.

The bed fluffs with an army of pillows, several warm blankets, and an oversized comforter woven in teals and golds. An elaborate framing of swirling tree limbs curves up and over the mattress, from which soft sheers hang. They flow gently in a breeze skipping in through the open windows along the room's far side.

The bed commands center attention; it's almost easy to overlook the settee and lounge, mirrored dresser and stool, or even the thin cabinet in which to hang your belongings. Should you actually have belongings to hang. At this moment in time, that's not me.

"My lady." Garr taps my hand. I jolt, not expecting the touch. He motions for me to follow, and he opens a small door at the edge of the room.

I get my own bathroom.

Holy Gaea, I love you.

Sorry, Ry. I am so staying here.

It's a cramped space, long and narrow, but I'll happily make do. It has a bathtub, a wash basin with small mirror; it even has a toilet. I duck deeper into the long, skinny space and discover another prize, a full-length mirror.

My head swivels in a double take. *I look horrible.* I stick my tongue out at my reflection, then exaggerate a frown and try to push back my crazy unruly hairs. Blonde and golden hairs. So much gold. How come I didn't know about this? I lift my braid, examine the hair strands, and then release and let the braid fall. My braid looks more like a cat shredded rope than a neatly weaved braid. I sigh and let my shoulders sag.

"All you need is a good bath and a decent rest, and you'll be back to your former glory," Garr says. "But if it's any consolation, you still are a true beauty." Garr inclines his head before ducking out of the room.

Please Gaea, tell me that guy did not just flirt with me.

I step back into the bedroom to find Ry stabbing the bed with his wands. I throw my hands on my hips. "Seriously?"

I don't get an explanation for Ry's behavior. When he's satisfied nothing is going to jump out of my covers, we take the rest of the tour. We climb a second staircase to the roof. From there, we have a lovely view of the virgin prison ward. In the center of the roof sits a small table with matching chairs. A few potted plants are gathered to one side, beside a wooden box filled of gardening tools, some rope, and tubing curled and laid to the side. Absolutely nowhere for a person to hide.

"Does it pass inspection?" Garr asks and heads back down the stairs, not waiting on Ry's answer.

"The accommodations are above adequate," Ry replies, following Garr. "She'll be quite comfortable. And it appears, safe, as well." He turns and grabs my hand. "Walk us to the door, Ana," he says and pulls me tight to his side. "I don't like this." I nod. "Be on your guard." His voice is barely a whisper. "Ultra-careful, and if any, and I mean anything, is off, use that sense of yours with everything you've got to call Jaden and we'll come running. You got that?"

I shake my head. "I think Garr can hear everything we say, no matter how softly we speak," I whisper in return. Ry's lips twist to the side.

We make our way down to the first level, but not before pausing in the bed chamber long enough for Ry to dump the bag Jaden gave him on the bed.

"For tonight," he says.

I respond like I know what he's talking about, but in truth, I really don't. I assume I'll figure it out when I dig into the bag later. Later, as in not now. Right now, I have other ideas, and I don't want to be rude or rush Ry out, but I'm looking forward to some alone time with my private bath. Hot water, bubbles. These things should never be taken for granted.

And I want Ry to immediately seek medical help from their local physician. Ry and Jaden, actually.

A soft knock beats at the front door.

Standing tall and gangly like a willow tree is a motherly lady, holding folded fabric. Her long ears droop toward the ground, and her skin is as dark as the wood all around us. She nods her head in greeting.

"Tegan," Garr says with gusto. "I trust you have something for our lovely lady here."

"Yes, sire." Her voice is soft and musical.

"Is this everything, or do you need measurements?" he asks.

"If all is as you said, then this should be everything. But I have the measurer here so that I may confirm." Tegan pulls out a small roll, much like a measuring tape. A horrified expression flashes across Garr's face.

He coughs, pulls his composure together, and turns to me. "Would you mind if Tegan measures you for a better fit?"

I can sense the uncertainty on my face. I glance at Ry for the answer. Ry's glaring at Garr through squinted eyes.

"Tegan can measure her upstairs, under my supervision," Ry responds. "You need not wait."

"That's a fine arrangement, Lord Ryland. I'll wait here for you..." He motions to the seating area. "... and we can walk across the bridge together." Garr moves swiftly across the room and takes a seat in one of the chairs near the fireplace.

Ry's irritation is evident in the press of his brow. This

situation is my fault for accepting Garr's invitation and not bolting like my brother had wanted. Only, I was so concerned about Jaden, and Velsa wanted to rest. Now, Jaden appears mostly alright, and I pray the horses are, too. I chew on my lip and let Ry guide me back to the bedroom.

Ry plops down onto the settee. He winces. He doesn't think I notice, but I do. I'm watching him closely. Just like he's watching Tegan closely. His distrust of Garr extends to everyone in the man's circle. Tegan is quick and efficient, moving the tape around my waist, down my leg, along my arm, all the usual. She prattles, pleasantly, while she works, speaking about their village and people. When she's done, she hands me the bundle of clothing.

"No adjustments are necessary, the sire provided perfect measurements," Teagan says with a tiny bow.

My face flushes. *How could he possibly know?* Our situation is getting stranger by the moment. I wrinkle my nose, glance at Ry

His face is red, burning and bloating like he's ready to explode. With a lightning speed snatch, he grabs the clothing from my hold and shakes them, crushing them with his hands.

"Don't you think you're getting a little overly crazy with the protective thing?" I ask, more for Tegan's benefit than mine or Ry's. Garr's knowledge of me is unnerving, and I am, admittedly, a tad freaked out. But Tegan is standing in our company, and she could easily be a spy for the Tree people leader.

"One can never be too careful," Ry retorts. "Haven't I told you that enough times for it to sink in by now? You'd be wise to learn it well and start living by that code."

I step back across the room and lean close to Tegan. "My

brother is a bit under the weather. Could you ask the physician to pay him a visit?"

"Of course, My Lady. Consider it done," she says with a slight head bow.

Ry throws the clothing on the bed, marches over, and ushers Tegan out of the room and down the stairs. I follow at their heels.

It isn't nearly quick enough before we are hugging and waving our goodbyes for now. We're in a strange, and slightly creepy place, and I shouldn't desire alone time, and yet I crave... even yearn... to wash the dirt from my skin and hair. I didn't realize how much I desired a warm bath until the option was made available to me.

Water may be a part of me I have yet to fully understand. It's inviting and never cold to my skin... not anymore... but that doesn't mean my body doesn't ache for the special kind of relief a soak in warm, or even hot, water has to offer. And I do make the water extra warm, bordering on scolding.

With a yank and a pull, I pry Dohlan's ring off my finger and slide the gold jewelry into my pants pocket. I carefully set my crystals on the counter—Kaia's pendant at my neck and both mine and Crystia's wristbands. It feels like forever since I removed them. I haven't felt safe taking them off since we left Yuromo's village. But for this bath, I have decided I will.

Without ceremony, I drop my battered clothing to the floor and then slip into the tub and the divine hot water... although, it isn't so hot that it's beyond enjoyable. The water is perfect, with slippery caresses soothing my skin.

I lay my head back on the edge of the tub, close my eyes, and allow my mind to go blank. It's perfect, until my mind pops full of all the conveniences I miss. Little things like cars and electricity, daily showers, hot water, and flushing toilets. When I am clean and standing outside of the tub, dripping wet and wrapped in a towel, I add one more thing to my list—a hair dryer.

Between all the items stocked in the bathroom and the items that magically appear in Jaden's handy backpack, I have everything I need to look decent for dinner. My face has a touch of color, my lips are moisturized, and my hair, while not completely dry, is pulled back into a comfortable ponytail, with loose tendrils framing my face.

The outfit Tegan left for me is tight yet comfortable, consisting of a white shell, a gorgeously embroidered deep green coat-top type thing that cuts down my sides and drapes in the back, and greenish-black pants that my boots lace up over nicely.

Thank Gaia, the Ivey City people didn't try to fit this princess into a pretty dress for the evening. Not in this place. Not on this adventure. For now, I prefer pants.

Once my luxury, pampering time is over, and I am dressed and ready to go, all I can think about is Ry. Ry and his health. Jaden and his odd behavior. Yuromo and her gender shifting ability.

I brave the bridge and meet up with everyone on the platform outside their accommodations. Yuromo links her arm in mine and pulls me to the side.

"I am sorry I did not tell you earlier," she says. I glimpse over her. She still looks like a boy. "I am the only one in my tribe with the gift of physical deception. I don't know what it's called, nor the name of my blood tribe, but it is something I have always been able to do."

My lips pull into a tight line. She is like me in more ways

than she previously pointed out. She is a species unlike those around her, and she is unaware of her origins.

"My mother did not explain it to me before I was sent away, and I have not seen her since."

My heart squeezes. I can't imagine being separated from your family at such a young age. Old enough to understand what was happening yet young enough that you felt you had no choice but to do as you were told.

"I should have warned you. I am sorry I surprised you in that manner."

"It was shocking. I'll give you that." I sigh and glance over my shoulder to Ry and Jaden. The four of us are walking the long path toward the main gathering hall. "But honestly, I'm glad you aren't trapped in virgin lockdown with me. You can keep a close eye on our guys." She nods in understanding.

"What was that weirdness when we made our way here from the horses?" I ask.

"I do not understand. What is this word weirdness?" She tilts her head.

"When you nudged my brother earlier and stopped him from saying something stupid," I reply.

Her mouth opens and head nods at the memory. "There was an odd surge of energy. It was a low-level frequency, and it felt like an attack to the senses. You didn't feel it?"

I did not. I bite my lip and study the path ahead. My mind plunges into that new bit of information, but it's foreign territory, and I don't know what to make of it.

"And you didn't warn us?"

"I did not think..." she stammers.

"That's a problem, Yuromo. You need to think. Think

often. About anything and every little thing that could in any way affect us," I say and heave a heavy breath.

She clamps her jaw shut.

I shake my head. I don't want to be a mean ogre, I just want her to understand. I sigh and glance quickly over my shoulder. "What about the guys?" I tilt my head in their direction.

"The physician made a visit to our room. He cleaned Lord Ryland's wound, treated it with some sort of medication, and applied a new dressing. He appears slightly better, wouldn't you agree?" She looks over her shoulder at Ry, and I follow her gaze. Ry's brows arch at the sudden attention.

"Talking about me, are we?" he says.

We turn back forward, leaving his question unanswered.

"And Jaden," I ask.

"I do not know what the situation is, or was, with him. Maybe he had an early and then prolonged affect from the energy surge? I don't know. But he seems to be his normal self now," she says.

I frown. Her answer is very ambiguous, and I find that extremely unsatisfying. I want... need to know Jaden is alright, and if something is affecting him, I have to know what it is.

We round a corner, bringing the main meeting hall into view. We are all dressed in fine, new threads, our overly-ripe garments sent off to the cleaners. Ry and Jaden are dashing in clean dark pants, clean-cut, cotton-sleeved shirts, and vests of various shades of brown and green.

Because Yuromo is camouflaged as a guy, she is dressed in a similar fashion. Of course, Ry strapped all his weapons and gear over his new duds, yet it works well, and I have no doubt the others have weapons hidden away somewhere, too.

The last leg of our walk is covered in silence. The anticipation of food and the delicious aroma wafting in the air
increases our stride and lifts our spirits. Nervous butterflies
attack my stomach lining the closer we get. Before we reach
the door, joyous chatter and laughter bleeds through the
walls of our destination. Ry stops us outside the main entry.

"Be careful of what you say and what you do while we
are in their presence," he says. "And never let your guard
down. Got that?" He looks each one of us in the eye. "Be
vigilant."

"And the food?" I ask.

"Right." He jabs his finger at me as if I just reminded
him of something important. "Be wary of everything you eat
and drink at the table inside. Anything could be drugged."

That really wasn't the direction I was headed when I
asked about the food, but he does have a point.

My stomach growls, pressing the desire for food in my
belly and the question of if I'll be able to eat or not. Will I
sense the panic and anxiety of the life set upon the table for
the feast? Right now, I'm so hungry, I don't even know if I
care whether the food is drugged or not. I'd likely eat up
regardless. I just can't eat anything that is screaming for help
or glowering at me in disappointment and fear.

Ry throws open the doors to the gathering hall.

The noise level immediately drops yet does not diminish.
Garr stands from his place at the center of the hall. With a
large wave of the arm, he beckons us to his table.

Everyone looks our direction. So many eyes on us. My
skin flushes. I detest being the center of attention. But this is
my doing. It's because of me we are here. I take a deep
breath, square my shoulders, grab Jaden's hand, and lead
the way.

Once we are in motion, moving about the room, the people return to their previous conversations, paying us no mind, except to greet us as we pass by. We weave between tables, happily engaging people, and all the while, I keep my gaze trained on Garr. He manages to clear four spots at the table for us.

"My lady, Might I say, you look astonishing." Garr bows his head and motions to the seat directly beside him. I thank him, politely smile, take my seat, and flash Jaden a nervous grin. He sits beside me. Ry takes a seat on the other side of Garr. I'm guessing this falls under the keep-your-enemies-closer strategy. Yuromo slides in next to Jaden.

Hot meals are swiftly placed before us. Steaming baked potatoes and green beans. I inhale a little too deep at the sight. *Gaea and God, bless these people for his hot meal.* I glance up and spy Garr watching me, an all too toothy grin on his face. I look away and poke my potatoes. Nothing happens. I attack my food with the utensils.

"My lady, might you share your story with me this evening?" Garr shifts in his chair to best face me.

I pause mid-chew. My stomach is growling. I'd rather eat than make conversation, especially conversation with him. I swallow, and the food gets lodged in my throat. "I don't really have much of a story to tell. As you probably already know, my mother fled in order to keep me safe. I was raised under a different name, so I didn't even know who I was." I glance across the table and motion to my brother. "Not until a week or so ago when Ry saw fit to tell me the truth." I shrug and take another bite of my potato.

It isn't until I stab my next bite that the room hushes. I blink and tentatively look up. Everyone's eyes are on me. Even Yuromo appears to be riveted by my lusterless story.

The only people in the room who don't appear to be hanging on my every breath are Jaden and Ry. They already know the story, including all the finer details I left out.

"You only found out your true identity a week ago?" Garr sounds incredulous. "I can't imagine." He shakes his head. "And what of your abilities? What did you think when they started to manifest?"

I choke, start to cough. Jaden pats my back. When I clear my throat, my plate suddenly holds all my attention.

"She did rather well. Channeled her strength nicely. She's a natural," Ry says, coming to my rescue. "We didn't leave her completely unprepared. I have been working with her for years, getting her ready for the inevitable."

"Interesting." Garr swivels toward Ry. "How did you accomplish such a feat when she didn't know who or what she was?"

"Does it matter really?" Ry's tone is sharp, a conversation stopper. "The important thing is that she's here and ready for what comes next."

"Yes." Garr slowly nods. "I suppose you are right. Very good, then." With a high wave of his hand, people scurry, and a moment later, the room fills with robust music. The chatter and laughter from earlier resumes, and I am able to finish my dinner without the heavy inquiries.

When dinner is finished and our plates have been cleaned from the table, Garr stands. "A toast," he says loudly for the whole room to hear.

He turns and collects two glasses filled with a shimmery green liquid from a girl holding a tray full of glasses. She moves past Garr and bends down so that Ry can take one. Garr hands me one of the glasses he is holding. Someone with another tray comes over and offers glasses to Jaden and

Yuromo. When everyone in the room has had a chance to grab a glass, Garr continues.

"A toast to our lady." He raises his glass to me, and I am overcome with the inability to move. I cling to my glass and peek sideways at him. "The Balance Bringer has returned to her homeland!"

The sounds of clinking glasses and cheers fill the room. I glance at Ry. He has dipped his finger in the liquid and is now smelling it, tasting it. He shrugs. I turn to Jaden and Yuromo. They both shrug, then sip from their glasses.

"Drink up," Garr says and taps my shoulder. I turn back toward him. He taps his glass against mine and swallows a large gulp. Nods for me to do the same. My lips timidly lift at the edges, refusing to follow through in a smile, so I cover and take a sip. Liquid shimmers and cotton candy lap over my tongue and down my throat in pure refreshment and sugar intoxication.

It's a wave of relief when we finally leave the gathering hall. Everyone is tired and longing for a good night's sleep. Although, at the moment, I'm not particularly tired. Not just yet, anyway. My entire system is buzzy.

This time, Jaden walks with me back to my luxury pod palace. The physician gave Ry orders to go to bed immediately after dinner. Although, he will likely not follow such orders, Yuromo is making sure he is a good boy and takes care of himself. He made sure to give Jaden a bunch of orders before allowing us to go. I would have been content to stay with Ry and Yuromo, only the guards at the bridge kept watching us. It made me itchy.

Jaden and I walk silently along the path, taking in the crisp air and pleasant scents of nature. From passing windows, snooping faces of virgins peek at us. I am a spectacle here, just as I was at Yuromo's village. I avoid their ogles and stares and take Jaden's hand in mine. His touch is warm and tingly, and I'm overcome with gratitude for his presence.

Night has taken hold, and lights twinkle through the surrounding trees like fireflies illuminating the path. Moonlight cascades off of the leaves, and paper lanterns hang from branches above. Despite the damper of Garr's creepiness, the world around us is quite magical. Something I'd expect to find in a fantastical dream or storybook. Being here with Jaden is setting my entire body to buzz with wonder and delight.

At my front door, Jaden lifts my hand, rubs it gently with his thumb and fingers, and studies it closely. "Remember that night you told me about Dohlan and his visits?"

How could I ever forget? I finally had the courage to open up to Jaden, and it was amazingly freeing. And then I fell asleep. My shoulders slump, and I shake my head. "Yes," I say in a small voice.

"I think I understand now." His fingers glide over my hand, back and forth and back and forth. My breathing is deep. In and out and in and out. "You said he visited you multiple times, and yet I was only aware of a few. I had trouble figuring out why."

"Yes?" I step closer, peer up at him, and bite my lip. My heart, it pounds with such a force, I fear it is digging a dent in my chest.

"Sometimes, when you sleep." He gazes into my eyes and pauses. We both stand motionless, not breathing. And then he blinks. "Something changes in your rhythm."

I shake my head. I don't understand. I'm not an A student.

"Your brainwaves shift, and for a while, it's not you I receive, but other variations of you."

My head jerks. "Like, other lifetimes?"

"Exactly that," he says, his breath washing over me. "I think Dohlan visits you when that is happening."

"But..." I gaze at Jaden. My body is buzzing, my brain is buzzing, and in the buzzing, I can't comprehend, can't think the problem properly through. "Is he causing the issue or using it as a cover?"

'That's the question, isn't it?" Jaden stands so close, and yet there is enough space between us that it's painful. Something inside of me yearns to close the distance. His gaze shifts from my hand to the landing beyond the bridge. I follow his line of sight to note the guards watching us. The virgin police. No doubt, they will collect Jaden if he doesn't return soon.

"Goodnight, Ana," he whispers. The guards are forgotten, and I turn my full attention to him.

He kisses my forehead.

He starts to pull away, and my heart skips. I don't want him to go. I don't want to be alone. Not in this place where Garr is the man in charge. My chest flutters, stomach hardens, and I tighten my grip on his hand. My mind reels, looking for a reason to keep him with me. Any reason besides admitting the truth.

"Wait," I say. "Will you come gaze at the stars with me? If only for a short while. Please." I bite back my embarrassment.

"What about the rules?" His gaze narrows, intensifies, and I sense he is searching my feelings. Can he sense the buzzing? Every inch of me is alive and crawling with want.

Want for *something*. Only, I have no idea what that something is.

Garr's words jump into my head, *this one has interests in deflowering her.*

My chest rises and falls. As good at reading my emotions as Jaden has proven himself to be, I'm certain he is already privy to the truth of my intentions. He knows my fear and my desire, but there is something else, something deeper that even I don't want to admit to myself. An inner unsettlement between him and Dohlan. One I fear Dohlan could win simply due to my lack of control in his presence. I don't want Dohlan to win. Not under those circumstances.

The last time I was near him, my lack of resistance scared me. And now, with the ring...

The ring!

I left the ring in my pocket. The pocket of my dirty clothing. The clothing some Treeite likely already collected for cleaning.

My heart hammers like an overactive gavel.

I close my eyes and breathe deep. Maybe the ring doesn't matter. *Maybe it's a good thing the ring could end up lost. I need to break Dohlan's spell on me.* Maybe, tonight, I can do just that. With Jaden in the comfortable bed waiting upstairs.

I shake my head. No. *No, no, no.*

"Who cares about warden Garr and his virgin penitentiary." Needing a quick break from Jaden's now curious watchful eye, I chance a glance at the bridge guards. They're still watching us. "We're only here for one night. What's the man going to do about us looking at a few stars?" Conflict rages in his eyes, and I suspect it's due more to my thoughts than Garr's rules. I need to dispel Jaden's discomfort. "Spend time with me? Please?" I raise his hand up to my face and gently kiss his palm. A warmth swirls through my body.

I close my eyes. Savor the moment.

Jaden is sincerity and passion, understanding and exhilaration, whereas Dohlan is intensity and boundary annihilation. Standing here amongst the twinkling lights, it couldn't be clearer which possible relationship would be exceedingly sound and desirable.

When I open my eyes, I cannot breathe. The strife within Jaden's gaze is deeper, now clouded with the pains and pangs of desire. His grip upon my hand tightens, and if my bones were made of glass, they would surely shatter.

He breaks visual contact with a sigh and slow eye-close. "Not here, in your purity protection quarters," He responds to my unspoken thoughts and laughs—at me? No. At the absurdity of the situation? Most likely. "But I will gaze at the stars with you."

His face is loving and beguiling, and his eyes melt to a molten jade with gold swirls around the pupils.

A chortle bubbles up my throat, and I pull him through the front door. Before closing the door, I glance at the guards and wave. Their mouths are hanging open, and their eyes are wide. The visual tickles my funny bone. I close the door.

The night is crystal clear, and the stars are like diamonds in the sky, a perfect night for stargazing. I make a point of waving to the guards from the rooftop so that they can see we didn't stop in the sleeping chamber to destroy my purity.

We lay out a blanket and relax on our backs, peer up at the stars. "This is different from home. I know the constellations there, but not here," I say. "Can you show me some?"

He shifts closer and wraps his arm around the back of my neck, pulling me into his side. My view should be close to his from this position. He points to the night sky, to a cluster of stars. "Can you see that line of stars there?" he asks. "It is somewhat similar to your Orion's belt"

"Yes, I see it," I say.

"That is Gradnar. You may be familiar with him."

"Oh." I involuntarily let out the tiny sound. "I've heard Ry holler that name at the craziest of moments." I remember the way Ry screamed to Gradnar's honor as he mowed over the gate to the mine.

"He was a famous Immortal Warrior," Jaden says. "He fought many battles before taking on the darkness at the side of the first Balance Bringer." I suck back a breath and search the stars he points out in the old warrior's constellation. "There is his broad build, and above his head, he is swinging a mighty axe. "And over here." Jaden's arm swings to the left. "Is the elven queen. The largest, brightest star is her head. Above that, you can see the slight glow of the stars that make up her crown."

"Yes, I say. I see it." A sense of awe fills my chest. Different stars lighting the night was one thing, but to have constellations that come with history and lore, it makes everything so much more..."

"And here." He points almost directly above us. He turns and looks at me, and I return the gaze. "That collection of stars is known as the lovers," he says without turning away from me.

"The lovers?" I say, feeling stupefied and peering into his ever-green eyes.

"Deona and Jove," he says at almost a whisper.

"Jove?"

"The first..." He's staring at me, and I already know what he is going to say next. The lovers are the first Balance

Bringer and her Tracer. That constellation could be us. Deona and Jove, Ana and Jaden, we could be one and the same, simply different incarnations.

But there's something else happening here. Something in the way he looks at me leads me to believe his thoughts aren't completely filled with the desire two lovers should share. It's almost like he's searching for something in my eyes. Or deeper yet, in my soul.

His search doesn't scare me, it intrigues me. I turn onto my side to better face him. Gazing upon him is preferable to studying at stars. "I admit, what you can do sometimes surprises and frightens me." I stop myself. "Confuses would probably be a better word. But I don't want that confusion over your gift to keep us isolated and apart."

"It shouldn't." He leans his forehead against mind. I close my eyes. "You are capable of the same. You only need to remember."

There's that word again, remember. What is it I am trying to remember.

"When we were young, you knew."

Younger me and a younger Jaden. I remember things. Sitting on a rock with him. Learning to shoot the bow and arrow with him. Burying treasure with him. Him falling off a horse and breaking his arm. Sigh. Why did that change?

I breathe deep and focus on the rhythm of his heart. The melody of his heart is the most appealing sound I've ever had the pleasure of hearing. It's a soft and steady beat, and if I listen closely, my name whispers in the tender rhythm. He is the forever calm in a sea of chaos. I am that chaos. Even now, in this clarity of night's serenity, my heart gears up for a race.

Buzz, buzz.

"Ana?" His breath heaves.

"Yes?" I open my eyes and tilt my head toward his. There is a beautiful urgency in the way he watches me. Draws me to him.

"There is something I need to do." His gaze sears through me, turns my body to liquid goo.

"Yes," I say. "Whatever you need." My arm hairs have risen to attention. My nerve endings are tingling, prickling.

"Don't be afraid." He shifts, bringing us eye to eye. His gaze is still deep and searching. What is he looking for? And why would I be afraid? His palms find the side of my face, slip through my hair, warm my ears. My eyelids grow heavy and my lips numb. And then, a frenzy of life. Buzzing, buzzing everywhere.

His lips are on mine, and my body responds, immediately and willingly, curving and melding to his. My hands find the warmth of his shoulders and then the thick marvel of his hair. His kiss is a feather's touch, whisking the dust from the recesses of my mind. A storm, tossing back the curtain and yanking away the blankets, exposing the brilliance of day.

The taste of him is cedar and sunlight. Every kiss turning the notch on my internal thermostat a level higher. My blood pressure is rising. My mind, expanding. Something is climbing out of the darkness of my soul. It's soaring toward the light, soaring toward Jaden. He is freeing something new within me and ripping something free from me. He is healing. Healing me with his lips, his kiss. A tsunami washing my soul clean.

His hands blaze against my skin, cleansing me with fire. Turning the buzz, the buzz, the buzz into a frenzy and finally, a blissful wave. He has brought serenity to my discord.

A small cough rumbles through his chest, and he pulls away. He coughs again, and it's like a dust storm rolling through his chest. "Sorry," he says in a semi-strangled voice.

I don't mind a cough, not even two. I enjoy the comfort of laying this way with him. It's somehow right. The rhythm of his heart is the music to which we both march... and dance... and live. I sigh, stargaze, and listen.

Hammer, hammer. Hammer, hammer, hammer.

"Jaden?" I say, tilting my head toward his face. He doesn't answer.

Seriously? Did he just fall asleep on me?

"Jaden?" I say again, this time sitting up and shaking him.

He gurgles, his head dropping to the side. He drops onto his back, stares up through half lidded, hazy eyes.

SIXTEEN

O h, my Gaea! "Jaden? Jaden?" I call his name repeatedly, my entire body revving into full alert.

I straddle him and grab his shoulders, shake. Shake hard. The motion reverberates through my limbs, and I tremble. My brain is rattled. My breath hitches and accelerates, attempting to compensate for his all-to-slow breathing.

"Ana," he mumbles, my name dropping from his lips slow and disjointed.

I drop my ear close to his lips and listen hard. "What's wrong, Jaden? What's happened?"

"It will be alright." His voice is forced and weak. "I am drained."

I jolt upright. Stifle a scream, a call for help. Would Ry hear me, or would Garr be the one to come running? I wish Ry had Jaden's ability, wish he knew what I needed and was here with me now.

I jerk to a stand, and with a clenched jaw and fist, peer out at where I expect Ry to stand—in front of his sleeper pod with his arms crossed. He's not there, and I fight back the tears that want to flow. *I don't know what to do.*

Drizzle starts falling from the sky, and there is the slightest scuff of Jaden shifting on the ground behind me. I spin around.

Jaden has his arm outstretched, his palm wide to the falling dew drops. He's trying to lift his head. "We should get you to shelter before your beautiful new clothes are all wet," he says, sounding drunk.

Drenched clothing. *So the least of my worries right now.*

I drop beside him and slide my hand behind his head. "Do you think you can move?"

"Sure."

He rolls to his side and into a sitting position. I help him stand and keep my arm around him for support. We stumble our way down the stairs to the main level. Someone is pounding heavily at the door. I throw the door open. Standing before me is the female guard blocking my path. I ignore her questions and push Jaden and myself past her and head for the bridge.

The guard follows us, even tries to grab Jaden, but I push her away. For all I know, it's the Treeite's fault something is wrong with Jaden. I start screaming for my brother as soon as I am close to the bridge. The guard at the other end of the bridge starts making his way toward us. In seconds, we will be trapped, guards on both sides of us. But before the guard can take two steps onto the bridge, he's pushed against the rope railing and Ry is standing in front of me, glimpsing over Jaden.

"What's happened?" He takes the burden of Jaden's weight.

"I don't know. He was coughing and then started acting

funny and collapsed." I follow Ry and Jaden back across the bridge, the male guard stepping out of our way. "One minute, he seemed fine, and the next..." I wave my hands in the air. "It's almost like someone slipped him a mickey. Is he going to be alright?"

"I don't know for certain, but I'm fairly sure he'll be alright. Whatever it is will most likely burn off quickly, given his blood type."

We step onto the platform, and the guards move in to help. Ry waves them away. "We got this. He should be fine in a little while."

"We don't want their help?" I follow him into the pod unit. Their entire space could fit into my front room and is designed to make the most of the space. Two beds are set into the wall, bunk bed style, and the third one is pressed into the opposite wall, above a table and chairs.

"No. In fact, I'd rather they didn't tell anyone about this, but I'm guessing that's not very likely. I'd rather no one here know you are currently down one warrior." He settles Jaden on the bottom bunk, looks him over for any apparent injury, pries Jaden's eyes open, studies his pupils, then lets out a deep breath.

Ry starts to step away, but Jaden's arm swings out and around Ry's neck, pulling Ry down until his ear as at Jaden's lips. Jaden whispers something I want to hear but can't. Ry nods, helps Jaden's arm into a comfortable position, and then makes himself comfy in a chair across the room.

"Why are you sitting?" My voice shrieks. "Shouldn't we be doing something?" I glance back and forth between Jaden and my brother.

"I am doing something," he responds without looking up. He picks up a knife and starts sharpening. *A knife!* What does a knife have to do with Jaden's situation? I want to smack Ry across the face. "Try to harness some patience," he says, calmly.

I glower at him and want to explode like a volcano. I look away. Look to Jaden. He's so peaceful. Looking at him soothes my rage. I ease onto the bed beside him and brush his hair from his face. I wish I could see his eyes. Find them clear and alert, but he's now sleeping.

He lazily opens his eyes as if hearing my wish. "Hey," he slurs, and I have to press close to hear him.

"Hey, yourself."

The muscles on his face strain, and his finger rises between us, as if he's trying to remember something. "Don't forget to hang the enigma loops."

Always thinking of me. Melancholia pulls at my face, and I press my lips to his ear, whisper. "I need you to get better, okay?"

He nods, closes his eyes. "Have something for you. Pocket," he says with eyes closed. A second later, he's softly snoring. I reach into his pocket and pull two pictures free. The one of Crystia with Caesar and the one of me, Crystia, and Ry. I smile at the memories, then kiss Jaden's temple and slip the pictures into my own pocket. I curl up beside him, lay my right hand upon his arm, and press my left hand against his chest. He's burning up.

"Ry?" I keep my eyes trained on Jaden.

"Hmm?" He's still sharpening his knife.

"What did you mean by Jaden's blood type?" I speak softly so as not to disturb Jaden and slowly shift to better see my brother.

"What's this talk of blood?" Yuromo steps into the room

through a side door. She looks well steamed and like a boy... still.

"Hey, Mo." Ry says.

Yuromo has a nickname? We are calling her Mo? When did this happen?

I watch Mo enter the room and close the door. Although it has only been a few days, in traveling with us, she has truly run the gauntlet. She deserves to feel like she belongs, like she is one of us. She has more than earned the right to be called by the more familiar shortening of her name.

Next to the door is a dresser, and, for the first time since stepping into the sleeping quarters, I notice the broken bit of glossy stone set upon the dresser's surface. I blink and my lips pucker into a frown.

"I was just going to explain to Ana that Jaden's blood is different from the human's she grew up with. He has Tracer blood coursing through his veins so whatever is disturbing his system should burn off fairly quickly. Hopefully, we'll have him back to normal in no time. Ry spares me a reassuring smile. "You just wait and see."

Mo moves deeper into the room, fluffing the moisture from her hair. One second it is short, cut like her guy version, and then next, it's flowing down to the small of her back. "What's wrong with him?" She motions to Jaden.

"Jaden seems have gotten himself stupefied or drugged or something. We need to let him rest and burn it off. Ana's visiting. She's concerned about him, of course." Ry delivers the news like it's something that happens all the time.

"Jaden's been drugged?" Mo steps urgently to the side of the bed.

At least she's showing the proper concern.

"Is there anything I can do?" She turns to me, and when

I look at her, it is the girl who has traveled with us for miles and days that is gazing back at me.

"I don't know. I have no clue what to do. When we came here, I thought he needed rest. Thought this place would provide that rest, but now I fear this place is absolutely no good for him at all." I sigh and lay my head against Jaden's chest. "You know what you could do?" She watches me, expectantly. "You could hand me that stone over there." I point toward the dresser.

Mo looks at the rock and then back at me. She's clearly confused by the request, but she grabs the stone and hands it to me, anyway. "If it helps..." she looks between Ry and me. "Legend says the Tracer is fortified with elven blood. Elves are one of the oldest and strongest races. One of the founders of all existence. They are not easy to kill."

Elves? I study Jaden's features with newfound interest and wonder.

"If that were true, then where are all the elves now?" Ry counters.

"They withdrew, of course." Mo's face is a shock of incredulity. "It's common knowledge that all the elves returned to the source world."

"Myth, created to cover a harder truth," Ry says, setting his knife on the table.

Elves and Fae and Immortal Warriors. *How different my life has become.* If the legends from fairy tales are true, then what else is real? What kind of being or thing could Garr be? He is clearly different from everyone in this tree branch city. I jolt upright. "I think we should leave, like now."

"We never should have stayed. But now, we can't leave with Jaden in this condition." Ry studies his feet, lazily looks up, motions from Jaden to me with a wave of his hand. "And you're denying the truth of your own exhaustion."

"I'm not tired," I lie. But it shouldn't matter. "What about the warrior thingy?" I mimic rubbing earth on my skin, like we did the night we went up against Dreya and the caves and doorway to get here.

"Warrior thingy?" Mo says.

"No." Ry's head rocks from left to right. "Not this time."

I leap off the bed. "What's wrong with you?" I pin him with a glare.

He flinches, tenses, and...

Oh my God and Gaea! My gaze drops to his stomach. Why didn't I notice sooner? Ry's coat is flared open, giving me a clean view of his white shirt. Only, it isn't white. It's spoiled with splotches of red, brown, yellow, and gross green.

I lurch forward, and he raises a finger to hush any forthcoming words. I freeze, my lower jaw hanging toward the floor.

There's a knock at the door.

The room falls silent. I jump and we all snap our attention to the visitor awaiting discovery. Ry stands, buttons his jacket, and moves past me, actually blocks me, to check who is knocking. He cracks the door a fraction open.

"Need I remind you of the curfew time?" a tired voice on the other side of the door asks. "I realize it may not be your custom, but it is ours, and Ms. Raine will need to return to her own accommodations." The voice belongs to the female bridge guard.

"Curfew time for all virgins," I mouth to Mo, and her guy version blinks back. *She doesn't understand my sarcasm.*

"She's pretty tired. Do you mind if I walk her across the bridge, just to be safe?" Ry asks the guard.

"Not a problem, sir. As long as you are not staying."

"Not staying. Let me collect her. We'll be out in a moment." Ry quietly closes the door and turns to face me.

I step back, sit on the bed, return to Jaden's side. Plaster on a firm face of defiance.

"Come on, Ana. Time to go." He offers me his hand.

"If I go, who will see to Jaden? Make sure he's alright?"

"I will. You have my word." Mo stands straight and tall.

"He's going to be just fine," Ry assures and grabs my hand. "You need to get some sleep, too." He pulls me to my feet.

"You promise me he'll be alright?"

"I promise. Now be a good girl, and go get some sleep."

"Only because you're making me." I wrap the stone firmly in my palm. It's too large for me to hide it from sight, but it doesn't matter. What matters is that I will have time to study it more. I move toward the door and stumble. Ry silently laughs.

"Told you, you were tired." He puts an arm around me and wraps mine around his shoulder. He leads me across the bridge and straight to my front door, the female guard at our back the entire way. With the guard's permission, he swoops me into his arms, carries me up the stairs, and deposits me in bed.

"You shouldn't have done that," I say, glancing between his hidden wound and his stubborn, straight face. A thin line of perspiration dampens his face. He silences me with the slightest of head motions and, from the corner of my eye, I spy the guard. She's waiting by the foot of the steps.

Ry pulls back the covers, helps me yank my jacket off, and waits for me to fall onto the bed, before tugging free my boots. They hit the ground with a thump. He then pulls several enigma loops from the bag he left on the bed earlier and starts tying them to the top of the bed frame.

"Before you go," I say. Ry turns and looks at me expectantly. I wave my finger at my jacket. The one he yanked off of me a moment ago. "In the pocket." He grabs the jacket and thrusts his hand into the various pockets until he finds the item I've sent him to retrieve. He holds up the pictures of us, of Crystia. "Thank you." I smile and blink slowly.

He sets my pictures on the nightstand where I can see them. "Okay?" he asks, regarding the picture placement. I nod, again, slowly.

"You promise he'll be alright?" I ask, snuggling into the pillow at the back of my head.

He stops meddling with the loops and heaves a deep intake of breath. "I promise. Now get some sleep." He draws the blanket up around me, tucks me in like Mom used to do when I was little.

"Okay," I say with barely a breath. "Goodnight, Ry. Love you."

"Goodnight, Ana. See you in the morning." Ry turns and follows the guard down the stairs.

"Love you, too," he says before disappearing into the darkness.

My eyes tease me with sleep, slowly drifting closed, then open, then closed, and then open again. The front door slams to a shut, signaling that I am all alone in a beautiful, yet strange environment—my own little pod palace.

The stone still resides firmly in my grasp. Its surface smooth and cool to the touch. Yanking the covers back, I pull the stone free and hold it eye level. There's nothing but the stone and hints of my reflection, and yet, I know what I saw. That day in my bedroom, I saw a face in the stone's reflection. A face that wasn't mine. It was a woman with brilliant red hair. *Definitely not me.*

"Hello," I say to the stone. "Is anybody there?" I wait. No face appears. "If you can hear me, Jaden is in need of help. He's not well and I'm scared. Scared for him. I assume you know him since he had this stone in his possession. Maybe you guys were arguing, or maybe I'm making a terrible mistake and you are a foe and not a friend. But if you are someone who cares about him at all, please... please help." Once again, I wait. There's no change in appearance. I set the stone aside. Drop back against the bed.

Sleep refuses to come. I twist left and right, trying to find comfort. It's hard to do when I am bound in slightly too tight pants. Reluctantly, I slip out of bed with barely enough energy to walk to the wardrobe. Hanging from the bar, for my sleeping comfort is...

Ugh.

Seriously?

A white cotton nighty.

First a potato sack of an outfit at Mo's village, now this. Is this entire world of Hiddenkel lacking in modern conveniences and comforts?

I shed my clothes, leaving the pieces where they fall on the floor, drop the nighty over my head, and crawl back into bed, pulling the covers tight around me.

Too hot.

I kick one leg free of the covers, turn on my side, and gaze at the pictures. Focus on the image of Ry in the photo of us three.

"First thing in the morning, we are out of here," I mumble a promise to myself. "Still need to fix the sisterly thing, but for now, that falls to second place on the urgency list. First order of business, find a cure for Ry and get Jaden as far away from this place as possible." I breathe deep, slip my hand under my pillow, and close my eyes. "Yes, that's the plan. Save my brother."

I slip and slide and toy with sleep like slumber is the ground and I'm on a teeter totter. The more I give in to the strong furrows of sleep, the more I fear another encounter with Dohlan. I need to find a way to control my subconscious, put a stop to dream infiltrations.

Even now, when I'm not fully encompassed by a nightly coma, I hear his approach. The creak of a floorboard, the squeak and press at the edge of the bed.

His hand slides along my uncovered leg.

"Please don't, Dohlan," I mumble and sigh.

"Who is Dohlan?" a deep, handsome voice answers.

I know that voice.

I bolt upright, knees to my chest, sheets pulled tightly up to my neckline. My equilibrium takes a second to catch up. Wide-eyed, and with mouth agape, I glare at Garr. "I can't believe you..." I wave my hand in the air between us. I need to finish that sentence. *Let yourself into my room. Touched me like that.* "What's wrong with you?" My voice hitches.

"I am sorry, my dear. I did not mean to scare you." His topaz eyes sparkle through the dark. "I thought you would be..." His words drift away, unfinished, and his gaze wanders inquisitively along the string of enigma loops.

"This is completely inappropriate. Explain yourself." I shuffle backward, as far away from his touch as I can get without leaping across the room in my flimsy nightgown.

"I agree, this may not have been the best way." His attention swivels back on me. "But I needed time with you, away from all the crowds and watchful eyes." He inches closer. "I need to know if you remember."

"Remember what?" When I first saw him, he seemed oddly familiar, but if it is because of a past life relationship, I can't retrieve the memories. I shiver. What sane man would think it's alright to let himself into a girl's room in the middle of the night? Let alone, a virgin's room in the middle of the virgin penitentiary.

Oh right, he's the warden.

He takes another step closer. Light from the window washes over him, and I notice he's not wearing the etched headband he'd been wearing during the day—the fancy piece he wore like a crown on his head. Without the band, his pointy ears and downward curled horns are clearly visible.

None of the other people here have pointy ears. In fact, their ears droop toward their shoulders, hanging long. I was right, he is not one of them. What is he?

"Remember what?" I ask again.

"I saw the way you looked at me when you first arrived. Are you saying you do not recall?" He studies me. "I see..." He allows the words to draw out and linger. "The fates are both kind and mischievous. They have brought us together once again, only this time, it may be too early. You do not even know who you are yet. You have not made the connection."

"The fates? Connection?" Something dark and slithery rises inside of me. It's bleak and dangerous and rolling in my belly. "Again?"

Sliding closer to me, he reaches for my hand and attempts to pry it free from my tight knee hold. I jerk back, shift away. With a weighted glaze and a heavy sigh, he slouches.

"We are at a severe disadvantage given you have yet to regain your memories. You will have to trust me when I tell you, our connection is boundless. Last time we found each other, it was too late. Not so this time around."

"Too late for what?"

"To clean up the mess Meira Morxisys Alastrine and Edea Virrie created." He's deep and thoughtful, and for the briefest of moments, I almost trust him. Almost. But as quickly as the feeling sparks, it vanishes.

"I have no idea what you are talking about. Who is Meira Morx... whatever her name is?"

"My dear..." He reaches, palm out, to caress my face. I turn away, causing his hand to miss my cheek. Instead, his touch skims down the length of my arm. Chills, ripe with disgust, explode across my skin and through my gut. "Let me remind you of us," he continues, his other hand swoops up to my far shoulder, sandwiching me in his grip. A slight smile wiggles across his face, and he leans forward.

Panic. Fear. Anxiety. A plethora of emotions erupt like a geyser. My body jolts, and I explode off the bed, pulling the sheets with, clutched to the front of me. I push my back against the corner of the room.

"I expected you to be receptive." His gaze drops to the ground as if pondering the situation, and he shakes his head ever so slowly, allowing a moment of silence to pass. "Please try to remember." He sounds exasperated. "Remember when you were Fianna." He looks up and extends his hand to me, but my attention shifts away from his appeal and drops to the show of his hooved feet beneath his ceremonial gown.

SEVENTEEN

Fianna. Fianna and hooved feet. A man, a thing with hooved feet.

Something between those two triggers a release within me. Be it the name Fianna or the sight of Garr's feet, I don't know, but the name Fianna reverberates in my head over and over again. The hail sounding like that of a desperate boy. A sad and frustrated boy. Could the boy be Garr?

Something feral and ancient climbs the walls of my soul to answer his call. The thing slips through the door Jaden earlier unlocked.

My reaction is instant and automatic, and I don't know what it means, but I have trouble believing it's anything good. Garr brings out the worst in me, my inner beast, and I sense myself becoming something unrecognizable in his presence.

Slow, steady steps take him around the bed, closing the distance between us.

Fury oozes from my pores.

I hiss, my vision reddens. "Stay away," I growl in a distorted voice.

Before I can blink, he pins my wrists to the wall and his body presses against mine. "She took you from me. It wasn't fair." His voice rings in my ear, sounding like a pouting child. "Do you remember now? I see Fianna's temper in you."

I slam my forehead into his, attempt to break free, but he holds firm. I thought I was supposed to be impossibly strong and yet... my mind shuffles through my options, his potential weaknesses. A millisecond later, I bring my knee up with all my force and connect with my target. He folds, and I shove him away.

Lurching to the side, I move toward the door, wanting to put as much distance between us as possible. His hand grasps my leg before I can get clear. The hold drags and tosses my momentum sideways. I fall to the bed and dig my nails into the mattress. The sharp, razor slashes of claws dig into my skin, followed by the sound of tearing fabric. Blood trickles down my leg prickling my senses, and with a yank from Garr, my nails break, releasing my hold upon the bed.

His hands are heavy and callous, and without a hint of gentleness, he twists me around and throws me back to the bed. He regards me with cold, determined eyes.

"You're crazy," I say and spit in his face.

It was a split-second decision on my part, a gut reaction. He sneers and briskly clears my stain with a wipe of his palm, temporarily freeing one of my hands. I swing, nails broken and jagged, aiming for his eye. Three distinct lines traverse his face, warm and wet to the touch. He growls. Smacks me across the cheek. A flash of fire erupts on my skin, and a coppery taste cuts across my lip.

His face contorts, flashes of confusion, frustration,

despair, fluttering on and gone. Something about Garr, his response, or temporary emotional state, provokes me. I flex and then relax. Ribbons of power race over the fibers of my being, melting away the tension and fight. Green, thrumming, flashes of light spit and sputter from my worn crystals. Even Kaia's crystal answers the call with a whining shrill. All fanfare and build.

A foreign state of awareness takes hold, as if I have been possessed by another creature or spirit. But that's not the case. The feral, unrecognizable beast within me no longer holds the reins, but has stepped aside, bowing to a more divine thread coursing through my system.

The red behind my eyes washes away, leaving the world before me in crystal clarity. Everything is brighter and intoxicatingly vibrant and filled with a matrix of energy dancing with life. Streamers of yellow and gold float at my side—my hair. I watch it swirl through the air as if caught in a storm of static electricity.

Fear swallows Garr's eyes, and in an instant, he is backing away from me and the bed. I don't pursue, nor visually follow him. I haven't the option. I'm not in control of my own body or senses. I remain seated on the bed, until I start to float inches above the covers.

Ghostly mists of blue and green, churn and twirl around the room, tossing, toppling, and bouncing items off surfaces, sending them sailing at Garr. He backs into the corner where I crouched only a short while ago.

My body floats, lifting and twisting my limbs until I am standing. One arm extends, finger jabbing, accusingly at him. "Garr Garrisian of the Ivey City Treeites, you are to leave this vessel in peace. It is not, nor has it ever been, part of your destiny." My lips do not move with the words, but the voice comes from within me, sounding like an angel song.

My hand flicks, and Garr is tossed across the room.

The power holding me releases, and I collapse, miss the bed, and fall in a heap on the floor. I'm sweaty and bloody and shaking.

Possession. It's the only explanation. That or I've gone insane.

Have I? Have I lost my mind? My free will?

My wild survey darts left, then right, taking in the room. Maybe it was all a nightmare. But... the wooden floor beneath my touch is *so* real.

Garr remains crouched in the far corner, fear seeping off his body.

Can't stay. Not a minute longer.

Stumbling forward, I make my way to the roof and gulp the night air in calming, deep breaths. That's what Jaden would tell me to do. When I was last on the roof, I was with him. Nothing of him now lingers in this place. It's dark and damp and dreadfully unsettling. I wouldn't want him to see me like this, nor Ry, not even Mo. Not in the light of whatever has possessed me.

A commotion erupts below. Voices shouting on the bridge, at the guard station. Garr is crossing, alerting his people to what, I do not know. I doubt he's telling anyone he accosted me. I can't go down there. Not now. They might take me back to Garr, the crazy, hooved-foot, horned man.

Through the hanging leaves above, I spy the stars twinkling in the sky. The stars whisper of possibilities and futures. The constellation of Gradnar inspires me to fight, but the stars of the elven queen sing the opposite. Flee, they say. Save your fight for another day. Gazing at the glimmers of hope, I wish the night away.

This didn't happen, I think. *It's all a bad dream. A terrible, most horrible dream.*

On the bridge, the guards huddle with Garr. They point to me standing on the roof of my pod cell. I drop to the ground.

Need to get out here. Flee as the elven queen said.

Keeping my body low, I crawl across the rooftop to the box of garden tools. From the contents shoved within and at its side, I yank free the rope and tubing. The tubing looks like something used as a waterline. Sturdy and flexible enough to hold a knot. I hope.

Judging the distance to the forest floor against the length of the items in my hand, it's questionable if I have a long enough escape line. Firmly tying the tubing to a side railing, I decide that what I have will have to do. I am becoming something other, and I need to put as much distance as possible between me and the rest of the world. At least, until I settle.

Footsteps move across the bridge. The sound reverberates through the night air like the thunder of wild horses. Adrenaline kicks in, and I know I must move quickly or find myself face to face with Garr once again.

With a slipknot and a loop to the rope, I make a lasso and curl the tool around my shoulder. Seconds later, using the tubing, I am swiftly and quietly propelling down the backside of the pod unit. In the glow of the moon light and with the light color of the shimmery pod, I'm less conspicuous in the white nighty.

That's one plus to the garment.

The length of the tubing only reaches a few feet below

the bottom of the pod. My feet swing in the open air. I climb to the lowest edge of the structure and yank the rope free from my shoulder. Burning in the night is a lantern on the outer tree circle, directly across from where I stand. With a swirl of the rope, I throw the hoop end of the line, hoping to catch the lantern and use it to swing free of this pod trap. My aim is off. The rope fails to catch and drops straight into a dangle.

I try again, and again. On the fourth time, I succeed. The art of lassoing, clearly something I need to work on. When the line is secure, properly taut, I release the tubing and grab the rope with both hands.

In one quick and swift move, I am swinging freely between pods and platforms, branches and leaves. My side scrapes the tree beneath the outer circular path. It's like an asphalt burn to the hip. I sway, roughly, to a stop and climb my way up. Looking back from where I came, it's clear that no one has made it to the roof yet.

With the rope wrapped around my shoulder once more, I take a moment to consider a descent between the trees, calculating distances. I square my shoulders, leap nimbly over the railing, hold to the side, and dive. My body soars through the air like an acrobat. I connect with the intended branch and spin around like a gymnast, landing securely on top. I splay my palms and study them, expecting them to be scraped and torn from the bark. They're not.

I'll think about that later.

After securing the rope to the branch and swinging the line around my waist, I hold tight enough to keep from falling while allowing the lead to gently slip through my grip, then run down the tree in a wide spiral motion. The rope stops several feet short of the ground. I release, slip through the air, and land on the dirt in a flat out run.

My feet are bare, and my gown screams, "Here I am." None of that matters. Not now. All I know, all I feel, is that I don't trust myself to be around the people I care for, and I don't trust myself to be around Garr. I could—might—kill him, and my soul isn't ready for such a heavy burden.

I run fast, hard, and far on the dew damp ground. I don't look back, and I don't know how much ground I am covering. But once the glow of Ivey City is no longer visible through the surrounding woods, my strength wanes, leaving me tired and worn and beaten. My speed drops to a drag of the feet and a sway of the walk.

I'd so been looking forward to a good night's sleep in that big, beautiful bed.

I wonder how much sleep I actually got, minutes, hours?

The nearest tree becomes a support. I lean into its dark bark, taking a moment to catch my breath and find my balance. Tonight, has been beyond strange, and I am teeter tottering between what is real and what is a fantastical nightmare. The feral fury that raged within me dissipated during my run, leaving me with a gaping hole through the center of my core. I don't know who or what I am anymore. If I ever did.

A raw throbbing churns in my belly. My arms hold me together as I lay my head against the tree and let a tear free.

I will not cry.

But ... Why did I run? What have I done? Where have I ended up?

The bushes and trees around me are quiet, eerie in the dim light. And the ground is cold with a bite of frost at my toes.

How will the gang find me? Will Jaden be able to do as Ry said, locate me even though he's been poisoned? My thoughts search Jaden out, and I pray he's okay. I whisper his name over and over, until the dam against my fear breaks and my tears turn into a stream.

Through my waterfall of ruptured emotion, I fancy the thrum of Jaden's heart and imagine him waking with concern for me and my plight. But it's nothing more than a silly daydream, for I am here lost among the trees, and he is far away, sleeping in a pod set high in the Treeite City trees.

Back flat against the trunk, I slide to the base, pull my knees in tight, and bury my head in my hands. How many mistakes will it take before I learn to react correctly? Running wasn't the answer. Leaders don't run or leave their teams behind. If this is who I am—the scared, runaway girl—then a leader I will never be. I need to stand up for myself, like I finally did the night of Crystia's death. That night at the party.

But that was back home... California, and I was standing up to a normal, bitchy high schooler. A human.

Still, I tried to stand up against Dreya the other night, even if everything turned inside out and Dohlan decided I needed rescuing. With a sniffle and a sway, I stomp my feet.

A gentle brush sweeps my hair from my face. I startle, and my head slams back, not hitting the hard surface of the tree. Dohlan is there, his hand cushioning me.

"*Luv*, why are you out here all by your lonesome, succumbing to tears?"

His voice is musically soothing, and a breath of relief escapes me. If Dohlan is present, then maybe, just maybe... *tonight must be a dream*. My heart clenches. Which means, I should awake safe and sound in that warm cozy bed, finally free of the nightmare that became Garr in my head.

I gaze into Dohlan's eyes, my hand slipping into his hold. "It will all be alright, now that you are here."

Nothing is as it seems, I tell myself as he helps me stand. A foreign and unrecognizable sense of panic and anxiety rips through me. I shake the emotions away. The feelings sparked by the experience with Garr should be left behind me.

A grimace flinches across Dohlan's face, and a growl jumps from his lips. His eyes roll over me, registering every cut and bruises and rip of my gown. "Who has done this to you? Tell me and I shall destroy them." Rage sparks in his irises.

The word destroy vibrates in my head, sets my teeth on edge. "I may have taken care of that already." The delivery is heavy and gets stuck in my throat, threatening to choke me.

"You?" Dohlan raises a brow. "Best I see for myself. Tell me who it was."

"Please don't push this," I say, my shoulders sagging. My body trembles and I pray he doesn't notice. I am ready to collapse. Of course, collapsing into him would be preferable to the ground. "Would you..." My throat closes, the words trapped within. Only hours ago, I had hoped I would never see Dohlan again and now... His face tilts closer to mine. He listens intently. "For now, would you please just stay with me?"

A fight clashes behind his eyes, betrayed by the intensity of his leer. His need to pummel something is challenged by his concern and, surprisingly, caring.

I am reminded of the conversation I had with Yuromo. What is Dohlan's end game? Why does he invest so much time in me?

"Come, let's have a look at you," he says, his movements and words gentle, like a father to a child. I am caught off guard. More often than not, I find him hard to discern, but in general, I suspect selfishness rules his actions.

"Let's not. I'm a fast healer and will be fine." I look away, unwilling to face his scrutiny. "I don't want to fuss over wounds or torn clothing. I'd rather you just let me lean against you." My thoughts are with Jaden and his soothing touch. But Jaden isn't here.

"Such a tall order," Dohlan teases, voice soft, slippery smooth, and his breath sweet as nectar. "Let me see what I can do."

Gently, he raises my hand, examines my broken nails, and, sparing me a glance, lowers his lips and kisses each finger softly. After each one has been christened with a kiss from the golden prince, he slips my pointer finger into his mouth, closes his lips around it, and pulls it free agonizingly slow.

Chills race over my skin; my blood warms, increases to a quick thrum. My breathing... I may have forgotten how.

My reaction doesn't slow him. He repeats the performance with each finger. As much as I try to fight the onslaught of triggered emotions, the battle is surely lost. My eyes flutter close.

"Why?" I mumble. "Why do you have this power over me? I can't even remember why I was upset."

A third finger. I'm not sure how much longer I can remain standing. Fourth finger. My legs wobble.

Dohlan wraps his arm around me and pulls me into the security of his warmth. "The last time I saw you, I didn't get the chance to tell you how much I enjoy the golden highlights in your hair." He twists a strand of my golden streaks through his fingers. And then the hair is forgotten, his hand working to slip the strap of my gown off my shoulder. My exposed skin presents an ugly, dark bruise. He bends down, breathes against my skin, and kisses the mark.

I gasp, and my legs finally give.

A heated explosion of fizzles and bubbles spins through my chest. Anger and jealousy. More emotions I fail to recognize as my own. I don't understand.

He holds me firm. "Oh Ana, what am I to do with you?" He speaks into the curve of my neck, the brush of his lips gliding up to my cheek.

A nervous laugh bubbles up my throat. "Why should you have to do anything?" My resistance is trying to rise, but I fear it is facing a losing battle. And still, jealousy courses through me. But why and of what am I jealous?

He laughs and attacks my cracked, bloody lip with a kiss and a sensual lick. I flinch to the sting but quickly melt into pacification. For a moment, I don't care that my lips were swollen before his touch and are likely puffier after partaking of his rousing appetite. For a moment, he is all that I want and all that exists.

And then...

Run. Run far away. The little voice starts chanting in my head.

Before I can protest, his lips are melded to mine and our hearts are beating in time. Yet this time, I sense I have more control. Want him, I do. Need him, maybe so. But give into him, no, I don't think I have to.

The jealousy gives in to frustration and rage. Is the feral thing within me the owner of these unfitting emotions?

The curve of my palm finds the chisels of his chest, and with a fraction of applied pressure, I push him away. He does not resist. "We can't do this." I shake my head. That isn't the truth I need to tap. "I won't do this," I correct.

"I thought this is what you wanted?" His face dims with confusion, frustration... dejection.

"No." I shake once more. "I wanted support. Not manhandling."

There may now be space between us, but it isn't much. The air could evaporate with a single step forward. He holds my elbows, locking us close, and his intoxicating aroma swims over me, challenging me to forget all that I said. My entire body leans back, pushing against his pull.

"Something has changed." He peers through me, making my inner core feel exposed to the cold of his blue eyes.

"Yes. Like the reveal that you are working with Dreya." I square my shoulders and attempt to yank myself free of his entanglement, but his fingers hold onto me like the tentacles of an octopus. He's strong like Ry. Stronger than me.

I'm suddenly curious if it has to do with his race or the incubus thing. I rather want to know.

"You need to trust me when it comes to that woman. I am not at her side because I want to be there, and being close to her only helps me better help you and your little band of followers." His lips pull into a tight line. "Didn't I help you get past her forces in the moss-covered forest?" His voice sounds like a sneer, but his gaze is intense with knowledge.

"I don't understand." I waver. "Why are you at her side if you don't want to be?" I stop fighting his hold and skim over his face, searching for the truth in his eyes.

"I have no choice. She has me bound. My will is not my own when it comes to many things. I am sorry, Ana. I wish the situation were different." He looks toward the trees. I'm no longer certain of the things I feel. I'm pleased to have my suspicions confirmed, but I suspect I am not getting the whole story, and that angers me.

"Let me go!" My body torques in my attempt to break free. More jolts of anger. Anger brimming on rage.

He holds me, his grip firm. "She is testing you. First the water, then the earth."

My struggle pauses. *Testing? For what?* The answer snaps into place almost as soon as I pose the question. She wants to know how far I have come in my transformation.

I wiggle, fight once more to break free of Dohlan's hold.

"Why are you acting this way? I would never hurt you. Have you not learned that by now?" His grasp tightens, stilling me, and he pins me with an inquisitive glare. "Is it this Jaden?" he says with distaste on his tongue.

I don't respond, merely look toward the trees, the grass, the darkness beyond us. Something is swirling inside of me—emotions and physical strains not belonging to me.

"I see," he says sharply while softening the pressure holding me in place. I fight the temptation to react. Some part of me doesn't want to hurt him. Doesn't want to leave him.

"Oh, my dear sweet Ana." He shakes his head. "You have so much to learn. It is so unbearably common for the Balance Bringer to become infatuated with her Tracer. And that's what he is to you, isn't he? Your Tracer? The two of you share a bond no other can fully comprehend. I am not ignorant. I can understand that. But are the things you feel around him real, or a product of magic?"

Dohlan's words pull my gaze to him like a magnet. He has tapped into my one major concern regarding Jaden. I can no longer feign indifference. Not now, after the question has been posed.

Dohlan's lips curl in a half-hearted grin, and he looks rather amused.

"Are the things I feel around, and about, you real?" I retort.

"Touché." His brows arch high, framing a mischievous sparkle in his eye. My fingers find his mouth, guided by his hand, and he teases me with the brush of his lips across my skin.

Something in my belly wiggles and squirms, causing my cells to sizzle with frustration. And the voice, once again, is yelling at me to run. It's a gut response to what he is, I tell myself. Yet knowledge does nothing to stay the emotions. I gulp and blink hard, push back against any thoughts of unreasonable reaction.

Dohlan laughs.

"You don't play fair." With a jerk, I snap my hand from his lips.

But rather than pull myself into a cocoon, away from Dohlan's touch, I allow him to linger on my skin, twisting his fingers in and along the lines of my hand until we are once more twined together like a vine, arms dropped at our side. I know it's a mistake, even as I allow the connection to continue. The hole I dig for myself where Dohlan is concerned will soon be a well with no chance of a return.

"I think you're wrong," I say, my voice calm and steady. "Jaden is more than infatuation. I can feel him in here." I tap my chest. "He's a part of me. A missing piece that makes me whole when we are together. I need him just as much as I want him. I'm sorry, Dohlan, but I chose him at the start... a millennium ago when I was the first."

Dohlan's lip twitches, and I sense my words burn. He

quickly recovers, his features and gaze burning with their normal intensity, as he leans his forehead against mine.

"Maybe," he whispers. "But it is my ring you wear."

As soon as the words are spoken, his eyes glint with fury. He yanks my hand into the space between us, twisting my palm to display my fingers, specifically my ring finger.

"Where is the ring?"

I gulp. How can I tell him that I honestly don't know? His fury is already pushing at the gates, waiting to break loose.

"Ana."

My name sounds from the darkness beyond the surrounding trees. My body straightens, and I turn toward the sound, happy for a distraction from discussing the ring, but confused by the direction my dream has taken.

Jaden emerges from the shadows.

EIGHTEEN

I'm taken aback. Jaden and Dohlan in the same dream. It's happened once, maybe twice, before, but never like this. Never so... interactive. And, with a third party, creepy Garr.

I jerk and shift my gaze between them, before settling my attention on Jaden. Last I saw him, he was extremely out of sorts, fighting a poison attacking his body.

"How did you get into my dream? I thought..." The sentence hangs in the air unfinished.

I don't know what I thought. Possibly that Dohlan, the dream incubus, controlled the dream world. Except, he recently told me I held the reins to my dreams. If only I knew how to control those reins.

Jaden slows to a stop and cautiously steps into a small patch of moonlight. The sweat lacing the sides of his face is alarming. As is the unusual dullness of his eyes. If I were dreaming, I would envision a healthier version of him. Nothing like the current state of the guy standing before me now.

"This is not a dream," he says; his arms rise at his sides in a show of amnesty.

His expression answers the puzzle I've been pondering. The odd emotions I've been experiencing and couldn't pin as my own, belong to him... our connection now a two-way exchange. It's his frustration and anger and jealousy I feel.

"Not dreaming?" The truth hits me like a Ryland-strength slap to the gut. Deep down, I knew the ugly truth, but I didn't want to believe. I still don't want to believe. My gaze shifts between the two guys. "Please don't confuse me. This has to be a dream. Understand? It has to be," I say, firmly.

Jaden takes a cautious step in my direction, his watchful glare on the man at my back, Dohlan.

A wave of annoyance and animosity leaps off Jaden and, although directed at Dohlan, smacks me in the face. My mouth pops open.

"Why must it be a dream?" Dohlan says, his face tilted into the curve of my neck and his breath warm against my skin.

I swing around to face him. "Because... If it isn't a dream. Then..." My eyes roll over him from head to toe, and my finger presses into his chest, measuring the resistance of his flesh.

Irritation and envy from Jaden scratch at my back.

I've seen Dohlan multiple times during this wild journey. He was walking with Dreya's army of undead, and he was by the magical rock tunnel. I wasn't the only one who saw him those times. Those times he was definitely corporeal. And I'm certain he was physically present when he came to our aid against the undead stealth troop in the evermold forest. That was when he gave me the ring.

But there were also times, exchanges, that I am fairly certain all took place in some sort of dream state. Like the other night when he came and Jaden chased him away with the enigma loops. Or when he pulled me into a sleep at the temple ruins, that time had certainly been a dream. A dream similar to the ones I used to have back home in California. Only scarier.

Real. Dream. Dream. Real. I don't know what's certain and what's not anymore. Nothing in this place is clear and obvious. I'm living a dark fairy tale, and that's the doing of the subconscious or... Maybe I died in the caves back home— or possibly even earlier than that—and everything since then has been my strange afterlife.

Did I die in the car that night with Jeremy, the night Dohlan first came to me?

Dohlan flashes me a weary and bored smile.

"You're real?" I whisper, looking up into his eyes, searching for answers to questions I don't even know to ask. "Are you here, in the flesh?" I pinch his sleeve. Dream or real, he feels the same as he always does. He's never felt *not* real.

A muscle in Dohlan's cheek quivers, and he flashes a glare at Jaden before taking a step back, putting more space between us. His hands drag slowly along my arms, tug lightly at my fingers, and reluctantly release. In that moment, I cannot only sense his desire to hang on to me, but I can also feel his desire racing over my skin.

Gentlemanly, he bows. "Of course, Ana. It is I, in the flesh. As I told you from the very beginning." He throws an arm wide, motioning to the world around us. "This is where I have always resided. On more than one occasion, I mentioned you would find me here."

My mouth pops open. I want to respond, but the words are a jumble. What is it I want to say exactly? He talked about Hiddenkel and his home, castle really, but at the time I didn't think Hiddenkel was real. I was a confused mess, raised on lies.

When I saw him leading the army of the undead, or anytime since then, none of it felt real. Everything has been too crazy to be real. Too unthinkable. And yet... I knew. Knew this was my new truth. I simply didn't want to admit it to myself.

I look down at my dirt-smudged, bare feet. Here I am. The girl who talks with water and has been known to levitate rocks.

"What will it take to make you believe?" Jaden asks. "You are neither dead nor dreaming. This is your life, Ana. I hope you can come to accept what is, accept me, and accept who you are." A chaotic outpour of emotions, some of them mine, some of them Jaden's, threatens to drown me.

"But..." My fingers rest upon my lips. I glance at my bruises and scratches. The tear in my gown. "All that really happened?" My hand swings forward, softly pointing in the direction of Ivey City.

My eyes, threatening to spill over with tears, find Jaden. One look at him and the truth is undeniably clear. Unlike Dohlan, Jaden would never deceive me. I understand that I am way past the point when I should have accepted this world for all that it is and all that it could be... once balanced.

The problem with accepting the truth is that I must come to terms with whatever divine or demon force can take control of my body at any time. I don't want to be a plaything in their game of create and destroy. I want to rise or fall on my own efforts.

Whatever took control of my body back there, pulsed with a godly strength and power, and it tossed Garr across the room like he was a tinker toy. And the ancient, feral thing that crawled up from my core... it seethed with festering anger. Her attack on the hooved and horned man was vicious and wild.

I backup, three more steps, and press my palms to the side of my head, attempt to muffle whatever monsters dwell within me. "Oh God. Oh Gaea."

"Will you stop me from being her savior this night and every night to come," Dohlan says, challenging Jaden. But despite his verbal incite, Dohlan makes no move toward me.

Dohlan's sharp, threatening voice floats over the jumbled confusion in my head, burrowing through the chaos enough for me to realize he views me as someone in need saving. I don't want to be the damsel in distress. I want to be my own knight. I want to do the saving.

I drop my arms. Sniffle and glare at him.

My eyes close. In truth, I want to go home, curl up in my bed with Crystia's cat Oscar at my side.

But that's not true either. There is nothing to be gained both mentally and emotionally by curling up and doing nothing. I want to be accepting of whatever crazy truth now resides around me, and I want to be strong enough to rise to the challenges presented. I want to be worthy of Jaden's kindness. I want a lot of things... but bringing any of those thoughts to fruition sounds so utterly exhausting.

Jaden's arms wrap around me, erecting a barrier between me and Dohlan. Jaden has made his move, effectively announcing that he will most definitely stand in Dohlan's way.

My heart thrums and my mind calms. I'd been so

worried about Jaden. So scared something was taking him away from me. I turn and gaze up at his face, fixating on his lips. The lips that were pressed to mine only a short while ago. It was a kiss of revelations. A kiss of clarity. And I want more, so many more. But I also want to know how Jaden recovered so quickly.

I reach up and touch his face. His physical and mental exhaustion washes over me. I blink, breathe deep, and allow my fingers to glide easily through the sheen of sweat masking his skin.

"I feel you," I say. "I feel so many things coming from you. Anger and frustration, for sure. But I also feel your desire, anguish, and impatience in regards to me accepting my role and destiny. I don't want to let you down." I press my forehead to his.

"I know," he says. "I feel you, too."

Dohlan still stands at my back, a growl vibrating through his chest. Unlike Jaden, Dohlan makes no effort to hide his jealousy.

"I'm so tired," I whisper, tears slipping down my cheeks.

Jaden guides me to the dirt floor in a wave of warmth. Healing surges through me, coming from both him and the earth. Mending energy sweeps through my system like dust particles in a cyclone. I sense Gaea's cradling touch.

I forget the conflict before me and simply exist, curled up upon the ground, with Jaden's arms wrapped securely around me. His presence reconciles my troubled mind and torn soul. I close my eyes and allow the healing to happen.

"Jaden?" Ry's voice echoes through the trees.

"Over here. I've found her!" Jaden calls out, dropping worry over me.

Dohlan grunts, but I'm aware of his burning glare upon us.

Why is he still here? Why hasn't he fled? I don't want to think about Dohlan watching me with Jaden.

The sound of disrupted plant life moves in our direction. The lack of stealth is so unlike Ry. My heart skips, fear for his health churning the situation and cranking up my concern. I open my eyes and peer through the night gloom. A fog has settled in, and the stillness is only interrupted by the occasional bug call... and Ry's thrashing.

Jaden's apprehension over Ry's physical condition bloats my own uneasy, all the more. I fear time is winding down and soon it will be too late to save my brother.

Ry steps into sight, his hand pressed into his side. His eyes are red, dressed with dark circles. His hair, damp with what I doubt is dew. He looks worse than when I thought he was dead at Dreya's hand.

"What is he doing here?" Ry says, pointing accusingly at Dohlan. Dohlan leans, cross-armed, against a nearby tree. It's quite clear, everyone can see Dohlan. There's no doubt he's physically here. I need to stop fooling myself. Jaden asked when I would start believing. Maybe now is a good time to start.

"Relax, warrior," Dohlan deadpans. "If I wanted to mar, or better yet kill, any of you, I could have done so a thousand times already. Since your arrival, you have made yourself easy pickings." Dohlan is a mask of boredom, and I'm starting to think that's exactly what his lack of emotion is, a mask. Only the slight clench of his jaw hints to anything other than indifference.

"That doesn't answer the question, *magroot*. What are

you doing here?" Ry's question is filled with animosity that seems misplaced.

"I am here for the girl, obviously." Dohlan makes no attempt to camouflage his condescending tone. "Where were you when she was beaten, huddled, crying against the tree?"

Dohlan's words are like a betrayal, cutting me to the bone with a dull knife. My gaze snaps to Ry. His face ghosts white, and his eyes pinch with pain. I hurt him more than I realized when I left the way I did.

Jaden, as well. He may be trying to quell his guilt and remorse, but I've already caught a whiff of the emotions.

Damn Garr. Damn Dohlan. Damn all this alpha male fighting. I want it all to stop. I want it to be over.

Jaden's arms tighten around me. I twist and bury myself in his chest. His warm woodsy scent is far preferable to the grown men tossing insults and threatening punches.

Dohlan and Ry continue to face off, their words becoming a muffle in my head. I'm almost too tired to care. But I love Ry and don't want him to get hurt in any way. And Dohlan... well, it's complicated.

Despite my desire to close my eyes and sleep, every other word drifts to my ear. There is mention of events of which I am unfamiliar. Things that happened here in Hiddenkel. Times and places that had brought them together. Family ties that date beyond my lifetime. And then the mention of Kaia snags my attention.

"You think pretty highly of yourself, a warrior and defender, but you failed with Kaia, what makes you think you'll now do better?" Dohlan says, a sneer threatening to engulf his face.

Without warning, Ry charges at Dohlan. Ry's such a jumbled mess, it's like watching a three-legged puppy storm a lion. With what looks like barely a flick of his hands, Dohlan deflects Ry and sends him flying into a moist moss puddle. Ry doesn't get up, but instead, rolls over with a groan and mumble.

Dohlan takes a step in Ry's direction. Visions of the black blur in the moss-covered forest flash across my memory. That blur was Dohlan coming to my rescue, destroying any threat around us. He wouldn't do the same to Ry... would he? Not to someone I care about. I can't take the chance. Ry must never end up like a mutilated undead soldier. A Dreya puppet. I jump to my feet and throw myself between the brawling boys.

"Stop this right now," I say, sweeping my gaze between them. "Dohlan and I merely had a misunderstanding, that's all. He was just leaving." I direct my attention to him. "Weren't you Dohlan?"

Dohlan smiles at me, clearly amused. Ry, who has righted himself and now leans back on his hands, appears mortified. His reaction confuses me, and I contemplate him through squinted eyes. Before I can ascertain what has him bothered, Jaden is behind me, covering me with his jacket.

"The moonlight highlights too much of a silhouette for your brother's liking," Jaden whispers at my ear.

Something spins in my chest, yanks at the back of my ribcage. I glance down at my white nightgown. Panic and embarrassment fight for control of the banging in my chest. I've never wanted to be more invisible than at this moment.

Dohlan's shoulders drop with a sigh. "You make too much of a fuss," he says to Jaden and Ry. "Her attire is more sugges-tive than indecent." His eyes lock upon mine. "You have nothing to worry about, my dear. Nothing at all. You are always a vision. And..." His leer finds Jaden. "If I had a jacket, I would have done the same. I would have gladly covered her and sheltered her from the cold." His gaze finds me once more.

Heat flushes over my neck and cheeks.

What did he see? Someone like him has probably seen it all, *but* he hadn't seen me... before now. Did that change tonight?

"Would you have preferred I'd left you alone..." He pauses and motions to our surroundings. "...out here, by yourself?" His head tilts and his eyes light with an emotion I can't finger. "Was it not better that I stayed and kept you company?"

I honestly don't know the answer to that question. I was upset and needed something, but his presence causes such conflict with everyone present. Which need, my need for comfort or my need for peace, should prevail?

"Enough." Ry pulls himself off the ground, shakily brushes away any clinging dirt, and extends his hand to me. His palm is clammy and white. "Come on, Ana. Let's get out of here."

"We should go before your brother drops," Jaden whispers at my ear. Under normal circumstances, I think Ry would have heard Jaden's words. But now, in Ryland's condition, I just don't know. His overall ability at... *well...* anything seems to be swirling its way down the crapper.

Dohlan clears his throat, commanding our attention. He doesn't back away or turn to leave, but rather stands his ground. With an exaggerated bow and the extended flow of his arm, Dohlan bids us farewell.

The gesture is a prompt upon which Jaden immediately acts. His arm tightens on mine and steers us toward Ry.

Jaden and I clasp our arms around Ry's back, and together we support his weight in our retreat.

"Where's Yuromo?" I ask.

"She'll meet us shortly," Jaden says.

Linked arm and arm, we keep moving until Dohlan is a fair distance at our back.

And then he's not.

Dohlan stands in front of us. He sneers at Jaden and Ry. Ry looks a tad out of sorts and doesn't appear to comprehend what is going on. He remains somewhat slack against my arm. But Jaden, he moves, his entire body shifting closer to Dohlan.

Dohlan slams his open palm into Jaden's chest causing him to shudder and stop. His face pinches and contorts.

"What are you doing to him?" I screech.

"All the times, the years, I visited with you, not once did I ever feed on you." His brows rise. "Have you ever considered that, my luv? I am what I am and all creatures... even monsters like me... need sustenance."

"Oh my Gaea! Are you feeding on him?" My head spins and my heart... my heart is deflating. I don't know what incubi do, but it can't be good, considering they are categorized as demons. I release my support of Ry and swing at Dohlan. Both fists slam into his hard, unmoving body.

A second later, I shiver and quiver and my body ignites with...

Oh my Gaea...

"He feels no pain. Look at him," Dohlan says. My head dips toward Jaden, and I regard him intently. "He's probably having the best experience of his entire life right now. Do you want to interrupt that?"

Jaden's features are slack, but internally, he is churning

with mental, physical, emotional delights. Delights shared with me through our connection. My breathing becomes labored, and a bead of sweat rolls down my temple. My deflated heart finds new life, bursting into a gallop. I gasp.

This is what it feels like to be fed upon by a dream incubus? Death by intoxicating false pleasure?

Dohlan's gloat shifts and narrows into scrutinizing consideration of me and my physical state. An animalistic snarl rumbles in his chest.

I slam my trembling fist into Dohlan a third, fourth, fifth time. And then his free palm presses against my waist, pushing me far enough back that I can no longer reach him. His gaze sweeps back and forth between Jaden and me.

"What is going on here?" he sneers.

"I don't know what you mean," I respond, voice shaking. His intense gaze narrows, glimpses over and evaluates me.

"You are a terrible liar." He peers at Ry, who fights for consciousness.

I silently pray Ry stays delirious until Dohlan disappears. If Ry becomes aware of Dohlan's nearness, he's likely to pick a fight, and Ry can't afford to get hurt more than he is already.

Dohlan sucks back a deep breath, releases it sharply, and snaps his attention back on me. "Think about what I said, Ana." His voice slithers over my skin like a snake.

My body goes rigid, aches with tension, and my heart ricochets within my ribcage. I refuse to respond, and yet I wonder which part of the many things he said I am meant to consider.

He moves forward until his face couldn't possibly be any closer without touching. He closes his eyes and inhales deep, taking a big whiff of me. He steps back.

"I now have his scent. I foresee pain in his future."

Whose scent? Jaden's or Garr's?

I decide he means Garr.

Dohlan's hand wraps around the back of my head, and he presses his forehead against mine. "Until next time."

He vanishes so fast I'm left wondering if he runs quicker than the eye can comprehend or if he is capable of appearing and disappearing like a magician.

Jaden lurches forward and gasps. A second later, he has regained his composure and is looking at me. "Did he hurt you?" he asks, his cheeks reddening.

"Has he ever?" I look to Ry. He's shaking his head as if trying to wake up. He stands a bit taller. Since Jaden and Ry were connected through their hold, I wonder if Dohlan's effect on Jaden spread to Ry, as well. That's something I need to investigate later.

Once again, I wrap my arm around Ry, just as Jaden strengthens his own hold, and we continue our forward motion. I'm not privy to our destination, so I let Jaden steer.

I lean forward, look past Ry. "Are you feeling alright?" I ask Jaden and think of all the sensations that rocked my body when Dohlan fed on Jaden. I can only guess as to what was happening in Jaden's incubus-induced dream, but I'm beyond curious to know if I was involved.

"I've been better," he says simply, without looking at me. "But I'm not the one we need to worry about."

I frown. I didn't expect Jaden to say he felt good. Only a few hours ago, he was practically unconscious with Gaea knows what. And I definitely want to know more about that, but right now I am curious about the affect Dohlan had on him. Dohlan said Jaden was probably having the best experience of his life. Does Dohlan's touch induce an experience or pull forth an already existing experience? Does Dohlan syphon energy, emotions, memories, what?

"I got really worried when Dohlan started feeding off of you," I say, trying a different tactic to gather information.

Jaden's eyes grow wide and then narrow, his face flushing with heat. "That explains a lot."

"Explains what?" I prompt.

He sighs. "You really want to talk about this now?"

"I do." I look straight ahead. Not at him. I was privy to the sensations, not the full experience, but the feelings alone are enough for me to understand I am tromping into personal territory.

"Do you know anything about succubi or incubi?"

My voice is weak, so I shake my head in response. I suspect I already know the answer to my question, and yet, my uncertainty causes me to press on.

"Well... he definitely took energy from me, and in my weakened state, I had little to spare." I open my mouth to say something, but he continues. "But, and I know this is the information you are digging for: in order to gain my compliance, he filled my head with pleasing ideas. Dreams, if you will. The kind of dreams a person doesn't want to wake from." He glances at me. "In my case, I'll leave it to your imagination to figure out what that might be."

My entire body flushes with a plethora of emotions gathered from both myself and Jaden. I chance a glance his direction and decide he's had far more practice at concealing his reactions.

"Did I really need to listen to that blather?" Ry says.

No one responds, and all conversation falls away into silence. I contemplate this new two-way exchange now existing between Jaden and myself. Being on the receiving end opens new avenues of understanding. The ability to feel the other's emotions is both a blessing and a curse woven tightly together.

The three of us move at a turtle's pace and hardly cover the distance of a trip around a school track when Mo, in female form, appears, approaching with haste. She is followed by Velsa, Belmiso, Timbers, and Clemens and has the Ivey City woman, Tegan, at her side. Tegan carries a carefully bundled satchel and large swath of fabric.

My posture stiffens at the site of the Treeite. My trust was given, albeit with trepidation, and that trust was betrayed.

Tegan stops several feet back from Mo and sets the satchel upon the ground. Waits.

Jaden leans across the front of Ry and catches my attention. "I asked her to come. I hope you don't mind." His lip twitches with uncertainty.

If Jaden asked her to come...

I straighten and study the woman. Like before, she is barefoot and wears nothing more than a sleeve of a dress in the color green. Her hair is down with no signs of clips or pins. I can't find a place on her person where a weapon could be concealed. At her feet is the satchel. If it holds any weapons, it is unlikely she can get to them before someone in our crew cuts her down.

I turn my scrutiny on the horses. They appear rested and well rubbed, for which I am grateful... and somewhat envious. I would have liked to have gotten more sleep. Any sleep, really.

The horses have also been fitted with odd looking saddles. Heavy blankets embroidered with ornate designs lay across the back of each horse. Above the blanket, a strange combination of carved wood and silk ties. It may not have the comfort of a conventional saddle, but I doubt any animal gave their life to make the strange looking seats.

Tied to the back of the saddles are inflated bags of supplies and what looks like thicker bed rolls than we've been using. All things to be thankful for.

Still, I hesitate to trust.

"My lady." Tegan steps forward, half bows, averts her eyes, and presents me with the fabric—a folded cloak. "My greatest apologies to you and your court." She peers up through her bangs, a timid expression upon her face. Her gaze darts between Jaden, Ry, and me. "For the trouble our sire has caused you. He spoke of you so often. We should have suspected. His species is lustful by nature, but he has his own entourage to care for his needs. Never before has he moved upon a guest. Never. Never ever. This event has caught us off guard and quite by surprise. Had we known he would be uncontrollably drawn to you, we would have taken more precautions."

"Lustful, you say? You're alright with this? You keep him as your leader even as he behaves so terribly?" I narrow my gaze upon her. She looks down and shifts her weight.

"He has managed many great feats for our people over the years. He is as old as the trees supporting our city. He knows many, many things. He is a gifted negotiator and has led our people through much strife to find peace and stability. Fulfilling his needs is a small price to pay," she says.

"It is a price that should not be required nor expected. You are worth more than the price he pays. I beseech you to rethink your leadership." I heave a heavy breath and turn away. I no longer want to talk about anything that makes me think of *him*. Whatever *he* is. I still don't know.

"Let's move," Ry says, pushing free of Jaden. "Thank you," he says to the Treeite, abruptly dismissing her with his tone and demeanor. He reaches into his jacket inside pocket and pulls free a dingy and crinkled paper, the map.

There's writing along the edge of the page, but I can't make out what it says. The note is marred with smears of blood. My heart slams into an erratic rhythm at the sight. After studying the scribbles for a millisecond, Ry folds the paper and flicks his finger, motioning Mo to approach. My brother slaps the folded map into her open palm.

Mo examines the map in her hand. Her thumb rubs over the texture of the paper, and she turns the page until the scribbles are right side up and easier to read. Her brow pinches, and she looks up at Ry.

"The choice is up to you." Ry glances around at all of us in turn. Me, Jaden, Mo. "We can continue on track and get you to the Palinot Woodlands and the old mystic as soon as possible. Or, we can make tracks to the location I provided Mo. At that location..." He weakly points toward the note in Mo's hand. "Is someone who might, and I emphasize the word might, know an antidote for what ails me."

Silence falls over us and the surrounding woods. I am the first to shatter the quiet, clearing my throat and pulling all eyes in my direction.

"There really is no choice to be made here," I reply. "If there is even a sliver of a chance of healing you and getting you back on your feet again, we're going to take it."

I glance over at Jaden. "Are you up to the ride?"

"I am." He looks past me to Ry. "But I'm not the one you need to be worrying about right now. Of course, we can talk about that later." His eyes avert to Tegan, the Treeite. She lingers at Mo's side.

Got it. No talking in front of her.

"I have more for you," Tegan says, pulling at the satchel she'd set on the ground. She holds it out to Jaden. "I brought a few things to help with his wounds." She motions to Ry. "It's not much, but it is all we have to offer."

Jaden graciously accepts her offering, tossing the bag over his shoulder. He pulls back the flap and starts rummaging through the contents.

"Not now." Ry moves to Belmiso, makes motion to climb onto the horse's back. "We can look through the gifts later." He lurches, swinging his leg up and over, and a second later loses strength. He drops to the ground. Everyone but the Treeite woman rushes to his side.

We all help Ry stand in a web of hands reaching and lifting. He reacts by attempting to brush us away. When we have Ry stable, leaning against Belmiso's side, Mo pivots toward the woman and quickly dismisses her. Without a word, Tegan turns and leaves.

"I think we need to take a look at the wound," I say.

"No." Ry's response is sharp and unyielding. He turns and in a blur of motion, successfully mounts his horse. The toll of his action shows in the new strain upon his face. "Time's wasting," he says, and starts moving away from us.

Life around us, the chatter of bugs and birds in the trees, bushes, and ground cover, have fallen deathly silent as if they, too, sense the seriousness of the situation. Jaden, Mo, and I rush to our respective horses and follow.

I want to sleep, but drag my eyelids to an open, needing to keep watch over Ry and Jaden. Neither man is in peak form, and I worry for their safety. I don't know what is going on with Jaden, but I find it hard to believe he has magically healed to full capacity in mere hours. And Ry, he appears to be a breath away from death.

Clemens moves to my side, and Mo leans toward me, holding the blood-smeared paper between us. Scribbled upon the paper is a location more than an actual address. Hushman's Meadow at Hillside and Listless River. "This isn't exactly close, but if we keep moving and avoid stopping we can probably cover the distance in a little less than a day's ride."

I glance at Ry's back. He's hunched forward and sways to and fro with Belmiso's movement.

"Do you think he has it in him?" I motion to Ry with a mild torque of the head.

Mo follows my gaze, but it is Velsa who answers my question.

I think not.

As if her words are the trigger, Ry slips sideways and falls from the horse.

NINETEEN

Before Ryland's name can leave my lips, I am off my horse and running toward him. I drop beside my brother. A moment later, Jaden is there with the bag of medicine splayed open before us. He shifts through the bottles and bags with a trembling hand. My lips remain sealed as my gaze wanders back and forth between Jaden's hands and Ry's delirious expression. I may remain silent on the outside, but inside I am screaming, cursing the world for all that has happened and is happening to the people I love.

It would be *so* easy to let anger control me under these circumstances. It really would. But I've witnessed what anger can do to people. If you let negative emotions rule your core being then you can evolve into a bitter, hateful person. That's the kind of person I never want to become. I promised myself I would never allow negative emotions to define me. I'm not going to break that promise now. I guess avoidance of such a nature is a difficult and treacherous path.

A tear squeezes free from the corner of my eye, and I am

quick to wipe away all evidence of its existence. I drop beside Jaden and glance over the many bottles and bags of ointments and medications. "Which one?" I ask.

He smells one, tastes another. Mo kneels on the other side of Jaden and adds her fingers to the push and dig at the contents. She plucks one from the jumble, regards the small bottle, and then passes it to Jaden.

"Yes, I think you're correct," he says, shoving the bottle and another small satchel into his pocket. "Let's move him over there and make him as comfortable as possible." Jaden motions to a flat, shaded area at our right. "Ana, can you get..."

"Already on it." I jump to my feet and pull at the ties around Ry's bedroll. Odd, but at that moment of need, I sensed I knew what Jaden wanted before he spoke the words. It could simply be logic leading me in the situation. Probably was exactly that, logic. But what if...

I don't finish the thought. My mind and emotions are flooded with concern for Ry. As quick as I can, I yank the bedroll free and lay it out on a flat patch of ground. Jaden and Mo carry my brother over and set him gently upon the cushion.

Once again, I pull myself tight at Ryland's side. "I hate the feeling of helplessness dwelling inside of me. First Crystia, then Kaia, now Ry. What kind of anticipated savior am I if I can't even help save my own family?" Tears well at the black of my eyes, but I am too tired and too dehydrated to let them fall.

The others are focused on my brother and don't acknowledge my confidence crash. Mo lifts Ry's head, and Jaden slowly pours a dingy-colored liquid down my brother's throat. Ry makes no motion to stop them. He makes no movement at all. Only once have I seen him so debilitated, and, that time, Kaia promised me it was nothing more than a nightmare. But what if she was wrong? What if that nightmare I had of Ry lying in a dead-like state was a warning... or worse... a prophetic dream?

My heart slams against my spine and drops into my gut.

"I can't. I can't." The words are little more than a whisper on the night air. Jaden has his palms pressed to Ry's chest, and I'm not sure if Jaden is trying to heal him or glimpse his future or something else. He pulls away, sits back, and yanks the satchel from his pocket.

Watching Jaden with a keen eye, Mo responds by pulling Ry's shirt back to expose his abdomen.

I gasp.

The wound has festered, bubbling and crusting with ugly globs of gold, brown, green set upon a bruised and reddened skinscape.

Jaden produces a small wooden bowl and fills it with a splash of water from the canteen and some powdered contents of the satchel. While he mixes, creating a paste, Mo spills the remaining contents of the canteens over Ry's tortured skin, in an attempt to cleanse the area. Ry shows no reaction to the touch of liquid. That changes the moment Jaden's fingers smear the newly created concoction over the infection.

Ry's body jolts, lurches forward, and his holler cracks my eardrum. For a moment, all I hear is the thrum of blood thrashing and crashing in my head.

Tears slip from the corner of my eye.

With a firm grip, Mo holds Ry's arms, and I hold his legs, allowing Jaden to cover the damage. Before he can complete the task, Ry passes out. My chest collapses, and I wish whatever earthly powers I possess to heal him.

Nothing changes.

I blink and stare and wish and stare and still... nothing.

Jaden nudges me, and I jump, jerk toward him.

"Did you hear me?" he asks. I blink in response. Had Jaden been talking to me, fighting against the chaos in my mind?

"I agree," Mo adds, pulling my quizzical gaze to her. "Lord Ryland shouldn't move for a while. We allow him to rest. I also think you both need to rest. I'll keep watch over him while you sleep."

"No, I don't..."

Mo stifles the tail end of my comment with a shake her head. "No offense, but the consequences of this night are evident on your person. You need sleep. And Sire..." She shifts, addresses Jaden. "You may have managed to chase her poison from your system, but you are not yet right." Mo's eyes drop to Jaden's hands. "If you do not take care of yourself, you will no longer be of any use to yourself, much less, her."

My back wrenches upright. "Wait. What?" My gaze darts between them, ultimately pinning on Jaden. "What does she mean by *my* poison?"

Jaden holds my gaze for a millisecond before his entire body slouches with what I take as resignation. "The Treeite leader..."

"Garr?" I add.

"Yes. Him. He managed to slip something in your drink before the toast. He must have been fast. I didn't see him do it."

"I did," Mo adds. "It was a smart sleight of hand. He took

a sip of his drink and then craftly switched and handed the one he'd already sipped from to Miss Ana."

"What? How does that work?" So, he took a drink from my glass. Gross, yes, but poison?

"I didn't realize at the time what he was, or I would have understood the significance," Mo says with a shrug. I study her with a keen eye. Maybe she didn't know what was happening, but she must have found it odd that he handed me the glass he'd already sipped from. I exhale, push away the desire to vomit.

"Garr is a member of the Faun species," Jaden adds.

"What is that?" I quickly ask.

"He is half man and half goat." Jaden's eyes are trained on me. Their usual luster is dull and strained. I know he needs to sleep, and yet I can't stop, not until I fully understand what happened.

"That explains the horns and hooved feet." I bite my lip and nod my head as I put the pieces together.

"He also has a tail," Mo adds, her eyes squinted.

And he was all juiced up and horny, coming after me. I don't even want to think about how that would work.

Jaden takes my hand in his. "I'm so sorry I wasn't there."

"It's not your fault." My body relaxes. "I never what you to think it was your fault. Sounds like you did some pretty big saving for me, as it was."

He nods. "I could sense, and finally pinpoint, the poison moving through your system. There were tiny blue specs sparking in your irises."

That must have looked cool, I think.

"When he handed you the drink with traces of his saliva, as soon as you drank from the glass, the drug was in your system. It wouldn't have killed you. Being that he is a faun, what he wanted, well..." Jaden adverts his gaze and shifts his weight. Irritation and ire slide off him and slip over me. "He wanted you worked up and lustful."

"Gross!" My nose wrinkles. "That explains the buzzing. My entire body felt like it was alive with electricity. But how did you..." I gaze into his eyes and recall our night together. The only thing, the only way he could have... the kiss.

He nods, as if responding to my thought. "I pulled all traces of the drug from your system when we kissed."

"You two." Mo leans forward and waves her hand between us. "You two kissed?"

Neither one of us answers.

"It's about time," she says, then turns and walks away. Walks toward the horses. "Guess that lowers my chance of getting a kiss out of him." The comment is low, but it does not go unheard. Jaden and I both turn our heads her direction.

"That's the long and short of it," Jaden continues. I cleared your system and then processed the drug through mine. Now I think I need to get more sleep." He turns and makes his way toward Timbers. I follow.

"But how?" I ask. "How did you take the drug and 'process' it, as you say?" My hands wave in the air as if I am framing the word process. It sounds so mechanical, unfit for the circumstances.

"I don't pretend to understand how it all works," he says, pulling his pack and bedroll free. "I only know that's one of the things I am able to do for you. I heal your state when you are in need. I saw a need last night, so I pulled the foreign substance from your body and made you well again." He unties a bag from the front of Timbers' saddle, steps over to

Mo, and hands her the bag. "Can I trust you to hang these around Ana's sleeping location tonight?"

"Of course." She takes the bag looking almost insulted by his question. With the transfer of the canvas bag, so has the responsibility of blocking Dohlan from my dreams been reassigned. But I'm healthy enough and fully capable so there's no real need for Mo.

I watch Jaden walk away once more, and again I pursue. "But how?" I repeat.

He drops his bedroll, lays it out, then straightens and looks at me. "Through the kiss itself." His expression is one of bewilderment. As if he thought I should already understand based on what I've already been told. Not during the kiss but through the kiss. Maybe I did understand. In fact, I'm sure I understood, but I wanted to hear him say the words.

I regard him, his answer, and my need for the spoken words, fully aware of the conflict pressing into my features. "So..." My hand rises before me, as if it can help me find the words I seek. "When you kissed me, you were kissing me to heal me."

"Yes," he says, eyes narrowed. My heart plummets into a cavern of crystalized tears, and the anchor line strains against my chest, pulling it stiff and taut. A second later, his expression opens. "No." His hand flares between us, like he means to stop the conversation, or maybe back it up somehow. "I wanted to kiss you. Believe me, I did." He moves closer, folding the space between us. "But I needed to heal you." He takes my hand in his. "Understand?"

I nod my head, three times quick. I understand, I do. I simply wish there had been only want in our kiss and no other objectives.

"You should get as much sleep as you can," he says. "We are all in need of rest, and I have a feeling tomorrow will be a rough day."

"Oh, I know. But..."

Mo's hand wraps over mine and, with a gentle tug, turns my attention to her. She shakes her head telling me not to pursue. "There will be time for your questions later." She looks to Jaden. "Right now, Sir Jaden needs rest."

"Who made you the group leader?" I snap. She winces and jerks backward. A lump lodges in my throat, and my stomach hardens. I shouldn't have reacted that way. It was completely callous of me. My shoulders and head droop. "I'm sorry." I wave my hand in appeasement.

Jaden watches on but allows me to fight my own battle and smooth my own error.

"Yeah, yeah," Mo says, waving her hand at me and looking completely irritated. "Just leave him alone so that he can rest. Lord Ry and Sir Jaden need to heal. Everyone needs rest. We all must be at our best possible health come sunrise. We have a long journey ahead." She walks away. Grabs the other two packs from the horses.

Jaden laughs. I spin around to face him. "I guess she's no longer intimidated by who and what you are," he says.

"You think?" I glance over my shoulder at Mo. "It's kind of refreshing."

"Ana." His hands slip around my waist and tug me closer. My head snaps back around, and I gaze into his eyes with hungry curiosity. "I'm sorry if you feel our kiss was tainted. Maybe you'll be willing to let me make it up to you sometime in the near future."

My bottom lip slowly drops, but I can't seem to manage

to thrust a single word free. *How about now*, I think. This moment is good. Kiss me. Kiss me, Jaden.

He leans into me, and his lips brush against mine, tender and sincere. They tease me, making me want for more.

"Goodnight," he says, leaning his forehead against mine.

"Goodnight." My voice is as quiet as a mouse. I cling to his hand as he pulls away. Slowly, reluctantly, I let him go. With a sigh, I walk away. Move toward my own bedroll that Mo so graciously laid out for me.

Mo sits on her own bedroll, laid out next to my brother. She sits straight with her arms wrapped around her folded legs. Her gaze is one of concern and determination.

"Ry, is he—" I ask, coming to stand next to him. Even in his sleep he sweats and looks anything other than peaceful.

"The medicine needs time. We shouldn't move him. Not yet, anyway," Mo says, clearly becoming rather comfortable with cutting me off mid-sentence. "What we gave him will not heal him, but it should slow his system and put him in a type of static state, giving us more time to get him the help he needs."

A deep breath meant to calm my system rattles through me, shaking my resolve. I clutch at sanity and suspect I am barely hanging on. "Is there a cure?"

"None known." She unfolds the map Ry entrusted to her. The one smeared with Ry's blood. "But it's possible that there is someone who knows more than we do."

Someone with more knowledge than the mystic we are seeking? Or just someone closer and easier to reach? It's not a question I expect Mo to answer. Like so many of my questions, this too will have to wait. I sigh, a sign of resignation.

"If we are to rest here for a few hours, then you need rest, as well," I say to Mo. "And after what happened tonight, I don't think Dohlan will bother me in my dreams. Not right now, anyway."

"One can never be too careful," she says softly and discreetly holds up Dohlan's ring between us. My mouth pops open.

"How? Where?" I trip on my words. Last I recalled, I'd slipped the ring into my pants pocket. The pants I left in a pile on the bathroom floor of my temporary prison palace.

"Tegan gave it to me when I gathered our supplies for departure. I think you should take better care not to lose this. At least, not until you understand its relevance." She slips the ring into my palm and closes my hand tightly around the tiny circle of gold. "She also gave me that piece of rock you took from Jaden. I put it with our stuff."

Right. The rock and the ring. I study my closed fist. "I'm doing such a horrible job at this Balance Bringer thing."

"No, you're not." She reaches forward and lays her splayed palm on top of my closed fist. "This has been a huge adjustment for you. You are doing quite fine. You've merely had a lot of logs to jump."

Guessing she means hurtles, I grant her a ghost of a smile, grab the end of my bedroll and drag it toward Ry, where I situate it at his side, opposite Mo.

"Is this where you intend to sleep?" she asks. I nod and sit down with my legs crossed. She jumps up and proceeds to get busy looking for places to hang the enigma loops. I move to help her.

"Sleep," she orders with a sharp point to my makeshift bed.

I frown. Mo really has gotten comfortable around me if she has taken to bossing me around. *I'm so happy she has chosen to step into Ry's boots while he is down for the count,* I think sarcastically.

I glance over at Jaden, making a visual check of his safety. He has collapsed into a coma on top of his bed. I smile at the sight but sense a grey cloud forming in my chest. I turn back, curl in on my side, and face my brother. He breathes heavy and steadily. My hand finds his arm, rests there, giving me a mild sense of reassurance that I will immediately notice any change in his status.

I unfurl my fingers and study the gold ring in my palm. The white nightgown I wear lacks pockets in which to hold the curious jewel. On my finger is the safest place I can think of, so I slip it into place on my right hand.

The ring, the one thing I didn't care to get back, is now in my possession. But what of my pictures of Crystia—Crystia with Caesar, and the one of Crystia, Ry, and myself? I placed them upon the nightstand so that they could watch over me through the night. And now look at what has happened? They are likely gone forever. I never should have taken them from the safety of Jaden's backpack.

Sleep does not come easy, but it does eventually find me, and it kicks me around in a restless state until morning arrives. I awake before the sun has managed to drag its body from the dregs of slumber. A mere shimmer of light works its way through the trees. Barely enough illumination to high-light the shiny square of chocolate waiting for me. *Someone* carefully placed it in the top corner of my bedroll, inches outside of my toss and turn zone.

Beyond the chocolate lies Ry. The sheen has been wiped from his face, and his breaths are soft and steady. He's a genderbent sleeping beauty, and if he weren't my brother, I would be tempted to kiss him to see if he would awaken. In

Hiddenkel, I wouldn't put fairy-tale outcomes beyond the realm of possibility.

"Good, you're awake." Jaden sounds like his normal, healthy self, and I abruptly swing around to verify his state with my own eyes.

His smile radiates with the light of a thousand and one suns and not only warms my heart but sets it on fire. I want to run to him, crush him in my embrace and verify his vitality with the strum of his blood, the rise and fall of his chest, and the goosebumps caused across my skin by his breath. And then, I want to cover him in kisses of elation.

But I don't.

Instead, my eyes widen, my breath lodges in my throat, and my butt remains planted to my bedroll like I've rooted in place.

"We should get moving," Mo says. I don't allow her to sway my attention from Jaden.

He points to the side of my bedroll closest to him. "I left you a change of clothing." I take notice of the backpack sitting beside me with a flash of a glance. "Why don't you get ready? We'll soon be needing your help."

One small phrase and my mood instantly deflates. A deep sigh rises and releases within me, my shoulders fall, chest collapses, and I turn, gaze upon Ry. I lay a kiss upon his forehead with the touch of my hand. "May God and Gaea watch over you in my absence," I whisper at his ear. Seconds later, I am disappearing into the tree cover, Jaden's magical backpack in one hand and the chocolate fortune in the other.

If ever I was in need of a lift, now would probably be the time. I unfold the foil before bothering to change. The need to be swift is essential. But so is my state of mind... essential.

My uncontrollable worry for the guys I now consider family could lead us down the wrong road if I can't stay focused.

I pop the chocolate in my mouth and flatten the shiny message. "Always follow your heart—it's never wrong." I nod and release the conflict in my mind. The conflict no longer exists. Saving Ry is the only mission that presently matters.

When I return, I am relatively clean and dressed appropriately for me, pants and boots instead of a gown. And... Dohlan's ring stored safely in a pocket instead of on my finger. After the incident with Garr, I would have preferred a shower or bath, but our present location doesn't offer up the option.

I help Jaden and Mo lift and secure my brother on top of Belmiso, and we get underway following the map to our next destination. Mo now leads our pack.

The travel is torturous in its length, and the view, which is likely sprinkled with many curious wonders, is lost under the chaotic blur of fear. Fear that we won't get to the desired location in time. Fear that timing won't matter because there is nothing that can be done. Fear that my brother will die.

My vision is clouded by the tears of frustration and despair. Tears that I keep blinking away, time and time again. I fight the desire to push Velsa at a run so that we may get wherever it is we are going all the faster. But a push would only tax Velsa and her team, possibly putting us at a deeper disadvantage. To remain calm, I focus on steady breaths and keep tabs on the shrinking and expanding shadows as the sun moves in an arc above.

As Mo promised, our journey is a full day's ride and lands us in an unoccupied stretch of grassy hills and deep-set meadows. There's nothing and no one in sight or ear shot. But that fact doesn't push confidence from Mo's features.

She studies Ry's scribbles along the edge of the map and continues to lead our weary and wounded caravan over hills, across arcing meadows or valleys, and around bends and folds in the landscape. It's along one of these bends that she brings Clemens to a halt. The night is bright with the crescent moon sitting high in the darkened sky, and there is nothing of obvious significance to warrant a pause in our progress.

"We have arrived," she says.

Arrived at what, I wonder. There is nothing in view beyond the surrounding grass and trees and lumpy hillsides. Are we waiting for a gopher to pop out of his hole and show us the way? Or a caterpillar on an overly large mushroom to talk to us, give us a magical cure?

Jaden points, directing my gaze.

Silly me for thinking of such things. Of course, it's not a gopher or caterpillar we seek. We have come here to find help from hobbits. In the side of the hill is a small door set against a dirt mound covered in long grass. The door is partially hidden by the overgrown grass drooping over the side of the hill.

Long-legged tree people or short hobbit people, I don't care, as long as they can heal my brother.

Mo is already off her horse and knocking on the small green and brown door. I suspect the color choice is meant to camouflage and make the door blend in with the surrounding land. She knocks, first softly, then with a thundering pound. There is no answer.

All this way to save my brother and no one here. No one to even peer out at window at us and wonder who we are.

At the thought, my gaze wanders to the side and upward, in search of anything hinting to a window or lookout. I think

I spot one, possibly two, higher up in the side of the hill, and above the hill, sprouts a large tree—more than large enough to hide a person within its bark. But whether the spot spied in the tree side is a knothole or scout hole, I can't say, and I detect no one peering back at me.

I jump off Velsa and move closer to the door... and Mo. Only silence teases us from the other side of the barrier. The spaces above that I suspect to be windows are all dark. No light shines from within. Either no one is home or they are hiding, hoping we will go away.

A thump, the sound of Jaden dismounting, strikes behind me, but instead of approaching, his foot falls move away. I turn, curious of his actions, He is descending into the field directly across from the small home in the mound. The field is thick with tall, heavily spikelet laden, yellow and lime grass.

He moves five feet, then ten feet away, maybe a tad more. The long grass hiding his lower body from view starts to move. Not in a sway in the wind kind of way, but in a deliberate path weaving away from him. He lurches and grabs. When he stands and turns back toward us, he's holding a small girl by the arm. She looks to be my age, with fair skin and long, tawny hair.

The feisty girl wiggles and tugs against Jaden's hold. His lips are moving, and I know he's trying to calm her, but she apparently won't listen. Her unrestrained arm lifts into the air, a large wicker basket in her hand. Fluffs and shreds of yellow and green, bleached by the moonlight, spill free, and she slams the basket on top of Jaden's head.

He bows with the shock, and the girl manages to squirm free. She starts running in the opposite direction.

"Hey, wait!" I scream at her back.

Her steps fumble to a stop, and she turns, looks straight at me. "Ana?"

My mouth drops. I'm immediately stupefied. I've been recognized as the Balance Bringer, but not as myself, with my given name. Not in this place. "Um... yeah," I say. "How did you..."

My words drop flat to the ground.

Her eyes are no longer upon me. Her gaze is searching, scrutinizing our tiny clan. A half breath later, the how jumps from her lips as she dashes toward Ry, calling his name. The sharp edges of her voice slipping toward panic.

TWENTY

"What happened," she asks, with heavy breath. She covered the distance from the field to us in the span of two blinks. She now stands beside Belmiso and stretches upward toward Ry's white, clammy face. She's such a petite thing, that she needs to press onto her tiptoes to brush the edge of Ry's chin. "I'm here now," she whispers. "Whatever the problem, I'll find the answer. I'll fix you."

My head buzzes with questions and concerns and suspicions. So many thoughts; they crowd my brain in a fuzzy chatter. But the loudest question of them all... who is this girl, and what is her relation to my brother?

I stand, silent and stupid, watching as Jaden informs her of my brother's condition. Everything he says is garbled, sounding like we're twenty feet beneath the surface of a lake. I'm trapped underwater without any water affinity. Strangely, the word distortion clears as soon as he speaks of the weapon used to impale my brother. When Jaden tells her the blade was forged in the Fires of Guardoone, her eyes widen and dread settles over features that were previously clouded with panic and fear.

Ry asked to be brought here. With what little strength he had left at the time, he entrusted Mo with the information that led us to this location. I don't know where I thought we would end up, maybe at some sort of hospital or at the home of a magical healer, but not in front of some hidden hermit hole, bearing witness to a young maiden girl who looks like she should be attending school with me.

"Help me get him inside," she says.

My senses snap sharply to attention. Moving closer, close enough to tackle her, should the need arise, I yank her arm and spin her to face me. "I'm sorry," I say. "Who are you?"

Confusion flashes across her face. The feeling is mutual, and I want the confusion cleared immediately.

"Apologies." She presses a gloved palm to the side of her face, as if holding a wall against a flood of emotions. "I assumed he would have told you by now." She flashes a concerned gaze over Ry. Mo and Jaden have lowered him off the horse. She breathes deep, straightens her gown, and pins her gaze upon me. "My name is Zarah of house Chronos. Ryland is my betrothed."

I suck back a breath. It instantly lodges in my throat.

Zarah's shoulders relax, and she grants me the weakest of smiles. "Honestly, Ana, I look forward to getting to know you personally." She glances nervously toward Ry again. "After we see to his needs." She doesn't wait for my reply. She turns, opens the front door of her camouflaged home, and motions for the gang to follow her inside.

All four of them disappear through the doorway, and I am left alone out front, standing with the horses. I bite my lip and study the surroundings.

"You should follow." Velsa nudges her nose into my side.

She's right, I should follow, but for some reason my feet won't unstick themselves from the ground. Has shock turned me into stone? All our time together and never once did Ry mentioned being engaged. Why would he hide that from me?

Don't judge. Don't judge. Don't judge.

This is Ryland. If he didn't tell me about the girl or their engagement, he had a good reason to keep it a secret. The imaginary roots holding the soles of my shoes retract, and I hurry into the house, hurry after my family.

From the outside, the house is barely visible. One has to be looking for the signs in order to see them. A door and two windows cut in natural lines, recessed in a wall of ground-cover, and hiding in the overgrowth of plant life. A hollowed-out tree atop the bluff makes for the ideal lookout tower. And once seen, the little habitat can't be unseen.

The place is a thing of stories and fairytales, and here I stand inside the doorway. The tawny-haired girl didn't impress me as the brooding type, and so I expect the interior to be cozy, despite being dark and cramped.

The entry inside the front door is modest with an immediate opening to my left and a wide curving staircase to my right. The walls are without corners, enclosing the space in a wide arc. Set into the wall straight ahead is a small door, shorter than me, that I suspect hides a closet. Beside the door, a meager table, upon which sits an apple-filled basket, not unlike the one the girl was holding when first spotted.

The place is quiet, providing no clue as to which direction everyone went.

The opening on my left hosts a simple but wide door. It sits slightly ajar, allowing only a hint of light to spill onto the floor at my feet. I push the door open, and my mind fails to make sense of the configuration of shadow and moonlight at play within. Running the distance from the far end to my feet is a line of light. It's a stretched beam of moonlight.

I expected dark, camped, yet cozy. The moonlight notwithstanding, the space is dark, definitely. Cozy, I can't quite tell... because it is dark. But cramped, I'm thinking not. In truth, it appears incredibly deep and wider than I ever expected based on the small hobbit styled door set in the hillside. I should know by now, appearances can be deceiving, especially in this crazy, nonsensical world of Hiddenkel.

A thump, followed by muffled voices from above, causes me to abandon the vacant room in favor of the stairs. My climb is swift, and my reward, the delightful aroma of jasmine and honeysuckle. I am standing in a spacious bedroom. Beside me is a wide and comfortable looking lounge area, littered with pillows and books. A large bed covered in a vibrant quilt, and shaggy throw sits in the center of the room. Clusters of narrow lamps hang at all four corners.

The far wall is a collage of niches, filled with jars and boxes and decorative items. Floor-to-ceiling windows, spilling with moonlight are set into the wall on either side. A staircase winds around one side of the room and disappears into the ceiling. Into the tree above, I presume. Mid- climb there is a small window nook. The window is partially open, and the sound of falling water spills into the cozy space. On the opposite side of the room from the stairs, a partially screened bathroom alcove. A small waterfall runs down the wall, splinters at a protruding rock, and drops into two different stone basins. One basin is large enough to serve as a bathtub and the other, a sink.

Ry has been placed on the bed, and Zarah appears to have put everyone to work. Jaden stands at the sink, ringing out rags, and Mo is setting fire to a powdery substance in an iron bowl. Zarah sits at Ry's side, her fingers resting at his temples. Her discarded gloves tossed to the corner of the bed.

I blink and take a step closer. A distortion runs over her skin, moving from her fingers, up her arms, to her shoulders.

"He has only lasted this long because he has her blood running in his veins," Zarah says.

Both Jaden and Mo glance at me.

My blood? As in Balance Bringer blood?

"He needs something more, though." Zarah glances around the room, her search falling upon Jaden. "You are her Tracer, are you not?" She waves him over before he can answer. For the brief moment, when she isn't touching Ry, the distortion across her skin ceases. When Jaden is close enough, she grabs his arm and closes her eyes. The second she touches him, the oddity resumes. It's perplexing.

My breathing is labored, and my heart heavy as I count the seconds of silence in the room. At the count of six, Zarah releases Jaden and glances over him.

"Oh honey," she says. "We need to fix you, too. I'm sorry, you just won't do in this condition." She pats the top of his hand, and I am reminded of a doctor delivering bad news. Her gaze shifts between Jaden, Mo, and myself. "How have you all made it this far?"

Dohlan's words replay in my head. *I could have [killed you] a thousand times over already. Since your arrival, you have made yourself easy pickings.* My heart bleeds at the mere thought of losing either Ry or Jaden. I can't. I won't.

"If there is a way to save him..." Zarah sighs and returns her gaze to my brother. A millisecond later, her head snaps up, and she pins a stare on me. "The secret is likely in your DNA."

What? I mean to ask the question, but no sound travels over my lips. I stand, gawk at the wavy-haired girl like it's the first time I've ever seen a redhead. Like I expect her head to burst into flames at any moment.

Zarah chews on her thumbnail and continues to study me, hope building and swirling behind her eyes. She waves me forward and I comply. Like she did with Jaden, she takes my hand. This time, I not only witness the distortion moving across her skin, I experience the sensation of information being yanked from me. Tiny, unreadable words and symbols rushing from me and over her in a flutter or quiver of her skin.

"What are you?" I ask.

She shushes me.

Unlike Jaden, she doesn't release me after a moment, or even five. She holds my hand until the minutes are way past awkward. I want to pull away, but suspect that whatever she is doing, she does for my brother, so I stay and wait... shifting uncomfortably.

With a tiny shiver, Zarah gasps, and her eyes pop open, but still, she doesn't release me. Her eyes are wide, and I'm suddenly nervous that she is aware of something regarding me that I possibly don't want to know. "What are you?" I ask again, fearing Zarah is some kind of clairvoyant who has just witnessed my death or worse.

"I am a chronicler," she answers rather simply, as if the

term should open a world of understanding within me. It does not.

"Wow," Mo says in a low and awestruck voice.

I glance at Jaden for clarification, but he is wringing his hands and muses into the empty space in front of him. My heart double taps. Zarah said he wouldn't do, was in need of fixing, too. What did she mean by that?

"Chroniclers were created at the beginning of time by the Elven Queen," she says. My attention swings from Jaden back to her. "We are few, but we are strong in our gift. We record the passage of time and all history encompassed within."

"How does that work, exactly?"

She smiles, but it fails to reach her eyes. "History is recorded in the DNA of all things touched by circumstance and change. The grass records the changing of the seasons or a traveler crossing its path. A lizard records the death of a fly or a near miss with a cartwheel. You record everything you have ever done or seen."

My lips pull tight at the edges, and my brow pinches.

"Yes." She nods her head. "When I touch you, I see it all. Everything in your past, anyway. But don't worry. I have seen everything you can possibly think of and then some. I let the information wash over me, and once it is recorded in the Urn of All, I let the information go. No reason to hold on to events and facts if it's going to make things awkward between us. Wouldn't you agree?"

"Um... sure." My answer is less than solid. "But I don't understand how looking at my history will help Ry's current condition."

"I had heard and read through the Chronicles of the All that the Balance Bringer is the same soul, reborn time and time again. If that is the case, then the history of each Balance Bringer, since the earliest start, should be coded within you. Stored and locked away inside here..." She taps the side of my skull. "...until you are ready to release and acknowledge the information."

My mind immediately returns to the ancient and feral thing that crawl up from the depth of my core the other night when Garr came into my room. My mouth pops open. Somewhere behind me, someone sucks back a breath. Mo. She's traveling the room with her bowl of burning red powder.

"It's quite the concept to wrap your thoughts around, I know," she continues. "But it would seem there is a lot left to be understood about who and what you are."

"What is that supposed to mean?" My body stiffens.

Zarah bolts off the bed and takes a step away. "Nothing really." She turns and hurries toward the niches in the far wall, grabs a bowl and moves to the table in the corner. "I'm going to need some of your blood."

"What?" I jerk. "Why?" The fact that she has left me hanging with a billion questions makes my head sway and pound.

Or maybe the stifling aroma is to blame.

Mo fans the plumes of stinky smoke out to the corners of the room. All the windows but the one far above are closed, trapping the suffocating fragrance in the suddenly tight space. I want to claw my way out and gulp a deep breath of fresh air.

"Your blood likely holds the cure," Zarah says.

I shiver. "Because it's Balance Bringer blood?"

"Yes. And because you are a gift from the gods."

I gape at her, unblinking. No one has ever called me a gift from the gods before. At least, not that I can recall. The thought of me being godly gifted stirs a seriously confusing emotion. I don't perceive myself as a gift or anything special, for that matter. What if I am a test for everyone around me? Or worse yet, a bad penny? Maybe that was a demon voice that spoke through me back in Ivey City.

Zarah holds the empty bowl in one hand and a small paring knife in the other. She means to cut and bleed me.

"You said Ry has my blood running through his system already. If it hasn't cured him at this point, what good will more blood do?"

"He has traces of your blood," she corrects. "It is not pure. What you have to offer is pure. I think I have found something in the older chronicles that might help."

Pure. I want to scoff at the word. My blood runs with mistakes and regrets and little much more. There is nothing pure and magical in that. But I don't speak my thoughts out loud. After all, I can manipulate water and maybe there *is* something within that affinity that is helpful. Something to save Ryland.

"I didn't see you check any chronicle or book," I counter.

"It was all in here." She taps the side of her head and then motions to reference me, as in my memories and biological makeup. Her consideration of me is sharp and unwavering.

"What are you doing? Are you still tapped into my genetic makeup or something?" I wave my hand in silent reference to her watchful eye and think mode. My brow pinches and my forehead crinkles to the sensation of an oncoming headache.

She laughs. "It doesn't work like that. I can't access your genetic makeup or anything so profound. I was merely probing the historical data collected throughout the centuries. I was searching for a solution once known but long since forgotten."

"You can do that?" I balk. "You can close your eyes and access all of history like some kind of electronic encyclopedia or Wiki?"

Zarah's lips draw straight. She blinks, and blinks and blinks. "Oh yes," she finally blurts, a smile pulling at her face. "Encyclopedia or Wiki, very otherworld terms. But, yes. I can access all the data ever collected by a chronicler, from any age. The information we collect is siphoned and stored in the elven Urn of All. Any chronicler can access the information stored within."

"Like a librarian?"

Again, she blinks. Then smiles. "Yes, that's rather similar."

Um... okay. This is so Neo and the Matrix weird. I glance at Jaden, and I am again reminded of Zarah's words... *you just won't do in this condition.*

"Would you be willing to give me a small portion of your blood?" Zarah asks, lifting the bowl and knife ever so slightly to emphasize her request.

I heave a deep breath. "You're ready for it right now? Don't you need to collect other ingredients for a potion or something?"

"No." She shakes her head and muses at nothing, again. "No. I don't believe I do... need anything more," she says. "You were created to be the worlds' cure."

My gut hardens. No pressure there in those last words of hers. My body now feels as if it is made of led. "Okay then," I say. If it will save my brother, I don't care if she drains me. I stretch my arm out as an invitation to do what she will.

"Are you sure?" Her eyes move over my facial features

with a sense of weariness. "I don't want to damage any trust between us."

I choke back the impulse to laugh. "We just met," I say. "We have yet to establish any trust. Therefore, there is nothing to be damaged or broken." *Except you, if you hurt my brother even more than his current ailing state*, I mentally add.

She nods once. "I'm sorry. It's just that I feel like I know you so well, having watched you grow up through Ryland's eyes. I sometimes forget that the experience is so very one sided."

I don't know how to respond. Her admission seems so personal. But then, if she is truly betrothed to my brother, I guess the two of them would be rather well acquainted. Instead of speaking, I present my arm to her, once more. I'm actually curious and anxious to see if my blood can cure him. "What do you need to do? Prick my finger? Cut my artery?"

Her eyes widen, and her body stiffens. "Oh, great Gradnar, nothing so severe. I wouldn't want you to bleed out in my bedroom." Her fingers firmly clamp over my hand. "This is all I need."

She quickly slices my skin on the side below my pinky. She has me make a fist and together, we watch the blood drip from the edge of my hand into the bowl. After a few minutes, she nods and steps away. Jaden steps up and presses a wet rag to my cut.

"Thank you," Zarah says, not looking my way. Ry now owns all her attention. She hovers at his side, whispering words in a language I don't understand.

"Come sit down," Jaden says.

I let him lead me to the comfy looking lounge area beneath the window. I take a seat and he settles in beside me, but my attention is elsewhere. I continue to keep a close watch on Ry and Zarah.

"It's all gone," Mo says with a yawn, lifting her stinky bowl in the air. The smoke no longer rises from the vessel.

"That's fine," Zarah says. She is swirling two fingers in my blood. Tiny white dots slip over her skin, down into the bowl. "It has served its purpose. Ryland is preserved in the moment."

"What does that mean?" I blurt, lurching forward in my seat.

Zarah turns toward me. "It means, we have frozen him in time and stopped the poison from spreading."

"I thought we already did that?" I counter. "Isn't that why we smeared that funky stuff on the wound?" My gaze shifts between Jaden and Mo. Jaden opens his mouth to answer but is cut off by Zarah's response.

"You curbed the process, caused the poison to move much slower than it would have organically." She blinks and looks between each of us in turn. "Thank goodness you did, or Ryland may not have made it this far. What we have done now, has paused the process completely. We haven't cured him... yet... but the poison will not spread any further."

"How did *we* pause the process?" I ask. "We didn't do anything."

"Your friend here did." She motions to Mo. "She burned the *everroot* and because my beloved..." She lays her hands upon Ryland and gazes at him tenderly. "inhaled its magical fumes, he will now be held in the suspended state for a full solar day, giving us time to act."

The problem with her statement is horrifically clear. Not only did Ry inhale the fumes, but so did we. How can we work to heal him if we all drop into a coma for a day?

"Let us work quickly before you all nod off," She continues and motions to Mo.

Mo covers her mouth, hiding a yawn. I glance at Jaden. He too is yawning. Everyone looks ready to drop. So why don't I feel it? Or maybe I do, in the drag and strain of my muscles.

"Would you mind grabbing the following," Zarah says to Mo, then starts rattling off different herbs she has stored in the various niches in the wall. She calls for caraway and comfrey, allspice and ginger, and a few other herbs with which I am unfamiliar.

Mo grabs each one quickly and, under her verbal guidance, tosses a pinch of each into a new, unused bowl.

"What we do now, is for your Tracer," she says, addressing me. Although, she does not look at me. She is focused on her fingers and my blood in the bowl. Her fingers rise from the bowl, drift to the space above Ry's wound, and hover. My eyes avert to Ry, taking in the depths of his state. He looks to be already dead. I want to scream.

My blood drops from her fingertips, land upon my brother's skin with a loud plop. It's completely unreal. It's like a drop of paint falling upon a still body of water, sending ripples cascading outwards. Only, these ripples cannot be seen, only felt and heard. The shock shifts through me, rattling my emotions.

When the air settles, a sound similar to static reaches my ears. I examine Ry, curious to know if he is the source of the new noise.

"Burn it," Zarah says to Mo. "And have him hold it near his chin, inhaling the smoke."

I blink and watch Mo comply.

Ryland borders death and Jaden... What is wrong with

Jaden? I find my voice again and ask the question. Jaden's hand drops over mine, as if he doesn't want me to hear the answer... or even ask the question. I won't let that stop me. I need to know. Everyone connected to me is in danger, and I suspect that somehow it is all my fault.

"Your Tracer has a parasite," Zarah says.

Another drop of blood. Another wave and, this time, I rock backward. A second later, I right myself... hear the faintest zings and zaps, like that of electricity. Something is happening to Ry. Something otherworldly. But I must, I must maintain my focus.

"A parasite?" My voice hitches.

"Yes," she says with a sigh. "And it has been with him an extremely long time. Lifetimes, I'm afraid."

The word *lifetimes* lingers on my thoughts, dipping in and out of the recesses of my mind. Lifetimes. Jaden has been with me for lifetimes. She has basically confirmed that fact. Not just any Tracer and Balance Bringer, but Jaden and me. Forever locked in eternity. He was my chosen. The one I kept coming back to time and time again. The one I keep coming back to this time, too. I am beginning to understand my intense, unexplained need for him.

But... he is unwell. He has a parasite. What does that mean? Like a leech or a tapeworm? Is it magical in origin? I need to know what it means and how I can extract it.

"I see the worry on your face," she says, pulling me from my uneasy state. "But I don't want you to be troubled. The gods have always smiled upon you. If what we do here today doesn't work, I have faith that something more suitable will come our way."

Maybe, I think. But if the gods really smiled on me, why

would they allow my Tracer to be infected and stay infected for multiple lifetimes?

Another question I don't vocalize.

"I wanted to tell you when I discovered the problem," Jaden says, and I torque my head to better see him. "But there were always so many Treeites around, or we were dealing with something more concerning."

"What are you talking about?" My brow pinching into my view.

"When we arrived at the Ivey City... actually, even before that. Right before that. I felt like someone was taking control of my body, choosing my actions, my words. I was trapped, unable to say or do anything to warn you of the situation." His chest heaves. "I was completely inadequate and unworthy as your Tracer."

I think about the crazy way he acted when we first met Garr and his flock of Treeite people. Now it all makes sense. Something or someone else was sitting in the driver's seat of Jaden's mind.

I lean into him, resting my head upon his shoulder. "I'm so sorry I didn't see it. If I have this same gift as you, I should have known. I should have been able to do something."

He reaches over and rubs his hand along my temple, weaving in and out of my hair. "It's alright. I want you to stop blaming yourself for things you have no control over. What could you have possibly done had you known?"

I gaze across the room and, despite the weighty subject, sense the space and moment owns a dreamy quality that has managed to enfold us all. I sit up, backbone straight, and study a sword hung high on the wall. A wicked and crafty smile pulls at one side of my mouth. "I could have pummeled the source of your issue." I raise a fisted hand. "And if I couldn't do that, I would have swept you off to someplace far, far away," I say with a somewhat dazed voice.

A heaviness washes over me, and I blink hard to stay alert. I catch Zarah glancing to my side. Jaden has collapsed, chest down, with his face at the edge of the sofa. Mo has also collapsed and is curled into a ball on the floor. Before she apparently passed out, she managed set the bowl of burning herbs at the base of the sofa. The fumes waft upward for Jaden to breath.

"They were both in need of serious rest. As are you." The hint of a sad smile tugs at Zarah's face. "You should sleep, while you can. There's no telling what the days ahead have in store for you."

A low bark of a laugh escapes my lips. It's uncontrolled and unexpected. My palm flies to my lips, and I blink again, several times. The ability to concentrate becomes more difficult with each passing breath.

What's wrong with me?

"Don't fight it," she says. "Let it happen." She looks away.

Let it happen, she says. But I can't let it happen. I don't know her. I don't know that I can trust her. How can we all sleep in the presence of a stranger? I blink and look to the two at my side. I am stronger than them. Magically created to be stronger than them and so many others. I don't need sleep. I can run on fumes forever.

I yawn, and my eyes widen, fighting the onslaught of dream demons. I slouch, sway, but remain upright.

Another drop of my blood falls from Zarah's fingertips, connects with Ryland's wound. A matrix of glowing gold and blue lines maps across his abdomen.

My mouth drops open, and for a moment, I cannot move.

A humming starts vibrating through my muscles and blood. It's like I am suddenly resonating at a higher state of being. Fluttering my way right out of this present nightmare. It's as if I am rising and rising. I fall backward to the soft cushion and become enveloped by the darkness of my subconscious.

A tiny voice in my head whispers *awaken*.

TWENTY-ONE

I stare at my hands, at the blood. Blood belonging to my sister Crystia. She lays, unresponsive, in the cradle of my arms.

It's my fault. Because I am the Balance Bringer, and of the three sisters born, only one may carry the torch and carry out our born-for mission.

Guilt. Undue guilt floods my dream.

A dream better defined as a nightmare.

A nightmare in constant shift. A morphing parade of scenarios that now pushes Crystia into the faded background and pulls Ry to the forefront.

Like it was with Crystia, I find myself hugging my brother's bloodied, broken, unresponsive body.

This too is my fault. Because of who and what I am, he put himself in the path of danger and paid the price. Tears cascade across my cheeks, falling like a downpour, drenching my brother's shoulder.

Guilt. So much guilt. First my sister, now guilt over my

brother and the wound working overtime to kill him.

I wish and pray, I beg for the healing of my family.

The word family reverberates through me like the dong of a bell, and for a millisecond, I envision Dohlan holding my hand, slipping a ring into place on my finger. A ring binding us as family. My heart clenches, and the image is gone.

I'm thrown back to the dreaded nightmare I had in the school swimming pool. That seems like ages ago—being in school, being with mom, living a normal, boring life—but in reality, I know it wasn't so far back. The event in the school pool was the beginning of this crazy ride my life has become. It was the first time I experienced a Tenebrousian—the dark and deadly shadow under Dreya's rule. Shadows Crystia tells me were once people. Trapped tortured souls.

I relive the dreaded vision from that first night, but it is not the Tenebrousian I am focused on, but the boy. Within my arms, I hold a dying boy, and after all I've been through, I know that boy is Jaden. My Jaden. The light in his ever-bright eyes is dimming, dimming, dimming, and I can't, simply can't stand for any of my loss to truly be.

A shrill howl swirls in the air above me. I look up, find Garr standing over us, clutching his blood tainted hands, and laughing to the sky.

If this nightmare ever comes to fruition, that too will be my fault. I know it to be true. Just as I know that whatever parasite has attached itself to Jaden is also my fault. Everything horrible happening to those I love is because of me.

I really am a bad penny.

"Alana Danika of House Raine." The old mystic's face is now all I can see. "Wake up."

I jolt, awake.

My temples throb, and droplets pool at the corner of my eyes.

My hopelessness from within the dream follows me into my waking. It's as if my chest is cracking and my heart melting, bleeding over my splintered ribs.

With a groan and a half-muffled whimper, I sit up, wipe the wetness from my face, and rub my eyes. Slowing my reeling emotional wheels takes longer. All the feelings refuse to let me go.

I never have studied the science of dreams, but I don't think it would be much of a leap to guess my dreams are a manifestation of my fears and personally assigned blame.

I try to shake the muddied emotions away. Gazing at Jaden's relaxed, sleeping face helps to chase away a portion of my anxiety. Careful not to wake him, my fingers trace the curve of his cheek. When my thumb rubs the edge of his lower lip, his face twitches. The simple action brings a smile to my face and a bloom of warmth to my chest. I sigh and lean closer, wanting to move closer still, but I hold myself a few inches away. I could gaze at him for hours. When he sleeps, he's so open, so heartbreakingly beautiful—inside and out.

Jaden and Mo still sleep beside me. The fumes from the bowl have dropped to little more than nonexistent, but the perfume is heavy in the air around me. The fragrance presses upon me like a mountain of stinky soaked socks.

My brother still remains laid out on the bed, unconscious, and Zarah is propped in the chair at his side, her body draped in slumber over his chest. His wound is hidden by the fall of her arm, so I can't tell if there has been any healing or not.

The space is silent with night, leaving nothing active to

distract me from the lingering state caused by my night-mares. I can't stop thinking about Crystia or Ry. I fear their fates are on me, on what I am. I don't want something similar to happen to Jaden. My beautiful, sweet Jaden. My lips find the corner of his mouth and press ever slightly.

The people I care most about seem to have a tendency to get hurt or left behind because of those that seek to control or destroy me. The thought stirs the desire to scream, punch something, kick all walls and barriers to smithereens.

Instead, I sit up, stretch my arms, and breathe deep. My stomach roils, complains, and vile lava thrusts up the hollow of my throat. I lurch forward, my hands fly to my lips, clamp over my mouth. A second later, I'm off the lounge, running down the stairs and out the door. Three feet beyond the little home, I vomit in the brush.

In that moment, all I know is the taste of nauseating defeat.

My emotions win the battle, sending my body into a shattered dance of shudders and shakes. I fall to my knees and let the floodgates against the tears rip open.

If I wasn't the Balance Bringer, Crystia would never have been in danger. Likely, Kaia, too. And Ry wouldn't have been attacked by Dreya... *I think*. The Tenebrousian prob-ably wouldn't have attacked my home, which means my mom would be okay. And Jaden... well... *I don't know*. Maybe I never would have met him.

That one truth hurts more than I anticipated. It's like a blunt vacuum tube plunging through my heart and sucking away all my strength and desires.

I sniffle and wipe at my eyes. I've cried far too many tears of late. There is a time and place for breakdowns, and the distinction appears to have been lost on me. I stand.

Suddenly have the overbearing need to run, run off the conflict in my heart and head. Run to catch my fleeting strength. But I won't, run.

Not now. I need to be here, with Ry.

A rush of anxiety gyrates in my chest. I fix my gaze upon the ground, concentrate on the shake of my hands.

Ry's going to be okay. He'll be okay.

I bend into my knees and breathe. Breathe deep. Breathe steady. The smell in Zarah's place was so sickeningly sweet. The air out here is fresh—clean—exactly what I need.

I pace back and forth, staying close to Zarah's doorstep. On the seventh pass, I pause, look toward the door and wonder. I narrow in on the doorknob.

I gave Ry my blood. Did it work? Is he better?

I step onto the front stoop and pull open the door. A waft of stinky sweet washes over me. My stomach roils. Nausea sloshes in my gut like a stormy sea. I turn away and jog out along the curve of the hill hiding Zarah's house. A mountain of vomit at her front door is not the kind of gift I want her to find when she awakes.

I can't make it more than thirty or forty feet before the desire becomes overwhelming. Once again, I lurch and let go. With a flick, I wipe the vile remnants from my mouth, and this time when I stand, a hum and buzz is pulsating over my muscles and through my blood. My head swirls with dizziness. My hands tingle as if falling asleep. And the world around me looks incredibly dull one second and wildly alive with color the next.

"What now?" I call out. "Must I constantly be on? Do I never deserve a break?"

Nothing answers.

And then something does... like a shock to my nervous

system, all my strength and mobility abandons me, vanishing with a whisper of the wind.

I collapse in a bed of dying grass. I want to call out, but my voice is gone. And who would hear me anyway? Ry is healing, and the others are sleeping. I want to get up and return to the safety of the house, but I can't move so I remain motionless on the ground, inhaling the potent stench of plant decay.

Anxiously, I await the onslaught of suffering that accompanies the change I sense rolling over my body.

The night grows darker, the ground chilly and damp, and the stiff grass scratches against my skin, stabbing at me like a plethora of tiny needles. The anticipated pain sweeps over my soul like a brush fire in a strong wind. I cannot scream, and I cannot sleep.

My only choice, to endure. To be brave and to burn and bleed, char with electricity and gasp at the invisible blows and stabs. My body convulses until I'm overcome with the sensation of being torn to pieces. It is then that my will gives and I pass out.

I am only vaguely aware of the shift in the ground taking place. Things changing from stiff and scratchy to soft and comfy. The earth encircles me, hugs me. A tangled web of plant and tree roots pulls me into the security of the earth's depth. And as I drift into the black drop of sleep, the earthen hug knits into a blanket meant to warm me against the raw night.

My spirit is morphing, turning a healthy green glow to match the world into which I am blending. Energy hums, hums, hums upon my wrist—my crystal bands—expanding in strength and coverage. Enveloping me in a serene protective gleam.

I whisper my thanks to Gaea and slip into eternal darkness.

Sleep is cool against my skin, gliding in and around me with a darkness that prickles through my blood and bones. Tingles with remembrance of me... the very first version of me. The initial Balance Bringer and her abiding mission. It is because of her that I now understand the roots of the dark I must combat.

Darkness is the dusk, the gloom, the twilight within each and every soul, and it is one of the elements I was created to balance. The purpose set upon my birth. For darkness will not exist without the light. That law was decreed at the beginning of life. The dark and the light need each other in order to find their own definition, their function, their eternal value. As the light dims, the darkness grows, and now it grows beyond the tipping of the scales.

My mind drifts, as if I am floating on air. Air fragranced with spice, and warm to the touch. Warm against my cheek and warm against my neck. Night braids its fingers through my hair, traces its touch along my form. It is a familiar and welcoming touch. It is a god-like beauty I have always known... and yet, I haven't always known that I knew. His reach scoops in beneath me. The shelter of my earthen blanket is lifted, ripped away, and I waver on the edge of awareness, but I do not fear, for the darkness that has come for me is taking me home.

But the process of change a Balance Bringer must endure refuses to release me, and instead, it thrusts my body, sending me crashing into a sea of broken glass. Followed by a deluge of knives to stab at me. A scream is lodged in my throat. I want to release the pain in a howl, but I can't. Can't move, can't speak.

Why must I endure? Why must I change?
No more change, please.

The dark warmth wrapped around me tugs harder, whispers in my ear to sleep, to allow myself to slip back into the peaceful caress of nothingness once more. I adhere, curling comfortably within my mind's safe burrow. In my mind's space, time holds no meaning. Anything I imagine can be. And the rules of reality don't exist. Crystia and Kaia can live. Ry is healthy, and Jaden and I are lovers, like the constellation in the sky.

My life can be perfect in my dark, safety burrow, but for one problem. None of it is real. And unless I choose to wake up, none of it can ever be real. For this reason, I know what I must do. It's time to awake.

Soft murmurs whisper my name, speaking to me in a language of old. I'm compelled to answer the mix of ancient magic and seduction. The words stir the desire to live, to awaken anew. I reach for the sound and envision Jaden beside my sleeping self, waiting for me to open my eyes. The calling of my name becomes a rescue rope that I use to pull myself toward awakening. In the never-ending landscape of black, a light blooms, shining from somewhere up ahead. Ignoring the physical aches and the cries to sleep, I pull myself forward into the glow of morning light. With the last thrust onward, I inhale deep and shove forward with everything I can muster. I sail for the light. Push for life.

With a flutter of lashes, light begins to filter through and chase away the shadows. A deep breath rattles through my chest, and my body moans with discomfort. Everything hurts, but...

I am awake.

I open my eyes, and white light explodes across my vision. There is nothing but blindness, everywhere.

And fire!

A blazing inferno sears the back of my eyes. I gasp and squeeze my lids shut.

Too soon! I woke up too soon.

My head pounds with more ferocity than when I awoke in Mo's village with one blue eye. I wouldn't have thought a more intense pain was possible, but the affliction I now suffer does not lie.

One blue eye. The thought lingers on my consciousness. When I underwent *that* transformation, I slept for three entire days. My body is now afflicted with many of the same sensations I experienced then, and none of those feelings are inviting. Must pain always accompany growth? And speaking of growth, have I successfully undergone another change? Have I slept away my days once more?

I lift one eyelid ever so slightly and seek out Jaden. Last time, he'd been so quick to soothe. He knew exactly what I needed to overcome the transformation process. This time is different. I'm lying on my side, on a real bed, in a place I don't recognize, and Jaden isn't sitting at my side. Instead, an arm is wrapped over my body. A touch radiating warmth, but nothing in the way the fingers glide over my skin is calming.

I close my eyes, breathe deep, and tilt my head back. My name drips like sweet chocolate from his lips, close at my ear. A frenzied hunger erupts across my skin, and a greedy need bursts to life inside of me. My body stiffens, and my eyes fly open.

The pain is instantaneous. A demolition crew breaks into full work-mode inside my head. They hammer and crush and pulverize my wellbeing. Lava rushes over my muscles and nerves, bursting from my pores in a surge of sweat. And my eyes, they might as well be swimming in a vat of lemon juice from the way they sting. But all these things, these physical miseries, are nothing compared to the personal plight within which I am now cornered.

In a single exhale, I spin and slip across the bed. My body objects to the quick motion with sharp stabs and white-hot pangs, but I ignore it all and hug the sheets to my body, narrow my focus upon Dohlan.

A wicked twist of his lips lifts his cheeks. "There you are. Ana, my sweet. Your sleep was long and troubled and wrought with fever."

My white-knuckled clench of the sheets redirects my thoughts from the pain squeezing my body. "How... Why..." The words are little more than a raspy whisper. My throat is scratchy and dry, and I long for water. Gallons and gallons of water. Like before.

I shake my head hoping it will help me hold a clear thought. It's pointless. My brain won't stop jumping. I want to ask Dohlan how I ended up here, wherever here is. I want to know how I ended up with him when the last thing I can remember is lying down in an unhealthy grass meadow.

A shiver rolls over me, and my skin breaks out in a sea of goosebumps.

"Still hurting?" he asks, a hint of concern in his tone. He's laid out on the bed with the sheets lazily lapped over his waistline. His muscular upper body is bare and distracting. He leans onto his elbow, resting his head upon his stretched fingers. I could reach out and touch him, if I wanted to. I don't want to.

No words come. Only my brow creases in response.

He nods as if understanding. "Soon the oils will alleviate your pain. You'll feel better then."

What oils? I chance a glance at my clenched fist. My skin does indeed shimmer as if an oil is working its way into my pores. I bite the inside of my lip and study him. Wonder at his intentions.

His brow jumps into a high arch, and something untrustworthy twinkles in his eye. "If you'd like, I'd be most willing to distract you until then." He shifts, pulling himself closer.

I slide back. Another inch and I'll be off the bed and on the floor.

"You're not afraid of me, are you?" He drops his arm across the pillow.

I shake my head and consider his hand resting all too close to me.

If I am in a bed with Dohlan, then I am clearly someplace other than Zarah's hidden home. My eyes wander from the pillow to the bed frame. In place of posts, long, elegant, and artful glossed branches twine from the frame toward the ceiling. The walls are bare, leaving the bed and a collection of small, delicate lanterns surrounding the bed the main focus of the room.

The sheets beneath my grip move, and I glance down at my all-too-bare skin, then direct my attention across the bed at Dohlan. He tugs on the sheets, once more. He probably thinks the action playful. I find it irritating.

"Why am I wearing so little? Where is my clothing?" I blurt, my voice hoarse and constricted, like it's lined with sand.

"Your skin needed to breathe. All that confining attire you were wearing was stifling the process." He grins, and I am reminded of every mad villain I've ever seen in a television show or movie.

I want to reach across the bed and smack him, but I am too afraid of exposing my indecent self any more than I am already. I'm not any more exposed that if I were wearing a bikini, but I never wear bikinis, and my current attire has me feeling naked. What would Ry or Jaden think if they were to barge in right now?

Oh my Gaea! Jaden! He's probably sensing everything this very minute. He was passed out when I left him, but what if he's well and good by now? It's highly probable, he's currently looking for me, using his Tracer ability to home in on my location. I definitely don't want him to find me with Dohlan. Especially, not like this.

Naked.

My mind screams the word even though I know I'm not truly naked. I'm just wearing less than I'd ever care to wear in Dohlan's presence, only my bra and underwear. Logically, I am not to blame for my current predicament. I was trapped in the transformation when he brought me here.

But what if...

I shake my head. I don't want to hear the thoughts in my head, but once whispered, how can I unhear them? What if Jaden isn't alright? What if he isn't looking for me? What if he has succumbed to the parasite?

No. No. I won't accept that possibility.

I huff and pin all my irritation on Dohlan with a nasty glare. "Why did you bring me here?" I demand. "And what makes you think you have the right to slip into my bed or rub oils on my skin?"

The smile slips from his face, and his hand snaps forward, clasps around my left hand, and tugs. I don't want to release the sheet and cling tighter, pulling my hand firmly to my body. From the look on his face, he takes my resistance as a challenge. The strength in his yank increases. Every part of my body still hurts from whatever I've recently undergone. My muscles and nerves scream, and yet, I hold my own against the powerful incubus in my bed.

In spite of my predicament, I'm rather proud to discover my strength in the face of pain. Pain that is lessening with each passing moment. In fact, my skin is starting to prickle. My head to tingle. My blood warms and swoons, and my nerves go numb.

My resistance ceases to exist, and I fall flat to the bed. Everything around me bends and morphs. My mind spins. I can't recall ever feeling so strange, like I'm trapped inside a carnival fun house mirror. Exhaustion presses through me, takes back the reins.

"That would be the effects of the oil," Dohlan says, plucking my hand free and caressing it with his own. He slips to my side, his body pressing against mine, and his fingers nimbly twist the gold band on my left ring finger.

"This, my dear, binds you to me. And, me to you." He splays his left hand and wiggles his fingers, showing off his matching gold band. His eyes meet mine, and there isn't an ounce of humor to be found within the lines of his features. "Your ring will protect you in your darkest hour. Do not take it off again."

Did he search my pockets to find the ring? He must have. How else could it now be on my finger? I gulp, try to speak, but all that emerges from my throat is an awkward squawk.

"You need water," he says and leaps from the bed. The sheets fall away, and I gasp at the sight of him. He wears nothing more than a tight pair of shiny black, butt-hugging shorts. His beautiful, golden body is as flawless as I always imagined. And now, I'm here gazing at his practically naked perfection. His incubus draw is overwhelming.

I slap my hand over my eyes. Maybe, if I don't see him, I won't be drawn to him.

How's that been working out for me so far?

"You will be needing lots of water." The mattress depresses, signaling his return. "I understand the process is dehydrating."

He gently removes my hand from my face. I turn my head away to avoid looking at him. Instead, I study the side table and its contents. The table is cluttered with candles and various bowls of what looks like different oils, or possibly cloudy water. My crystals soak in two of the bowls. My bands in one and the clouded pendant in the other.

My crystals. What is he doing to my crystals?

My head throbs, and my throat squeezes shut. I want to yell at Dohlan, but my lips don't move.

His arm slides beneath me, across my back, and he slowly lifts me to a sitting position. "Look at me," he says.

Like a stubborn child, I refuse to turn my head toward him.

He repeats the request, this time with more authority. I bite my lips. I don't want to look, but for some reason, I do. My eyes narrow, and I turn to face Dohlan.

"That's good," he says with a smirk. "You stay angry. It will only increase the passion in our love."

My jaw drops. He laughs, then raises the glass to my lips. "Remember, small sips. We wouldn't want anything to revisit us, now would we?"

I lift my hands to the glass and attempt to inhale it all.

No, I don't want the water to come back up, but I'm also parched. I want all the water I can get to my lips.

"Slowly." He pulls the glass from my mouth forcing me to ease my intake. "You must listen to me if I am to help you through this transition."

If the transition he speaks of is what I believe it to be, then I've managed to survive it once already. Why would I need his help this time? I fail to see the answer. What I do see, though, is an opportunity this situation has provided.

For some reason, Dohlan has a magnetic power over me. Maybe it's his incubus nature Ryland spoke of, or maybe it's something other. A basic chemical attraction between two people. I don't know. I always find myself in the midst of confusion when I am in his presence. Part of me wants to run from him like he is the devil, and the other part of me wants to throw myself into his arms. Those two parts of myself can never find a cohesive harmony.

The way things are presently, I couldn't be physically closer or more vulnerable to his influence. Maybe, here in this place, is where I will strangle that part of me that desires him. I can cut her free from the rest of me. Toss her into the deepest darkest hole, never to be found.

His finger loops over a tangled strand of my hair and pulls it from my face. With tender care, he smooths the unruly hair into place with the rest. I open my mouth to say something, and he guides the glass back to my lips. I eagerly drink.

I close my eyes and think of Jaden. My heart squeezes at the thought of him feeling or experiencing my current predicament... because I refuse to believe he is anything but healthy.

Jaden is my chosen one, I remind myself. And I do care

for him. Maybe even love him. But that part of me that craves Dohlan... damn her.

Ry once told me that I should be able to block Jaden when I so desire. Somewhere within myself, I must hold the key to such knowledge. Especially if what Zarah said is true, and it is me—my soul—that keeps reliving the journey of the Balance Bringer lifetime after lifetime. Our souls store it all, even if we don't remember, don't they? Every experience, every tidbit of knowledge, every love, and every loss.

All I need to do now is dig through my muddled mind and figure out where the information is hidden. I encounter what I believe to be a workable answer quicker than expected. Using a mental exercise, I imagine a wall going up around me and blocking me from the world beyond.

Jaden and I promised there would be no more secrets between us, but nothing good could ever come out of him knowing about these moments with Dohlan. Moments with the golden prince are always unpredictable and dangerous, and my lack of willpower in his presence is embarrassing. I don't want any knowledge of what happens here to cause Jaden pain. Hurting him is the last thing I want to ever do.

I push the thought of Jaden from my mind. Or at least, attempt to. It proves to be incredibly difficult. The fact that I am worried about him and about the parasite Zarah spoke of keeps him on the forefront of my mind. Not to mention, my current situation feels like a hideous betrayal. I keep thinking his name, seeing his face, his eyes. Maybe that's a good thing considering the difficulty I used to have remembering Jaden's existence in Dohlan's presence.

I must be getting stronger. If only I knew what triggers connected Jaden to my emotions. Would merely thinking of him let him know where I am and what I am doing?

I sigh. Blink hard. Shift my thought to Ry.

Squaring my shoulders, I visually search the room for my clothing. I've always known Ry to be the strong one. The one who came to everyone else's rescue. But now he needs me, and I must get back to him right away.

On a chair across the room, I spot a soft pile of colors. I make a safe bet that the pile is my dirty wardrobe. Holding my head high, I glance at my bare shoulder, my bra strap, the sheets clutched to my chest. Then I glance at Dohlan. In the mere flash of a second, my decision is made. Ry is my brother and he needs-me needs me, in a life or death sort of way.

Confusion and concern inch into the creases of Dohlan's face. "What are you doing?" His hand wraps firmly around my arm. It's a touch that demands attention, not a hold meant to detain.

"I need to get back," I say, sliding my feet off the bed. "My family will be worried and... and... Ry needs me." Dragging the sheets clutched firmly as a modest barrier, I stand beside the bed.

"You can't." He reaches for me, but I step away.

"Watch me." I take one step, and the room starts spinning. My arms fly out in search of purchase. My knees buckle. I sense my world toppling and crumbling. Dohlan catches me.

"You aren't ready," he says, lifting me into his arms and setting me back on the bed. He pulls the covers up over me and tucks them neatly beneath my chin. "You have been here thirty hours. They have barely woken from their slumber."

Thirty hours! "But Ry. He's dying." The desperation in my voice taste like stale chips. My body is limp, and my eyelids are half open, pressing against the desire to cry, the desire to give up, give in to sleep, and the desire to get up, kick ass, and get back to Zarah's.

No tears come. My eyes are dry.

Dohlan looks down at me from where he stands beside the bed. His body heaves a heavy sigh, his shoulders drop, and he sits beside me on the bed. Concern once again plagues his features, and he bides time tucking more of my hair behind my ear.

"You speak of Ryland Norde Sorlonte, Warrior of Whilystda?"

I blink at the mile-long name. For so many years, Ry was simply Ry or Ryland Cale at school. Both our last names turned out to be a lie, and he is a Raine, just like me. "Ryland Raine," I correct.

"If Ryland Norde Sorlonte Raine were to die protecting you, then it is as good a death a warrior could wish for." He takes my hand in his and starts tracing his fingers up and down my own.

"I don't want my brother to die." I close my eyes. The sting at the back of my irises has multiplied. Some eye drops, and an aspirin would be nice, if we had any. Maybe Jaden has both in his magical backpack.

"Half-brother," Dohlan responds.

My face crinkles at the distinction. I don't open my eyes. Half-brother, full brother, honorary brother, it doesn't matter. I love him the same either way. I'd trade my life for his.

"You need not worry, my sweet Ana." His fingers trace the side of my face, curving around my cheek and along my jawline. I release a shallow breath. "You took him to Zarah of house Cronos, did you not?"

My forehead wrinkles. How does he know these things?

"And you gave her a sample of your blood, correct?"

My eyes blink open. Has Dohlan been following me? Spying on me?

A silent laugh rumbles his chest. "Yes, indeed you did. Like I said, you need not worry. Your Ryland will pull through. Of this, I assure you."

I pull my arms back and start to sit up. "How..." I'm prepared to interrogate Dohlan. He knows far too much for someone on the outskirts of my tribe. I'm mentally ready, if not physically ready, to give him a piece of my mind. But before I can get a sentence past my lips, red-hot needles shoot through my skull, straight through my left eye.

My entire body jerks, slams to the bed with the force of a collapsing house. The bed rattles, the walls shake, the table at my side topples. My glass of water, the bowls of oil, the candles, they tumble and fall, crash to the floor.

Internally, my psychic wall plunges into darkness, and in that split second, I see Jaden. Not a memory or thought of him but him, in his physical form, wherever he is currently. He jolts upright from his bed laid out on the dirt, somewhere outside. He's no longer at Zarah's, and I have just woken him from a night's sleep. He's been looking for me, and now he's found me. We are connected in a far stronger way than our previous two-way encounter. The experience is incredibly more tangible than he led me to believe.

"What?" My voice is mousy, unrecognizable. "What's happening to me?"

Dohlan throws a leg over my body, straddles me, clutches my face between his palms, and leans forward. "Let me distract you." His voice is warm and seductive in my ear. When he pulls back and looks at me, his face fails to match his alluring invite. He's pressed with concern and fear.

Fear.

My eyes widen, and my heart takes off like a racehorse at the sound of the starting bell.

The candles. The fire. Beside us, fire from the candles laces up the wall, reaching for the ceiling and for us on the bed.

Dohlan's lips crash into mine, and everything—the worry and pain and impending danger—evaporate into waves of red and purple... wanting, needing, desire, passion, lust.

TWENTY-TWO

The waves of emotions summoned to the surface by Dohlan not only crash over me, but crash over us, and the bed, and everything around us. I am soaked in craving and confusion and fear. Probably sweat, too. Whatever it is I sense, it is too large to be contained within myself. This mix of me can no longer be stifled or hidden.

Every muscle and tendon in my body pulls taut toward the floor. Only Dohlan's arms around my body, his lips upon mine, hold me from being tugged into the earth. But the strain is exorbitant. My chest is clasping, my breaths shallow, oxygen lacking. My heart thump thumps, thumps, and then thumps no more. I sense the drag succeeding, wrenching my soul into the grassy patches of an indigo ghost.

Dohlan and the bedroom disappear.

Everything ceases—pain, longing, thirst, heat, light, breath.

All are gone.

I find myself standing barefoot on an emerald lawn. Above me, a royal sky peppered in cotton puff clouds.

"What just happened?"

No answer comes. Only the tiny chirps of bugs. I am alone. I turn in a circle, taking in everything around me. Land, and land, more land, a tiny village, and a tree. An unworldly large tree. The tree is by far the most interesting thing within my view. It's clearly ancient, pulsing with ribbons of history and knowledge and life. The wonder sits upon a hill overlooking the tiny village.

"Where am I?" I ask of the open air.

The hill is littered with offshoots of the main tree. Or maybe it is all part of the same tree. My body tingles with the thought. Yes, the tingle sensation means yes. The hillside is covered in one massive tree that deceivingly looks like a forest of trees. The heart at the top of the hill looms like a beast ruling over a kingdom. Blooms of pink lotus flowers sprinkle the upper branches. And from my perspective, the flowers glow.

Surrounding the giant tree are large megalithic stones. It's unlike anything I've ever seen in any book or documentary.

I glance down at the small village and imagine miniature fairy folk going about their daily business.

"This can't be to scale?" I say to myself, half expecting to find the answer float up from my subconscious.

"Right?"

I startle, jerk sideways, and balk at the sight of Crystia.

"Oh my Gaea!" Without thinking, I throw myself at her. I'm already in motion when I realize my mistake. She's a ghost. I'll fall straight through.

Only, this time, I don't. She is flesh beneath my grasp. I

clench my arms around her. We laugh, cry tears of happiness, and hug each other as tight as our strength will allow. "Am I dead?" I finally ask.

"Don't get used to it." It's not Crystia who answers me, but Kaia. I'd know her voice anywhere. I release Crystia and spin around to face a blonde-haired, color-crazy-eyed version of my older sister.

My mouth pops open, and my eyes bulge.

"Not what you are used to. I know." Her lips pull tight, puckering her cheeks. "It's strange for me, too. But this is what I look like without the old mystic's magic." She grabs a strand of her hair and flicks it. "I'd grown rather fond of my shiny chestnut locks." She heaves a sigh and her shoulders drop.

I throw my arms around her and hug her so tight she'd probably have trouble breathing if she weren't already dead. "You look like one of us now," I say, swaying left to right while holding the hug.

"That she does," Crystia agrees. "The three goddesses, just like I told you."

"Not exactly," Kaia responds with a tinge of sarcasm.

I snort, then suddenly jerk. I step back and look between my two sisters. Ghost sisters. "So... I'm dead?"

"Like I said, don't get used to it." Kaia's lips twist into a crooked smile.

"Not all death is permanent," Crystia adds. "You know Jaden won't let you stay dead."

"What can he possibly do? He's too far away," Kaia argues.

"Jaden?" I ask. "Where is Jaden? Where am I... or... was I?"

"Dohlan will save you," Kaia deadpans. "He's on top of things." The tiniest of silent laughs rocks her chest.

Crystia rolls her eyes and half-kiddingly slaps Kaia's arm. "Don't listen to her," Crystia says about Kaia. "Jaden will come through. Believe in him." She grabs my hand and holds it firmly. "But don't forget what you've seen here. Got that?"

I nod and open my mouth to ask exactly what is it that I've seen.

The pain of a flung boulder slams into my chest. I fall straight back to the grassy ground. Crystia and Kaia stand over me, look down, and do nothing to help. Another slam to the chest, yet there is nothing visible attacking me. I can't breathe.... Not that such a thing should matter. I'm dead.

My question is lost to the invisible attack. Another blow. Cracks splinter through my ribcage, blood flows, oxygen inflates my chest, and Crystia and Kaia vanish in a blinding light.

Dohlan emerges. His hair is a drippy mess, his eyes are squinted in concentration, his lips are muttering something undecipherable, and his hands are linked, pressing on my chest.

I gasp. Choke. And he is gone.

There is nothing but golden warmth and the embrace of Jaden's calming touch. Wherever I am, whatever I am, I am no longer physical. I've left my corporeal form behind. I simply am. And I am with him, Jaden.

I don't hear his words. I sense his message, my mind adding the sound of his voice in the translation.

"Don't let go," he says. "Fight, Ana. Fight for life."

I do as he asks. I breathe deep and open my eyes.

The room is covered in shadow, and I still lie on the same bed as before, only now, the bed and I are soaked in a thick coat of sweat, and everything about my being screams of horrible, wrenching pain. Dohlan sleeps on his belly beside me, his face is turned toward me, and his breath warms my cheek. His arm is slung across my shoulders, and he too is covered in sweat. He appears frighteningly drained.

A tiny moan passes over my lips, and I close my eyes once more, wish the pain away. I whimper. My body is falling. Falling through the bed. Falling away from the tiny room and everything.

"Fight, Ana." Jaden's urgent voice whispers in my mind once more. I don't respond. I no longer know if I want to fight. Living is painful, and it's so much easier to let go, especially since I am beyond exhausted. Besides, I have Crystia and Kaia waiting for me on the other side.

"Please..." A hint of desperation I've never before heard creeps into Jaden's words. "Please don't leave me," he says. "I need you."

I'm still falling, and the cool, seductive embrace of night wraps around me, welcomes me.

"I love you," he whispers.

My eyes slam open.

The room is covered in darkness; the only light is the flickering flame of one candle, burning in the corner nearest to me. The chatter of birds whistles beyond the walls of the room. It's the song of predawn. Soon the sun will rise, waking the world to a new day.

Unlike the coming change of day, my body doesn't appear ready to wake. My arms and legs refuse to answer my request to move. Sleep paralysis, I hope, and nothing more traumatic. At least, I don't hurt like I did the last time I awoke in this room.

Breathe. Just breathe. *Everything will be fine. Neither Jaden nor Dohlan will allow anything to happen to me.*

My fingers twitch. A tic jerks my shoulder. I open my eyes and sense a barely there smile grace my lips. I glance to my side. The side where I recall Dohlan sleeping. He is no longer there. My smile flips upside down.

My toes twitch and my frown pulls into a straight line.

Wish I came with an owner's manual.

"You scared me." Dohlan's voice floats over me. He sounds exasperated, something I've never experienced where he is concerned. "I feared I'd lost you."

"Sorry?" I'm surprised my voice sounds solid, not scratchy or tiny like before. Especially if I was previously dead. I try to lift my head to pinpoint his location, but my body ignores the request as if it is locked into some sort of body armor that weighs thousands of pounds.

"You have nothing to apologize for," he says. I catch movement out of the corner of my eye, and I manage to twist my head enough to somewhat see him. His hair is still a mess, even though it's no longer dripping wet, and stubble covers his chin and upper lip. How much time has passed? "I suspect the error is mine."

Something slithers across my abdomen. It's the first sensation, outside of my fingers, toes, and shoulder, I experience since opening my eyes this time around. I shiver.

Dohlan sighs. It sounds like a sigh of relief. "Any pain?"

I shake my head. "No," I say. "I hardly feel anything at all."

"Yes. These oils have worked well at blocking the pain receptors." His hand drops onto my shoulder and glides down the length of my arm. His palm is slick with oil and slips easily over my skin. "You were screaming so much, it was the only thing I could think of to ease your discomfort."

I don't remember screaming. But there seem to be a lot of holes in my timeline, and I definitely felt pain. Lots and lots of pain. *Maybe I blocked that bit of time from my memory.*

"Sensation and mobility are starting to return. Let me know if you experience any discomfort."

I nod and lift my head. It's a slight lift, but it's something. More mobility than I was able to manage a minute ago.

Dohlan's hands skate down my waist, over my hips, and along my legs. If he didn't look so worn I'd probably be anxious about the intimacy of his actions. But as things stand, in this instance, I trust his motives.

His voice hums an unfamiliar tune as he rubs my calves, feet, down to my toes.

"You must allow the oils to absorb directly and fully into your skin," he says, interrupting his hummed tune. "They will help you find balance and should not only quicken the next transition, but lessen the pain involved. The magic is ancient, but it is proven."

I haul myself up onto my elbows to better watch him work. The effort is a task that should be simple and is so often taken for granted. It is with great strain that I hoist myself up. "How do you know this?" I ask.

He falls silent and studies my toes while he massages my foot. I know his silence isn't because he didn't hear me. His silence is because, for some reason, he is reluctant to answer. I repeat the question anyway. He sighs, gently lowers my foot to the bed, and looks up.

After all the years of thinking I knew him, I believe I'm seeing him, really seeing him, for the very first time. The facade has been stripped away, and the heart and soul of the man behind the incubus now sits bare and humble at the edge of my bed.

"The knowledge has been passed down through the generations on my mother's side," he says, his gaze trained on me, awaiting my reaction.

"So?" I suspect my reaction disappoints. His disclosure as spoken means nothing to me. Just because something has been passed down from generation to generation, that doesn't mean it holds any credibility, especially in something like this... an ointment to help the Balance Bringer through an elemental transition. Who has experience in that stuff?

"So." He repeats the word blandly, nods his head, all the while his gaze remains glued to me. "So..." He racks his hand through his hair, brushing his damaged bangs out of his face. "According to family lore, my great grandmother, many times removed, was one of the original elves present at the ceremony when the first Balance Bringer was created."

With newfound strength, I jerk into an upright sitting position. "What? Why didn't you tell me this years ago?"

He stands and turns away from me. Paces across the room. Stops and looks out the window, laughs. When he turns back toward me, he is the Dohlan I've known for the past two years—confident and cocky. "You know nothing of this world, Ana. Elven ancestry is not something one speaks of openly."

"That's crazy. I don't understand." Finding I have full mobility, I shift onto my knees and move closer to the end of the bed. "Elf, Fae, Treeite, Nymph, Pixie. Why should any group be discriminated against?"

He shakes his head and looks away. "It's not discrimination."

"What then?" I push. "Help me understand."

His hands comb through his hair, clench and hold there. "Around the time of the first Balance Bringer, the seven houses of the elven nation retreated from this world and returned to the mother's core. By traditional thinking, no member remained behind." He drops his arms, shifts to look at me and tilts his head. "Only the two houses of Fae chose to stay behind."

My forehead pinches, and I jerk my head back.

"The two houses of Fae were originally elven, Elenari, to be exact." He watches me keenly as he speaks. "Fae was originally a family name. Not a species distinction. But it would seem history has forgotten that tiny fact."

My knees relax, and I sit back on my feet. "So, I'm elven, too, then?"

"Yes and no." His grin fails to fully commit. "I imagine you have traces of elven blood, but over the centuries the Fae have forgotten their true selves and many of the elven abilities can no longer be found in their family lines. They have changed and are now something other. And you, sweet Ana..." He leans forward, bringing his face close to mine. "Have a bloodline deeply polluted by generations of Immortal Warriors."

Overcome by modesty, I slide back, away from him, and crawl under the covers. "Was that an insult? Because that felt like it was meant to be an insult."

"I'm sorry." He massages his forehead, rubbing his fingers across his brow. "I don't want to talk about this anymore."

"I don't understand why any of this..."

He slams his fist into the wall at his side. "No more."

I pull my knees to my chest and hug my legs. I silently study his movement, watching for a marker signaling the next mood change. He stands at the window, peering out at whatever lies beyond. Is it a garden? A village? I want to know, but I choose not to move from my position on the bed.

Instead, my gaze starts to wander the room. The space was probably once rather charming. Now, it's a bit of a mess. Is the mess because of me? A pile of damp sheets lies on the floor next to hastily swept together bits of broken glass and pottery. The walls and floor are streaked with a mixture of scorches, oil, and water. The water should dry... eventually. The oil may cause damage. And the scorches... I recall the fire started when the candles fell from the nightstand. What I don't recall is anyone drenching the fire and putting it out. But obviously that happened at some point.

I glance from the damp pile of sheets to the bed beneath me. The current combination of sheets and blankets appear to have been rapidly set into place. The bed itself is somehow changed. As to how, I currently can't quite put my finger on the difference, but I'm sure it will come to me. I study the bedposts and try to remember how they looked when I first saw them.

"Any pain?"

The question catches me off guard. Dohlan's been quiet for so long I'd stopped waiting for him to resume our conversation. And now he's asked a question without turning to look at me. I ogle his back, my gaze traveling the glistening lines of sweat and oil highlighting his defined muscles. For the first time, I detect a flaw, and it's a flaw that only makes him more beautiful. More perfect. A hard-earned scar marks the left side of his lower back.

"Ana?"

I blink. He has turned around to face me. My mouth is agape. I snap my mouth shut and meet his gaze.

Question. He asked me a question. What was the question?

He takes a step toward the bed. "Are you alright? Do you hurt anywhere?" He takes another step toward me.

I don't hurt anywhere. I find it oddly discomforting. "Truthfully, I feel pretty good. Do I have the oils to thank for the lack of a transition hangover?"

"Possibly." His eyes narrow, as if spying something new in me. Something in need of serious study. "From all the tales I've heard, the earthen transition is one of the more difficult for the Balance Bringer to endure."

"Earthen?" Water, now earth. This should come as no surprise. All the signs have been present, waiting to be recognized, ever since my first tear drop turned the dead grass green.

"When I found you, the earth had wrapped herself around your sleeping body. You were encased in a grassy cocoon. I had to pull you free from the ground. She had firmly weaved her tendrils all around you, and she fought hard not to give you up. You should try to remember the connection you made with her that night, the new part of you that has awoken."

Strange. I don't sense as if anything new has awoken inside me. I may feel good, but I pretty much feel the same. After the first change... I stop, think back to that first time. Waking up in the tiny hut, my entire body hurting, discovering my blue eye. I connected with the water before that transformation. I'd felt the bond when we first dropped into the lake upon our arrival. Was it always so, connecting beforehand?

Following the butterfly in my mind back to that night when I ran from Zarah's cottage and dropped in the dying pasture a few yards away, I understand. The grass and plant life were withering. Everything looked and smelt ugly. My knees buckled, not because I was tired, but because change was taking me over. I'd been utterly exhausted, yes, but that seems to be the nature of my transformations. Did anything else happened while I was there?

I nod once, answering my own thought.

Gaea answered my cries of sorrow. I felt her wrap around me, like a warm nurturing blanket. Even in my exhaustion, I knew. She spoke to me, comforted me, while at the same time taught me. My body may have been sinking into the ground, but my mind was rising through the trees, reaching for the highest of all branches.

When I succumbed to the darkness, I sensed every granule in the soil. Just as I was aware of everything that moved through or on that soil. I was mindful of every plant and tree root system, and the sensations traveling through their branches and limbs. They spoke on the wind, and I heard them. Understood them.

Where did that knowledge, that connection, go? Is it my fault that I can no longer recall any part of my latest gift? Am I fighting who I am meant to be?

I shake my head and study the bedcovers in my lap. I am meant to embrace my change like the butterfly. I am supposed to be the butterfly.

I am the butterfly.

The thought has barely finished forming in my mind—Embrace change. Be the butterfly—and a surge of information and knowledge smacks into me like a panicked student driver in the school parking lot; rough and rigid and without mercy. The new download floods my system faster than my synapsis can absorb. My body drops, begins to convulse. My legs and arms kick and swing, flailing like an out of control child.

I am assimilating the earthen element, and a new me is awakening... only, it's hacking its way through doors and walls to get here.

The pain of this birth sears through me like the never-ending flash point of fire. Blue flames sweep over my body, devouring me, over and over and over again, turning me to ash. My ashen bits are pasted back together only to be scattered in the spirally wind of a blistering tornado. Fragmented me is slung, slammed, and smashed to the dirt. Sucked through the earth. Buried alive. My fingers dig and claw to pull myself free. My nails break. My fingers bleed. There is no relief. I can't see. I can't hear. I can't breathe. I can't find release.

I still. Give in. Succumb to the crushing chill.

TWENTY-THREE

I don't recall my awakening to the water element being so traumatic. It's possible I slept through the transition. Maybe. I was out for three days that time. If I were to judge the passage of time taking place during this transformation based strictly on the change of shadows in the room and on Dohlan's face, I would venture a guess that this time around things are taking as long if not longer.

Dohlan said the oils were supposed to help speed up the transition. This doesn't seem speedy. It seems drawn out and torturous. Could it be this particular transition normally takes much longer than what I am experiencing?

Maybe I misunderstood, and the oils are meant to help with the next change I'll have to undergo. Wherever the truth lies, I want *this* experience to end, and end now.

The pressure upon me blasts apart and is tossed away. Water and sand douse my flames, and a limelight chases my pain into the darkest recesses of my soul. The prickle and tickle of grass and ferns and everything green ripples over my skin. Flowers bloom across my nerves. Vines twists and bend with my muscles. New sensations sing and delight in the rousing stimulation.

Relief.

Electrification.

My back arches and my body moans.

Kisses. Kisses in places where I've never been kissed. Kisses and... other things. Things I... I've never...

My eyes open. A tiny whimper leaves my lips. I am alone on the bed.

Or, I was alone.

Dohlan glides up my body, his skin smooth against my own. He kisses the bare skin between my breasts and gazes up at me. His hair drops lazily across his forehead. His aura is bright, energetic, seductive. "You see. A little distraction works every time."

My eyes flutter in acknowledgement. The bed beneath me burns my skin, and the water in my belly boils. What just happened? And... Did I *allow* it to happen?

Something's off. Abnormal.

Wait... did something actually happen?

A chasm rips open in my chest. A massive black void torn between me and Jaden. The boil in my stomach explodes like a geyser. My muscles tense, and my teeth clench. I'm shaking. Shaking with a whirlwind of memories and emotions. The bed rumbles, and I pin Dohlan with a seething glare. I slide back, press my spine to the headboard, and, clutching the sheets to my chest, swing, palm flat, slapping him across the cheek.

Only, he's not in front of me like I expect him to be. Truth be, my hand slices straight through the image of

Dohlan stretched out before me. He vanishes like the night-mare... or memory... he was.

"Must have been a wicked dream," Dohlan says, a crooked smile spreading across his face.

Dohlan, the here-in-the-now Dohlan, is standing at my side. He isn't even on the bed.

It doesn't matter. My emotions are still charged and directed. At the sight of him and his devil grin, I wish him away from me.

A luminescent charge of energy explodes in the room with me as the source. The phenomenon emanates in a room-wide wave. Dohlan is lifted and thrown. The bed posts come to life, sprouting, stretching, and curving into a wall of bars encircling the bed. It may look like I'm a prisoner, now held within an earthen made-cell, but in truth, the bars stand between Dohlan and me, keeping him at a distance. Keeping me safe.

The wood of the bed sprouting to life happened so fast, as if driven into creation out of instinct. I don't know how I made it happen, and I don't know how to make it happen again.

Dohlan sits on the floor, his back pushed against the wall, the same place where he came to rest after being slammed into the barrier. Unlike his usual form, he is neither angry nor excited. He reeks of exhaustion. It's evident in every aspect of his body and soul.

"You sure can be feisty," he says, rubbing the stubble on the side of his face. "If I wasn't so tired, I'd be thrilled." He stands, rolls his shoulders, and stretches his arms. The move-ments make sure I get a good look at what I'm missing.

I pull the covers snugger and gaze down at the bedsheets. *I'm mad at Dohlan*, I remind myself. *Mad at him for his constant interference*. I bite my lip, frown. My chest is tight, so tight, and a sour taste is swimming over my tongue.

"Well... this sure didn't end as I had hoped."

I raise my gaze. Dohlan runs his hand through his damp hair and crosses the room, moving toward the spot where his clothing is meticulously laid out. His shirt and jacket are neatly draped over the back of a chair.

"Very little of this..." He waves his fingers between us. "... transpired as I had anticipated. But your transformation seems to be complete, and that was the end goal." He grabs a towel that was dropped on the floor and dabs lightly at the oils on his skin. "And as it so happens, we managed this transformation rather quickly."

"You call that quick?" I blurt out. "Look at you. Look at this room." I swing my arm out and gesture between him and the damp, scorched wall and floor. "You're both a disaster. Clearly we were dealing with my transformation hell for a long time."

"I'm fine, Ana. I simply didn't take the time to shower, shave, or sleep." He pulls on his pants.

"Maybe you should have."

He raises his gaze and a brow, then, without responding to my jab, grabs his shirt and slips it on.

"And the wall?" I ask.

Dohlan sits in the chair and starts pulling on his socks. He's left his shirt unbuttoned. "You did that. Don't you remember?"

My lips press into a half-puckered frown. I remember the candles falling and the fire springing to life, crawling up the wall. But then Dohlan's lips were on mine, and anything about the room and events happening outside of our kiss got sucked into a vortex of *never mind*.

Dohlan pulls on a boot, drops his foot to the floor, leans forward and buckles the straps, one and then the other. "When the candles fell, a small fire started. Your need was greater than the attention the fire demanded, so I ignored it. I would have eventually dealt with the blaze, would have been forced to, but then water started seeping up through the floor, moving in a most unnatural fashion, and before I realized what was happening, water was everywhere. Not only did the water kill the flames, but it doused us and the bed beneath us."

He pauses and smiles at something he's clearly not vocalizing. "When I realized the water was responding to you..." He slips on his other boot. "I decided to let it play out." He glances at me sideways, the seductive Dohlan glowing in his grin and gaze. "It added an element of excitement to the distraction tactics."

He drops the sex god facade with the slump of his shoulders. Snagging his jacket from the back of the chair, he slips into his dark duster without the usual Dohlan style flare. "It all happened rather quickly, if you ask me. From start to end, this transformation took less than three days."

My mouth drops open at the time lost. Time away from Jaden... *away from Ry!*

He volleys his hand in the air as if silently saying, "*sort of.*"

"I'd estimate, fifty-seven, fifty-eight hours in total." He buttons his shirt, leaving the few buttons at the top untouched.

I chew on my lip. I don't know what to say. It's likely Dohlan has somehow helped me, but he took me without my permission. That's never alright. And he took me away from my group, leaving them to worry for hours upon hours. Days, even.

I should have been with Jaden for the transformation. He is my Tracer, not Dohlan. Something within my gut stirs. Zarah's words float to the forefront of my thoughts, and I am suddenly wrought with conflict.

Jaden has a parasite. He may not be trustworthy.

I silently shake my head. The thought is a lie. I refuse to let any such fears derail me. Dohlan, on the other hand, may not have a parasite, but he consorts with the enemy. He surely can't be fully trusted.

His gaze is set upon me as if waiting, but I have nothing to add to the conversation. My mind is racing over what I remember from minutes ago. Dohlan was on top of me, but the Dohlan that was kissing me, the one I tried to slap across the face, and the one standing before me, reeking of exhaustion are clearly not the same. They were the same Dohlan, and yet they were not. I'm so confused.

As a dream incubus, can he be in two places at once? If so, did I experience the dream incubus version while the real, physical version was actually standing in the room beside me?

Nah. That doesn't feel right.

I scratch the back of my neck and twist my lips into a confused frown.

"You can find clothing in the closet that fits you. The wardrobe here will help you blend in better. You'll look much more like a local. If you aren't interested, your dirty rags are downstairs in the alcove by the backdoor. I attempted to clean them." He sounds exasperated.

"Oh." My voice is tiny, tinged with the confusion that is swarming my system. I'm anxious over my time spent here with Dohlan while at the same time, I'd be a fool not to notice the lengths to which he has labored... labored for me.

"Take anything you like. The lady of the house will no longer be in need of them." He gazes out the window, at something unseen by me. He nods so slight it's almost imperceptible. After a moment, he turns his attention back to me. There are no games, no facades at play in his features. Standing before me is the raw, undiluted Dohlan. "I'm on your side, Ana. I've always been on your side. I am sorry that you no longer trust me. But believe me when I say, everything done was for your benefit."

My breath heaves. "What exactly was done here, I mean, besides the obvious transformation. I'm having trouble understanding the need for all the oils and attention."

Dohlan squares his shoulders, stands as if he is being interrogated. Maybe he is. Maybe that's exactly what I am doing, pulling answers out of a reluctant witness.

"I don't expect you to understand everything yet," he says. My mouth pops open, and my head jerks back. "There are bindings you will be in need of later. The oils are working to strengthen and expand your internal matrix so that you may more readily accept and adapt to your new constitution each time one is presented to you.

I blink and say nothing.

He sighs. "In your original state, your mind was accepting the information with the speed of a goat, using your gift as one would start a fire with the rubbing of sticks. Now, you can gather the new intelligence with the speed of a running cheetah and invoke abilities as one would start a fire with flint rock—instantly."

Now that sounds like a most pleasant and useful upgrade. I'm grateful, only... "And the distractions..."

"What about the distraction?" He cuts me off, a sharp edge to his voice. "It helped you forget the pain. Did it not? If only for a short while."

"Yes, but..."

His gaze sharpens, eyes narrow. "But what, Ana? You didn't seem to mind at the time. You kissed me back, held me tight. It felt wanted. Have things changed so much since then? Do you honestly believe *he* can make you happier?"

"Jaden is none of your business," I retort, Dohlan's comment having sharpened my hackles and inciting an instant need to defend my Tracer.

His breath heaves, and he turns, heads for the bedroom door. "Your friends should presently be on their way. *He* will be able to track you, now that you are fully awake." Dohlan grabs the doorknob but doesn't open the door. "And the other..." He pauses and appears to struggle with something internally. "He is still healing, confined to bedrest. You need not worry."

"You're leaving?" After all we have been through, all that he has disclosed, the only words I am able to scrape together are the obvious. My face warms. His departure was what I wanted, but I never expected him to actually leave. My stomach flops, is suddenly sick.

"I am." He glances back to the window and the tiny table set beneath. Three bowls sit on the table. The three bowls that used to be on the nightstand. He turns to me and nods toward the window. "Let your crystals soak for as long as possible. The juniper oil is helping to clear all the negative energy they have absorbed. When they are clean, it's possible they will help absorb some of the transformation energy next time. Maybe they will help you stay conscious."

After all that I've experienced from the transformations,

I don't think I want to stay conscious. Sleeping through the entire ordeal sounds pretty good to me. Of course, I don't say any of that to Dohlan.

He opens the door and pauses, peers into the space beyond. His hand tightens around the doorknob, and his eyes close. I watch him in his silence, watch the way his chest rises and falls in a slow-tempered rhythm. "You have been on an epic journey to find the old mystic since before you set foot in Hiddenkel."

My tension releases, and I shift on the bed, moving closer. My Bringer sense whispers, telling me Dohlan holds knowledge that I need to know. "Yes."

"You think the old woman will help you. You believe she will save your sisters. It's true, the old woman may be able to help you better understand yourself. She may even help you hone your God-given and elven abilities. But your sisters..."

At the sound of the words *but* and *sisters* in the same sentence, my heart pauses, as does his delivery. I'm holding my breath, counting the seconds, sensing the room grow heavier by the nanosecond.

Tell me, Dohlan. Tell me.

He opens his eyes, turns and looks at me. "Your sisters have always been within you, Ana." His eyes are tender, graced with sadness and understanding. "You don't need anyone to grant you access to them. They are waiting for *you* to open the door and let them in."

I lean forward on the bed. "But Dreya has used black magic to break our connection."

"Illusions," Dohlan says with a flip of his hand. "She may have more magic than most in this realm, but no one can break your bond with your sisters. You are the Balance Bringer. A power as ancient as time. Far more ancient than

Dreya, and although she likes to think she wields enough strength to do anything she pleases, she does not." He looks away, steps through the threshold.

"Dohlan," I call after him. He pauses in the doorway. "Why?" I ask. "Why do all this, tell me so much?"

"Because I love you." He does not look at me. He turns to close the door, keeping his back to me.

"But you are an incubus," I say.

His head snaps up, and his devastated gaze sets upon me. "Do you find it so impossible for an incubus to love?" I'm struck dumb. I sit on the bed, mouth open. "This incubus was once a boy. A boy who understood love and honor and loss." He turns away, closing the door between us. His footfalls recede down the hallway. He does not return.

Dohlan's admission has frozen me, mind and body. I fall back on the bed and stare at the ceiling.

Dohlan loves me.

I press the heels of my palms to my forehead. "Dohlan loves me." I taste the words on my tongue, and I can't decide if it is bitter or sweet, or bittersweet. For so long, I desired him, wanted for only him. But things are different now, and I... I don't know what I'm feeling.

If only Jaden's arrival could clear up the cloud that fills my head. Set all doubts and fears to rest. But such a thing is unlikely to take place. His entrance will no doubt press more confusion and uncertainty and internal conflict upon me.

If I knew for certain that Dohlan was on my side, unwavering despite Dreya and her foul notions, would I have a better handle on my emotions? Unlikely.

And what of Jaden. I don't have the same level of an established relationship as I do with Dohlan...

I raise my right hand and gaze at the gold band upon my finger.

Dohlan loves me.

I shake my head, attempt to clear my thoughts.

If only I could remember the multitude of lifetimes Jaden and I have spent together. Maybe that memory would eclipse anything I feel or could possibly ever feel for Dohlan. Maybe the memories of such a bond would clear my confusion.

Dohlan says he loves me and Jaden...

Jaden's on his way here.

We said no more secrets, but when the words were spoken, I never anticipated anything like this happening. My wall fell, and so I know he knows it all. Knows what I've done and knows I tried to hide it from him. He knows about Dohlan's distraction. And worst of all, he knows the chaotic emotional storm that rolls through my heart and soul.

I sigh. A second later, I pound the mattress with my fists.

Dohlan. Dohlan. Dohlan. If he truly loves me, then, how could he have done this? And why... oh Gaea, why can't I remember all the minutes?

I slam my head to the mattress two times. After the way I treated Dohlan today, he may never tell me another thing. Not ever. Only he knows what truly happened here. What I did and didn't do. How will I ever know?

"*We can tell you. We can even show you.*"

Startled, I sit up, spin around. There is no one here. I am alone. Or so it seems when viewed with normal vision. But already, my bringer talent has taught me that there is so much more to the world. So, I ask the question. "Who's here?"

"We, the trees. The guardians of Gaea. Lay back and let us alleviate your confusion."

Not ants or termites, but trees. As in my earthen ability at work in the bedroom. My gaze is drawn to the bedposts made of tree branches. As I watch, a small leaf presses free from the old wood and unfurls in a vivid green. My gaze wanders the full length of the posts and the added bars of branch encircling me. I note the handful of pink blossoms now blooming along the limbs.

"Trust," the tree encourages.

Slowly, and a tad reluctantly, I lower myself to the mattress. I am unsure of what to expect, and so I fixate on the ceiling once more. With a sigh, I close my eyes. "I am the butterfly," I remind myself. It's true, I am the butterfly. I need to learn to accept the change and blossom like the tiny flowers around me. Talking to trees isn't that much different than talking to insects or animals or water.

"Remember," the branches say in unison.

Instantly, I am there, in the moment. My body reacts immediately with a whimper. Dohlan prompts my nerves to sing and my body to delight. Even though I watched him leave, he is here with me. His hands and kisses exploring my body, even the off-limits areas.

My eyes snap open. A mere suggestion of Dohlan remains, like I am looking at a faded hologram. A hint of the physical sensations lingers, my body reluctant to let go, but I know now that the feeling is not mine to own. I did not lie with Dohlan. Not in that way. Never in that way.

What I experienced was a memory of long ago. Something that happened in this room and on this bed. At a time when the room was bright with love and not dreary with neglect.

For those involved, the memory may have faded to time. Dohlan probably doesn't have a clue what I was reacting to when I attempted to slap him. But in that moment of my awakening, the memory was overwhelming.

The bed, or the living bed frame, remembered. It's possible, it may never forget since the event is recorded in the tree's time-keeping rings.

I was not the first girl Dohlan entertained in this place. That explains how he knew about the clothing.

"Dog."

I glance around the room and think about cleaning up. Dohlan looked wrecked when he left. I suspect I look a lot worse. I came out of the last transformation looking rather horrid. That knowledge kindles a fear to look in any mirror. But if I don't look in a mirror, I will never know.

Know. I want to know lots of things where Dohlan is concerned. Even if I don't want to openly admit it to myself, the desire to know more about the girl with Dohlan in the memory the trees shared nags and pushes me to learn more. Only, experiencing that particular memory, especially so intimately, is like an invasion of their privacy.

I take a moment to contemplate my dilemma. Decided, I release a heavy sigh. It's not my memory to revisit, and so I will not look again. I wouldn't want others looking back at things I've done so I will show the kind of respect I'd prefer to receive.

"It's kind of cool, you know," I say to the room as I slide to the side of the bed. "Trees with memory." I grab the post, untwine my legs from the sheets.

"Memories," the bedframe whispers.

In a flash I see, hear, feel everything. Everything I never

wanted to know. I leap off the bed and wiggle, shiver, shake off the slimy ick slithering over my body.

Dohlan and Kaia. "Dohlan and Kaia?" I scream to the bedroom walls.

Realization charges.

"Kaia?"

Truth slams into me like a Titanic-sinking iceberg, knocking the breath from my lungs. I back against the wall. A frigid frost rolls over my skin, turning my bones to slush.

TWENTY-FOUR

Dohlan and Kaia were a thing, and *that's* why the mention of her name pulled a reaction from him. I get it now. But I'm not sure how that fact honestly makes me feel. I breathe deep, then look around the room with new interest, and a lump of bile stuck in my throat. This was Kaia's bedroom. Kaia, my sister. The older sister I've only ever known through dream walks. She dwelled here. Touched things, loved things, made plans, and had dreams here.

I glance at the bed. And had sex here.

I shiver. *Yuck.*

If I can't have her with me, I can at least feel her here, in this place, if only for a short while.

I wonder if I'm in the family castle?

I yank the top sheet off the bed and wrap it around me. The bars of branch that separated me from Dohlan now cage me in the corner of the room with the bed. My face twitches with thought. I'm fairly certain I can get out of the surrounding tree cage if I so desire.

Holding the sheet in place, I step forward and place my hand on the corner bed post. The raw wood scratches my palm. Oddly, I enjoy the prickle. It reminds me that life comes in all forms. All of it, Fae, human, horse, water, tree, grass, bird, everything, it's all important. Each one plays an invaluable role in the balance of our world. Destroy one and the rest will experience the detrimental rippling effect.

My hand caresses the wood, and I lean closer to the post, as if I'm preparing to whisper a secret. "With your permission," I ask softly. "May I pass?"

The entire bed sprouts to life. The posts were already showing tidbits of growth, but now the branches press to the roof, bend, and reach across the width and length of the mattress, connecting with one another above the bed's center. The branches twine together and explode in a blanket of leaves and flowers. At my side, the wooden bars part, creating a path through which I may pass.

I step through and rush to the window, gaze out the bubbly blown glass. I spy a much-neglected garden, and, when I lean against the glass to see what I can of the building, I glimpse a thatch roof.

Not a castle.

Of course not. It wouldn't be the castle. Dohlan warned me not to go to the family's home, the family home being the castle. He wouldn't warn me not to go there and then take me there himself. That would just be...

My heart beats a double thump.

I turn my back on the window and glance around the room. Everything is so beautifully earthen. The use of natural materials is exquisite in the space. But why the space at all? Kaia would have been safe had she stayed at the castle. Father, mother, Ry, and who knows how many warriors were there to protect her. Why did she wander to the meadow? Why did she have this place?

I recall the memory of Kaia sitting in the meadow, moments before Dreya showed up. Moments before Kaia's fate was written on Dreya's sword. I think about the beautiful blonde boy Kaia adoringly watched as he walked away.

Dohlan.

The boy too beautiful to be a good thing. Had he masterfully manipulated her? Delivered her directly to Dreya?

I breathe deep and blow out a long, thoughtful breath.

And now he is messing with my head. Does he plan on handing me over to Dreya, too? Would he do the same to Crystia if she were not...

My breath catches and my heart squeezes to a full halt.

No. My eyes sting with the want for tears. My head shakes against the thought forming in my mind. I saw her that night. The night she died. Saw Crystia arguing with a blonde-haired guy dressed all in black, one of Dohlan's favorite apparel colors.

Did Dohlan... could he have... killed Crystia?

My knees buckle, and I slide down the wall. Drop butt to the floor and fold in on myself, hugging my legs tight.

I can't. I can't.

"It can't be."

He's insanely good at what he does. Incubus. Demon. Deceiver.

His lies smell and taste of vinegar and work like a drug, numbing my body, numbing my soul. I remain sitting and watch the shadows of the day on the opposite wall shift and eventually slide away.

When the moon is high and its glow slips through the windows, I decide the time for wallowing is over. I stand and go in search of a washroom. I find one immediately. A washroom is connected to the bedroom, the only two rooms on this floor. The washroom is rather large for what I am guessing is a small place overall.

Keeping with the naturalist theme, a lot of stone and wood decorate the washroom, giving it a warm and inviting feel... or at least it would, if it were clean. Unlike the bed and nightstands, the washroom is half-cleaned and half-covered in a thick layer of dust. Totally peculiar. It's like someone started cleaning and then stopped for some odd reason.

An odd oval seat with a hole in the middle is the closest thing to the door. I assume it is the toilet, but there is no tank and no handle to flush. *Kind of scary.*

I go straight to the sink. A stretched mirror shaped like an ornate window hangs on the wall above the sink. It, too, is covered in dust. I wipe my hand across the grime, and a scary swamp monster peers back at me. I jerk and wipe at the mirror more. I want to believe the vision before me is the result of a filthy mirror and not how I really look. The mirror doesn't want to comply. It remains spotted and streaked.

I turn my attention to the sink. It is set in an old barrel. When it is clean and the wood treated and glossy, I bet it looks cool. The actual sink is simple, as is the faucet, looking much like a spout or spigot you'd find at an old well pump. Which is exactly what one needs to do in order to get water out of this faucet—pump. Only, no water comes no matter how many times I crank the lever. The line may be broken or the well empty. Either way, I'll need to find other means to clean up.

My gaze wanders over the room, taking it all in before I

start my hunt for water. A giant shower takes up the back corner. It's meant to be a waterfall shower. The design is evident. The wall is a serious eye catcher, with its stacks and layers of various stones.

I wonder if it still works.

Next to the shower is a large tub carved from a grey granite boulder. It sits against the far wall and is filled with water and fading bubbles. At the base of the tub, a small box with a slip of paper set on top.

I cross the room and pick up the note. It's a one liner from Dohlan telling me to light the fire. I glance to the bottom edge of the tub. Something juts out at the side. Further investigation informs me that the tub is set up with a water heating system. The box is filled with what would be the equivalent of matches.

I glance between the tub and the note. Dohlan not only made sure I had the comfort of Kaia's things but an awaiting bath ready to be warmed from the timbers below. He clearly thought through my needs, and even anticipated not being here to fill them. Somewhere deep within his pit of a soul he must have known I would be angry and would kick him out.

There's a knot in my stomach, and it's making me nauseous. I squeeze my eyes closed tight. "Great. Now I have remorse. I don't want to have remorse."

I crumple the note and walk out of the room.

I wander into the hallway and down the stairs. The same path Dohlan took when he left me.

Dohlan. *I wonder what he really did to me.* I can't even begin to guess.

My hand glides along the railing made of a long, knotted branch. Slats of wood, set an inch apart, run from floor to ceiling creating the dividing wall that encloses the stairwell.

Four steps from the bottom landing, the slatted wall ends at a quick turn in the descent.

The view opens to an all-in-one room cottage. There is a large stone fireplace in the center, serving as a barrier between the kitchen and the entertaining or family gathering area. From where I stand, plush seats are gathered round the stone centerpiece. I envision Kaia curled up in one of the chairs, enjoying the warmth of the fire.

My fingers drag along the wall, a wall that feels like hard-packed clay, as I make my way across the room. Many of the furniture pieces are made of wood. Some are carved directly from tree trunks, leaving no joints or separate pieces. The craftsmanship reminds me of the log bench in my mother's meadow. The meadow my father planted with a sea of Nerine lilies.

On the other side of the hearth, I discover the kitchen. Large cooking pots hang on either side of the fireplace, leading me to think the structure doubled as an oven. In the center of the room is a semi-large table surrounded by chairs. The dinner table. Another table, looking similar to some of the old dough tables I've seen in antique stores, is shoved up against the wall. Also against the wall is an empty rack, a sink married with a short counter, and a shelf packed with supplies, likely far beyond their shelf-life date.

A wide oval window, framed in the wall, allows the moonlight to filter into the space. The hints of light high-lighting dust motes as they float in the open air.

I pull out a chair at the dining table and take a seat. This seems as good a place as any to discover the new manner of me. Probably, a right perfect place because there is no one nearby to get hurt. I inhale and exhale a deep breath and relax. Take a mental check of myself. I've changed a lot this year. I've grown into abilities I'm only just now beginning to understand. I'm melding with the elements one by one to become something I can't even comprehend.

How does one girl balance the world?

No idea.

But I will. Somehow. So I've been told. But before I can even consider the job for which I was created, I need to know myself. I must recognize what is within my ability, and I mustn't hesitate when it comes to the gifts I have been given. Which means I must explore, investigate, and practice.

I close my eyes and allow my mind to wander over every sense and thought lingering within the package of me. Somewhere, among the many memories, wishes, and jumbled knowledge, lurks my new side, nature. Its power waits to be explored and tapped.

One thing I learned from my experience with Dohlan is that I want to be able to pull that power to the forefront on a second's notice. I want to wrap my clutches around the ability, keeping it at my disposal. But I also want to be able to hold reactions at bay in situations where reflexes come into play, such as surprises, shock, dreams, and nightmares.

Currently, I'm not sure if I would classify Dohlan's distraction tactic as a dream or a nightmare.

Up until the water in the bedroom above, I'd never used my ability at such a powerful level without being fully aware. Except, possibly that one time, when I buried a guy alive. I shake my head. *I don't want to think about that.* Maybe, if I practice and work hard enough, I may gain some deeper understanding of what I'm *becoming*.

Several minutes of steady breathing, quiet meditation, and gentle probing, and my vision is washed in green. I close my eyes and even the darkness is tinted green. I imagine the inside of my head brimming with flowers and meadows. When I open my eyes, there is now plant life where before there is none. It dawns on me that I may be staring my earthen ability in the face. It wants to be seen. And it wants to interface with me.

Scanning the kitchen, I wonder where I should begin. *It's probably best to pick something small.* I have yet to figure out what I am doing. My gaze pauses on a dusty mug placed at the far end of the table. The image sends my thoughts skidding sideways. Did Kaia leave the mug there? Or had Dohlan been the one to set the mug on the table?

I try to imagine Kaia here, going about a normal day's routine. Sitting at this table, sipping her tea. I wonder if she was happy here. If she had chosen this place on her own or been held captive by our mutual pretty boy. I decide I prefer to imagine her happy and here of her own volition.

The place is cute, but it doesn't seem to fit what I know of her. She was a force to be reckoned with. And this place is so, well, sweet. Except the walls. The walls are drab. A total blank canvas of dirt and clay.

Maybe she hadn't gotten around to decorating yet. If she had, I'm sure she would have done something about the boring walls. Hung paintings or tapestries or something. Maybe weapons. This small home needs color. As soon as I think it, I know it's true. The cottage is in real need of color. Everything is so grey and brown and orange—like the dirt beneath the house. I imagine wisps of green added throughout.

As if on command, lush vines slither up from the floorboards. Their movements are slow and steady. The process takes several minutes, definitely faster than paint, and soon the place is decorated in an array of varied green lines almost covering the full height of the walls. It's a different way to decorate, but I like it.

Something about the scent, the feel, the look appeals to the new me. Kaia won't mind me redecorating. She can no longer use the place. And if Dohlan doesn't care for it, maybe he'll prick a finger on a thorn.

The thought causes me to smirk, then fall somber.

I wander through the first floor of the cottage, admiring my work. I can make things grow, like my mother. She is touched with a smidgen of the earthen gift. I wonder if she actually knows why she has an affinity for all things floral. If only I knew then what I know now, maybe I may have been able to better help her at the shop. I cause vines to spring from the ground, and, most importantly, I can turn life on the verge of death green again. And that, I imagine, is the real treasure, the purpose in my gift.

I turn away from the cottage's interior, in favor of heading out to the front yard. The moon appears to be mostly full and should provide sufficient light for what I plan to do. But before I reach the front door, something shoved into the corner of the room catches my eye. I pause and then change my path.

Pushed behind a cabinet, with only a portion of it visible to the room, is a full-sized mirror. An old blanket has been thrown over the top. The tattered blanket hangs at a crooked angle and doesn't cover the entire piece. The frame is made of hefty wood blocks the size of railway ties.

Being careful not to topple the mirror, I pull the blanket free. It releases its hold in a billowing cloud of dust. I cough and wave my hand in front of my face. My nose tickles. I fight the desire to sneeze. When the dust settles I blink away any dust remnants and gaze at my reflection. I barely recognize the girl looking back at me. I expected many things—greasy hair, dark circles, pale skin, and overly chapped lips. None of that is what I witness. What I discover—I've morphed into someone else.

Not exactly, but my immediate reaction is one of confusion and unknowing.

I don't know her—the girl in the mirror. Her complexion is a healthy pink, and the birthmark at her eye is almost invisible. She gazes back at me with one blue eye and one green eye.

Goodbye sectoral heterochromia.

At the top of the overall change, the girl's dishwater-blonde hair is weaved with obvious strands of gold. Sure, evidence of Dohlan's oils dampen my hairline and lower strands, but it is the gold that pulls at my attention.

I stare and my mouth pops open. So does hers. I stare more.

"Will Jaden recognize me? What will he say?" I bite the edge of my lower lip.

The girl in the mirror disappears. She is replaced with a vision of the countryside at night. I jerk. A second later, I'm leaning closer, squinting at the image trapped within. It's Jaden. He's standing, fidgeting actually, beside a tree.

"Is this for real?" I position myself in front of the mirror, crouching to better view him.

"This is now."

I glance to all sides of the mirror and finally check at my back. Still alone. "Seriously?" I say. "A talking mirror? This is so Snow White?"

My gaze finds Jaden once more. I am watching the real him wherever he is at this very moment. My fingers skim the mirror at the edge of his image.

"Not mirror. I am the tree."

I spare a quick glance at the mirror's bulky wood frame. "Like the bedframe upstairs?" When I look back at Jaden, his hand is skimming the air and he appears to be looking at me. How can that be?

"We are all the tree. The world tree."

At the mention of a world tree, a vision from my walk on the other side of life comes to mind. While I was dead, I saw one massive tree feeding all the other trees. Maybe the one tree was the world tree. Crystia told me to remember. A ton of questions pop into my head at that statement, but the thing I want to know most is... "Where is Jaden?" Is he okay? Is he far? Does he know about Dohlan? Is he mad, upset, frustrated?

"He is there, in the mirror."

"Yes, but where is that?" Jaden is calling my name. I drop down so that I am level with him, place my hand on his heart and answer. "I am here, Jaden. I am here."

The tree does not answer. Mo comes up behind Jaden. "I'm ready," she says. Jaden waves her away and talks to me. "I am coming for you, Ana. I will find you."

"How am I seeing him?" I ask. "How does he see me?"

"He does not see you. Only you see him. The share is one way."

But he's looking directly at me. Talking to me. One-way share, that can't be true.

"It is the mother's mirror," responds the tree. *"It can, will locate loved ones. For the mother's peace of mind."*

Super handy. *Does it come in a travel size?*

"My loved ones? Like Jaden and Ry?" I gaze at Jaden. I miss him more than I had allowed myself to admit. I honestly wish he'd been with me these last hours, days, whatever timespan my change swallowed. Dohlan *was* the distraction from my true want and need.

"*Ryland—Ry Maitias Cale Norde Sorlonte Raine*," the tree says.

I jerk backward and glance up at the top corner of the mirror, the spot where I imagine the face or mind or whatever of the tree to be. The thing just barfed out a chock worthy collection of names for my brother. It sounded like the tree knew them all. His name here in Hiddenkel, before and after my mother's second marriage, and the name Ry used while living in California.

The image of Jaden vanishes from the mirror.

"No," I yell and throw myself at the spot where Jaden was visible a second earlier. But another image is coming into focus. One of my brother. I sit back and study everything about him. He's no longer white or covered in a sheen of sweat. His hair is messy, but who wouldn't have bedhead after spending days laid up.

Zarah steps into the picture, taking a seat on the stool beside the bed. "How are you feeling?" she asks.

"Tired but worlds better, thanks to you," he says.

A smile immediately curls across my lips. Ry looks good and sounds good. *Thanks be to God and Gaea.* I was worried sick about him.

"May I?" Zarah asks.

"You may do anything you like," he says with a tease in his tone. My face falls flat, and I blink hard. Never have I heard Ry talk that way. It's strange to hear. "And so much more." He finishes with a smile, and I think he is trying to look smooth, debonair or something. In my opinion, he fails.

He reaches for her, tugs at her waist with a weak hand. She kisses his cheek and easily redirects his hand to rest on his chest. She pulls back the sheets and checks his wound. There is no sign of a puncture. The infection has completely cleared. All that remains on Ry's abdomen is some minor bruising and a finite network of faint blue and gold lines. Strange to know my blood caused that healing artwork.

Zarah ruffles his hair and produces a small vial from her apron pocket. "Take your meds?" she says.

"Whatever the doctor orders." He obediently leans forward and opens his mouth. She slowly pours the concoction down his throat. I frown. I don't like not knowing what it is Zarah is giving him, but she has managed to bring him back from death's door, so I should probably trust her. After the last swallow of the medicine, Ry's hands reach out and weave through Zarah's hair. He pulls her to him and they kiss. And kiss some more. They keep kissing.

I roll my eyes and look away. Clearly, he's feeling better if he's up to fooling around. I exhale and smile. His love for Zarah explains so much I didn't understand before. When I look back at the mirror, Zarah is laying on the bed, curled up against him. He is on the verge of nodding off.

My heart swells at the sight of him happy, mostly healthy, and resting peacefully. The glimpse is a gift for which I am deeply grateful. "Thank you," I say, looking up to the top of the mirror's frame.

A tiny knock comes from the mirror, and I glance back down, watch as Zarah stirs. She's careful not to wake my brother when she extracts herself from his hold and the bed.

The knock comes a second time, and I spy someone standing outside the glass doors in the back corner of the room. When Zarah realizes who waits on the other side of the glass, she pauses and looks back at Ry before making her way to the awaiting visitor.

The fact that Zarah felt it necessary to look back at my brother before answering the door has caused my chest to tighten. I watch keenly, unsure of what I will do if danger waits with the knocker at the back door.

The image in the mirror is focused on Ry so the scene currently playing out is in the background, hard to discern. I must squint and focus.

When Zarah opens the door, she puts her finger to her mouth and steps to the side, allowing the visitor to enter. My heart slams into the wall of my chest and drops into my gut.

Dohlan steps into the room.

TWENTY-FIVE

Dohlan and Zarah? Why would he visit her? He's clearly no stranger to her. Ry hates Dohlan. If he knew his *fiancée* was meeting his enemy behind his back, he would be livid. I want to jump through the mirror glass straight into Zarah's hobbit abode. I want to give them both a piece of my mind.

They step outside, out of sight.

"Follow them," I say.

"This is a mother's mirror, not a spy glass." The wooden frame sounds indignant.

I drop back onto my butt and huff. My head is sweltering. Frustration and anger are swirling into a tornado inside of me. I'm thinking hard, trying to figure out how to hear what is being said between Zarah and Dohlan.

Crystia.

Crystia or Kaia. They are both on the spiritual plain. They can find out what I want to know.

"Show me Crystia," I say to the mirror. No image appears. "I said, show me Crystia." I wait, but nothing happens. "Show me Kaia." Again, no change. Maybe the mirror needs to recharge. But the tree isn't talking or responding in any way. Could it have gone to sleep? It is night. Do trees sleep?

My shoulders droop. Energy evaporates off my skin, and exhaustion floods my blood.

The changed, unrecognizable girl in the mirror peers at me. She blinks and frowns. She is my butterfly, the change I must accept. I study her, taking in all the changes, and hope that the longer I watch her the more accepting I will become of all the differences.

Your sisters have always been within you. Dohlan's parting words echo at the back of my mind. Did he mean they are literally within me, trapped in my head or something? If that were true, it would explain why the mirror showed me my own reflection when I asked about them. If that's the case, how do I release them?

I shake my head. Dohlan is a liar. A deceiver. He probably told me that stuff about my sisters to send my off course from my original journey.

I want to be at Ry's side, and I want to be there now, but I have no idea where I am and which way I must travel to find my brother... or Jaden. But Jaden is on his way. He is coming for me. That means, I wait.

Waiting can be painful, like now.

Overcome with a sense of anxiety, I think about lying down on the bed upstairs. A flash memory of Kaia and Dohlan instantly changes my mind. I shudder, then leave the mirror and shuffle toward the front door, my original destination before being distracted by the mirror.

After sleeping for days during this latest awakening, being tired now is absurd. It seems I have managed to spend more hour sleeping than I have spent doing much of anything else since I have arrived here in Hiddenkel.

Now that I am someplace where Kaia actually spent time and made memories, I want to learn things. Discover things. And since my time here is limited, I should investigate and learn as much as I possibly can before Jaden arrives and takes me back to my brother. I am, after all, curious about Kaia's life and the location of her cozy cottage.

I step outside and stand on the tiny porch, soak in the moonlight. There's a magic in the moonlight I never before understood. The sun is warm and radiant, but the moon is equally radiant, only on a different frequency. The relationship between day and night is part of the balance between the dark and light that I suspect is too often overlooked. I have never experienced the current of the moon and the night tingle through my system as I do now. My latest change has strengthened my connection.

The moon rejuvenates me. I suspect, with what I am becoming, I will never have need for another warrior's ritual. I will gain my energy boosts organically.

With the thought of the warrior's ritual, my mind once more wraps around wishes and concerns of Ry. I bet he will be blown away with my latest metamorphosis. His reactions to my transformation are almost embarrassing.

Ry sleeping, depending on Zarah for his health and care. Zarah slipping out the door to talk with Dohlan. Dohlan who probably killed Crystia and set up Kaia.

I am a volcano about to erupt. I grind my teeth and clench my fists until my nails cut into the skin of my palms. My foot slams to the ground, and I let out a scream. If I were a cartoon, my face would be red and steam would be spewing from my head.

Dirt explodes on either side of the porch, blasting away from me.

I suck back a breath. My emotions caused the destructive reaction. That, right there, is what I need to learn to control.

Deep breaths slowly calm my rage. There is nothing I can do about Zarah and Dohlan from where I am, and stressing over the Ry-Dohlan-Zarah situation won't do any good. My lips pull into a tight line, and I throw my focus onto something else. Anything else.

The cottage is set in a large clearing, surrounded by a densely packed army of trees. The wide expanse of open space between the cottage and the forest would make it difficult for anyone to sneak up on the place. Smart planning. When I look back at the home, I immediately recognize it as the one I saw in a previous flash or memory. I saw Kaia greeting the mystic here.

My heart swells. Until the moment I placed that memory here, I didn't realize a part of me desired confirmation of Kaia's presence. Now I have that confirmation, and I have no doubt that Kaia was here because she wanted to be here. I meander the side path, move closer to the garden.

In the memory, Kaia was standing at the edge of a garden. The garden that now slumps, neglected at the front and side of the cottage. So much of the plant life is dead or near dead. The same goes for the pasture spreading out in all directions. It's browning. The trees at the front of the forest fortress, their branches lay limp and leafless. A few fallen trees and land scars speckle the area. At the sight of them, my imagination spins with images of an intense battle with Dreya. Trees torn from their roots. Dirt and grass exploding.

I blink the images away.

Wild imagination.

But something destructive happened here—once—that much is clear. The state of the landscape rips a massive gash in my heart. Sorrow rolls down my cheek and falls to the grown. When my tear hits the yellow thrush at my feet it instantly turns a healthy green. The speed of the change is jaw dropping, and I must snap my mouth shut.

What has happened before my eyes is a miracle. The change isn't that much when you look at the bigger picture. The new grass is a circle the size of a soup can, and I need to heal the world. At this rate, it will take years far beyond my lifespan.

Not that I know how long my life will be. But still... There has to be a better way I am meant to go about inciting change.

Dropping to my knees, I lay my hands on the ground, dig deep into the farthest nooks and crannies of my soul and pull forth the spirit of life. Love and life, gratitude and serenity fill my being, my request, my message, flowing freely from me, spilling out onto everything around my hands. The energy is like a growing puddle of warm water. Something greater than me has turned the faucet all the way on, allowing the hot waves of growth to rush down my arms, through my hands, and into the land.

The breath of life extends faster than water from a garden hose. The change spreads in an arch, moving away from me toward the trees. At the forest line, the regeneration of life climbs each tree individually, lifting branches, and filling their height with an abundance of rich leaves. Flowers of purple and white bloom in patches along the pasture, producing a haphazard path to the cottage. A doorway framed of vines outlines a path into the forest ahead.

My tongue has turned to sandpaper. A droplet of sweat meanders down the side of my brow. Each limb aches and my elbows threaten to fold. I have reached my limit.

For today, anyway.

A waning thread of exhaustion beats at me with an invisible broom of twigs.

I pull my hands from the grass and sit back on my feet. My thirst for water bubbles like a geyser. Something inside of me fizzes, prepares to overflow. The earth beneath me grumbles. The grumbles turn to rumbles, shifting away from me and toward the edge of the clearing. With a crash of thunder and the roar of a rockslide, the ground by the tree line caves, drops, and fills with water. My water ability has abundantly answered my thirst.

A babbling brook, weaving in and out of the forest, now runs along the front perimeter of the cottage.

I exhale and slip back, landing butt to night-chilled grass. Never did I ever imagine I could do so much. Although, I am drained, I am stronger than ever before. My accomplishment has left me with a solid sense of empowerment. I wouldn't be surprised to find myself glowing with satisfaction.

The grass becomes a temporary bed, and I gaze at the moon above.

Still thirsty.

Seeing water and hearing water does not fulfill my need, my desire to drink.

Water seeps up through the ground, filling my curled palms.

I bolt to a sit. *Oh my Gaea!* I glance at my hands. The

water spills when I sit up. My hands fill with water once again. I cup my palms together, the water level increases, and I quickly gulp it down. Every time I cup my hands and focus on my thirst, water appears, rising out of nowhere. I repeat the action time after time until my thirst is quenched.

Content, I lay back on my earthen bed. The bedsheet I've been dragging around me adds a layer of protection against the night. My heavy eyelids tease of sleep, but my mind continues to poke me awake.

Kaia was here with the old mystic. Why was Kaia here? Why did she need or want this place when she likely had more than comfortable lodgings at the castle?

So many times I have dreamed an experience from the view of another. That ability is in my blood on my mother's side, an Immortal Warrior gift. Learning from the mistakes and successes of our ancestors is what makes the clan formidable in battle. The battle I fight is different than that of the warrior clans. I do not fight an army with weapons of steal.

Dreya has her army, yes, but she is not the ultimate bad. Not as I am coming to understand the true battle being fought.

I close my eyes and hope that the immortal blood flowing in my veins will allow me to access Kaia's memories.

I relax, focus, and close my eyes.

Drift off.

The intensity of the colors surrounding me is unworldly. Above, the moon is swallowing the night sky. Smoke rises from the cottage chimney, and a warm, inviting glow emanates through the open front door.

I am dreaming... I think.

A tiny sound of awe whistles through my lips. I hadn't properly studied the cottage until now. The entire back half of the house is built into a hill. In a way, it's like Zarah's place, only this home isn't trying to hide its presence. The hill drapes over the top of the house, reminding me of a car pulling out of a garage. The garage being the hill. Ferns and flowers hang over the roof line, cascading toward the windows and doors in nature's imitation of ribbons and bows.

Kaia steps from the cottage, moves to the edge of the garden and waves. I peer in the direction of her attention. The garden, the forest, the night, it's all so alive, on a level meant for a C.S. Lewis story. Fireflies dance in the dark sky, pixies play among the trees, and tiny gnomes are at work in Kaia's garden. Either she is so used to the sight that none of it surprises her or she doesn't see what I see.

The fact that I can see her means I am not viewing the scene from her point of view but from the angle of an outsider. An outsider unseen by her.

Standing here with my bare feet buried in the grass—I look down... my feet are *made* of grass... I blink, swallow, and return my attention to Kaia—I understand that I don't need to be in Kaia's head to know what happened. Everything in this place is made up of energy, and where there is energy, there is life. Where there is life, there are memories, and the imprint of memories.

I am not only an Immortal Warrior or a Fae family member, I am coursing with water and earth. Our connection on all levels helps me see beyond the obvious. Past the barriers and layers and folds. I am the knife piercing the veils. And I am something else, too. I sense it swimming in my blood.

My skin tingles.

I am Elenari. A hidden descendant of the seven elven nations. A marrying of species in the first offering of peace and balance among all, elven and *other kind*.

There is so much about myself that is a mystery. I fear I will never know nor understand it all. My journey is in the baby steps of the beginning.

Kaia abandons the garden in favor of running the path toward the forest. The old mystic steps through the vined gateway at the tree line.

This is the memory I was hoping for.

Kaia throws her arms around the old lady, and the mystic hugs Kaia back.

"I see you found the place," Madame Marrouske says.

"I did, and it is simply charming." Kaia takes the mystic's arm and leads her toward the cottage.

"I do not approve of this." Madame Marrouske pulls them to a stop. She wearily considers the cottage. "The home has seen much loss. That changes a place, you know. Seeps into the walls. The foundation."

"So you told me," Kaia says, urging the mystic to continue moving forward. "Now I will counterbalance the sadness with an abundance of cheerful thoughts and memories. I will fill this place with a free-spirited, happy family."

Madame Marrouske pulls them to another stop. "I disapprove. This life is not yours to live. What you plan to do is unfair. Cruel, even."

"I don't believe you," Kaia counters. "It's been thirty years, and I am still a single child. Your prophecy is wrong. I'm tired of waiting," she says flatly. "I'm ready to live my life. A life of my choosing. And I choose to start that life here."

Madame Marrouske shakes her head. "Foolish"

"Maybe." Kaia tugs at the mystic's arm. "But even if we disagree, we can enjoy a cup of tea and conversation without arguing, can't we?"

Madame Marrouske pulls away, tears her gaze from the house and pins it on Kaia. "There is no need. I can see all that I need to from here. The magic remains as strong today as it did when I conjured it. As long as you are in the house, and I do mean physically inside, no one may cause you harm. You will find the dagger we spoke of hidden in the back-room." She turns to leave.

Kaia leaps after her, grabs her arm. "You're going to leave like that?"

Madame Marrouske's return gaze is a face of indiffer-ence. In that instance, she reminds me of Dohlan. I shiver. The old woman doesn't speak, but tugs Kaia's hold free, and starts walking away.

Kaia's hand wraps around the mystic's arm once more, causing her to pause. "How will I find you if I need to?"

Madame Marrouske's gaze slides over Kaia, assessing her. "If you are correct and my prophecy is wrong, you will have no need to find me. If you are wrong and my prophecy is indeed correct, the memory waters have had a pool on this plot of land for as long as I can recall. And that is an extremely long time. If I am correct, you won't need anyone's help finding the pool." She frees herself from Kaia's hold and disappears the way she came.

Kaia watches her go.

Kaia didn't think she was part of the Balance Bringer Triune. Can't say I blame her. She spent years and years preparing for something and nothing ever happened. I would find that more than a little disheartening, too.

At least now, I sort of understand why the cottage. She probably needed time away from those who would press the responsibilities of the Balance Bringer upon her. But did that mean she would sneak back and forth, show up at the castle in an attempt to keep up appearances?

My gaze shifts from Kaia to the cottage. The house is magic... or was. Within its walls, no one could cause Kaia harm. Would that magic extend to me? I bite my lip and continue to study the cozy cottage. The magic wasn't put in place with Kaia in mind, but it would continue to work for her, or so the old lady implied. In theory, that means protection should extend to me. I think. Which means, Dohlan couldn't have done anything to intentionally harm me.

Emotions. Jumbled.

Every time I think I have him figured out, another kink gets pushed into my impression.

The colors on the horizon change. The dark is now slashed with shades of cobalt and aquamarine, the calling card for sunrise. I glance down at the sheet I still hold clutched to my body. This is not the way I want to be dressed when Jaden and Mo arrive.

I wouldn't mind finding the memory water pool, but it could be anywhere from the garden to the open field to deep within the surrounding forest. Walking the landscape playing the part of a human divining rod could be time consuming. I'll try to locate the pool after I get dressed.

I head for the door of the cottage, noticing as I walk, that all remnants of the memory have faded, taking with it all hints of fireflies, gnomes, and pixies.

If I wanted to play it safe, I would head directly upstairs and get dressed, but I don't. I think about the mention of a backroom, something I didn't notice when I walked through the house. Somewhere, hidden in the spoken-of backroom, is a dagger possibly holding some kind of importance.

I start at one corner and walk the back wall all the way to the other corner. There is nothing but wall and furniture. No doors. Only one piece of furniture is large enough to hide a door. I push the tall cabinet out of the way and discover what I am looking for... a door. Somebody purposely hid the door from view. From the design, it wasn't originally meant to be hidden.

I try the knob. It's locked, and I don't have the key. I could break the lock or door, or I could look for the key. I kick the door. The door looks ancient. It splinters and gives with ease. A sigh of relief floats through me. I recognize it as belonging to the door I broke. A small black cloud of dust mushrooms from the top of the old wood. The release is followed by a rapid reknitting and reunification. Within seconds, a new looking door swings in the doorway.

"You could have just asked."

"Sorry," I whisper and make my way into the room.

The space has no windows. I guess that makes sense since it is at the back of the house, putting it in a position that is completely surrounded by earth. The room is cool and dim and a little smaller than the bedroom upstairs, and it also has a bed. Only this bed looks like it has been sitting here since the dawn of time. The musty smell is an affront to my nose.

An odd collection of furniture pieces has been shoved in the room. All furniture and no boxes or trinkets. The way the wall is coated, there definitely aren't any hidden compartments. To be thorough, I look under and behind all the furniture pieces in the room. Behind a bookcase, I find another door, cut into the hillside.

I open the door and peer into the darkness beyond. *It's incredibly dark.* Images of the inky black shadows race to my mind. Just like the night Ry and I raced from my California home. The Tenebrousian bend and stretch, reaching for me.

I squeal and stumble backward.

TWENTY-SIX

Jumping to my feet, I throw myself at the door and slam it shut. Lean my weight against it. Shudder and wait. Nothing happens. Nothing pushes from the other side. Nothing reaches beneath the door or tries to turn the knob.

Nothing can harm me inside the walls of this house.

I heave a deep breath of courage, turn around, and study the door. It's just a door. A very old but extremely ordinary door.

An ordinary door that leads to a tunnel in the hillside.

Does the no harm thing extend to this room?

I decide it must. The room was here when Kaia moved in, and Madame Marrouske made mention of its existence even as she boasted about the magical protection of the cottage.

I open the door.

It's blacker than oil within the tunnel, but there are no Tenebrousians waiting to attack me. It's nothing more than utter darkness in a chilly, echoey tunnel. *Totally normal.*

I close the door. This definitely requires investigation but at another time, when I'm feeling braver and wearing the proper attire. A bra and underwear, wrapped in a bedsheet is not ideal for exploring dark, creepy holes.

A tiny tremor rolls over me.

Creepy, having a dark tunnel in your house. I understand why someone would hide its existence.

I close up the room, leaving it the way I found it, and head upstairs.

Realizing I don't need a working pump for me to use the bathroom facilities, I enjoy a warm bath followed by a hot shower. The water line was fine, and the well was full so whatever the problem with the pump was, it was likely mechanical. Turns out, if I ask the water to come, it comes. I dry off using the bedsheet I've been hauling with me all throughout the property. The towels are simply too gross.

I rummage through Kaia's closet, tossing all the pretty gowns to the side, in search of something both appropriate and kick ass to wear. I settle on a made-for-action pants outfit in burnt umber. Further forage at the back corner of the closet gains me a sword with a hip strap. It's not the sword with which she fought Dreya, but a good sword, nevertheless.

Light filters in through the bubble-blown windows, telling me that sunrise has officially arrived. I discover a small dressing table hidden behind a privacy screen. I take a seat in front of the mirror and style my hair, using my fingers in place of a brush. My hair appears longer and fuller, which makes it that much easier to braid.

After drying my crystals and clicking or snapping them into place, and before abandoning the room, I decide to make a quick check for anything useful. I pull out drawers, shift through garments, shoes, and personal items. Most of what I find is cosmetic, things to make her more like a girl than a warrior. Maybe I don't know her the way I thought I did.

From beneath the bed, I pull a long wooden box covered with intricate carvings. The grain is rich and deep. In contrast to most things found in the cottage, the wood of the box retains a healthy glow. I study the meticulous designs, run my fingers along the beautiful illustrations. Some of the bends and curls remind me of water, but I have no idea what any of the representations mean. Even without understanding all the meanings etched across the wrapping, the box is still gorgeous.

I lift the lid to find the pressed silk outline of one large, and missing, dagger. My chest is suddenly heavy. My hopes had taken flight that I'd found the dagger Madame Marrouske mentioned. I wonder what the deal is with the dagger, anyway. I am certain Kaia was not hurting to get her hands on any weapon. As the daughter of a Fae king and a Warrior Immortal commander, she probably had access to anything she wanted.

I close the box, scoop it into my arms, and head downstairs. Before heading out the door to look for the memory water pool, I stop at the giant mirror.

"Where is Jaden now?" I ask. "Is he close?"

"Close enough." An image of Jaden and Mo appears in the glass. I startle.

"Velsa is a unicorn?" Velsa walks beside the them and their fellow horses. Her pure white main shimmers with silver and gold. Colors that match her long, twisted horn.

"*A rarity,*" the tree says, shortly.

"Clemens and Timber, too? How did I not know this before now?"

"You were blind, like so many."

"Are there many unicorns here?" I marvel at the splendid creature. I knew she was unusually gorgeous, but now it makes so much more sense. According to so many stories, she is magic incarnate.

"Very few. Her herd is the largest in all the world," the tree says.

I sigh and drop into a casual sit on the floor, placing the box at my side. Four horses, that's the largest herd to exist. "This world used to be abundant with magic, didn't it?" I think of how the area around the cottage looked when Kaia was here. Since my arrival, I haven't seen much magic, and of what I have seen, most of it has been frightening.

The tree does not answer.

"Tell me about the world tree?" I say, remembering the tree said all trees were the tree, the world tree.

"All are the tree," it says. *"All trees are separate yet one. We are born of the one. The world tree. We forever are the world tree, feeling each joy and each sorrow as one. When one of us falls, we all feel the pain."*

"That's horrible," I blurt before I manage to stop myself.

"It simply is."

Indeed. But it's still horrible. The pain part, anyway. "If you are all one big tree..."

"Separate but one."

"Right. But if you are all the world tree, what about the Tree of Life?"

"The Tree of Life is the source of life, brought into existence at the beginning of all. We are all born from the Tree of Life. From the Tree of Life comes the World Tree."

History was never my favorite subject. I want to blame that fact on my teachers. They were dull, their delivery boring, but the truth is, it was probably all me. I was too busy thinking about my plans for Hollywood to spend massive brain power trying to remember dead presidents and long-ago wars. Remembering who was born from whom and went on to do what, it was never my strong point. But this, the world tree is comprised of all existing trees. They all come from the Tree of Life. I think I can handle that fact. "I think I got it."

The tree does not respond. I didn't expect it to. I smile at Velsa the unicorn and change my focus. "How's Ry doing?" My throat thickens, practically choking my words. I press the heel of my palm to my chest. It hurts. I should have checked on my brother sooner. I allowed myself to get distracted.

I'm suddenly looking at Ry. The mirror shows him sitting in a chair somewhere outside. Someplace unfamiliar to me. He's sipping from a mug and watching something I can't see. His condition is a huge improvement from the nearly dead warrior I left days ago. He actually looks really content, considering I am missing from his life.

My lips pucker, the edges slipping toward the ground.

There is movement behind him. The edge of a door swings in and out of view. Zarah appears with a plate of food, takes a seat in the chair next to his, and places the plate on a small table between them.

I glance out the window. It's barely past sunrise. Ry, always up with the roosters. Even when he was on death's bed a few days prior. I shake my head.

"When can we expect Ana and the others?" Ry asks Zarah.

I laugh out loud. She didn't tell him. He has no idea that I went missing. He's going to be livid when he finds out. My laugh stops short. But what of Dohlan? Something happened between him and Zarah, even if it was only the exchange of information. I want to know.

"Show me Dohlan," I ask.

The tree does not respond.

"Come on!" My voice spikes with irritation. "Show me Dohlan."

"Dohlan is no more. He ceased to be when the Ice Princess touched his heart."

My shoulders slouch and brow creases. I mull the information in my mind. He ceased to be. "Because he is now an incubus? Is that it?" I ask.

The tree does not answer. I take the silence as affirmation. *Dang Dreya.* I can't spy on Dohlan with the mother's mirror because he is no longer pure elven or whatever he was. He is now an incubus and an agent of Dreya's, the Ice Princess. Is she called that because her heart is frozen? I wonder. "Oh." My back straightens. "And you couldn't show me Crystia or Kaia because they're dead." It's a statement, not a question, so I am not surprised when the tree, again, doesn't answer.

"Okay, then." I tilt my head and tap my finger to my lips. "Show me Dreya."

"You consider Dreya a loved one?" the tree asks.

I'm a little taken back. This is the first question the tree has fired back at me. "She is family. My father's sister, to be precise."

The tree remains quiet. The silence drags into the minutes, and I become uncomfortable.

"Dreya stopped being family when she fell through the ice."

My mouth pops open. "What? What happened? When did that happen?"

I get nothing but silence for a response. I splay my hands, enjoying the stretch, then I cross my arms over my chest and heave a sigh. "Fine." I can't know or do anything about Dreya or Dohlan. The mirror has zero information for me regarding my sisters. Ry looks good, but there is something fishy there I will need to investigate. And Jaden and Mo are on their way here.

"When will Jaden get here?" I ask, hoping the tree will choose to be more helpful.

The image of Jaden takes over the mirror once more. My heart inflates and then shudders at the sight of him. I need him. I miss him. I'm scared to face him.

"Can you show me images that are not from now?" I ask the wood surrounding the mirror.

"The mirror does not tell the future."

"That's not what I want," I say. "I'd like to see something from the past."

"One should be careful with requests. Knowing too much about events for which they were not present can often come to a bad end," the tree warns.

"I'll take that under advisement." I watch Jaden in the mirror and take a deep centering breath. Wish I could tell by the landscape how far away he is right now, but I know nothing about this world of Hiddenkel. "Can you show me Jaden when he first felt me again, after or during my transformation?"

"Some things should not be seen." Silence passes between me and the tree that is the mirror's frame. *"You have been warned."*

"So I have," I whisper. "No secrets." The words are barely audible.

My reflection in the mirror swirls away and is replaced

with a new vision of Jaden and Mo. The sun is out, and they are riding through a field of long yellow grass. Yuromo calls my name as they ride.

"It's no use," Jaden says. "She's a complete void. That means, wherever she is, she is deep in the grips of another transformation."

Mo shrugs her shoulders and calls my name yet again.

Jaden jerks, his arms automatically pulling on Clemens's reins. The beautiful, chestnut unicorn pauses, side steps. Jaden searches from left to right, a frantic frenzy in his eyes.

"I feel her. I feel her," he declares, with enthusiasm. "She's... she's far from here. We need to go..."

He yanks on the reins, adjusting Clemens's direction. He doesn't finish his sentence. He's frozen, glaring into a void no one but he can see. He snarls. I twitch, pull away from the mirror. I keep watching. Jaden's snarl turns into a yell, and he pushes Clemens to top speed.

I drop my face in my palms. "Oh god. Oh Gaea. What have I done?" Tears threaten to break free. I press at the space below my eyes, discouraging any breakdown.

"I'm coming, Ana. I'm coming."

Jaden's voice pulls my face from my hands. I watch his expression morph as he rides, knowing that each change, each frown and show of anguish is because of me, of what he's experiencing because of me.

"What?" he hollers, and Clemens skips, kicks his front legs. Jaden's nostrils flare, his teeth clench, and his eye twitches. "A ring? Are you kidding..."

A tear escapes. I look away. I've never seen Jaden anything but gentle and accommodating. Yet, I asked to see this. I asked for this pain. I didn't ask for the pain I have caused him, but I asked to know.

Would I want to not know?

The answer is no.

His reaction only proves that he is real flesh and not something falsely made.

But I've caused him so much anguish...

"She's gone. She's gone."

The panic in his voice is another dagger to my soul. My head snaps up, and I focus on the scene playing out in the mirror once more.

"It will be alright," Mo placates.

They are no longer on the horses. I wonder when that happened. Or why it happened.

"Come on. Let's keep moving." Mo leads him back to the horses. "We know the general direction. If we keep moving, when you sense her again, we'll be that much closer." Jaden nods his head and quietly mounts his horse.

I shake my head, watch them set out and ride once more. Coming here, the time with Dohlan, none of it was my idea. None of it was planned. All I wanted to do was get clear of the sickening sweet aroma all over Zarah's place. I should have stayed put and remained indoors at Zarah's house. Everything. My fault. Always.

Even when he doesn't know the terrible things I am up to, I am causing him pain. There is no win for us. For me.

I watch them move at a trot. Jaden looks like someone just killed his dog. His eyes suddenly widen. He feels me once more. I remember why he couldn't. I erected a wall in my mind to blind him to the vision of Dohlan. I thought nothing good would come of him living that experience, but clearly, he had already experienced enough at that point. It was already too late when I blocked him. I also remember the moment my wall failed.

The traumatic pain shattering my body. Dohlan's hot and heavy distraction. A kiss unlike any ever before bestowed upon me. The rush of emotions—irritation, frustration, ecstasy, to name a few. Only, looking back now, I'm not sure all the feelings are mine.

When Jaden experiences that moment between me and Dohlan, his entire face falls. Clemens rears and Jaden topples to the ground. He pushes up on his hands and stays there, unmoving, focused on the dirt. But I know what he's really seeing. He's seeing Dohlan kiss me, long and fevered. He is seeing, feeling, experiencing me kiss Dohlan back.

Jaden's hands stretch into ridged claws, fold into tight fists, then slam into the dirt.

My chest erupts with rage. Rage that isn't mine, but his. The damn breaks and my tears rush down my cheeks. Again, I bury my face in my hands. There has been so much misery and suffering since I awoke. Could more of what I am experiencing belong to Jaden?

"Enough," I say, my voice cracking. "I've seen enough."

The image on the mirror shifts, and I am once more looking at my own reflection. I have two different-colored eyes, my birthmark is hardly noticeable, and I have enough gold strands in my hair to weave the Fae king's new clothes, but it's still me. Clueless, confused me. A confused me I can't stand to look upon anymore. My gaze drops to the floor.

I can't stop thinking of Jaden's clenched fists in the dirt. His fists slam to the ground again and again. And then they are slamming into Dohlan's face, once, twice, three times. He's yanking me free from the bed. Like a mini movie on replay, the sequence rolls over and over and over.

My shoulders jerk straight.

That hadn't happened. Where did those thoughts come from?

Jaden's name falls off my lips in a whisper. Again, his fists slam to the ground, only this time his skin is bloody and marred. With each impact against the ground, the surface flickers back and forth between dirt and Dohlan's face.

My hands fly to my lips and I gasp.

Somehow, I've managed to channel Jaden's emotions— his anger—from moments already gone by.

I bite down hard on my lip and taste the coppery taste of blood. In an instant, I am reminded of licking the blood from Dohlan's lip during a previous kiss. I'm overcome with an inundation of images—me with Dohlan, Jaden beating Dohlan, Jaden shaking me senseless.

I fold in on myself and sob. Living with no secrets is excruciating.

And crying. I so hate crying. But the waiting... in this instance... the waiting is far worse. It's the dread of not knowing.

Nasty anticipation courses through my veins. Jaden's seen it all, and there is nothing I can say to make things better. I am a slave to the pain of waiting for what will unfold. My body is at war with itself. Fire and acid crash and burn my insides. Nerves shaking, eyes stinging, I gather the wooden box and make my way upstairs to watch and wait in the bedroom window seat.

When Jaden finally arrives and is here in person, will I hold my own, or will I crumble? Will we hash out our feelings, or will we stay silent, allowing them to bubble and fester inside?

I am aware of their arrival long before they step foot on the property. The sound of the horse hooves hitting the dirt carries through the earth to my ear. They have a couple more miles to cover. I still have time.

My heart is so tight in my chest I can't breathe.

I train my gaze on the garden below.

A gentle mist has begun to form. It matches my mood. I keep vigil at the window, eyes fixated on the well outside. I don't remember the well from the first, second, or several other times I looked out this window. And I definitely don't recall it being present when I was in the garden earlier. It's the oddest well, with no borders or walls. It's nothing more than a perfect circle of water set upon the ground. It's as if... I blink... it's magical. *The memory waters.*

I raise my head, focus on the bubbles trapped in the window glass. My heart has stilled, my breathing stopped.

The pounding of Jaden's heart sounds like the quick and constant hammer of a race car piston. My heart zips into action, matching his thrum. My ribs are going to crack. I take a deep breath and turn around.

He is standing in the bedroom doorway.

TWENTY-SEVEN

When I was in junior high, my teacher Mrs. Elliott thought it would be a great idea for all the students to pair up, interview each other, and then introduce their paired partner to the class. She called it a get-to-know-you exercise. In theory, it may have sounded great, but for the execution, it was horrible. I got paired with Skylar, who has never liked me. Like never ever liked me.

She asked the most embarrassing questions. Answering them was a minefield. A no win situation. No matter what I said, I knew she would twist the words around to make me look ridiculous. And she did. She stood at the front of the class and made me sound truly wretched. At the time, I considered it one of the worst days of my life.

Thanks to the Bringer-Tracer connection, Jaden has now been exposed to the ultimate get-to-know-you exercise. There is no way to twist or untwist the events that transpired between me and Dohlan so that I come out looking, sounding, and smelling good.

I stand and face Jaden. He is across the room, braced in the doorway, and he is looking not at me, but at the bed, his face contorted into a mix of emotions. The most predominant of which I suspect is anger. Anger with Dohlan and anger with me, no doubt.

I have had hours to prepare for this moment, to figure out what to say. The moment is now, and I have no words. They won't come.

But he's peering and glaring, non-stop glowering at the bed. The bed in which Dohlan and I kissed. My heart is trying to beat its way out of my chest. I need to say something, anything.

"You came?" *Stupid, stupid, stupid.* I bite my lip. Hold my breath.

His shoulders drop and his head lifts. He meets my gaze. My heart skips and pauses. His beautiful green eyes are glossy, wet with unshed tears.

I did that. Caused that.

We're like statues at opposite ends of the room. Neither one of us speaks or moves for endless, torturous seconds.

"Ana, I..." He chokes on the next word, falls silent.

The moment of truth is here. I steel myself against the coming onslaught.

"I was..." His voice is so soft, so hushed I tilt my head to better hear.

"I need a minute," he says, pressing his hand to his forehead. He turns his back to me.

I don't move. I wait. The air is dry and dense, hard to breathe. Something has sucked all the oxygen from the space. I tug at my collar.

Outside, the horses huff and shift. They, too, are waiting. Mo sits in the garden. She chews on an apple she recently plucked from the newly bloomed apple tree. I sense them all. All but Jaden. I have no idea what he's going to do or say. He has clearly erected a mental wall to keep me away.

My heart is fluttering. Fluttering up into my throat. I fear I am coming unhinged. Disconnected from the world. I'm floating away on a cloud, but I can't hold on. I'm going to fall. I've been terrified to face Jaden, but despite that, I assumed that he cared enough to work through the pain. What if that is a lie?

My strength dissolves. I collapse onto the seat in the window.

Jaden spins around, it's a blur of color and motion. "Are you alright?" The distance between us folds, and he is here now, at my side—his palm gentle against my upper arm.

I shake my head. Everything is blurry. I can't see. I blink and tilt my head to gaze at the blur I know is Jaden. "I may never be alright," I say.

"You can't believe that." He sits beside me. He's moving, doing something, but I can't make it out. It's all a mush of color and fuzz. "You'll find your balance. I believe in you."

"You do?" I hate how pathetic I sound.

He huffs a half laugh, and I hear so much in that simple sound—skepticism, hurt, reluctance, tenderness.

Something scratches my eye, and I jerk back.

"It's alright," he says. "Don't move."

I obey and slowly, softly, he dabs at my eyes. He clears the tears I didn't know I cried. I blink the last trace away.

He holds the cloth out for me to see. My tears are frozen. They froze over my eyes. *I can't even cry correctly.*

The thought makes me want to cry more... but I won't.

I peer at Jaden through the cover of my lashes. I find myself leaning, leaning closer, watching the swirl of his green eyes and searching for the truth of his feelings where I am concerned. As my Tracer, he is stuck with me. But does he want to be... stuck with me?

His shoulders hunch, and he twists the cloth in his hands. "I'm not going to lie to you, Ana. I know none of what happened was intentional on your part, but it hurt, and I may need some time..."

"Of course," I say, cutting him off. I'll give him time. I'll give him all my meals. I'll give him all my tears. I'll give him anything he wants if it will make up for the way I made him feel.

He nods. Doesn't look at me, but molds his palm to my thigh, giving the softest of squeezes. When he releases, he splays his open hand before me. "Let me see."

I'm confused by the request, so I study his hand and make no attempt to move. And then it dawns on me what he's asking. I place my left hand in his.

His breathing is heavy, deep, as he spreads my fingers and studies the tiny gold band on my ring finger.

"Can you remove it," he asks.

My eyes widen, and I stare at the band of gold like it's a trap. The kind of trap that will cut off my finger if I try to go against Dohlan's wishes. Twice I have removed the ring, and twice Dohlan has shown up, scolded me, and put the ring back on my finger.

"I didn't ask you to actually remove the ring," Jaden clarifies. "I simply want to know if it's possible."

I shake, silently, in a nervous response of uncertainty. I haven't even touched the ring since it was slipped on my finger this time. I don't know why, but the sight of it, the thought of it, evokes a flee response.

Am I suffering from PTSD or something?

Jaden looks away from the ring, gazes into my face. He's studying something. I'm afraid to jinx us, so I keep my mouth shut and don't move. I get the sense that I am wide open and he is receiving everything—thoughts, feelings, all of it.

"He put you through a lot," Jaden says, finally breaking the silence. I don't trust myself to speak, not yet, anyway, so I simply watch him. "I could kill him for what he's done," he says, full of venom.

My eyes fly wide. The last thing I want is for Jaden to be maimed or killed.

His head tilts back and shakes. "You don't think I can take him."

"I didn't say that," I blurt and shift to better face him.

"You didn't have to." He stands and offers me his hand.

My breath is stuck in my throat. I consider the offered hand that I am unworthy of taking. His hand flips, drops over my arm, and pulls me to a stand.

"Stop it," he says, pulling me from the room.

"Stop what?" My feet quicken to keep up.

"Stop doubting yourself." We descend the stairs and make our way through the main living space. "It amazes me that you have all this strength and magnificent abilities..." He motions to the vines covering the walls and ceiling. They've grown so much in a day. "...and you still cower when it comes to people and relationships."

His words are a slap to the face. They sting, but they are true. I've always had trouble where talking and sharing is involved. I'm not a good people person. I've never denied that fact.

He pulls me through the cottage, out the front door, and into the garden, where Mo and the horses wait.

"And what of you?" I ask, quickly shuffling my feet to keep up with his pace.

He glances over his shoulder at me. "What do you mean? What about me?"

"You know, your problem." I wave my hand in the air as if the silly motion clarifies my comment. He looks at me funny and squints his eyes as if to better peer through the chaos my mind is currently generating. "The parasite," I whisper for only him to hear.

He turns his attention forward. "Don't you worry about that," he says, which I take to mean I definitely need to worry about it... about him. The problem remains unfixed.

At the sight of us, Mo leaps to her feet and tosses an apple she was eating. "Finally."

Jaden thrusts me toward Velsa. I stumble with momentum, crash into her side. Jaden grabs Clemens's reins and turns him around.

"Um..." Mo wipes the back of her hand across her mouth. "Before we go, I thought you might like to know that there is a puddle of water over there..." She flings her arm toward the side garden. The area visible from the window seat in the bedroom. "...that keeps calling Ana's name."

Jaden and I both freeze and ogle Mo.

"The memory waters," I mumble. A second later, all three of us are rounding the edge of the cottage, making our way to the side garden.

The memory waters sit upon the ground like a perfect circle of black glass. It shimmers and reflects, while remaining perfectly still. A strange tingle itches at the back of my head inciting the oddest sensation that I have once stood in this spot, gazed at the same dark water. If I have, the memory is just beyond my reach.

"It's not saying anything now," Jaden says, studying the water at our feet.

"Just wait," Mo says. "It's intermittent." She crosses her arms and tilts her head to the side.

I don't doubt the water called my name. When I sat in the bedroom window seat, something was constantly drawing my gaze to the large puddle. And once I saw it, noticed it, I was mesmerized.

A series of ripples expand from the center of the memory water, like a tiny pebble has been dropped in the center. Only, there are no pebbles and none of us have moved.

My name dips and rises with the liquid's curl and fold, sounding like a whisper spoken from a deeply channeled crevice beneath the surface. The melody is chilling with both dread and beauty.

"Anala," the waters call my name, again. Treading on new territory, I'm unsure what I am meant to do. Such is the case with everything I seem to come across in this world. I drop to my knees and lean closer. Jaden's hand clamps over my shoulder, and I somehow know he means to yank me backward, away from the pool, at the first sign of danger.

"I am here," I say.

Mo snickers and I shoot her a stop-it glare. She clamps her lips shut and looks away, tossing her hip out with the motion.

"Join us, Anala Danika Raine. Join the waters of remembrance," the voice hums.

I glance back at Jaden, and he frowns at me with uncertainty.

"I know nothing about any memory waters," he says. "Please be cautious."

As if he even needed to speak the words. I smirk at him

and then gaze down at the water. "How exactly do I join you?"

"*Closer.*" The word whispers through my head. "*Closer. Closer.*"

Right. My gut constricts. I reach out, hesitantly, and dip my finger into the water.

"*More. More. Closer. More.*"

Jaden's grip on my shoulder tightens. He's sensing my apprehension, my agitation. I want to pull back, forget about the water and leave this place, but I know I can't. There are things I want to know, need to know, and if this dark little pool of water can help me with any of those answers, I'm going to stay and follow through.

I dip the fingers of my other hand into the water and close my eyes.

The cool, sliding sensation of ancient belonging glides over my arms. The feeling wraps around my biceps and over my shoulders like a serpent.

"Wooha," Mo says, her feet shuffling backward.

Jaden tugs on my shoulder. I yank back, and he releases. Whatever is happening, whatever they see, I am alright... so far.

The calm wash of waters continues to climb, its fluid fingers inching up my neck and through my hair. Like a veil, the awareness of what the memory waters is and what it has to offer slips over my sight and mind.

"*It is time, Balance Bringer,*" the water says, sounding like it is all around me.

Time for what? I think but do not speak.

"*Time to awaken.*"

"To awaken my inner Balance Bringer?"

"*No.*"

I am startled by the response. I was so certain.

"Time to awaken the world. Heal her and all the magic that dwells upon and within."

Such a tall order for a now high school dropout. I am but one girl. *One girl who can apparently manipulate water and plants.* "And how do I do that?" I ask.

"Be, and be not," it says, as if I should understand exactly what that means in my situation. *"Share your energy with everything around you."*

"I was hoping for a little more guidance than that," I grumble.

The water does not respond. It falls stills, remains intensely quiet.

Three ripples of time swim by before the water delivers its next message. *"Remember."*

With a soft nudge, I recall. Not a lot. Not the answers to all that I seek. Not even the extent to what purpose I was made. But one thing, a most important thing I remember... and it is a lie. It is a thing I cannot accept as truth.

I gasp and drop onto my butt. Water splashes all around me.

"Are you alright?" Jaden asks.

I examine the pool of water, it is receding, as if being sucked down a drain.

"What happened?" He drops to my side, and my cheek itches from his scrutinizing peer.

"That was unreal," Yuromo says. "The water from the pool slipped over your arms and head like some kind of body armor. Jaden hushes her.

The pool disappears down the small, imaginary hole, and the ground at my feet is as it was before, with no hint of ever having been wet. My gaze shifts to the garden before me, then to Mo who is staring at me with saucer-wide eyes, and finally, I look to Jaden.

"Are you all right?" he asks again.

Slowly, I shake my head. "Like I said before, I may never be all right. Never again."

"Your heart and mind are plagued with discomfort," he asks. "What happened? What did you learn?"

"Something that can't possibly be true," I blurt. "The water lies. It seeks to deceive."

"And what is this lie?" Jaden wraps his hand over mine and, with a soft tug, encourages me to rise. We stand, facing one another, and as much as I care for Jaden, I wish my brother was here. Ry would know the truth... wouldn't he? He could tell me if what the memory waters said is true.

"Tell me, Ana. What is troubling you? What did you learn?" Jaden's hands glide the length of my arms, his touch comforting and easing my distress. Not by magic but because it is him who offers me ease.

With a deep breath that reaches to my core, I find my courage to speak. "The water reminded me of my sisters' origins."

The origin memory presses firmly at the front of my mind. A hand holding a twig. One long twine that breaks into three smaller stems. "On this day, the one shall become three," the voice said. Her fingers trace the line of the wood, bending the other two branches to slowly curve back toward the center stock. "Until the time when three must again be one." Magically, the wood binds, and the three are once more one branch, with a bowed separation at the center of its length. The owner of the hands holding the twig is unknown to me and the memory is focused on the magic she is creating, rather than who she is or what she looks like.

Jaden's gaze is both soft and questioning. He waits for me to continue.

"They are not my sisters," I say with a hitch, thinking of the curve and bend of the branch.

His eyes cloud with confusion and, still, he waits.

"They are pieces of me!"

TWENTY-EIGHT

The ride back to Zarah's little hobbit home is both long and miserably silent. We ride and ride and ride some more. I know I didn't cover this much distance when I ran out the other night, attempting to clear my head. I find it incredible that Dohlan managed to carry me so far. Or had he? Maybe he transported me by some means I fail to remember.

Dohlan's words keep nagging me, whispering in my mind, over and over, on an endless loop. *Your sisters have always been within you, Ana.* The key word is *within*. Was he privy to the knowledge the memory waters shared? Did he know my sisters *are* me? I struggle to understand how such a thing is even possible.

My grip on Velsa's reins tightens, chasing the blood from my fingers.

Velsa has chosen to follow, rather than lead, our return, and I chose not to fight her. Under the circumstances, I want to give Jaden any and all space he may require. He hasn't spoken to me since we set out, and I have decided not to push things. I don't want to force him into a conversation he isn't ready to have. I want him to brood, then forget any indiscretions, remember his heart, and come back to me.

So for now, I find comfort in the rock and sway of Velsa's forward canter. From my position, I have a perfect view of Jaden's backside. His shoulders are tense in their movements, and I imagine him simmering in a stew of emotions. Ugly, unwanted emotions.

Occasionally, Mo will glance over her shoulder at me and then over at Jaden, but she never says anything. She probably doesn't want to be the first one to break the silence. If I were her, I'm fairly certain I would feel the same way.

I glance between Jaden and Mo, my gaze wandering to the majestic unicorns carrying their weight. Jaden and Mo don't even know... they have no idea of the magic surrounding them. Magic that *apparently* only I can see.

For now.

I'll change things so that everyone can experience the wonder. Somehow.

When we left the cottage, the flora was rich with verve and speckled in vibrant colors, half of which I was unfamiliar with. The farther we travel, the duller the colors have become. It's astounding how quickly the scenery here can change. One minute, we're surrounded by suffocating plant life, and the next, the terrain is wide open in yellow-green pastures, and of course, the occasional crooked tree.

It's in one of these pastures that the sensation washes over me. The nausea one gets when riding in a car that is weaving and spinning around a winding, mountain road. Or when your plane hits a pocket of turbulence and makes a sudden drop. My stomach flips and churns, my muscles ache, and bile climbs up my throat.

It's the rank, nauseous feeling of death. My gut recognizes it immediately.

I reach for my newly birthed earthen gift, hoping a connection with the land will help me distinguish what is awry. But as quickly as the sense washes over me, it vanishes, and I am once again my normal, confused self. Nothing has changed—or so it appears. Only our physical location is different, due to the horses continued forward motion.

Since the feeling is gone, I say nothing to hinder our trek back to my brother. I miss him and I'm anxious to see him. I need to verify that he is alright and beautifully healed. But the incident, the gut response to something ugly that I can't see and only sense, has left me wondering. The memory waters basically said that I will awaken the world's magic by doing pretty much nothing. How does that work?

Does that truly mean my mere presence is all that is required to wake up and heal the land around me? I feel like I should have to do something. Master a grand quest or speak a major enchantment. Doing nothing seems so wrong.

Or maybe, without actual intention or planning, I am predestined to do whatever needs to be done to heal the world... or worlds.

If only I knew.

I let out a deep breath and survey the landscape.

An open pasture is fading at our back, and we're making our way into a pocket of Hiddenkel bursting with ferns so tall that even as I sit upon Velsa's back, I can reach out and touch them. Growing up in the California desert, I didn't see a lot of ferns, except in my mom's floral shop. Ferns have always made me think of rain. I'm not sure why they invoke visions of moisture, but for some reason they always have.

The ferns we pass by now are pale in color, looking yellow or turning tan with singed edges. The only thoughts of water they induce is a want, a thirst. This space is a need, and I suspect water is only a portion of what is missing here.

A shiver rattles through me, and a dewy sheen slips over my skin. As if reacting to me, ferns start to twitch and wiggle—a few even stretch up to my hand.

I startle. *Am I subconsciously doing something?*

Dull yellows and browns become golden apricot and saffron. Like the traveling current of a spilled bag of skittles, color races and spirals across and over the surrounding ferns, bushes, and trees. Shrubs blush in shades of chardonnay; a potpourri of aquamarine and turquoise flood the ground-cover, and trees that previously looked like collapsed straws plump to the size of small houses.

I know Jaden recognizes the change. I sense his astonishment. Something inside of me flutters and warms. *I sense him!* But despite his curiosity and wonder, he remains quiet. He doesn't even turn his head to look at me. Sadness pinches my nerves. And, to my surprise, guilt twitches his shoulder and tilts his head.

Still, he doesn't speak and doesn't look my way. We are trapped in a cone of silence filled with only the thrush of the unicorns' hooves upon the ground and the drip, drip, drip of the dew off the overhanging canopy of leaves.

Mo drops back, bringing Timber to trot at my side. Her eyes are gigantic windows into her marvel-filled soul. She chews on a native fruit, hands one to me. I take a bite. The greenish-orange fruit is sweet and juicy, and I thank her with a happy nod.

"You did this?" Her finger swirls in the air, motioning to the colorful trees and ferns.

"Pretty sure." I wipe away the sweet nectar working its way down the side of my chin and survey the multitude of colors among the plant. The sight reminds me of the wide range of flowers my mother would work with in her shop. She was a painter without a brush. An artist working with the living. I never understood how she did it before now, but she could produce any flower in any color and create bouquets that would melt the recipient's heart. "Guess I'm an artist now."

Mo gives me a funny look and takes another bite of her fruit, as do I. "What do you mean artist?" she asks. "You are the Balance Bringer."

"I only meant..."

A cry, a plethora of screams sears through me, cutting and slicing at my ear drums. Every muscle tightens. The horses whinny, nervously dance, and Jaden throws his hands over his ears. Mo's head swings left and right, taking in our reaction to something she doesn't appear to hear.

I yank at Velsa's reins, turn her in a circle in an attempt to distinguish the direction the sound is coming from. My searching gaze bounces off Mo's confused expression, to the ferns at our feet, to Jaden's probing watch, to the path we have yet to travel.

It is there, up ahead, from where the outcry originates. The sound is neither humanoid nor animal. It is something deeper and something combined. It is as if the pain of the world has been mashed together in a horrid melody of chaos and agony.

"Go," I whisper at Velsa's ear, and we take off at a run.

We run from the fern filled garden into a fungus laid

land. A thin, rocky stream, heavily laden with mushrooms and moss, zig zags across our path. Velsa leaps over tiny villages of tall, gumdrop topped mushrooms and outcrops of short, fat sprouts. There are even mushrooms that flare out like large pixie umbrellas.

Everywhere I look, there is moss. Moss that grows like fine grass upon the rocks, and starburst moss in unorganized patterns on the stones or on nearby trees. Poking the ground, moss grows in clumps like little caps, as if trying to emulate mushrooms.

It's peaceful. A kind of serenity I would never tire of, and yet...

My stomach churns, my head pounds, and a pressure settles into my chest making it difficult to breath. Nausea gurgles in my gut... a sensation similar to what I experienced earlier. Only that time, the physical discomfort came and went so quickly it was almost like it was never there. Such is not the case this time.

Suddenly, I'm lurching forward, leaning over Velsa's side, and letting go of all the food I haven't eaten. My ears are ringing, filling with a high-pitched opera of dying and darkness.

A soft brush of a hand pulls my hair out of the way and rubs down my back. It's Jaden and I don't want to look at him, take the chance of exhaling something vile in his face.

"I'm fine," I say, not really sure if I mean the words or not. I keep my cheek pressed against the damp and clammy fur of Velsa's neck. I don't look back at Jaden but train my eyes forward, seeking out the source of all the painful cries.

A second later, I spy something worthy of investigation.

Slipping off Velsa's back, I proceed on foot, moving away from Jaden, Mo, and the team of unicorns. I ignore Velsa's disapproving whinnies and stomps and set my sights on a murky line twisting through the soft mossy ground. This line is similar to the one I saw in the forest beyond Mo's village. The only real difference between that line and the one I now approach is that the first line didn't scream as this one now does.

Of course, it could be that line *was* screaming and I simply couldn't hear it. Not yet, anyway. The ability had yet to awaken within me.

The closer I get to the line, the louder the hollers become, and the more pressure jabs at my chest and stomach.

I step up to the line, bile rising in my throat.

The ugly line appears to glint and wiggle. There is something oddly animated about the dark, gooey crevice. It's as if the line is slowly searching, reaching forward, splintering in multiple directions. The one major vein is probing the land and using small tentacles to determine the best direction or directions in which to move. And its movement is so infinitesimal that it's almost invisible to the naked eye. But my eyes, one green and one blue, perceive it well, taking in the glint of the glossy surface and the Jell-O like wiggle.

I kneel and tentatively reach forward but don't touch the line. My hands hover in the air, undecided. Without warning, Jaden's hand wraps around one of my wrists and pulls me back. I snap around. His head slowly shakes, expressing disapproval of my intended actions. He gazes down at me, but his eyes are obscured in a swirl of green and white.

He's witnessing something... and then I'm observing that something, too.

I'm no longer kneeling beside the moss-framed stream. My knees are pressed into the hard and cold edifice of a tower. The tower upon which I have met Kaia in past dreams. The stout scent of sulfur prickles my nose, makes me want to sneeze. I don't need to glance over the wall to know where the smell originates. The land to the left of the tower is barren, ravaged by fire or something as destructive. To my right comes the crash of waves upon the stone structure and rocky foundation.

In front of me, looking out over the rooftop wall, stands a woman with wavy, blonde hair. She wears what on first appearances looks like a dress made of black and gold brocade, but the flairs of the skirt camouflage her gold pants. Beyond her, and the tower, I notice a small castle sitting upon an island that floats in the sky. A long, curved staircase connects the island with the land below.

I suck back a deep breath.

"You have made me wait," the woman says. "And I so detest waiting." She turns and sets her gaze upon me. The blonde woman is Dreya. If she wasn't so disfigured with distrust, dislike, and rage, she would be the kind of beauty that would drive men to conjure nations. Her lips pull taut, and both brows rise. "Well, well. This is unexpected. What exactly is it that we have here?" She closes the space between us and snags my left hand, lifting it to better view.

The warmth of another is weaved into the grip of my right hand. I glance over. My hand is dropped at my side but is clasped with a guy's hand. And one wearing a gold band matching the smaller one Dreya now examines. I blink and look up into Dohlan's eyes. He shrugs.

My body jerks, my hand slams to the ground, catching my fall. In that instance, I am no longer standing on the tower or looking into Dohlan's eyes. I have somehow managed to pull myself from the vision, and I am gazing down at my hand pressing into the moss at the inky line's edge. Jaden's grip is still firm around my other wrist.

A scream echoes through me, I yank back, away from the cutting dark line inciting my cry, but it's too late. Whatever evil resides within the inky earthen cut it has successfully wrapped its influence around me. I fall backward to the ground, falling not onto the grass, but into a well of thick, suffocating darkness.

Everywhere around me, there are visions of Dreya laughing. She laughs at my recklessness and inexperience and sensitivity. She sneers at me, and for my benefit, she yanks Ryland from the ground at her feet and slams her hand through his chest, digging her fingers deep. When she pulls free, she not only holds his heart, but a broken rib, and bits of other internal organs.

But it can't be. The mother's mirror showed me my brother. He was safe and healing in Zarah's care. Only, I don't know Zarah. And I don't know if she can be trusted. I scream and slip backward through the inky goo, tumbling into a new room trapped within.

I'm still screaming, eyes closed, my hands pressed firmly to the side of my head, but the ground beneath me is now solid and goo free.

Someone tugs at my hands, attempting to yank them free from my ears. It's a gentle tug, and I reluctantly give in. I open my eyes, discover Crystia and Kaia standing at my side. They're transparent while being clear and distinct. Each sister takes one of my hands, weaving their fingers with mine. Together we stand, three sisters, stronger through our connection.

"She is a sad lady, full of hate and vengeance," Kaia says. "She cannot be allowed to win this fight." With a tempered smile, Kaia looks away and studies the wall of black on the other side of the room. High, arched, double doors, carved of dark wood, are set in the center.

"What she said." Crystia's smile brightens her entire being. She holds my gaze. "Didn't I say Jaden would save you?"

She's talking about when I died during my last transition. It was a short death, but I know it could have been longer. It could have been forever. At the time, I kind of wanted my death to be permanent. But Jaden's call pulled me home. My save was bittersweet. I returned to the living only to have a wedge of friction shoved between us.

"Her heart wouldn't have started back up if it hadn't been for Dohlan," Kaia says. I can't argue her point. Dohlan was persistently working to stir my heart back into action.

My sisters tug me to a stand, and I tighten my grasp on each of their hands. Thankfully, neither one of them speaks another word regarding Jaden and Dohlan. I don't care to consider that confusing situation any further.

My sisters are here... and yet... to the memory waters, my sisters are me. I don't know what to think, say, or feel.

Kaia lifts my hand between us and ogles the golden ring on my ring finger. She bites her lip and says not a word. A creek from the opposing wall jumps our focus to the large double doors. Kaia lowers our hold and carefully wraps her hand over mine, hiding the ring.

The double doors fly open, and Dreya strides into the room. Again, she is blonde. We take a step back. The back of our calves hit something ungiving. Momentum throws us off balance, and we collapse onto a firm sofa at our back. In front of us is a highly polished wooden coffee table. A melted candle, nestled into a large candle stick, sits at the top center of the table. The table also hosts a small stack of books and several more that have been laid out and left open.

The book directly at the front of me boasts a drawing of the floating island. I skim the image, blink, and look away. We are sandwiched between wall-to wall-shelves of books. It would appear we are in the middle of a personal library. A rather grand one, at that.

"Welcome to my family's library," Dreya coos. "Your father and I spent many a long hour in this room. He did love it so."

"And you?" I ask, keeping my butt seated.

"I took a liking to one or two books in particular."

I glance back down at the sketch of the book opened on the table. "Any books about the floating island?"

Her smile is wistful, filled with remembrance, and in those seconds, she is pretty. It doesn't last. Her hair morphs to red and then to black, and her smile curls into a sneer. "I see you found your sisters."

I don't correct her—sisters or other parts of me. I chose not to answer.

"They are merely a projection. A smidgen of their essence. They will be of little use in their current state."

My blood boils, and yet I somehow manage to maintain a straight face. So far, every time I have come up against Dreya, she has been able to get the upper hand. I want that standard to change. I am stronger now, and I merely need to be wise about how I proceed.

I want to tell Dreya that she can't know with certainty what my sisters are or aren't capable of in their current state. Just like she can't know what I can or could do. She is limited by what she has seen from me, which at this point hasn't been much, and little of it has been good. But I'm changing every day, becoming a new, more gifted person, and an individual with a stronger will. But I don't say any of that. I sit still and study the room, looking for clues that will give me insight into who she is and what drives her.

The books are many and most are pristine. Above, the ceiling is several stories high and decorated in a remarkable design. Four chandeliers, looking to be made of ice crystals, drip from the ceiling's center at measured intervals. Sun shimmers through the cut glass windows at my back, highlighting floating dust bunnies. A glimpse over my shoulder catches the sight of a family portrait. Four beautiful, blonde family members, all with pointy ears. Two parents, a teenage son, and a sweet little girl—Dreya.

Aside from the presence of Aunt Dreya, the room is warm and inviting and a place where I wouldn't mind hanging out.

I frown.

"I decided not to invite Dohlan to this gathering. He's been a might unpredictable lately." She closes the doors behind her. "I assume I have you to blame for his bad behavior." She turns a crooked smirk in my direction.

I haven't asked Dohlan to do anything for me. I haven't even asked him to help me where Dreya is concerned. I have yet to figure out what fuels his actions. My forehead wrinkles and I bite my lip. Dreya and me, alone. No enigma loops to protect me.

I have a bad feeling about this.

"Welcome home, Princess of nothing," she says with a sour tone. "This is how the room looked when I was young." She casually motions to the family portrait. "It's changed a bit since then. Nevertheless, the family home is rather spacious, with plenty of rooms to pick from. You could move in today... if I let you." She waves her arm over the room setting, white ice, and crystals to quickly cover everything in sight. Even Dreya's dress, hair, and skin turn white.

"My family used to be warm and friendly, the grandest in all the land. Then one day, ice ran in their veins and everything changed. The family blood turned bad." She reaches up to a large bun on top of her head and pulls two small daggers free from where they were hidden within her hair. "The family blood is bad, Ana. That includes yours."

Holding the blade out in front of her, she moves around the coffee table and makes her way toward me.

Crap. Crap. Crap.

I haven't a weapon. Nothing to fight with.

"The books," Crystia says.

"The candlestick," Kaia yells.

I grab the open book off the table and hold it up as a shield in the nick of time. Dreya's dagger pierces the book. The book filled with the floating island pictures.

She screams.

My hand wraps around the weight of the candlestick. I lift and swing, connecting with the side of her head. Then I turn and run, candlestick still in hand.

The ice and crystals on the walls and furniture melt, turn to dirty water, then black sludge. I slip and slide, fall into a bookcase. Everything is turning dark, the walls, the books, Dreya and her dress. I'm not blacking out. The darkness is swallowing the space.

Someone's grip hooks under my arms. I swing, hit something unseen, then slid sideways. Clinging to a shelf, I right myself and blink, trying to adjust to the new dark.

Again, someone wraps around me. A familiar tingle signals Jaden's touch. I yelp and fall backward. The darkness of the room blinks away, and I am once again among the trees and plants of Hiddenkel. Jaden's arms are wrapped around me, holding me where I fell.

"I can't believe I did that," Jaden says.

"How did you pull me out of there?" I say, turning to look at him. The crystal around his neck glows with the same wild swirl of colors as my crystal wristbands.

"I don't know. You were always here, physically beside me, but your mind was somewhere else. Seeing something else. I reached out for you, mentally, and yanked," he responds, sounding somewhat out of breath.

"I was with Dreya," I say. "But I didn't start there. At first, it felt like I'd managed to slip into one of your visions. Is that what I did? Was I actually able to see what you were envisioning?"

He shakes his head. "I saw you there, on top of the tower. How did you do that?"

"I don't know," I mutter. "It just happened. It almost felt like you tugged me and took me with you. I started feeling the two-way connection the night outside Ivey City, but I've felt even more connected to you ever since you arrived at the cottage to collect me."

"Yes, I've felt that too." He takes my hand and helps me stand.

"After the tower?" I ask, my stomach in knots. He saw me at the tower, holding hands with Dohlan. I can't imagine what would take me there with Dohlan or why I would hold his hand, but none of it can mean anything good for Jaden and me.

"A psychic attack. You slipped right out of the vision and into Dreya's grip. It was horrifying." His hands hold tightly to mine. "I was under the impression she used Dohlan to locate you for such attacks. But Dohlan isn't here."

I bite the edge of my lip and look to the dark cut in the earth. It's not calm like it was before. It now gurgles and pops with bubbles.

"I think..." I say and pause, study the black goo. "I think she found me through that." I point at the line.

Jaden doesn't say anything. He doesn't need to. I can *feel* him agree. Now we know, Dreya is likely the source of the cracks in the land, and the decay that comes with those lines. She is infusing her anger and resentment into the land and inhabitants of Hiddenkel.

The unicorns neigh, their hooves stomping and clawing at the ground. I look over my shoulder at them and follow their line of sight. Mo is kneeling by a break in the dark crack. She pokes it with a stick, and it's like a scene out of the old horror movie; black sticky liquid is climbing the stick.

TWENTY-NINE

I launch myself at Mo, plow into her chest full force. She drops the stick, and we tumble clear from the dark sickness, landing in a jumbled heap with her bag of fruit spilled at our side. Scrambling to my knees, I clutch her shoulders, twisting her body from side to side and every which way, looking for signs of infection. She's clear.

"What was this about?" She rubs the back of her head and then gently removes my hand from her body. She leans away from me, sending me a clear message—*give me space.*

"I was saving you," I say. Her eyes are wide and waiting. "It's just... I thought..."

Jaden offers his hand to Mo. "She was worried you might get infected by the darkness."

"Right." Mo's gaze darts toward the searching, stretching crack in the earth.

"There's no telling what contact with that stuff could do to you. I'm sure it wouldn't be anything good," Jaden adds.

Mo nods with agreement, and she slowly rises to her feet.

My hands move quickly snatching and grabbing the scattered fruit, shoving them all back into the bag. I hand the bag to Mo. "I'm sorry if I hurt you," I say, the word hurt reverberating through my mind. My eyes pop wide.

Mo glances between me and the dark crevice. "It's more like you startled me. I owe you great thanks," she says. "You may have just saved my life." She smiles. I barely hear her. The word *hurt* keeps spinning in my mind.

Ry.

My gaze snaps toward the direction that will take me back to my brother.

"What's wrong?" Jaden asks, taking my hand and pulling my attention, albeit temporarily, to him.

"I need to see my brother, like now." I let my hand slip from Jaden's hold, then turn and move toward Velsa. Jaden follows.

"Ryland is fine. I told you he was recovering nicely when we left him to find you," Jaden assures.

"I remember." I take hold of Velsa's saddle and pull myself up onto her back. "Back at the cottage, I saw him in the mother's mirror. He was doing exceptionally well." Jaden jerks at the mention of the mirror. "But just now, when I slipped from your vision into Dreya hell, she showed me a horrific sight, and that's why I need to get back to him, make sure what she showed me hasn't happened. If it hasn't, then I'll protect him so that what I saw never comes to pass." I close my eyes and see Dreya yanking Ry's heart out through his chest. I shiver, shake the image away, and tell Velsa to take us home.

Velsa bursts into a run, leaving Jaden and Mo to flounder behind us, scrambling to catch up.

Garr and his obsession with me. Dohlan and the golden

ring on my finger. Dreya and her creeping vine of darkness and death. My sisters not being my sisters but actually being me. Jaden being in the grips of a parasite. All these things weigh upon me, press into every thought, every worry.

But for now, each of them remains shoved behind my worry for Ry. I need, I *need* to see my brother. Need to touch him, crush him to my chest.

Velsa maneuvers across the terrain and through the obstacle course of trees and bushes, carrying me with unmatched speed back to Zarah's. Back to my brother. Everything at my sides is a blur, a mass of blotched color, until Velsa slows in the approach of our destination.

I sense tension in the surrounding plant life. Anger and frustration bristle the leaves, and sadness weighs upon the moss, grass, and dirt. Moments later, Ry's voice carries to my ear. My heart squeezes to a stop. Anticipation holding my every system on pause. The stillness within me broken only by the sounds of Zarah's sobs.

My heart thrums with the beat of a gallop while Velsa drops to a gentle advance.

"Please, Ryland," Zarah begs.

"I can't believe you hid this from me," Ry says.

"I know. I'm sorry. But please, please don't go." Zarah's voice is heavy with unshed burdens.

The desire to fade into the landscape itches within me. I haven't forgotten what the mother mirror showed me—Zarah talking to Dohlan, while my brother slept a few feet away. But my suspicions are only that, suspicions. I didn't hear what was spoken, and even though I no longer trust Dohlan, I cannot condemn him or Zarah of any crime without solid proof. It's clear Ry has strong feelings for the redheaded history keeper, and for that reason, I hate to hear their discontent.

I bite my lip, stretch my tight muscles, and round the bend. Jaden and Mo are at my side when we come into view of the hidden home in the hillside.

Zarah stands on the front doorstep watching Ry as he tightens Belmiso's saddle and reins. My heart swells. Although, Ry is wrapped in irritation and frustration, he is healthy and magnificent. No discolored skin or sweat along his brow. His stance is sturdy and tall. I blink back tears of delight and allow an all-too-wide grin to stretch my lips.

Belmiso stands between us, an all-too-stunning unicorn. As a horse, he was gorgeous. Seeing him for the first time as a unicorn, I have no words. He is the purest of blacks. A depth of color that can and will touch your soul. He is the existence of all colors at once, with hints of the rainbow in the curve of his shoulder or the bend of his knee. The mere sight of him is magnificent and mind boggling... but currently, I only have eyes for Ry.

Velsa stops. As if unspoken communication is taking place between the horses, Belmiso nods and trots back, around Ry's grip. Ry clucks as he follows the horse's backward canter. Ry probably thinks Belmiso is being fussy, but the purpose of the action is immediately evident to me. The unicorns wanted to give me a better view of my brother. A rainbow of colors dance around him —an aura unlike any I've seen.

I gasp.

Zarah's head snaps up, her hand flies to her lips, and she sucks back a breath.

Reacting to Zarah, Ry looks our way. Like the wax of a melting candle, his anger and frustration slide into relief. His chest rises, filling his body and soul with a plethora of emotions, and he abandons Belmiso in favor of rushing toward me.

My heart feels like it could explode at any minute. I slip off Velsa's back and run to Ry, throwing my arms around him and hugging him to my body, my heart, my soul. I never want to let him go. "I was so scared," I say in a mousy voice, tears welling at the corner of my eyes. "I thought..." I choke. Swallow. "I thought you might die."

"And yet..." He steps back and holds tight to my shoulders, looks me over like a scrutinizing mother. "I'm in perfect condition." He releases my shoulders and swings his arms out to his side in a theatrical presentation. "A fine specimen, if I do say so myself." He jabs his finger at me. "But you, you have been a bad girl. Leaving the safety of my hideaway, allowing yourself to undergo your next change without Jaden or myself at your side, and getting mixed up with Dohlan. I disapprove." His arms fall to his side, and he sighs.

The levels of my joy or overflowing, stretching my grin stupidly from ear to ear. "I'm so happy to have you back." I throw my arms around him once more.

"Not the reaction I was expecting after that speech of mine." He hugs me back.

"Good to see you mobile and back to your old habit of mothering our girl," Jaden says, tapping Ry on the shoulder. Both Jaden and Mo walk by with Timbers and Clemens in tow. "Why don't you two take some time," Jaden calls over his shoulder. "Mo and I will take care of the horses," Mo agrees with a nod and motions for Velsa to follow. She does, as does Belmiso.

"Hello, Ms. Zarah," Mo says, waving. They walk to a nearby patch of shade cover.

My gaze wanders from them to Zarah, who still stands in the doorway, wiping at her eyes.

"Why have you upset your fiancée?" I pin Ry with a steady glare.

He steps back and shakes his head. "Don't start that, Ana. You weren't here..." He turns, starts to walk away.

I grab his arm, halting his retreat. "I heard the way you were talking to her. If you love her the way you say..."

He turns on me. "Never doubt my love for Zarah." He grits his teeth. "But she kept me in the dark, even as Jaden and Mo set off in search of you." His hands fly to the sides of his head and shake. "You could have been seriously hurt or worse."

"Yeah, I could have been hurt. I could have even died." The memory of coughing into the harsh reality of life, brought back from the afterlife by Jaden's words and Dohlan's actions flashes across my thoughts. "But in the messed-up state you were in, what could you have possibly done to help me?"

His shoulders drop, and he exhales. "Let's never talk of that again." He cracks a half smile. "I hate thinking about how incapacitating that situation was."

"Consider it forgotten." I say the words to please him, but know I will never, for as long as I live, forget how mortal my immortal brother really is.

He wraps his arm around me and directs me toward the house. "How about you tell me everything I missed."

I smirk and look off to the side. "I will consider an informational exchange, if you make nice with Zarah." I swing my head to look at him and grin.

"Informational exchange?" he repeats.

"Yes. A few minutes ago, you inferred this place was

yours, not Zarah's. Tell me about that and about why this location. And tell me why you never bothered to mention you were engaged." I frown.

"Somethings are better left unsaid than trying to come up with an acceptable explanation that works with the cover story you are living." We make our way to the front door, where Zarah stands, waiting. Ry's arm drops from around my shoulders, and he steps up to her. "Sorry I upset you, Hon. I don't always handle my frustration in the best possible manner."

"It's all right." Her gaze sweeps past him to me, then blinks back to him. "I never meant to lie to you. I only wanted you to allow your body to heal."

"I know," he says, and his palm fuses to the curve of her cheek. "I love you for every thoughtful choice and action." He leans in and kisses her, allowing his lips to linger on hers.

I look away. Take note that Jaden and Mo have disappeared with the horses.

"Let's grab a drink and get caught up," Ry says.

My attention snaps back to him. "Okay," I say and follow him into the house. Instead of heading up the stairs to the space I am vaguely familiar with, he pushes open the door to the left side of the entry and strides into the room I have only glimpsed in the dark.

"Hungry? Or do you just want to quench your thirst from the ride?" Ry asks as he moves past sofas and chairs and tables to an open kitchen.

"Um." I stop in the doorway and take in the room. My voice has gotten lost, slipped away in the surprise of the view. "I could do with a snack," I finally say, not tearing my focus from the décor.

The floor is similar to something I would expect to see in

a nicer home back in Cali. Tiles of flat rock in shades of grey and rusty orange. The difference between Cali and here, the tiles would likely all be cut in uniform shapes, like square or rectangle. Here, each rock is organic in cut and curve, and they fit firmly together without any grout. The walls are a combination of wood beams and stone, crisscrossing in an artful design.

Keeping with a theme, the furniture is all made of organic materials such as wood, cotton, suede, or leather. The dining table is a half mile long with high backed chairs. I half expect armored knights sitting at the table, holding session. The lounging furniture, overstuffed, deep, and inviting looking.

The kitchen area runs along the far-left wall. Like the bathroom above, water cascades into the sink from some unseen source. Beside the sink, stretches a long counter fitted with a thick wood countertop. Sharp knives and forks are clipped to the wall above the space. On the opposite side of the sink, a long built-in box with a latched lid. An ice box, maybe?

Between the stretch of kitchen and the rest of the room, stand two small walls or ledges that arc away from the back counter, and into the room, circling around and stopping short of a cooking fireplace. The entire room can enjoy a warm view of the dancing flames within the copper framed fireplace.

The ceiling looks to be eight feet or so high on the right side of the room, the side above which the sleeping quarters is located. Midway across the room, the ceiling bends and reaches to a height of two stories or more.

Beyond the sofas, chairs, and large table, is a wall completely peppered with windows and glass doors. The window glass is thick and wavy and sometimes cuts the entering light into long rainbow ribbons. And although the room appears clean, rays of sunlight highlight floating dust particles, making them look more like glints of magic powder than dirt.

"We don't have any processed stuff here. No canned goods, chips, and so on." Ry lifts the latch on the chest beside the sink, opens the lid, and reveals an ice box. He reaches in. "I can cook some meat…" The sound of shuffling items comes from within the box. I move closer and look over his shoulder. "Or offer you some fresh veggies or fruits."

Colorful veggies and fruits sit in a small box within the bigger latch-lid space. Everything is situated as if in a giant ice box, only there isn't any ice.

"What is that?" I point past him to what looks like white rocks that Ry is shuffling around in order to find the various foods packed within. He picks one up and holds it out to me.

"Check it out," he says and smiles.

My gaze darts between him and the rock in his hands. Before I am even holding it, I am tingling. My earthen ability is swirling around the stone and rushing information back to me. It's not a stone at all. It's something unlike anything on earth. I take it in my hand. Despite its appearances, it's light, soft, pliable, and plenty cold.

"That there," Ry says, nodding to the stuff I am squeezing my fingers around. "Helps keep our perishables fresh and edible."

"What is it?" I ask, then throw my finger up, halting his response. "No, wait. I know." I turn the white thing over in my hand allowing its information to flow through me. "Oddly enough, it's a member of the crystal family. Formed from minerals we don't have on earth." I hold the white rock up and study the way the light seems to get trapped within its inner folds and knots. "Curious," I say.

"Yes," Ry says, snatching the white pliable stone from my hand. "It's pretty cool. It doesn't melt like ice does, and it keeps everything chilled and fresh. What more could we ask for?"

"Ketchup?" I say with a smirk.

"Very funny." He places the bit back into the large cooler.

"Why is it called xaedosos?" I ask, knowing the name as a result of bringer.

"Don't know," he says. "Maybe because it's cold, and the root of the name means frost."

My lips pucker and twist.

"Why?" He closes the cooler lid and turns to look at me.

I shrug my shoulders. "Because it's really a byproduct from the secretion of an ice dragon."

He laughs. "There are no dragons. I told you that, Ana." He turns back to the counter and grabs a dish from the far edge. "Gods bless that woman of mine," he says to no one in particular, then whips around and holds a dish between us. "I have the perfect snack, and you're going to love it."

With the slight gesture of a push, he directs me to the table and motions for me to sit. I do, and he places the dish in front of me then hands me a roughly hammered out spoon. "This stuff is amazing. Dig in. I'll grab us something to drink." He walks away.

I scrutinize the stuff in the dish. It sort of resembles apple crisp, if apple crisp was mixed with peaches. That combination doesn't sound bad. I carve out a bite and savor the flavors in my mouth for glorious minutes before swallowing. Whatever this stuff is that Ry has me now eating, it is by far the best thing I've had the pleasure of tasting since my crazy journey began.

"Now, before you start slamming me with questions, I'm going to give you the quick rundown." Ry sets a couple of drinks on the table and takes the seat across from me.

"Go for it." I take a swig of the drink. It's water with a hint of kiwi or something.

"Zarah and I have been engaged for a long time. Since before you were born. We were in the midst of planning our wedding when the whole thing got set on the back burners while your father dealt with your aunt Dreya. As you know, things escalated into war. The next thing I knew, I was ushering our mother to the safety of another world, and you were on your way."

"Why didn't you bring Zarah with you?" I take another bite of the apple, peach goodness.

"No time," Ry says bluntly. "When your father started making plans for mother's relocation, I intended to bring Zarah along. But then, without out any warning beforehand, King Marduk was thrusting a map into my hands and pushing mother and myself into a hidden passage. The passageway took us through long ago closed off corridors and caverns and eventually dropped us at the foot of the dimensional door. I had no choice but to leave Zarah behind."

"But you came back because she's still here, and she waited for you," I say. "After all these years, that's love."

"I did come back. As often as I could. I secured this place here." He motions to the house around us. "And moved Zarah in. I originally intended to bring her back, have her live with us or something. But Zarah is a smart lady, and she suggested staying here so that she could keep tabs on the war and Dreya and anything else." He smiles, a crooked, partly wicked, smile. "She is brilliant when it comes to intelligence gathering."

"Yeah, that talent of hers." I set down my spoon and narrow my gaze. "You don't find that intimidating?"

"Nope." His gaze searches, as if he is sweeping the contents of his life to the side to check for hidden secrets.

"Okay then." I straighten my shoulders and give him a satisfied grin. My meal is done, and both drink and food were filling and delicious. "And through all this you haven't gotten married?"

"We've been waiting for it all to end, for the chaos to calm, so that the family could attend and actually enjoy the moment."

"Makes sense," I say and lean into the table.

He sits back and, with arms crossed, leans into the wood of the high back chair. "Your turn. Hit me," he says with a snap of his fingers.

I suck back a deep breath. One that reached into the center knot of my belly. Then, releasing the breath slowly, I relax my shoulders. "Well..." My gaze wanders off to the side. "I did something stupid when I stepped outside of this place the other night. But it was not my intention to actually run away. I simply planned on clearing my head and catching some fresh air. The healing aromas filling the interior space that night were too thick for my senses." I toss him a super quick glance. His face is open, patiently waiting. "But whatever I did and for whatever reason, it all turned out alright. I *did* make it through the next transformation."

For the first time since I started speaking, I let my gaze linger on Ry. He's beaming, stupidly so. Like he did when he addressed my changes back at Mo's village. When I awoke to discover one eye was now blue. I sigh and roll my eyes.

"Your green eye. It's earth, right?" he asks.

I nod.

"I hear, feel, all that good stuff of the trees and grass and dirt, so on. Oh!" I blink. "And I was at Kaia's cottage, a place Dohlan appeared to be rather familiar with."

Ry is no longer smiling. His face has crumpled into an ugly picture of hatred. "I don't like you having anything to do with that guy."

"I got that. Are you going to tell me why you dislike Dohlan so much?"

Ry doesn't say anything, so I drop my counterattack.

"Why is Zarah then allowed to talk to Dohlan?"

The question leaves Ry looking pained but not surprised. "Their relationship predates the one I have with Zarah. I will not be the bully type of fiancé that dictates who she can and can't see."

I narrow my eyes at him. "It's okay for her but not me?"

"I never said you couldn't see him. I only said I didn't like it," he corrects.

It's true; that's what he said.

"But he is not the same person Zarah first met," He adds. "He is an incubus now, a dangerous thing, a thing you'd be best to stay clear of. But should you insist on communing with him in any way, I want you to be informed of what you are dealing with and never ever let your guard down."

I nod, taking note of my brother's cautionary advice regarding Dohlan, and focus on the table for a moment before continuing the synopsis of my adventure. "I was at Kaia's cottage," I say. "and it was there that I saw you in the mother's mirror..." his expression turns to one of surprise. "I saw you were healing. The mirror also showed me Zarah talking to Dohlan..." he doesn't look surprised by the reveal, so I rush onward. "And the memory waters spoke to me. Oh!" I jolt.

"Slow down. There's no rush to get the words out," he says.

He's right. my lips have been moving like a couple of pebbles racing down a hill.

"Did you know that Kaia's house is protected against Dreya?" Ry's brow arches. "And not just that. No one could have physically harmed Kaia while inside that house. Well, the Balance Bringer, really... I think. Kaia, the Balance Bringer. They are one and the same. So that means the protection also extends to me. Or maybe it's a protection of the cottage owner." I pause, blink in thought. "Or a general protection spell, protecting anyone within the home's walls."

"Alright, hold on." Ry waves his hands to stop my story vomit. "Are you saying Kaia had some sort of magical spell placed on a tiny house she hardly ever visited?"

"Oh no. Didn't you know?" I lean into the table. "She fully intended to live there. She was going to leave her life at the palace. She wanted to make a life with Dohlan."

Ry takes a deep breath. It's accompanied with the slightest sound of a growl. "Guess that didn't work out so well for her."

"No," I say with a nod. "But she had it bad for him. I wonder why she never told me." I gaze out the window and muse. "Was she waiting for me to figure it out?" I say more to myself than my brother.

"What? You think Kaia wanted you to figure out she had a horrible crush on the incubus Dohlan?" Ry asks, now looking confused.

"He wasn't always an incubus," I say softly, wondering

how that horrid status fell upon him. "But no. I meant, she was waiting for me to figure out we are the same."

"The Balance Bringer, you mean?" he asks. "That's silly. Of course, you would know that."

"Yeah, but no." I turn my gaze from the window, focus on him. "That we are the same person. The same soul. She is me and I am her. Just as I am Crystia."

In one quick motion, Ry pushes away from the table and is standing across from me. Glaring down at me with his brow pinched and eyes squinted. "What the fuck does that mean?"

THIRTY

M y eyes are wide, and something heavy tugs my ribcage to the floor. My breath, knocked backward by Ry's words, blocks my throat.

I cough, breathe through my nose, and shake my head.

"Your reaction was off the Richter scale... a giant leap over the top, don't you think?" I hold my fingers an inch apart to emphasize the overkill of his response.

"I don't know. Was it?" He paces left and then returns to stand beside his chair.

"What I said was..."

"I know what you said." He cuts me off. "I want to know what you mean by that bull spittle."

I throw my hands in the air as if they will somehow magically help me explain while at the same time calm my brother. "It's confusing to understand, I know, but from what I have learned, Kaia, Crystia, and myself are all of the same soul—something like, different incarnations of the same person."

Ry leans into the table and slaps his knuckles against the hardwood. "How can that even be possible when you and Crystia lived your lives at the same time."

"I..." I blink and drop my gaze to the surface of the table. "I don't know." I sound bewildered in my admittance, and even though I hadn't wanted to admit the one soul idea as fact, the long ride home has removed a few barriers and cleared my mind. Something within me knows—fears, even —the new knowledge is a golden truth.

"There you go..." He waves his hand into the air. "You must have misunderstood. You..." He jabs his finger at me. "Are not your sisters." He turns, looks out the wall of glass, his head shaking in disapproval. "We'll get you to the mystic, and she will explain everything. Fix everything, too."

"But I thought maybe..." I say under my breath.

"What is that?" Ry turns back and peers at me, having heard my tiny whisper. I don't know if I should finish my sentence. Admit to Ry that I have an unexplained attraction to Dohlan, a person my brother clearly despises. A kind of attraction I don't believe is the result of Dohlan's incubus nature. An emotion I was most recently thinking—hoping— was a remnant of Kaia's emotions where Dohlan is concerned and not a conflict of my own personal feelings with regards to Jaden.

"Did I hear mention of the mystic?" Zarah steps into the room. She's holding Yuromo's bag of fruit. Both our heads snap in Zarah's direction. She falters, looks between us. "I'm sorry. Did I interrupt something?"

"Yes," I say at the same time Ry says no.

"Oh." Her voice wavers, and her gaze appears uncertain as to which of us to settle upon. "From what little I happen to hear, I was hoping there would be a trip in our near future."

"Very near," Ry says with gusto.

I push my seat back and stand. "Isn't it too soon for you to be traveling?" My question is directed at Ry.

"Nah." He shakes his head with steeled determination, but his gaze wanders to Zarah, as if seeking her confirmation. Her eyes are wide, and she hesitates in a response. Ry takes her silence as an opportunity to close the space between them. He takes the bag from her and pulls her close, kisses her long and slow.

My gaze drops to the table surface. I scratch at the back of my neck. Start counting the ways my brother can make me feel uncomfortable. A tiny squawk of astonishment snaps my gaze back to them.

Ry pulls away and Zarah appears almost dazed. "We can do this thing, can't we? You did a great job healing me. I feel perfectly fine."

Zarah spares me a glance. "I think a visit to the mystic would be good for you both." She takes the bag back from Ry and moves to the kitchen where she sets Mo's bag of fruit beside the sink. She removes each fruit in turn and washes them beneath the running water, setting them out on the counter to dry. Her hands work methodically, as if this practice is something she has done countless times a day.

Ry follows her across the room, sweeps up behind her, and slips his arms around her waist, hugging her to his chest. "I'm glad you think so. I'd like to head out in the morning, after everyone gets a good night's sleep."

"So soon," Zarah and I say at the same time.

Still bound within my brother's loving hold, Zarah turns

to face him. Her back arches over the sink so that she may better gaze up into his face. "What about the horses?"

I jerk. "What does that mean?"

Ry doesn't spare me a glance. "The horses will be fine. They came from the wild, they can now return to the wild."

"The wild? I don't understand?" Zarah's confused gaze shifts to me and then back to Ry.

"Some of the fun you can look forward to, working beside my sister," Ry says. "Her way with everything in nature around us. The water, the land, the animals. It's nothing short of miracles. All of it." He glances over his shoulder and smiles at me. "We were on foot when the horses came and agreed to help us make the trip."

I could point out the errors in my brother's little speech. I could also point out his unwanted up sale on my abilities. But I don't.

Zarah blinks in clear astonishment. Ry leans forward and kisses her forehead. Zarah's muscles relax, and I think, if she weren't made of flesh and bone, she'd be melting all over the kitchen floor. Their hands hover in the air, touching and feeling the skin of the other in a lover's foreplay.

My skin flushes, and once again, my gaze drops to the table. I study the swirl and curve of the wood grain, looking for any hidden designs. I spot the hint of a horn, and I think of the horses.

"Why don't you give it a day before we go," Zarah says. "We can use the time to organize and gather any supplies."

Curious of my brother's reply, I look up. Ry has lifted Zarah so that she is sitting on the counter. He has also captured her hands and pulled them behind her back, holding her firmly in his embrace. They gaze into each other's eyes as if they are the only ones in all the worlds.

I glance at the door, thinking maybe I should leave them alone. I haven't a clue how long they have been apart. But something Ry said is bugging me. I need to know what he meant.

I cough.

With only a mild reduction in their passion, they look at me.

"Why won't we need the horses?" I ask.

Zarah caresses Ry's cheek, plants a sweet kiss upon his lips, and then slips off the counter and steps free of Ry's enclosure. She continues to keep a strong hold to his hand. She smiles at me, glances at the wall of glass windows and doors, then back at me. "Because, from here, you'll be traveling by water."

My mouth pops open, and for the first time since my arrival here, I have a desire to look out one of the many windows and see what drew Zarah's attention, what lies on the other side. I hastily make my way past the multitude of chairs to the nearest window. Pressing my hands into the frame on either side, I gaze out onto a surprisingly different world beyond.

This side of the house appears to be built directly into a cliff, in front of which is a wide ribbon of waterfalls. But from where does the water come? When I stood outside the front of the house, all I could detect was the grass and tree above. And, when we rode the horses around the bend there was no sound nor sign of water. I rub my forehead and contemplate the waterfall mystery.

There's a terrace, so I quickly find a door and step outside. It is the same terrace upon which I saw Ry sitting and eating one of the times I viewed him through the mother's mirror. While tight, the space manages to remain comfortable. I guess it's all in the decorating. Zarah's decorating. I lean over the railing and take in the scene below.

White crescents and blue swirls. Solid and soft sprays. Water. So much water. All of it rushing, rushing away.

To the far right, I spy a staircase. One option is to climb upward to the sleeping quarters. I choose to go down, closer to the rushing river. The staircase spirals, taking me deeper beneath the upper level. It's as if hundreds of years, probably more, of the waterfall hitting the bottom and swirling outward and up carved out a circular indentation at the bottom of the cliff face.

The bottom landing is a wood platform, pieced together with footlong two-by-fours in an alternating pattern of board and space. The result is almost like looking at an organic version of a bagged floor mat. The design allows for any overspray landing on the deck to easily drain away.

The deck is spacious and is enclosed with a basic, rustic railing. It even has a slide gate to be used should anyone dock a boat at the platform's edge. Currently, no boat is docked.

Beyond the gate, a short extension of the landing—the dock. Behind me, in the cliff wall, is a camouflaged door, one meant to be invisible to the average eye, similar to the front of the home. I am only aware of the door's existence because I can sense the difference in the stone. Right now, the door is not what I want to explore.

I lean over the railing and the water's spray moisturizes my face and arms. I can almost reach out and touch the ripples. I lean closer and closer still, trying to figure out where the water is coming from. It's almost as if it is suddenly there, coming from nowhere and hurrying to get away. I close my eyes and breathe in the marvelous, moist air.

I think of nothing. I simply choose to be, exist in that moment, free of thoughts and emotions.

All is silent, stay the rush of the water beneath my feet.

Quiet and still... until the thrum begins. It starts with a beat, one and then two, followed by a drag. The sound repeats and repeats until it is a steady thrumming. The rock, the water, the earth speaking. If only it could be heard by more than just me.

I open my eyes, reach out my hand, palm to the sky. Water dances in a thread, up from the river's surface, through the air, to my fingertips. With a gentle touch, it wraps around my palm and wrist, glides up my arm.

Tickles.

"Ana."

The water splashes back into the river. I blink, shake my head. At almost the precise time the water dropped from my arm, I'd swear a large tail slammed against the river's surface. A mermaid-type tail. Only, like the wall behind me, the tail was camouflaged, appearing to be carved of clear, flexible ice. the rushing water of the lake being visible through the skin and scales.

My body jerks upright and my backbone yanks straight, as if by an invisible rope. I spin toward Jaden.

"The group is gathering upstairs. Zarah is about ready to put dinner on the table. Will you be joining us?" he asks.

Involuntarily, I glance between the water and Jaden. "Yes of course." I push away from the railing and pull myself to a stand. I move to step past him, and he grabs my arm, causing me to pause. Through our touch, I sense the depth of the wound I have daggered through his heart. I am frozen in place awaiting his move.

"You've begun to open up and feel our connection.

That's good, but with the ability comes a great deal of learning. Emotions are a complicated thing to navigate. Please, don't be quick to judge or act until you have mastered the ability." His gaze stays keenly glued on me.

"Of course," I say and wait for him to release me. But he doesn't release me. Instead, he closes his eyes for a moment.

"I have failed you in the gift of prophecy and now this." He releases my arm, flaring his palm to his side before letting it fall flat.

"No." I shake my head adamantly. "You haven't failed me."

He waves his hand, silencing my words. "It appears I was compromised long before my current incarnation, but let's set that aside for now."

"What do you mean?"

He raises a finger, and I fall silent once more. "I don't want us moving forward under the wrong assumptions."

"Which are?" I ask.

"I cannot deny the fact that whatever is happening between you and Dohlan is troubling. Of course, there is his incubus nature to take into consideration. All the same..."

"But Kaia..." I say.

"I know that you think Kaia is the source of your conflict," he rebuts. "But is that the truth?" He narrows his gaze on me.

I open my mouth, but no words come forth this time. I don't know if Kaia is the source of my conflict or not, and I hate that I don't know my own heart.

"As I thought." His chest rises and falls. "You were previously worried that I was attracted to you by magical means, but what if it's the other way around? I think you should now take the time to figure out what and who you want to be a part of your future." He moves away, turns toward the steps.

"Wait." I lurch forward and grab his hand.

When he turns back his eyes are filled with wonderous beauty and sadness. The sight squeezes my heart dry. I want nothing more than to kiss away all his pain and repair all my mistakes.

He steps close and fits his open palm perfectly to the side of my face in a heartbreaking caress. I lean into his touch, and the wetness of a tear slips into the spaces between our skin. "Don't worry, Ana. I'll know when you've figured everything out." He kisses my forehead, then turns and leaves me alone on the deck.

Oh my Gaea and God! Did I obliterate any chances of ever having a relationship with Jaden?

I take a deep breath, wipe my face, and decide I'm over-reacting. Hopes for us are not anywhere near dead.

I follow ten spaces behind him, climbing the stairs back to the great hall. A large plate of cut bread sits on the table where Ry and Mo are seated. They're already chowing down. Zarah is pouring drinks into their cups. She looks up and smiles. Mo waves at me and Ry grins.

My smile pulls into a tight, puffed line. I pick a chair on the side closest to me and near the middle of the table. Jaden sits on the other side, near the corner. Hopefully, I am giving him enough space while I *sort things out*.

Zarah sets out a hearty meal, and we all fill our bellies. I contribute little to the conversation, only answering when asked a question and stealing glances at Jaden often. Ry sets forth the plan and makes sure everyone knows what to expect. A day and a half from now, we will head out on the next leg of our journey. Thankfully, Ry isn't trying to push a break-of-dawn departure upon us.

After all that has happened and all that I have discovered, I no longer know how I feel about everything... the mystic, my sisters, my Tracer. All I know is that I am changing, and even though I thought it would be scary, I am kind of digging it.

After dinner, Mo shows me where to find the horses. At the front of the home, to the extreme end of the bluff, there is a hollow hidden by drapes and ribbons of plant life. The space is accessible from the outside as well as by way of a narrow cavern that runs directly to the lower level of the house.

When Mo opens one of the doors in the great hall's side wall, the cavern is revealed. Upon first inspection, the door's proximity to the kitchen left me to think the space was a pantry. I need to stop making assumptions.

When we enter the hollow, I find all four unicorns in glowing splendor. Most of them are resting, Clemens is definitely asleep. But there is something about their proximity to one another that makes each of them more brilliant. As if they weren't already fantastical enough. Their coloring pushes the boundaries of otherworldly, and their auras double in reach. I try not to be overcome by the presence of a unicorn, but it's hard not to become that wide, glossy-eyed kid gawking at the most marvelous, magical carnival on earth.

I assign myself a task. It's quickly completed. The unicorns already had a fair amount of food and water, I merely top off each. There is nothing more they need... except an explanation of the plan. The fact that we will be leaving without them in a day and a half.

Sensing I have something heavy upon my heart, Velsa nods her head and whinnies, drawing me to her like any horse lover is drawn to a magical beastie. I rub her cheek and kiss her nose and check to confirm that Mo is no longer in the hollow space with us.

She is gone, and I am alone with the unicorns brilliantly hiding as horses.

I step back from Velsa and look over her sleeping herd.

"I've been told that we leave in just over a day's time," I say.

"*As expected.*" She turns her head so that she is watching me with one eye only.

"I've also been informed that you will not be coming." I rock once back and forth on my feet and weave my fingers together.

Velsa turns her head to look over her heard. "*You will go by way of water?*" I nod. "*Understood.*" Her nose drops toward the ground.

"I'm so sorry." I step forward.

Her head swings up. "*Do not be sorry. It has been our honor assisting you and yours. We look forward to hearing of your progress. Of seeing your work in action. And should you need us again...*" Her head nods once. "*We shan't be far.*"

"You've been so kind." My fingers trace the edge of her nose. "Is there anything I can do to repay you."

"*The assist is payment enough. But promise me, Bringer...*" She presses her head forward. "*You must not delay in finding your way to the mystic.*"

"I won't. I need to see her. I need her help. What do you know of her?" I ask.

"*Only that whispers of her existence go as far back through history as those of the Balance Bringer. The lives of the two have always been intertwined."* She gentles herself down to her knees. *"Now you have things you must do to ready yourself... and you must sleep. As must we."*

"I'll see you in the morning."

She lowers her head in understanding, then lowers her body all the way to the ground to sleep. I turn and leave, glancing over my shoulder at them once more before I disappear into the narrow hallway leading to the house.

When I return to the kitchen area, Zarah is present, packing up a few items for the upcoming trip. There is already a small collection of packs on the table. It looks as if Ry was actually thinning out the items we have been carrying around in our packs. A large starburst crystal has been pulled out and set off to the side.

I forgot about this. My hand glides over its sharp edges and curves.

"Ryland wasn't sure if you still wanted to tote that around or not," Zarah says.

I nod at her and gaze into the crystals glossy surface. A stronger Ana than I am familiar with peers back at me. "I think I do," I say.

"Ryland is quite organized as I am sure you know," she says to me. "With the help of Jaden and Mo, they packed everything they felt we might be able to use. It wasn't much. I don't believe the journey will be all that long."

I nod in understanding.

"I already sent Ryland up to bed. I also showed Jaden and Mo where the extra bunks are. I have a few sleeping options to present you."

My lips twist to the side. I look past her to the balcony beyond the glass doors. "If it's not too cold tonight, I think I'll simply curl up in one of the chairs out there." I point to my intentions, the terrace.

My decision seems to surprise her, and, for a moment, she is at a loss for words. "If that is truly what you want," she finally manages. "I shall get you some blankets and pillows." She stops her current chore and disappears from the room.

I look over the room. I've barely had a chance to familiarize myself with Ry's little abode, and now I will be leaving. Same as Kaia's cottage. Same scenario, different location. Will I get to stay in any one place for a decent length of time?

I sigh.

Using a mitten, I pull the kettle from the fire and pour myself a mug of hot something. I have no idea if the liquid is weak coffee, strong tea, or something unknown to me. I take a tentative sip. It's neither coffee nor tea, but it isn't unlikable. I walk out to the balcony with mug in hand. I take a seat against the railing and dangle my feet over the side, muse at the surrounding darkness and listen to the musical serenade of the water.

A soft swoosh and scoot accompany Zarah's approach. She sits beside me.

"I hope you don't mind that I approved Ryland's desire to get underway," she says.

I don't look at her. Nor do I answer immediately. I contemplate her question and wonder if I do mind. I don't actually know the answer. I continue to study the subtle lines and shapes within the encompassing mass of dark beyond the railing and decide that I don't mind her approval. I suspect that if anyone has the power to make Ry stay put when he wants to move, it would be her. Her veto of the plan could have forced him to stay and rest. But I can't picture anything good coming out of all of us being cooped up in this little house with a grumpy Ryland. More traveling, more adventures is what Jaden needs. What I need to bring Jaden back to me.

"Nah. It's fine," I say in a comfortable tone "He was always going to get his way. We both know that."

She snickers. "He is good in that way. When he decided he wanted me, despite all the hundreds of thousands of reasons we should not be together, all the reasons I should not be with anyone, he didn't care. He refused to give in to anyone or anything and in the end..."

I blink and turn toward her. "Why shouldn't you be with anyone? Why should anyone be denied the chance at love?"

She sighs. "I know this is all new to you, but because I am a keeper of history and because of what my touch can do, it is best for my kind to not become romantically involved."

"That's so... unfair," I say and bite my lip, think about how her touch pulled memories from me as easily as one would drink water from a glass.

"Each of us caries our own burdens." She looks at me pointedly. "But I've been lucky. Thanks to unexpected blessings and the kindness of people like Dohlan, I escaped what could have been a lonely existence of captivity and found my way to this life." Her hands flip out at her sides and then drop and pat the floor beneath us. "So, here I am. From one cage to another."

Dohlan's name rattles through my bones. I startle, spilling liquid from the side of my mug. I quickly set it down and turn to face her. I want to know more about how Dohlan has played a part in her life, but her mention of being caged seems a far more pressing matter. "What do you mean, cage?"

She sighs and waves her hand between us. "I don't mean it the way it sounds. Believe me. And Ryland never meant for this place to become such a long-standing situation. A cute home and hideaway, but still a cage of sorts. But with all that has happened, with the never-ending battle in which darkness now holds the upper hand, this place became one of the few places I can feel safe."

"I had no idea. I'm so sorry." I throw my arms around her.

Our embrace is warm and tingly and...

Oh no.

I pull away, but she holds firmly to my hands. Her gaze seeks mine, but I don't want to look. I fear I already know what I will see. Finally, I can't ignore her any longer. I look.

I didn't know so much sadness and pity could be packed into one set of eyes. The last thing I want is her pity. My shoulders stiffen.

"I'm so sorry, Ana. I can only imagine the difficulty of your current state." A tiny smile of platitude pulls at the side of her face.

Yeah, well." I yank my hands free. "No one said being the Balance Bringer was going to be easy."

"But your sisters," she says.

"Yes. My sisters." I fall silent.

Neither one of us speaks. There is only the music of the water, the clatter of the plants rustling in the night air, and the thrum of the stones... the earth. I listen. I feel. I welcome.

And I realize.

"In little over a day, we will leave to find the mystic. And find her we will. I may have my sisters within me because they are me, but we will break whatever magic is binding those parts of me and keeping me from accessing them. And once that is done, I will get to the bottom of the stupid spell that ever cut my soul into three to create sisters for me." My chest rises and falls. "That was a mean, terrible thing to do, to any person. Why should I be forced to grieve sisters who never really were sisters in the first place. They were only parts of me." I shake my head. "So, mean."

"Yes. But..." Zarah says, raising her hand between us. "You liked, even loved your sisters, which goes to show that you actually love yourself... even if you aren't willing to admit it. If they had never been pulled into the form of another living being, it's likely that you would have been less willing to accept those various parts of your personality."

Her words drop over me like a bucket of ice. She's right, I do love my sisters. And yet I often find fault with myself. Would I love those parts of myself that represent my sisters had they never exited? I mull over the thought, then glance at Zarah.

It must be horrible to have a wedding planned and then have to wait decades without any hope for a commitment date in site. If Zarah were any normal person, I would squeeze her hand. But she isn't normal, and a mere touch gives away a lifetime of secrets. I've given her too much already. I settle upon a grin, and gaze at her with purpose brewing in my belly.

"Dreya's tyranny must end so that you can finally have that wedding you've been planning... for like... ever," I say.

She smiles and it's one of warmth and love and sisterhood.

When I first laid eyes upon Zarah, I never would have expected that in so few days, I would be prepared to consider her a sister of sorts. But the bond has already begun netting together.

"And Dohlan?" she asks.

I falter, stunned. As for Dohlan, I don't know. Part of me never wants to let him go. Never wants to have to make that do or die choice where he is concerned.

Acknowledging my inner conflict, she nods, releasing me from any obligatory answer. "You have time to figure all that out," she says.

I hope that's true.

"Trust your heart," she adds. "As an incubus, Dohlan is more attractive now than he ever was. Never forget that a portion of your attraction to him is a manifestation of his magical state. He may believe he loves you, but it was Kaia who really stole his heart so long ago."

She stands, drops the pillow and blankets on the chair and turns to leave. "It's late. You should get a good night's sleep. Knowing Ryland, he will have us all in constant motion tomorrow, prepping for our soon to be travels." She steps inside and closes the door between us.

Now it's just me, the balcony, the nature beyond, and my promise to myself.

I raise my left hand into the air in front of me. Raising a golden ring from a guy who once loved a part of me. But I am so much more than the Kaia side of me.

I twist the ring. Twist it back and forth and back and forth. It clings to my skin like glue, but the seal on any glue can be broken when enough pressure is applied. I twist and yank. It gives with a sharp tear of my skin. I wince and pull the golden symbol free. I study the wrap of etched designs that hold no meaning for me.

"Good bye, Dohlan," I say and toss the ring to the river water below. "Water below me and earth beside me, carry my farewell message to the man and incubus who would have me as his own." I smirk at my lack of rhyme. I don't know if using the elements as mail delivery is within my realm of possibilities, but I won't ever know if I don't try.

Putting an end our relationship feels hollow. Somehow, I thought it would be liberating, but the hardest part of my course still lies ahead—regaining Jaden's trust. No matter how long it takes, I won't give up. I am committing, right here and now, to give us my everything.

My feet swing freely; my hands rest palm down upon my thighs. The music of the night, the world around me, tempts me like a siren's call. I am a pinpoint in the midst of unmeasurable splendor. My palms slide forward, free from the comfort of my legs. They flip upward, welcoming the air and gentle spray of water. Droplets dance upon my skin, sending shivers across my nerves. Something within me stirs. My back straightens, arms rise, extending into the open air. Never have I felt more alive—connecting with the worldly elements.

The breeze around me whispers at my ear. It calls my name, tells me the mystic is waiting. "I'm coming," I respond. The crazy lady has found so many ways to reach me during my journey so far, I don't expect she'll give up until I am standing before her. Hopefully, that will only be a matter of days from now. "I'm coming," I say again.

A sound from the sleeping quarters above catches my attention, and I turn my ear to Zarah's delighted giggle, followed by Ry's playful growl.

If I'd grown up with a normal life, with Ry living as my brother, under the same roof, I might knock on his door and make a wisecrack. But life has been anything but easy for him. I understand that more now than ever before. And although I was skeptical upon first meeting Zarah, I now believe that she is exactly what he needs in his life. She fills his desire to be on constant vigilance because of her ability, and she fills his want for deep satisfying love.

The rightness of Ry's and Zarah's relationship makes me warm and tingly. I want to give them the wedding they started planning so many years ago.

Such a want only adds fuels to an already burning desire. A need, really. I gaze into the dark and imagine what steps will need to be taken in the coming days. What things I must learn and what actions I'll have to take in order to stop Dreya's dark and treacherous reign.

I nod, acknowledging to myself and the watching world, invisible to those who are not me, that I am ready. Ready to know the true me and ready to take action.

I have *become,* and I am *awake.* The time is now, here, to empower myself and my gift and discover all that I have been, all that I currently am, and all that I can be.

Time to empower this Balance Bringer.

The end... For now.

The adventure continues. Keep reading in:
Empowering: The Balance Bringer

If you enjoyed this action-packed YA Fantasy Adventure, then you may also enjoy the nonstop paranormal-fantasy adventure in *Moorigad*. A mystical carnival, dragons, and

supernatural beings...what's not to love? Check it out here:
http://books2read.com/u/4AYnnJ

To secure your sneak peek at future Balance Bringer stories,
and ensure notification when new stories are released, sign
up for Debra Kristi's newsletter.
https://www.debrakristi.com/claim-your-free-gift/

BEFORE YOU GO...

Dear Reader,

I hope you enjoyed *Awakening: The Balance Bringer*. Thank you so much for joining Ana on her journey to self-discovery, empowerment, and balance. As are all stories of growth, this one is long and full of highs and lows. I look forward to bringing you each new installment as quickly as I possibly can. I have a lot of plans for Ana and her crew, and I'd be more than thrilled if you came along for each new adventure. I plan to explore the origin stories of the first Balance Bringer, as well as Ryland, Dohlan, and Dreya, to name a few. If there is a character you'd particularly like to hear more about, let me know. I simply love writing in this world.

Readers and reviewers like yourself make up the foundation of our author world, and we love you madly for all you do! That being said, I have a favor to ask. If you enjoyed this read, I invite you to post a review of the book. Your review needn't be more than a line or two. Not only do I love receiving feedback, but reviews also help other readers find what they are looking for.

Thanks so much! Until next time, keep the magic real.

∼ Debra Kristi

MEET THE AUTHOR

Debra Kristi was born and raised a Southern California girl. She still resides in the sunny state with her husband, two kids, and several schizophrenic cats. Unlike many of the characters in the stories she writes, Debra is not immortal and her only super power is letting the dishes and laundry pile up. When not busy drumming away at the keyboard spinning new tales, Debra is hanging out creating priceless memories with her family, geeking out to science fiction and fantasy television, and tossing around movie quotes.

Find me online and connect!
Discover more about me and my books on my website:
http://www.debrakristi.com/

And join me on my Facebook author page for updates, news, discussions, and more:
https://www.facebook.com/DebraKristi.writer/

Follow *The Balance Bringer Chronicles* **on Facebook** for 'Bringer'-inspired motivational posts and fun series extras and shares: https://www.facebook.com/TheBalanceBringer/

GLOSSARY OF TERMS

Aubadetruss: Wristband that harnesses the sun.

Aura: The invisible energy radiating from an individual.

Balance Bringer: Chosen individual born to the warrior and Fae races, bringing balance to the realms at the hand of a higher power.

Chronicler: Created at the beginning of time by the Elven Queen, chroniclers record the passage of time and events and deposit all historical information in the Urn of All.

Dream Incubus: A demon who takes on the appearance of a man in order to syphon the energy with women.

Dream-walk: Living an experience, past, present, or future, in a dream-state.

Era: A measure of time marked by a calendar of events.

Equinox: Time of year when day and night are of the same duration.

Faun: A half man, half goat lustful creature.

Feline Preservation Center: Home for large, endangered felines.

Fires of Guardoone: Eternal flame capable of killing immortals.

Gaea: Mother Earth, the universal mother and goddess.

Gradnar's Honor: Hiddenkelian warrior cry honoring the great fallen leader, Gradnar.

Hiddenkel: Homeland from where Anala Jannsen Raine originates.

Lightning wand: Weapon harnessing light used against the Tenebrousian.

Lles dei Luz: Hiddenkelian for, "I grant thee light."

Mãnah: Hiddenkelian for, "mother."

Ondine: Water spirits.

Puteri: Princess.

Purusians: A group of believers that revere the sanctity of virginity and protect their purity through separation from the majority.

Tenebrousian: Hiddenkelian name for the dark ones or shadows.

Treeite: A resident of Ivey City, the community built high in the trees.

Toran: Gateway between worlds.

Toranik: Stone marking a Toran defense area.

Usoda: One of twenty-four warrior tribes spread across the vast lands of Hiddenkel.

ACKNOWLEDGMENTS

Eden Plantz. Editor, and friend. Thanks for always pushing me to make the story that much better.

Tiffany Johnson. Editor, and friend. Thanks for always believing in my talent.

Rebecca Hamilton. Mentor and inspiration. I'll never forget the fine example you set.

Rebecca Frank. Thanks for making the story come to life on the cover.

April at Under Wraps Publishing for the perfect book design.

Ren at Renflowergrapx, for the amazing world maps.

Brandee, for helping me acknowledge my muse.

Christy, for writing at my side and always nudging me.

Danielle, for providing me a semi-regular outlet for 'crazy' talk.

Lily Sheen, for helping me to "own it."

My extended family, for your never-ending support.

Mom.

Scott.
My kids.